A SEAL Never Quits

HOLLY CASTILLO

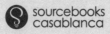
sourcebooks
casablanca

Published by Sourcebooks Casablanca, an imprint of Sourcebooks
P.O. Box 4410, Naperville, Illinois 60567-4410
(630) 961-3900
sourcebooks.com

Printed and bound in Canada.
MBP 10 9 8 7 6 5 4 3 2 1

Chapter 1

"Hi!"

The cheery voice and enthusiastic wave of her hand did nothing to quell his temper. No one had told him when he took over this ranch that there were going to be other people—outside of the ones he had selected—working there. She could be a spy for all he knew.

She strode toward him across the field, a bright smile planted on her face, and he felt some of the tension leave his body. He was being too sensitive. She was naive to the entire operation. There was no way he could hold her accountable. But he would certainly do his best to get rid of her as quickly as possible. They still had a lot of work to do on the main house, and, at the moment, she was proving to be a distraction.

"Hi," she said again, a bit breathlessly, and he was instantly *very* distracted. Her voice was husky, with almost a raw quality to it that made it sexy as hell. "I'm Dr. Anya Gutierrez. I'm the local veterinarian." She seemed to feel the need to tag on the last part of her statement because he had yet to accept her outstretched hand and was no doubt looking at her as if she had lost her mind.

"Oh, hello," he replied absently, taking her small hand into his large mitt and giving it three solid pumps before letting go. "I wasn't aware we had made a call for a veterinarian."

"Oh, you didn't," she replied quickly. "There's nothing wrong with any of your cattle. I'm just doing a routine check to make sure we're ready for calving season."

"Do you do that for all the ranches you serve?"

She looked at him quizzically. "Yes, most of them. Didn't the veterinarian at your last ranch do the same?"

He tilted back his cowboy hat and gave her what he hoped was a rueful smile. "It's been years since I was ranching," he said. He had been a teenager the last time he'd been on a ranch. "It seems a lot has changed in the years that I haven't been involved."

"Oh? What took you away from ranching?"

Time for his story to begin. It all came with being part of an undercover operation. He couldn't tell her who he really was now, but he could tell her who he used to be. "The rodeo circuit. Ranching had always been something my parents did, but the call of the road set me on a different path. But my last run-in with a mad bull reminded me how short life is, and it's brought me back to the life of ranching."

"Oh, no," she said with heartfelt sincerity, and her eyes searched his face as she laid a comforting hand on his bare forearm. "You weren't hurt badly, I hope."

Good grief, have mercy on me. He couldn't remember the last time a woman had reached out to touch him as if she genuinely cared about his well-being. And on top of that, it was a beautiful, smart, and sexy woman touching him. "I'm fine," he responded cryptically. "Though I don't know if the bull will ever be normal again."

She paused for half a moment, then broke out in laughter, and it brought a smile to his face. He liked her laugh as much as he liked her smile. He needed to get going. "So, are the cattle okay? Are all of them on track for calving season?"

"A majority of them, yes. But it looks like we may have a small handful that will be late dropping their calves. And there are a few that I'm concerned about. They have narrow hips, and the birth canal may be a bit tight for them. But I'll swing by every day or two to check on them and make sure they're in good shape."

She dug into her back pocket and fished out a business card for him. "It has my cell number on there, so you can call me anytime you need help."

He didn't know what made him do it. But there was something about her—something that made him unwilling to dismiss her as quickly as he had wanted to earlier. In an about-face that surprised the hell out of him, he said, "I'm looking to grow my cattle operations rather significantly. I'll be going to some auctions over the next few weeks and could use some guidance..."

"Considering you've yet to tell me your name, I'm not sure how I should respond," she said, a teasing lilt in her voice. He was momentarily mute. Her voice was mesmerizing.

"Sorry about that. My name is Amador Salas. Though those closest to me call me Stryker."

"Stryker? I'm sure there's an interesting story behind that. Please, call me Anya. And I'd be thrilled to go with you to the auctions over the next few weeks. Though we'll need to be selective about which auctions you go to."

"Why's that?"

"Because the cattle you have here are all pure-bred Santa Gertrudis. You can't go to just any auction to maintain the bloodline."

Stryker shook his head at himself. "I remember, now that you say it. So you'll help me, then?" Why was he asking this of her? It was going to be sheer torture traveling to different auctions with her. If only she weren't so alluring. But he had no one else to turn to with the wealth of knowledge that she could bring. As long as she was able to tone down her overly enthusiastic routine, he'd be fine. Maybe.

"Of course. Count me in. I'll do some research tonight on the best auctions for us to go to."

He nodded. "Thanks, that'll be a big help. We're still doing some remodeling at the house that I need to get back to…"

"Oh, please don't let me interfere. I'm glad to see someone is giving this place a face-lift. It has needed help for years. Your ranch will become the envy of all the other ranchers around Hebbronville."

Her words made him pause as he was turning to leave. He pivoted back to her and pinned her with what he hoped was his most intimidating glare. "About that—I'm a private man. As are the men joining me over the next couple of months. We'd really appreciate if you didn't tell anyone about the ranch house, or the improvements we're making to the land…none of it."

She tilted her head slightly and raised an eyebrow, then shrugged and held up her right hand as if she were taking an oath. "On my honor, you won't have to worry about me. I won't say a word about our new neighbors at the Bent Horseshoe Ranch. You'll find I don't believe in town gossip."

He gave her a half-hearted smile, then finally turned and left for the ranch house. She was going to be an interesting part of the new chapter of his life. An unexpected part that he was looking forward to. It wouldn't be long before the rest of his team began to arrive. It was going to go by fast.

———⁓———

Lieutenant Amador "Stryker" Salas had still been high on his latest successful mission infiltrating the city of Juarez, Mexico, releasing a hostage, and disabling a notorious gang. Twenty-four hours after that, they'd been on their way home.

Much to his surprise, his former commanding officer, Admiral Haslett, had tapped him on the shoulder when he arrived back stateside and taken him to his office. Several months earlier, Haslett had transferred to the naval offices in Corpus Christi from Coronado. Stryker had thought Haslett no longer worked with the SEAL operations, but Haslett quickly informed him that his move to Corpus had been strategic. He had moved with plans already in place to continue as Stryker's CO on a dedicated assignment. Only Haslett and a few other senior officers knew the true reason for his move.

"I made the transfer here specifically knowing we would utilize you for a covert operation," Haslett had said, watching Stryker in that intense way he had. Stryker had never been the type to get nervous about an assignment. On the contrary, he looked forward to whatever Haslett had for him.

"We have reason to believe there's a terrorist cell operating out of Mexico and Central and South America that's going to launch an attack on U.S. soil sometime in the not-so-distant future. We've purchased a ranch just an hour away from the border that will allow you to keep your ear to the ground for information and also give you solid cover to work your way into the community and identify those who are working on this side of the border. There are a lot of unanswered questions, and I'll be doing my part to help your team gather intel."

Stryker had learned years ago that it was best not to ask questions until Admiral Haslett was finished, which he obviously wasn't. "This is black ops unlike anything you've experienced. If you or any of your team get caught in the process, we'll disavow you. I'm not saying that lightly. There are things already moving, and I need you in there now. What we've been able to pick up so far is random information, and the NSA has come to us with coded conversations that even they are having a hard time cracking. What little we have is enough to necessitate the formation of this team. It isn't going to be like most of your missions. However, you will have tremendous resources at your fingertips, as well as the ability to build your own team. Choose wisely, as these will be the men you spend the next few years with."

His CO had handed over a flash drive, and Stryker turned it over in his hand, waiting to hear the rest. "Everything you need to know is on there. The main house is being remodeled to suit the needs of your team. You'll arrive there within the week to oversee the changes. You'll start with a team of six, but there's a good chance more will join you as the investigation and operations expand. Do you have any questions?"

"I'll read up first, then let you know, sir."

"I'm not going to say that I'm pleased to lose you.

You're one of the best, and I have no doubt you'll pick some of my other top guys to bring with you. But I'm glad you were handed this assignment. It suits you perfectly."

"Thank you, sir. I won't let you down."

Haslett smiled. "That's what I'm counting on."

"*This* is our new headquarters?" Derek "Brusco" Delgado said in surprise as they stepped into the large foyer of the new compound.

"There are still a few things being upgraded, but the short answer is yes."

"Nothing says 'undercover' like a posh, large house sprawling across a massive ranch. I'm sure it hasn't raised any questions at all." Isaiah "Snap" Flores spoke with heavy sarcasm dripping from his voice.

"Always the optimist, aren't you, Snap?" Stryker grinned. "Trust me, the appropriate contractors were used, and there's a reason there are large plantings around the house. Not even satellite imaging can pick up the size of this place."

Brusco ran a hand through his dark brown hair and drifted farther into the building that was now going to be their home, followed by Snap and Stryker. "How many of us are there supposed to be again?"

"Six for now," Stryker answered, meandering into the giant kitchen and peering into the refrigerator. He raised an eyebrow when he saw it was fully stocked with some of his team's favorite foods—namely, beer. He grabbed one for himself and two more for Snap and Brusco.

"What do you mean 'for now'?" Snap asked, his voice sounding distant in the large house.

Stryker followed the sound of the man's voice and found him and Brusco kicked back on a large leather couch, their feet propped on the coffee table in front of them. There was a massive sixty-five-inch TV hanging on the wall in front of them, and they were both looking around with appreciation. "Whoever set this place up did a sweet job, ése." Brusco rolled a toothpick around in his mouth as he talked and barely lifted his eyes to catch the beer that was tossed his way.

"We're into it with six SEALs right now. But I've been warned more may come our way, depending on our needs."

Snap lifted his chin and a mischievous glint entered his eyes. "We'll show them what the six of us can do together, and they'll leave us alone." Then he winced at his own words. "That came out wrong."

"Pervert." Brusco laughed, then stood to continue exploring the house. Snap shrugged and followed behind him.

Stryker could hear them moving through the first floor, and he was tempted to catch up with them. But he knew the rest of the team would be arriving soon, and he didn't want to wander too far from the door. He made his way back into the large foyer and studied the incredible rock and wood décor of the home, the high, vaulted ceilings, and the strong angular lines of the structure. The contractors who remodeled this compound had "Man Cave" stamped across the top of the blueprints— Stryker had made certain of it.

"Hey, Stryker!" Brusco yelled from down a hallway. "Who gets this killer room?"

Stryker smiled. "I do," he called back.

"Bullshit."

"Didn't you see the sign? It said the guy with the biggest dick gets that room. So, you know." Stryker smiled as he brought his beer to his lips.

"Then it must be mine."

The voice came from the front door and Stryker grinned. "Santo, man, is it good to see you." Hunter "Santo" Gonzalez was an expert sniper, so his stealth didn't surprise Stryker. But Stryker had seen Santo's truck pulling up from a distance and had known the man would be on their doorstep in just a few minutes. Stryker had been on many missions with Santo, too many. Because every time they were paired together, someone was destined to die. At least, with Santo behind the trigger, it was usually a quick death.

"So, what is it that has my name on it?"

Stryker shook his head and led the tall man into the home. Santo let out a low whistle. "This is an upgrade from our usual undercover digs."

Santo was still dressed in military fatigues, having just arrived back stateside that very morning. But his expression, always passive and calm, didn't show any signs of exhaustion. Originally from Venezuela, his family was wealthy and directly descended from the Spanish who had arrived in South America in the 1500s. His lighter complexion and slight accent gave him the best and worst of two worlds. Sometimes he could blend with many different nationalities and ethnicities. Other times, he didn't seem to fit in anywhere.

"It's certainly nice," Stryker replied, grabbing a beer for his friend and comrade. He wasn't going to tell anyone that he had seen to it that the place would be built in a way he knew his men would appreciate. He'd let that remain a mystery. "I haven't had a chance to go through the entire compound with the guys yet. We still have a couple of men on their way."

Santo nodded as he looked around, and Stryker knew he was sizing up the facility for areas of weakness in case they ever needed to defend themselves. It was the same way Stryker had been looking at the place from the moment construction had started.

"Who's here already?" Santo asked, taking a tentative sip of beer, then a longer pull at it.

"Brusco and Snap are cruising around here somewhere. Two more are on their way."

Santo lifted an eyebrow, but Stryker just smiled back at him. "I'll let you be surprised with the rest of the team."

Santo turned away and began exploring the house on his own. From the excited chatter down a hallway, Stryker could tell Santo had caught up with Brusco and Snap. Stryker went to stand at the door, watching as dust plumed, telling him another truck was coming down the long stretch of dirt road that led up to the ranch.

When he saw Joseph "Buzz" Gomez exit the passenger side, unfolding his long, muscular body, and Enrique "Phantom" Ramirez get out of the driver's side, his big boots striking the ground, he smiled. Phantom was easily his best friend, and the man he had worked the hardest to recruit. He was as his name indicated—a phantom in the shadows, a ghost in the light. He had saved Stryker's life more times than he cared to admit. With Phantom there, they would be able to tackle whatever came their way.

His team was in place. All they needed now was a mission.

—∿∿—

It was dark and the team had turned in for the night when Stryker began his walk-through. Besides the kitchen and the living room, there was a sizable dining room with a table that could hold up to twelve people. Terra-cotta tile covered the floor from the kitchen to the dining room, and the colors on the wall were similar to an old Spanish kitchen, with the rock and the wood combined in such a way that Stryker felt he had stepped back in time two hundred years—a very relaxing feeling. It was exactly as he had pictured it would turn out.

As he wandered farther, he came across a game and media room with another giant TV, a pool table, and a foosball table. It was clear how much thought had been put into making this a relaxing and fun location for his men. He wanted them to be able to unwind after a difficult mission, and they could either do it with games and fun in the ranch house, or by checking the fences and working the fields with the cattle.

The area he had been walking was one giant circle, with corridors leading into different wings. When he'd first arrived during the restoration project, he'd discovered those wings led to spacious bedrooms—more than the six he had originally requested. It was obvious this covert operation had different mission parameters than his SEALs were used to.

He climbed the stairs to the second floor and found a few more large bedrooms, another media/game room, and then, finally, what he had been searching for. He

would have missed the entrance if he hadn't been looking so hard, and he knew if it was hard for him to find,
when he had been the one to design it, it would be virtually impossible for someone else. He pressed on a knob
in the wood next to the thin seam he saw between the
wooden boards, and there was a soft *whoosh* as the panel
slid open, revealing a substantial communications and
tactical planning room, equipped with a separate conference room at the very back.

Everything was mostly dark, and there was something
about the small buttons flashing and the soft beeping of
data being received and recorded that made him decide
to leave the lights off and wander the room strictly by
the glow of the data signals.

Everything he had asked for was there, from live satellite imagery, to a bank of computers that could log in
to just about any database in the world, and an interac-
tive imaging and mapping system at the center of the
room. It was all prototype technology—stuff the rest of
the military hadn't even gotten their hands on. But his
special missions had given him insight into the type of
intelligence the government had been pulling together.

He stood in the room for several minutes, taking it
all in and wondering what would come next. He knew
the tech team was still making some adjustments to the
house, as well as to the command room, but it was practically finished. There was no point trying to guess what
assignment was headed their way. Whatever it was, the
CO had picked him to lead the task force.

He took one final glance around the room before
heading down to his bedroom, praying he'd be able
to get some sleep and not be plagued by a nightmare.

Whoever claimed the job didn't take a toll was lying. There was no way you could enter the bowels of hell and come back unscathed.

He hesitated at his door when he saw a makeshift sign hanging on it that said BIG DICK. He chuckled to himself, shook his head, and walked into the oversized master bedroom. Yes, things were going to be interesting around here, that was for sure.

Chapter 2

DELAYS WERE NOT ACCEPTABLE. HE KEPT STRICT TIME-tables for a reason. They were often being watched, so when he took action, he had to be fast—otherwise, he would be caught. And that was simply unacceptable. He wasn't worried about the cops. They were nothing to him. He was worried about his competition.

A car approached slowly in the distance and his jaw clenched. *How dare they make me wait!* He watched the car coming through his side mirror. He would have to dole out punishment. He couldn't show any sign of mercy. He had expectations of his men. And they *would* obey him.

The initial stage of their business went smoothly. When the man and his colleague turned to leave, however, Jefe cleared his throat. "Our transaction isn't complete."

"What will you do? Kill me? That won't get you any closer to the information you want. What will you give me to make this worthwhile for me?"

Jefe advanced on him and heard his driver follow-ing closely on his heels. The two men began to reach into their jackets for their guns, but Jefe made a slashing motion with his hand. There were two distinct pops and both men fell to their knees, clutching their thighs in agony as blood spilled between their fingers.

"You *shot* me? You arrogant son of a—" The man began breathing heavily. "This information could get us both killed."

"Lack of information will certainly get you killed."

The man's eyes darted back and forth. "I-I don't know much." He fell backwards as Jefe approached, landing on his back. Jefe leaned over him and pressed his foot into the man's chest.

"Tell me at least what you promised already."

"The-the Americans... There is talk. There is suspicion. And their eyes are set on everything south of their border. I've heard their government is setting up a special force to come after all the illegal activities."

Jefe lightened the weight of his foot pressed on the man's chest. "Tell me more."

Anya Gutierrez was rarely intimidated. But the impressive man who had first met her as the new owner of the Bent Horseshoe Ranch had intimidated her. He had also made her pulse race for different reasons. It had been a long time since she had been so intimately aware of the presence of a man. But every fiber of her being had been aware of Stryker Salas, and she wanted nothing more than to move closer—which frightened her. She had never been drawn to a man so strongly.

So the thrill of excitement as she talked to the burly man had surprised her. And she had acted like such a fool. She had been overeager to please him and to try to get a smile on his hard face, and somehow she had succeeded. Cracking open the man's armor just the smallest amount had made her day.

She wanted to know more about him. There were few who knew any details other than that he had recently moved there and had started rebuilding the ranch. Even her best friend, Elena, who trained the horses out at his ranch had known little about him. Where was he from? What was his story?

"He certainly likes his privacy." Elena shrugged. "We met briefly when I was there a couple of weeks ago. He didn't seem happy to have me there. Once he saw that I was sticking to the barn and the arena, he left me alone. My only real interactions with him have been when I bring him the winnings from the horse shows. He seems kind enough. Why? Was he rude to you?"

Anya shook her head. "Not really, I suppose. He's just very—"

"Rough?" Elena supplied with a grin. "Most real cowboys are. You've just gotten spoiled by all the city slickers out here pretending to be ranchers."

Elena's words had made her laugh. But she was beginning to doubt her decision to take him cattle shopping. It would be a long drive with just the two of them cooped up in his truck together. And then there would be the auction itself, where she would need to stay close to him so she could tell him which calves and heifers would be the best to purchase.

She stared at her image in the mirror and took a deep breath. "You can do this," she said firmly to herself. "He's just another rancher." But he was more than that. She could tell from his eyes that he was kind and gentle, that he was smart and had a sense of humor, though he tried to hide it. He was a man with a soul and a story to tell, though it was clear he really didn't want to share it. Not yet, at least. She drew a deep breath. "He's just another rancher," she repeated to herself. "He's a man you can trust. Have. Fun."

The small pep talk in front of the mirror helped restore her self-confidence, and she nodded firmly to her own image. She grabbed her things and was out the door quickly, and reached the ranch thirty minutes later. It was to the east of Hebbronville, and down a long dirt road, so getting to it wouldn't be easy if she didn't drive a truck.

As she pulled up, she noticed several other trucks parked on the property and wondered if the men he'd mentioned would be living there had finally arrived. She hadn't been in the house since it had been remodeled, and as she walked up, she saw it had been greatly expanded. The trees and landscaping had kept it hidden from her before, and she was amazed at the size of the house.

The exterior of the home had also been changed. Where there had once been plain wood side paneling, there was now rock and cedar, giving the home a modern yet rustic look. She wondered if the group of men were all friends who had won the lottery and gone in together to make the home so attractive and expansive.

The front door was massive, and it reminded her of how she had felt standing next to Stryker. The man was large. That was putting it mildly. He stood at least four inches taller than her and had massive muscles that bulged beneath clothing that he seemed to wear to hide his strength. But she had actually felt that strength…when she had put her hand on his bare forearm as she had talked to him the first day. She could feel his muscles moving under her fingers, and she had been too mesmerized to take her hand away.

She could almost still feel the silky hair that covered his warm, taut skin and the tendons as he shifted in reaction to her touch. She hadn't wanted to stop touching him, which had surprised her.

She had just lifted her hand for the doorbell when the door was yanked open by a man who could have been Stryker's brother. His skin was lighter, and while Stryker's hair had a slight wave to it, this man's hair was straight and cropped rather short. He was tall, and, in his simple T-shirt and jeans, his muscles were obvious. He looked at her, then smiled, though it seemed it wasn't something he was used to doing.

"You must be the veterinarian," he said, and held the door open a little farther. "Come in."

A wave of cool, air-conditioned air welcomed her into the foyer, and her eyes drank in the beautiful architecture and design of the house. She couldn't see anything that reminded her of the previous house. It was as if the entire place had been gutted, and they had started over.

"My name's Phantom, by the way," her door greeter said, extending his hand to her.

She smiled up at him as she shook his hand. "I'm Anya Gutierrez. Are you—do you live here now too?"

He nodded. "I'm here, along with Stryker and four other men. Buzz is the newbie to the ranching world, so if you see a guy who looks totally out of place, that's him."

Anya grinned at him. "I'm sure you're going to educate him just fine."

A sly smile crept across Phantom's face, and Anya suddenly felt very sorry for Buzz. "Oh, yeah. Buzz is in good hands."

The sound of boots on the hardwood floors came from somewhere within the house, and Stryker suddenly rounded the corner and faced both of them. He eyed

Phantom for a moment, then turned his full attention on Anya. "Are you ready to go?"

He was dressed in a navy-blue button-down shirt and a pair of jeans that fit him perfectly. Anya felt like asking him to turn around so she could get the full picture. *Good grief, this man is turning my mind to mush.* She felt the heat of a blush burning her face. "Y-yes," she stammered. "I'm ready to go."

"Be back later," he tossed over his shoulder to Phantom, as he opened the door and placed his hand at the small of Anya's back, guiding her out the door in front of him.

The feel of his hand through the cotton of her polo shirt sent a small thrill through her. She had to remind herself to breathe as he escorted her to his F-250, which already had the gooseneck trailer attached to it. It was a big trailer, and she knew they'd be able to bring home at least ten or more calves. It would be a good addition to his current cattle, especially since he had about twenty-five head that were ready to be auctioned off to make room for some heartier heifers.

The ride to Kingsville was punctuated by the sounds of the latest country music coming through the radio. Anya had come prepared for the drive with her ledger and a stack of invoices she needed to record before mailing them out. Stryker had taken one look at her paperwork, raised an eyebrow, and then returned his eyes to the road.

They hadn't talked since the first day she had met him, and only briefly when she had called to tell him about this sale. She'd hesitated even to call him, but she'd made a commitment. She hadn't expected him to say yes.

They pulled up to the sale arena where the

Kleberg-Kenedy County Junior Livestock Show was held every winter, and Anya remembered with fondness her years showing cattle and goats and even some turkeys. She had won the title of County Stock Show Queen when she was sixteen, and then had gone on to win the County Rodeo Queen when she was seventeen. She still had her tiaras and sashes.

"What on earth has put that look on your face?" Stryker asked. She realized at that moment they'd parked and she was still sitting in the truck with a goofy look on her face.

"Dreams," she replied with a smile. "Haven't you heard of them before, Stryker?"

Her quip at his expense seemed to take him by surprise. He shook his head at her, then left the truck. "Well, you're about as much fun as getting a root canal," Anya said to herself, before her door was yanked open and Stryker stood looking up at her impatiently.

She hopped down from the truck and instantly had to scramble to get her feet set right underneath her on the muddy ground. Suddenly Stryker's muscular arm snaked around her waist, and he pulled her to him, holding her tight.

She was hit with the scent of his spicy cologne, leather, and man—pure, hearty *man*—and her hands immediately pressed against the front of his shirt as her feet settled beneath her. But her mind and body were far from settled.

He leaned down and the feeling of his lips brushing lightly against her ear caused her heart to thunder so hard, she was afraid it would beat out of her chest. "Just for your information, I can be far more fun than a root canal... You just have to know what to ask for."

Chapter 3

SHE WAS BLUSHING TO THE TIPS OF HER EARS, AND HE WAS enjoying every second of it. Especially when she had drawn in a deep breath, which only served to press her more intimately to him. He could smell the sweet scent of honey and lilies on her skin and in her hair, and wanted nothing more than to nuzzle the warmth of her neck. How long had it been since he had craved a woman this much?

His body had started to respond, so he'd quickly set her away from him, a muscle jumping in his jaw. She wouldn't meet his eyes, and in fact turned away from him and set off toward the show barns. He couldn't tell whether she was embarrassed, angry, or a combination of both. He *had* just made a very strong innuendo to her. Perhaps too strong.

He followed her to the show barns and tried his best not to watch her the entire time. He needed to make connections, meet people in the industry. He needed to blend in with his undercover role. That was what he was there to do. He nodded to several people as he passed them, memorizing faces, registering those that struck him as out of place and those that seemed right at home.

Anya was just too damn appealing in his mind. She wore a simple pair of boot-cut jeans with a belt that had a touch of rhinestone embellishment, though not so much that it made the thing appear gaudy. She wore a pale pink polo shirt tucked into her jeans, the perfect color to complement her tan skin and dark brown hair, and accentuate her narrow waist.

Stryker felt a growl growing within his chest. He stepped forward until he was alongside her and cast a look around, noticing several men giving her appreciative glances. He wanted to slide his arm around her waist and hold her close. These men needed to know that Anya Gutierrez was off limits. She was with him.

The thought startled him. It had been years since he had felt such a way about a woman. He had thought he was incapable of feeling such things ever again. But there was something about her innocence, her wide smile that she cast as she moved through the crowd, that made him want to protect her from all the big, bad, ugly things he knew were in the world.

They checked into the show and got their bidding number, then went to find a place in the stands. There were far more ranchers there than Stryker had expected, and he was worried the cost was going to be driven up because of it. While it was technically still the government's money he was paying with, he wouldn't pay an outrageous amount just because he could.

Several ranchers stepped over to say hello to Anya, and Stryker bared his teeth in the semblance of a smile as she introduced them. *I need to be making friends*, he reminded himself. This was all part of his undercover operation. Anya was a surprise he had discovered on his land and had no part in his undercover role. But he'd realized after the first day he'd met her that she could help him. Being credible to her made him that much closer to being credible to other ranchers, and eventually clients, as he cycled through his cattle, pulling out the weak ones to build an even stronger herd.

As if reading his mind, Anya spoke up suddenly. "Have you decided when you're going to sell the twenty-five head you have that are ready to go to auction?"

"When do you think would be a good time?" She looked startled by his question. "Keep in mind," he said, "it's been many years since I've been in this game. So you tell me when you think it will be a good time to auction them off, and I'll tell you if I agree."

"I'd sell now if I were you. The market is strong, and your calves are already a year old—perfect size and weight to sell. They're actually bigger than most of the one-year-old calves I've been seeing, so this could be a great opportunity for you. If you wait any longer, you may lose this chance."

He fought the urge to smile. What was it about this woman that made him feel the need to smile, to laugh, to be…the man he used to be? That was a sobering thought that quickly took away the urge to smile. "I agree," he said, turning his attention to the ring where they led in a massive bull.

The auctioneer's voice blared over the intercom, and Anya leaned into him, her lips against his ear. "They're going to get a high dollar for this bull, but anyone with common sense should stay away."

"Why's that?" he asked, turning his head so he could speak into her ear, giving her the same torture she was giving him.

She turned back to him, and when she did, she unconsciously placed her hand on his leg. "His front legs are splayfooted. You can't tell unless you're looking for it.

Most likely hereditary. So any of his calves will have a high probability of also having the disfigurement. It could impact an entire herd if it isn't kept under control."

Stryker looked back into the ring and noticed she was right—the bull's hooves were curved inwards. That wasn't stopping the ranchers from bidding like crazy for the tall, muscular beast. He turned back to Anya. "Good eye," he said against her ear, and she blushed. She suddenly seemed aware of where her hand was, and her blush deepened as she pulled it away.

He wanted to tell her to put it back. He liked the feel of her hand on his thigh, of her body pressed against his, of her lips against his ear. He liked *her*. But he knew she was more than a casual fling type of woman. He could see it in the naive way she touched him, talked to him, teased him. She wasn't aware she was playing with fire.

Nearly an hour later, they began to bring out calves that were freshly weaned from their mothers, and things started to get interesting. Anya provided a running commentary in his ear about which calves stood out the best and which ones he should be wary of. He knew most of it on his own, but he wasn't about to stop her from leaning into him and pressing against his arm every time she turned to murmur in his ear. It was a sweet torture, and he couldn't get enough.

At the end of the day, he had bought ten calves, all the right size to start raising into future foundation animals for his herd, and Anya seemed very pleased with his purchases. "You got two bull calves," she said with excitement as they headed back toward Hebbronville. "Are you planning on putting them into the rotation?"

"The thought has crossed my mind," he said, and

again he had the desire to smile. She was so different than any woman he'd ever met.

"I can just see the kinds of calves you're going to have in a couple of years! They're going to be phenomenal. Are you going to take them to any shows or do any competing with them at all?"

"Let me guess. You know how to show cattle."

Anya made a scoffing sound. "I wouldn't be worth my mettle as a cattle veterinarian if I didn't know that. Just think, we could hit the road, go to a few shows, and get the word out about the herd you have—you'd have buyers lining up in no time."

"You want to go on the road with me?" He didn't know why he was asking her. He couldn't show cattle with her. His emotions were already in knots just being around her.

"Of course. It would be fun."

"Yeah. It would be." What else could he say? "But I couldn't take up your time like that. I know enough about cattle to get by."

"Seriously? After that cattle auction, I'd say you need your fair share of help." She was teasing him. She seemed genuinely interested in helping him. Did she feel the same burn he did every time they touched?

"Now you're judging me, not the cattle." He chuckled. He had actually chuckled. *What is this woman doing to me?* He needed to move on to another subject.

Right at that moment, one or more of the cattle shifted drastically in the trailer, causing the truck to lurch. Anya gasped and clutched the seat tightly. The cattle shifted again, and he had to focus on his driving rather than Anya.

"We're going to have to check the cattle," he said, glancing in the rearview mirror. "One of them might have fallen, which could be why—"

"Stop the truck."

"There's a rest stop up ahead. It will be best—"

"Please, stop the truck now."

He glanced over at her and noticed she had gone pale. "It isn't safe on this road. Just wait a minute longer."

Her grip on the seat tightened until her knuckles turned white, and her lips pressed into a thin line. The sign for the rest stop came into view, and he turned in with relief. Something wasn't right with her, but she looked like she was on the verge of throwing up, and he didn't think now was the time to ask her questions. He slowed the truck and the cattle shifted again. He cursed under his breath.

The truck hadn't even rolled to a stop when he heard the passenger door open, and it was only through sheer willpower that his arm snapped out and caught her slender wrist. He heard her cry out, and from the sudden hard tug of her arm, he knew she had fallen. He brought the truck to a complete stop, and, using his left hand, put it in park. Then, with both hands, he pulled her back up into the cab.

"What the hell were you thinking?" he demanded, stunned and angry. He was angry at her for making such a rash move, and furious with himself for allowing it to happen. He should have realized she was in flight mode.

"Let me go, Stryker, please. Let me go!"

The sight of tears glistening in her eyes surprised him, and he reluctantly released her. She scrambled out of the truck as he exited his side. He knew he needed to check on the cattle, but Anya was a bigger concern at the moment. He rounded the front of the truck in time to hear her retching in the grass on the side of the road.

Immediately he went to her side and wrapped an arm around her waist, the other hand pulling her hair back from her face. Her body trembled, and she remained hunched over for several long moments, finally straightening, though she kept her face turned away from him.

"I-I'm sorry. I don't usually react that way…" She shook her head and swallowed hard.

"Hey…look at me. Anya, look at me."

Slowly, she turned her face toward him, her eyes glassy with tears. He kept his arm wrapped around her, holding her close. She still trembled, and he wasn't certain what caused it. She couldn't possibly be afraid, right? She wasn't afraid of *him*, was she?

"What is it? What caused you to panic like that? Did I do something? Say something?"

"No. No. You did nothing wrong. Please, just go check on the cattle. I don't want you to see me like this."

"I'm not leaving you until I know you are okay."

"I'm fine. Seriously, Stryker, I'm fine." She looked embarrassed and nervous, though she didn't try to pull away from him.

"Then tell me what just happened." She was still trembling some, though it wasn't anywhere near as bad as before. She forced a smile to her lips.

"It was a panic attack. I don't have them often. I'm sorry you had to witness that."

A panic attack. He had seen plenty of soldiers go through them in the heat of the moment, and he'd usually had to save their asses. But he knew there was always a reason for one to start, and he couldn't think of anything that would have done so with Anya. "Don't apologize for something like that. What triggered it?"

"I'll go with you to check on the cattle." When he narrowed his eyes at her, she added, "I'll tell you about it after we make sure the cattle are okay."

Reluctantly, he agreed to her suggestion, and they went to the trailer. She didn't try to move away from him as he kept his arm around her waist. In fact, she almost seemed grateful for the support and leaned into his body. The urge to protect her spiked.

As expected, one of the calves had fallen and was scrambling to get to its feet. Reluctantly, Stryker released Anya, opened the rear door, and began to push one of the panels in, helping the calf to scramble upright. He secured the panel closer to the calf to prevent it from falling again. He hopped out of the trailer, and Anya locked the door in place behind him.

Anya smiled hesitantly, and he nearly reached over to tuck her hair behind her ear. He stopped his hand midway and redirected it to his own hair. "The cattle are okay."

"I was in a car accident when I was younger. I was just a kid, but I remember it like it was yesterday. We were hauling cattle, and the trailer jackknifed. There was nothing we could do. The trailer snapped free from the truck, and then we flipped. There was glass, and blood, and the cattle—oh, the cattle…" She broke eye contact with him. "It was horrific."

"I'm sorry, Anya. Was anyone hurt?"

"I broke my wrist. My mother was in the hospital for weeks. My father blamed himself, but there really wasn't anyone to blame. But the cattle… We lost a few that day."

He frowned, and she gave him a wobbly smile. "Is that what made you decide to become a veterinarian? Witnessing their death?"

"I suppose it put a seed of the idea in my head. I'm sorry I panicked on you earlier. Just the feeling of the trailer lurching… It brought back those horrible memories unexpectedly. I haven't had a panic attack like that in years."

Stryker shook his head. "There is nothing to be sorry for. I'm sorry you had to go through such a thing and the memories still haunt you so much. Will you be all right for the rest of the drive home?"

She nodded, though her expression was nervous. "I should be. I've hauled cattle trailers myself many times before and haven't had this reaction for so long. I don't know why today made it all rush back."

He didn't stop himself this time when he reached out to tuck a strand of hair behind her ear. Her eyes widened at the intimate touch, but she seemed pleased as he let his fingers trail lightly down her face.

Slowly, he pulled his hand back from her smooth, soft skin. "Let's get you home."

He appeared every inch the consummate businessman. In his slick Armani suit and shoes that shined enough that he could see his image in them, he was dressed for the part. His hair was cut in what he described as "the overpaid-white-business-guy trim," and he had even gone to the hassle of getting a manicure. Yes, he looked the part.

But if anyone could see the man beneath the slick

and shine, they would be terrified. He had lost count of the number of people he'd killed, and was eager with anticipation for his next kill. He only wished it was his full-time responsibility.

He glanced down at the signature scorpion ring on his finger as he waited for his "business partner" to arrive to their meeting. He wasn't used to having to wait for anyone. The last time he'd been made to wait had resulted in dire outcomes for the two men who'd made that mistake.

Yet here, it was all part of the American rat race. Foolish men and women running around like they were important without having a clue about the real chaos right under their noses. *Fools*. They were all fools. They made life miserable for people around them just so they could climb an invisible ladder and step on everyone else to get to the top.

Americans made him ill to his stomach. All they cared about were material things. More money. More cars. Bigger houses. And more often than not, they didn't have the money to pay for all those things, and they depended on their government to bail them out.

Things in Mexico were far different. Most Mexicans had to work hard to get those things. And if they couldn't pay, they usually died. There was no government hand-out ready to save them. If you could only afford to live in a shack, you lived in a fucking shack. Yet there were leaders making sure that people couldn't advance to create better lives for themselves.

Those leaders were working with the Americans to keep the poor close to poverty and make the wealthy even more powerful. The Americans were helping destroy his country, and ruining their own country at the same time. The people who wanted to be a part of the system didn't see the corruption, didn't see the problems. He did, though. And very soon, he would be teaching all of them a lesson they would never forget.

His cell phone rang, and his hand clenched into a fist before he reached into his jacket pocket and pulled out the slim smartphone. "I'm in a meeting," he said curtly, knowing his irritation at the interruption was clear.

"We may have a problem."

He rolled his shoulder that ached from the time one of his "business associates" had decided to try and fight the inevitable. "I'm listening."

"It's best we talk in person. There's a new player in the game."

Again, his hand clenched into a fist. He had his men working overtime to find out about the potential threat. Now, they might finally have a lead. If only the people plotting to bring him down knew that a prominent leader in Washington, D.C., played a key role in his plans, they might not be so focused on him. "Are you certain?"

There was a pause on the other end of the line. Finally: "New guy. Just bought his dream ranch to run with his 'friends.' Doesn't look right."

"So you want me to go off your gut instinct and meet you out in the middle of nowhere to talk? Is that what you're asking me to do?"

Again, there was a pause, but the voice came back, strong and firm. "Yes, sir. Something isn't right."

"I'll be there in two days. In the meantime, gather as much information as you can. This better be worth my fucking time."

"Yes, sir. I'll take care of—" He hung up on the man before he could finish talking.

The door suddenly opened and a tan, fit man—probably in his late fifties, judging by the white in his hair—came in, barely casting him a glance. "Sorry to keep you waiting, Mr. Davila. It's been a very hectic morning. My assistant informs me you have a proposal that could take our tech industry even further into the area of coding and encryption. Now, we don't actively participate in encryption, but the area of coding appeals to me."

Davila fought the urge to flex his hands and pop his knuckles. Lies. The people creating the corruption were always telling lies. He looked forward to killing this bastard. And he'd make sure he felt every agonizing second of it. He'd make the man squeal before he finished him. But this man wasn't his final target, and, as such, he couldn't kill him yet. He could threaten him enough to make his life a little easier, though. This man was just the starting point. He needed to make an example of him, so no one would be willing to double-cross him again.

Then he would go after the tech department. But not in a way they would know. He had hackers in place, ready to break into the system. He realized it could cause more death to acquire the codes, but he was willing to take that risk. The more he got to practice his hobby, the better and better he became.

A slow smile spread across his lips as he stood and walked around the large conference room table, pausing long enough to lock the doors to the room, and then he finally stopped, standing directly above his quarry. "Yes, Mr. Jameson, I'm sure we can work out a mutually satisfying agreement."

Chapter 4

CALVING SEASON HAD ARRIVED. ANYA FELT LIKE SHE belonged in some episode of *The Walking Dead* as she pulled around the back of the clinic. The past two nights she'd been out on call. One of the ranchers had called in time, and she was able to save both the mama and the calf. The other had called too late. Even though she had spent hours trying, she could only save the calf—the mama had already lost too much blood.

Elena had been checking on her daily, knowing this was the hardest time of the year for her. She stopped by multiple times with a packed lunch or dinner, something Anya could take with her if she had to race out the door for another emergency call. She didn't know what she would do without Elena. They had become best friends while at Texas A&M and been inseparable since.

One of the benefits of living at the clinic was that she was always ready for what might come at her and the bed was only a room away when she needed her sleep. The downside was…she lived at her clinic.

She unlocked the back door and went into her room, ready to rinse off and get into fresh clothes and, if she was lucky, maybe get a half hour or so of sleep. She pressed her head to the cold tile in the shower when her phone began to buzz on the sink counter. No rest for the weary.

She hastily turned off the water and grabbed a towel

and quickly dried her hands, snatching up the phone before it could go to voicemail. "Dr. Gutierrez," she said out of habit.

There was a pause on the other end of the line, then: "Anya?"

Stryker. She would recognize the husky baritone of his voice even in a loud room. Just the sound caused her heart to jump. It had been nearly a week since she'd seen him. She'd been too busy to check on his cattle as she'd planned. But part of her was also embarrassed to see him again after her panic attack. No one had ever witnessed one, and she felt betrayed by her own mind for giving up her secrets.

"Yes?" she replied, suddenly anxious. Most calf births happened overnight. It was nearly six in the morning. Something must've gone wrong.

"Anya, one of the heifers, one that you were concerned about because her hips are narrow… She's been in hard labor for close to four hours."

"I'll be there in thirty minutes or less."

True to her word, less than twenty-five minutes later, Anya punched the code into the gate and watched the gates open with agonizing slowness. She drove up to the house at a breakneck speed and pulled a medical bag from the passenger seat. She was heading for the barn when a sharp whistle drew her attention. She turned to see Stryker riding up to her on one of their workhorses.

"She's out in the field," he said and extended an arm down to her.

Anya hesitated only a split second before reaching up and grabbing his forearm. The direct skin-to-skin contact was jarring.

She looked up into his dark eyes and saw something flash. Was it possible he was feeling the same thing? But whatever had been in his eyes disappeared almost instantly as he lifted her quickly, setting her in front of him in the saddle. He spun the horse around and spurred it into a gallop. Anya reached for the horn of the saddle, but suddenly Stryker's thick arms were around her, holding the reins while securing her in a tight embrace.

Anya drew in a deep breath and was struck by the smell of horse, leather, and man. She felt a little light-headed as she clutched tightly to her medical bag. They had gone about a quarter of a mile when Stryker finally pulled the horse to a stop. Anya could hear the weak cries of the heifer, but couldn't move until Stryker did. Fortunately, he was in as much of a rush as she was, and he dismounted quickly, then pulled her from the horse and set her firmly on the ground.

She shook off the goose bumps that had pimpled along her skin and hurried in the direction she'd heard the cow. Stryker stayed close to her, and she began to fire off questions. "As of now, how many hours has she been in labor?"

"Hard to say when her first labor pains began. But it's been close to four and a half hours since she really began bearing down as if she was ready to give birth."

She cast him a sideways glance. "And you're just *now* calling me?"

He frowned. "She seemed to be progressing just fine, same as the others. And we know that it usually takes longer for a first-time mama. But then she started thrashing around and seemed to be in a lot of discomfort. More so than would be considered normal. She took to ground right about the time I called you."

Anya was already yanking on her long, latex gloves as they rounded a large mesquite shrub and the heifer came into view. It was obvious she was in the middle of labor as her body strained against another contraction and she let out her distressed cry.

"Try to keep her calm while I check her," Anya said softly, trying not to frighten the animal.

Stryker went to do as she asked, placing a knee on the heifer's neck, preventing her from lunging to her feet. Anya did a quick examination, and it was as she feared. The amniotic sac had already burst. The cow's hips were very narrow, almost too narrow for the calf's head and feet to fit through. Almost.

"I need to twist the calf." She looked up at Stryker, and he was watching her intently.

"Okay. So what do you need from me?"

Anya focused on the task at hand. "Hold her like you are, but brace yourself. She's going to try to move."

Stryker frowned at her a little deeper, then braced himself. Anya reached into the heifer's birth canal and felt the head of the calf. There was a very high percentage it was going to be stillborn, depending on how long the calf had been without the amniotic sac to protect it. Carefully, she turned the calf's head, then reached for the legs that were already pointed in the right direction of the birth canal.

She waited until she felt the start of a contraction by the tightening of the heifer's muscles, then pulled hard on the calf's legs. The next contraction almost immediately followed, and the heifer tried desperately to push.

Suddenly there was a give in the calf, and the heifer pushed again—hard.

The calf came out so quickly, Anya was propelled backwards into the mesquite bush. She felt thorns dig into her flesh and winced at the burning, stabbing pain, knowing they were going to hurt like hell when she pulled them out. It hurt like hell already. She drew in a deep breath to keep from crying out at the fiery ache.

"Let her up," she said to Stryker, and he lifted his knee from the heifer's neck. Instantly she propped herself up on the ground, staring at the unmoving object she'd given birth to. With a few grunts, she went to a standing position on trembling legs and began to lick the slickened calf.

A minute passed by, and Anya grew anxious that the calf wasn't moving. She couldn't lose two in one night... But as faint streamers of light appeared in the sky, she realized it was no longer night. A new day had dawned.

"I should've called you sooner. Thanks for trying..."

"Shh!" Anya exclaimed, wincing as she extracted herself from the mesquite bush. The calf was moving.

"Have you had a lot of calls this week?"

"Ouch! Yes. It has been busy."

"Have all the calls been as bad as mine?"

"No, and yours wasn't so bad. If you had waited much longer, it would have. I lost a heifer last night because the rancher waited far too long. It breaks my heart every time I lose one of my animals." She drew in an audible sharp breath.

"Sorry. I can't believe how many of these you have in you! You do realize that you'll probably have a rather painful reaction to this?"

"Trust me, I'm already painfully aware of everything involving these damned thorns right now." Anya stood leaning against the horse they had ridden out to the pasture, her eyes squeezed closed against the pain as Stryker removed each agonizing thorn one by one. He wished he could take the pain away from her and take it upon himself. Fortunately, her jeans had protected her from some of the smaller, more difficult thorns, but several of the long thorns had penetrated the thick denim and would certainly leave sores.

"This is my fault," he said with sincerity.

A smile touched Anya's face. "If you knew all the stuff I've fallen into over the years, you would realize this is nothing. I once fell into a cactus. So this is definitely not the worst." She hissed out her breath through her teeth when he pulled out a thorn that was deeply embedded in her upper thigh. Because of the way the thorns had gone in, it was far easier to pull them out with her jeans still on, much to his disappointment. The thorns had literally pinned her jeans to her body.

His hands roamed over her back, feeling for any additional thorns he might have missed. Then his hands moved lower, and he could feel the tension in her body. He wanted her to trust him completely. It was a thought that suddenly disturbed him. Why did he want her to trust him? What was it about her that had him dreaming about her, thinking about her as he went about his work, even looking forward to the next time she would come to the ranch? *It's because she challenges you in*

*a way no one else ever has. She makes you want to be
a better man.*

"You have some more…" His hands continued to
trail over the backs of her thighs.

"Believe me, I know. I can feel every single one
of them."

He frowned, and she turned her head to look at him.
He was pulled into her light hazel eyes. It seemed as if
there were a thousand colors in those eyes. She gave him
one of her smiles that he'd wondered if he would ever
see again. The soft, carefree smile that had intrigued him
from the moment he met her.

"You've got this, tough guy. Don't go fainting on
me now."

He could feel the corner of his mouth pulling into
a smile. "I was feeling a bit woozy there for a second.
Would you revive me if I passed out?"

"Not a chance. I'd finish pulling out the thorns myself
and ride your horse back to the ranch. You could walk
back once you came to."

Stryker was dumbfounded for a moment, unsure how
to respond to her comment. Then she chuckled. He shook
his head. "Woman, you have thorns sticking out of your
ass, and you're in the mood to joke?"

Still laughing softly, she replied, "Who says I'm joking?"

Stryker plucked out one of the thorns, and she drew
in a sharp breath. "Because I know you, and you could
never be so cruel."

"You *think* you know me."

His mind flashed back to that horrible night when
she'd tried to get out of the truck. He could still feel
the tug on his arm when he knew she'd fallen. She had

risked serious harm just to get away from his truck, from her nightmares, from *him*.

He kneeled and his eyes were level with her ass. If it wasn't for the thorns sticking out, he would be mesmerized by its perfect heart shape. She was a small woman, and many would probably say she was too thin. But he recognized her strength and her muscle and knew she wasn't thin. She was lean, like a well-trained athlete. He plucked the last thorn loose, and he lightly ran his hands over her ass, checking to make sure there weren't any that he missed.

Damn, he was getting hard just touching her! But he had another motive as he was kneeling there. Quickly, he leaned down and lifted up the leg of her jeans, and there was the evidence of road rash he had suspected.

He stood and turned her to face him. "You *did* get hurt that night. Why didn't you tell me?"

"Seriously? You really want to rehash that night again?" Her eyes held shock and…pain.

He should have realized the subject would be a delicate one for her. He wanted to rewind and take back his words. "I don't mean to bring up old feelings. What you went through was terrible. I just can't believe you tried to jump from a moving truck."

"I know," she whispered.

"At first I thought it was something I'd said, or done. But then… Wait, what?"

"I said, I know. I know what you were trying to do. But that doesn't make it any easier to relive my embarrassment. I don't want anyone to know I had a panic attack. Can we just forget it ever happened?"

Why can't I let this go? I've just got to make it right.

She's still hurting. "No." His answer made her gaze fly up to his in confusion.

"I thought you would want to move forward as if it never happened, so to speak." Anya watched him, her brow furrowed in puzzlement.

"Having a panic attack is hardly anything to be ashamed of. In fact, it makes you a little more—well, real. You were coming across a little too perfect to be human." He smiled when her lips twitched. "I want you to trust me. I want you to feel like you can be yourself around me." *I want you to like me again. I want to be blessed with those smiles again. I want to feel your sweet body pressed against mine again. I want you to touch me again. I want you.*

The realization was jarring. He wanted her. He wanted her to be his and only his. The idea of another man receiving the same attention brought up an unexpected jealousy. He didn't want to be feeling these things for a woman. And yet, this woman…

"I would like that too," Anya said softly.

Had she been reading his mind? Was she saying… No, wait, she was replying to his earlier comment. "So you think we can go back to the way things were?" He wanted to put his hands on her waist. He wanted to kiss her.

"Yes. I just… I don't know how to explain it. You're the first person ever to see me have a panic attack. You won't tell anyone about it, will you?"

He smiled down at her. "Not a soul. Well, you're finally thorn-free. We can head back now."

She smiled up at him, and he quickly mounted the horse, then offered his hand down to her. She grabbed

ahold of his forearm, and he lifted her up and in front of
him again. She leaned back against him and settled in
comfortably. Which meant her ass was nestled directly
against his crotch. He was in trouble.

Chapter 5

THIS TIME, HE SLID HIS ARM AROUND HER WAIST. THEY weren't running at full speed, so there really wasn't a need for it. But it brought her a sense of security she wasn't aware she craved. They were traveling at a leisurely walk, and even though Anya knew she had a thousand things to do when she got back to the clinic, she didn't complain.

She could feel the muscles of his chest against her back, and her mouth suddenly went dry. The man was incredibly handsome in spite of his often surly attitude. Even beneath his ranch clothes, she could tell he was muscular, but feeling his biceps flex as his arm curled around her, she knew he was even more so than she'd originally thought. And it was hard not to look at him.

His face was just as fierce as he was, with strong, angular lines and a square jaw. His jet-black hair and dark eyes only emphasized his olive skin and full lips. He was a man who knew what he wanted and would stop at nothing to get it—at least, that was what his expression said every time she looked at him.

The warmth of the morning sun beat down on her, and she found herself relaxing deeper and deeper into his embrace. His arm tightened around her waist, and she smiled. The next thing she knew, his lips were against her skin, murmuring softly. Then she felt a small kiss behind her ear, and she slowly let her head fall to the side as he layered kisses down her neck. Heat built within her lower belly, and she didn't want it to ever stop.

"I'd love to stay like this all day, but I think the horse might get a bit irritated with us," he whispered in a husky voice against her ear.

"Mmm," she replied, wanting more. His arm tightened around her gently, then began to release her, and her eyes opened slowly. They were back at the ranch house, sitting atop the horse near her truck. She had been asleep! *Had it all just been a dream? A sweet, wonderful dream?* "Oh!" she said, sitting upright, unaware she'd grabbed ahold of his forearm. "I'm so sorry I fell asleep."

"I'm not," he said in a deep, rumbling voice, sending vibrations through her chest, and her nipples tightened in response. The man exuded everything masculine and sexual, from the way he moved to the way he spoke. And she was practically draping herself all over him. Reluctantly, she peeled herself out of his warm embrace and instantly felt cold and lonely.

He dismounted quickly and pulled her down gently, letting her body slide down his. She felt him inch by agonizing inch until her feet were firmly on the ground. His cologne was intoxicating—a warm, heady aroma of spices, leather, horses, and the delicious scent of man.

She needed to control her wayward mind. She had so many things to do, and standing here fantasizing in the arms of this man wasn't going to get anything accomplished.

He reached up slowly, as though approaching a skittish young filly, stroked some of her unruly hair out of her face, and hooked it behind her ear. "Where do you go from here?" he asked softly.

"I leave from here to the clinic. We don't open for another hour, so at least I'll be able to get some paperwork done and freshen up a bit. That is, so long as there isn't another call for a calf birth."

"You look practically dead on your feet as it is." Had his words not been framed by his expression of concern, she would have been offended. She gave him an amused shrug of her shoulders.

"I get to sleep when all the calves are born."

"That could be weeks!" When all she did was shrug once more, he frowned deeply and slid his arm around her waist again in a protective gesture.

"Come inside." He said it as if it were a command, but she decided it was a request, and her heart began to beat wildly in her chest. This man was…dangerous. She could feel it in the leashed power of his muscles, see it in the mystery stirring deep in his dark eyes, and knew it from the way she could sense he hadn't been completely honest with her about his past. But somehow, deep inside, she believed he wasn't a danger to her. The way he looked at her, the way he had so carefully removed the thorns from her, the way he wanted to protect her now… He wouldn't hurt her.

She nodded, and he kept his arm around her waist as he led the horse to the patch of green grass near the house. He released her only long enough to tether the horse, then returned to wrap his arm about her, holding her against his side. It felt natural, as if that were where it belonged. She wondered if he could feel her racing pulse.

A wave of cool air washed over her as she stepped into the magnificent foyer of the home, and she smelled the scent of bacon wafting about the house. She heard men talking and laughing boisterously, and hesitated. Stryker's arm tightened around her. She looked up at him, suddenly filled with doubt. "I...I really should go back to the clinic. I didn't mean to intrude."

"You aren't intruding. I invited you in, remember?" His voice was still a low rumble, and it was making her insides quiver. What was it about this man? She had never felt this way before. Maybe she was getting sick.

She drew a deep breath and nodded again, and he smiled down at her. Suddenly she didn't care about the other men in the house, didn't care about her thundering heart or the butterflies low in her stomach, because she thought she was going to melt into a giant puddle on the floor. "You should do that more often," she said softly.

"Do what?"

"This," she whispered, and before she could think better of it, her fingers lightly traced his smiling lips. His eyes darkened, and the smile slowly slipped from his face.

"You're playing with fire, bella." His reply was soft and almost seemed to caress her.

Her eyes searched his face intently, but she felt no fear. Instead, she wanted to be closer to him. She suddenly felt flushed under his scrutiny, but she didn't turn away. There was just something about this man that made her long for things she'd never known.

"Boss man is back, and he brought a woman with him."

The man's voice jarred her out of the trance she seemed to be in, and she looked over to see a man she hadn't met before. He was tall, with a light olive complexion. His hair was deep brown, and his eyes were a magnificent hazel.

"Thank you, Santo, for the grand announcement," Stryker growled and pulled Anya forward. "Anya, this is Santo. He's usually very quiet, but he seems of a different mind this morning." Stryker's voice dripped with irritation. But Santo looked at Stryker, and something in that brief gaze carried a message to Stryker, because Anya could feel him draw in a slow, deep breath.

Something had happened. Or was going to happen. She couldn't tell which one it was. And she couldn't tell if it was good or bad, because neither man looked concerned.

"Hello, Santo," Anya said, extending her hand. "I'm the veterinarian." That was the best introduction she had? She needed to work on that.

"Ah. So, were you able to save the heifer? She woke up Brusco with that damned cry of hers, and he was just about to shoot her and put her out of her misery."

Anya recoiled in shock at his words and nearly didn't catch the wink Santo gave Brusco as he rounded the corner. "Don't believe a word he says," Brusco said, giving Santo a none-too-gentle elbow to the ribs. He grabbed ahold of her hand and squeezed it gently. "Nice to meet you, Doc. I'm Brusco. The only sane one of the bunch."

"Oh, please, just call me Anya." She felt so tiny standing next to the three burly men. They were all lean, tall, and muscular, and seemed carefree. But there was an undercurrent of tension, something she couldn't put her finger on.

"I really should return to my clinic," Anya said, turning toward Stryker and finding his eyes watching her intently. "I don't want to interfere."

"You'll be hurting my feelings if you leave." Another

large man came walking toward them, a wide grin on his face. "I've already made extra food for you to have breakfast with us." He dried his hands off with a towel and extended one to her for a handshake. "I'm Snap."

"Hello, Snap," she said politely. "I wouldn't want to hurt your feelings, especially when everything smells so good."

His grin broadened, and then he motioned for her to follow him. "It's serve yourself around here. And I recommend you get to the food before the rest of the men, or you'll end up with crumbs."

"Does that mean you're finally done cooking?" a male voice called from around the corner, and two more men stepped forward. Anya thought she must be seeing things. How could they all be so muscular, so powerful and confident?

Distantly, she realized Stryker was rubbing her back through her shirt, soothing her. He must have sensed she was becoming nervous around so many intimidating men. He leaned into her, and her heart raced as she felt his whisper against her ear. "If you want to leave, I completely understand."

Anya drew a deep breath and squared her shoulders. She wasn't going to be intimidated by all these men. Especially not in front of Stryker. "I don't want to let Snap down," she said, her lips tilted in a half smile as she looked at him.

"All right. Just don't say I didn't warn you. These guys can be savages when it comes to food."

"And what's funny is that Stryker is usually the worst of all of us."

Anya gazed up at Stryker and noticed him cast an

irritated glare in the direction of the man who said it. Then he looked back at her and a lopsided grin touched his face. "You've already met Phantom. And the one with the big mouth is Buzz. Guys, in case you didn't catch it, this is Anya. She's our veterinarian and will be helping us with all the animals."

She shook hands with each one of them, amazed by how small her hand was compared to theirs. Did they all spend hours upon hours a day at the gym? Were they all somehow related by larger-than-life relatives? That had to be it.

Stryker led her around in the home until they came upon a large, open kitchen that allowed her to see the dining area and the living room. These men were certainly spoiled. Their house was easily one of the most exquisite she had been in around the Hebbronville area. Farther outside of Hebbronville were some lavish homes, but even they seemed to pale in comparison to this one.

He handed her a paper plate and guided her to the stove. "Snap loves to cook, and he does one helluva job at it. So we let him run free—in the kitchen, that is."

She looked down at the lightweight paper plate in her hands, and her lips twitched at the thought of any one of these men washing dishes, but that didn't change the heat in her cheeks. Stryker still had his arm around her waist, and now only shifted so she could get access to the food. "What about you?" she asked, noticing he didn't hold a plate.

"I'll get mine when the men have gotten theirs." He spoke low and soft, as though he didn't want the men to hear him.

There were eggs, bacon, sausage, pancakes, and even chorizo and egg with tortillas on the side. Anya's mouth watered just looking at the food. Finally, she settled on a chorizo-and-egg taco and was going for the chile when Stryker's arm tightened around her. "Careful. It's muy picante."

"What makes you think I don't like things hot?" she asked with a coy smile and looked up at him. The way he was watching her made it very obvious what *he* liked hot, and she was feeding the flame.

"Remember what I said about playing with fire?" His voice was low and husky.

No man had ever spoken to her in such a way. She had sworn off men after the disaster with her boyfriend so many years ago, but the things promised in Stryker's eyes made her wonder…

"The men are waiting," she said softly, trying to change the subject.

"And they can continue to wait if necessary, bella."

She struggled to tear her eyes from his and snagged a pancake, then let him escort her to the table. He pulled out a chair for her, then went back, following his men into the kitchen. It wasn't very long before she was surrounded by five large men, all of them talking and laughing. Stryker had been right: Santo was the rather quiet one, but he threw in quips when needed, well-timed and delivered with perfection so they always hit their mark and often left the men either slack-jawed in pretend offense, or laughing so hard they had tears in their eyes.

None of them touched their food as they waited for Stryker. It was odd, in these times, to see that level of courtesy. She marveled at it. These men were disciplined. She glanced over at the man who was approaching the table—the man who was making her heart and stomach trade places.

Stryker joined them quickly, and she noticed not one of them had made a move toward the head of the table where Stryker now sat. So he was the "boss man" as they had said. She supposed they had to have someone as the leader of the ranch or dysfunction could quickly follow. And Stryker seemed a natural born leader.

He had come back to the table with his plate heaped as high as the rest of them and grinned as he looked around the table. Instantly, the men interlinked hands, Snap grabbing hers on the left and Stryker grabbing her right, and Stryker led them in prayer. Anya was surprised. She had never thought hard men such as these would be the type to pray before a meal. But she'd been wrong.

"Amen! Let's eat!" Snap said, and Anya smiled at him. It seemed to be a contest between Snap and Buzz over which one could be the loudest and proudest. They all had great qualities in her mind.

For a few minutes there was silence at the table as the men enjoyed the food. Anya dug into her taco with gusto, unaware of how hungry she was after having been up all night. The chile was hot, but not more than she could tolerate. And the flavor was fantastic. As she finished the last bite of her taco, she suddenly became aware that all eyes at the table were on her.

She wiped at her mouth with a napkin to make sure she didn't have grease all over her, and her eyes scanned the table. "What?" she asked hesitantly.

"If you can eat Snap's chile, you can eat with us whenever you want." Phantom's lips twitched.

Anya's gaze shot to Stryker, and he was watching her intently, but he wasn't smiling. Instead, she saw the same fire burning in his eyes as she'd seen when she had touched his lips earlier. Before she lost the ability to speak, she turned back to the table. "Well, if he wants to make it so weak, anyone can eat it."

"Oh!" The collective shouts around the table as fingers pointed at Snap made her laugh at their antics. She glanced back at Stryker, and he still watched her intently, his gaze never leaving her face.

"Can you pass the butter?" she asked, squirming under his scrutiny. She felt as if his eyes were peering into her soul, searching for all her hopes and dreams, fears and nightmares. And if she let him, he would have access to it all.

He broke his gaze with her and handed her the butter and the syrup, and returned to the last of the food he had on his plate. She drowned her pancake in butter and syrup, and her eyelids fluttered in bliss as the fluffy, sweet morsel melted in her mouth. She was almost disappointed it was a paper plate. Because she was seriously tempted to lick the plate clean.

"Snap, you sure can cook," she sighed contentedly. "I think I may be able to make it through the day now that I've had that delicious meal."

"You're going to give him a bigger head than he already has," Brusco grumbled good-naturedly.

"At least let me help with the dishes," she said, as she stood and began to collect the empty paper plates from around the table.

Phantom stood and took the plates from her, shaking his head. "You're a guest in this house. You don't need to do the dishes."

"But I want to help…"

Stryker stood, immediately drawing her attention, and she was captured by his gaze. He looked…pleased. "You have your clinic you need to tend to. We won't make you stay and wash the dishes this time. But next time…" He shrugged. "Next time might be a different story."

Anya tore her eyes off him and gazed at the rest of the men at the table. "Y'all are wonderful," she said with a smile. "I've thoroughly enjoyed spending time here, and I hope one day I can learn how y'all earned your nicknames. I'm sure you have some incredible stories to tell."

The men exchanged glances around the table, then grinned up at her. She was suddenly reminded of the Cheshire cat from *Alice in Wonderland*. Then, she felt Stryker's hand on her upper arm, the warmth of his skin seeping through into hers. She turned to look at him, struck again by how powerfully handsome he was.

"I'll walk you out to your truck." His hand slid down her arm to her hand, and he gripped it lightly.

Anya turned back to the men with a smile. "Thank you, all of you, for the wonderful breakfast. And for the great company." They responded with nods, and all of them stood as she left. She couldn't remember the last time she had been around men who had so much respect for a woman. But as soon as she left the dining room, all her attention was focused on the man who made her feel as if she were already melting in the hot Texas sun.

—⁓—

Her hand felt so small in his giant paw. She was a petite woman, but she had more fight in her than women he'd met who were twice her size. And she had a sense of humor that had shined through as she joined in the banter at the breakfast table. Maybe she wasn't human. Because she seemed too good to be true.

They came to her truck far too soon, and she turned to face him, a small smile lifting the corners of her mouth. "Thank you."

"I should be the one thanking you. If it weren't for your skills, I'd have lost both the calf and the heifer this morning. You're amazing."

"I'd hardly go that far. If it weren't for your help, I wouldn't have been able to save them." Her gaze traveled around, looking at the improvements to the arena, the cattle chute, and other areas they'd been working on for the past week. "I can see you're starting to remember ranching life."

"It's in my blood." He still hadn't released her hand. He didn't want to. He didn't want to let her go. And that very idea was what made him drop her hand and take half a step back. "Thank you again. I hope that's the last heifer we struggle with."

She looked confused for a moment, then nodded. "So do I. But just call me whenever there's even the slightest concern. It doesn't matter what hour it is."

He nodded and reached around her to open the door to her truck. "Be safe. I don't want you to fall asleep driving back to town."

She chuckled, a husky, rich sound that made his heart

pound hard and heavy. "It's impossible to fall asleep on these bumpy roads."

He closed the door when she had slid into the truck, and she gave him a small wave as she drove away. He simply nodded to her. Then he turned and stomped back to the house to take a cold shower.

"I think I'm losing my mind," Anya groaned.

Elena chuckled as she fastened the horse into the stanchion. "What happened this time? Another bizarre calving story to share with me?"

Anya cast her a frown as she moved toward the horse. "I don't know how to explain it. The things I'm feeling... There's something special about him, Elena. He's so strong and smart and kind—"

"Yes, you're losing your mind," Elena interrupted. She smiled at her best friend. "But I've known that for years. What you are suffering from is far worse, I think."

"What are you talking about?" Anya asked, running her hands down the front of the horse's leg, checking it for swelling and tenderness.

"You think he's hot."

Anya's head jerked up, and she frowned at Elena. "Don't be preposterous." She returned her attention to the horse. "I only recognize he's a good man."

"I've *never* heard you talk about a man that way. What happened to us being confirmed bachelorettes for the rest of our lives?"

Anya laughed. "It's not as if this is going anywhere. I'm allowed to appreciate a good man, aren't I?"

"It sounds like a lot more than appreciation." Elena

shrugged, her curly, black hair bouncing on her shoulders. "Don't say I didn't warn you."

Anya looked away from her best friend and concentrated on the horse. "Whose horse did you say this was again?"

"Jonas Franklin's."

Anya pulled a face. "Ugh. That guy gives me the creeps. I don't see how you can work for him."

"I rarely have to work with him. All I do is train his horses and compete in shows for him. I avoid him whenever possible."

"Good. That's one guy I can say is *not* a good man."

"Returning to the subject of good men," Elena said, unwilling to let go of the juicy tidbit her friend had just shared. "What makes you so certain this Stryker guy is a good one?"

Anya ignored her for several moments as she concentrated on the horse. Then she urged it to lift its left front hoof for her. "How long has she been lame?"

"Nice deflection," Elena said wryly, then sighed, accepting the fact that Anya had donned her veterinarian hat and wasn't going to take it off until she had answers. "About a week ago she received new shoes. I thought that was where the problem lay. Figured the farrier had trimmed her down too short. But the problem should have worked itself out by now."

"She's got a hoof abscess," Anya said, her voice muffled as she leaned over the horse's hoof to examine it. She straightened and turned to face Elena. "The farrier should have caught it. I'm sure getting her hooves trimmed and a new set of shoes aggravated it. We'll have to drain it and treat it."

"Jonas will be thrilled to hear that."

"So long as you keep him away from my clinic, I'll be happy. I'm glad you brought the horse in here so I didn't have to make a trip out there."

Elena gave her a goofy smile. "What's a best friend for?" They walked back into the clinic, and Elena grabbed a candy off the counter, popping it into her mouth. "So, you gonna tell me how you suddenly have magical powers and can tell if a guy is good or not?"

Anya groaned as she sat down in her chair and made notes in the chart for the horse. "You're not going to let this go, are you?"

"This is the most fun I've had in weeks."

"I had a panic attack on our way home from the cattle auction."

Elena's joking face immediately fell flat. "Oh, shit, Anya, I'm sorry."

Anya waved a hand dismissively. "He took care of me. He wasn't irritated or bothered by it. He held my hair back while I threw up. Not one of my best moments, but he didn't care. Not even my own parents reacted that way when I had a panic attack. He's a good man, Elena. I can feel it."

Elena watched her closely as she twirled the hard candy around in her mouth. "If he takes care of you… If he makes you smile, then he's okay in my book. You know how I feel about men."

"Yes, and it isn't healthy. Not all of them are going to be like that jerk. You need to live again, Elena."

"All I'm saying is, be careful. Don't let him hurt you—and I'm not talking about physically. I'd hate to have to hunt him down if he broke your heart."

Anya smiled and grabbed Elena's hand. "We've got a long way to go before there's a chance of that."

Elena gave her a speculative look. "You're more than halfway there already. I can see it all over your face."

"Ugh! Enough! I never should have told you. Now you're going to harass me nonstop. C'mon. Let's go take care of your horse and get ice cream from Dairy Queen when we're done."

"Oh! Did you hear they have a new Blizzard flavor out this month?" Anya couldn't help but laugh at Elena's excitement. For the rest of the afternoon, her thoughts were occupied by Elena's latest adventures, and not the dark eyes and warm touch of the man who filled her dreams.

Chapter 6

"WE BELIEVE HE'S BEEN IN AND OUT OF THE U.S. AT LEAST ten times in the last year. But he's a ghost. We've tracked surveillance from the border patrol cameras. We've also pulled images from the buildings we know he's been in or around. Every time we think we've found something, there is a blip on the screen, or a portion of the data has been erased. It's like I said... The man is a ghost."

"A ghost." Admiral Haslett ran a hand down his face wearily, then studied the commander sitting across from him. The man was competent and had worked hard to gather intel. But they needed more. So much more. Whoever this ghost was, he was wreaking havoc. "This ghost is costing us time and money. How the hell does this guy keep slipping past us?"

The commander frowned. "He has connections in a lot of places. More than we even know at this point. He may have been tipped off that the U.S. government is tracking him. He may be onto us." The admiral stood and paced the office for several moments, contemplating what the commander had just said. They had barely started operations with the undercover unit in Hebbronville, and already there were problems.

With a heavy sigh, he sat down and the commander spoke again. "We don't know who he is, but we think we know *where* he is. We've had a few people indicate that a man of average build and height had come in for an appointment with each one of our victims prior to their death. One characteristic mentioned over and over again has been that he wears a ring with a scorpion on it. Then most of the people say he looked nice, or professional, or other vague observations that help us very little."

A fluorescent light above them buzzed and made a soft popping sound, and the light flickered. It wasn't helping the admiral's mood any. He was already nearly blinded by the all-white interior of his office that he'd tried his best to cover with framed diplomas and certificates to break the monotony. And the temperature in the office was so fickle, it would go from freezing to sweltering in a matter of thirty minutes. At the moment, it was close to sweltering, and he could feel sweat rolling down his back. But part of that had to do with the report he was receiving.

"This type of ring is one of a kind. Here's a sketch of it that one of the associates of a victim provided. We've been doing some research. We've found a man who wears a ring like this, and we're pretty sure he's a match for our ghost."

"Are you telling me you have an idea who this man is? Spit it out. Tell me who your ghost is." He needed good news. He needed *actionable* news.

"Benicio Davila. He's the leader of a drug cartel in Mexico called the Scorpions."

Admiral Haslett leaned back in his chair, digesting the information. "You mean to tell me all the technology and information we've been losing has been going to a drug cartel?" Just that week they'd received notice that one of the largest tech corporations in America had been hacked and that key data and technology applications had been stolen.

"Yes. We intercepted some of their communications… They're using the applications and data that were stolen from us to help move their product secretly. They're using some of the stolen encryption and coding techniques, but it goes far beyond what we've seen before from the NSA. They obviously have a very talented coder on their side. And even if we were able to raid the cartel, the odds of catching Davila are slim."

Admiral Haslett frowned and looked at the file he had opened on his laptop, full of gruesome pictures of men who had been murdered for their knowledge, apparently only to gain intel and technology to further the operations of a drug cartel. Most of them were low-level tech guys from various companies. Others were high-ranking corporate officers, which he supposed was intended to frighten other companies into handing over their information. No, something didn't add up. The cartels were getting more sophisticated, he knew that. The military had been battling their encryption codes for years already. There was more behind this. They needed to find out what it was and stop it immediately. And he knew who to use to make it happen.

"Thank you, Commander. I'll review this information and determine next steps." He stood and the commander also stood, sharply saluting him before turning on his heel and leaving the room quickly. Admiral Haslett shook his head, looked back at the images on his computer, and sighed heavily. This project was going to require specific skills and talents, things that weren't easy to find. But he knew exactly where to get what he needed.

—∿∿—

He had been sweating bullets from the moment he had set foot on the property. Getting around the security system had been one of the most complicated jobs ever. But that was why they paid him so well.

The house had significant foliage around it, making it hard to see how large it really was. He had been about to creep up on the house to get a few pictures when the sound of hooves pounding the ground forced him to dive for cover.

A man came riding up toward him, and for a moment he feared he'd been found. But the man was focused on the woman in his arms, who appeared to be asleep. He saw his opportunity and took it, getting several pictures of the two of them. The man who'd hired him for the job would certainly be pleased.

He was even able to snap a few photos of the men who greeted them at the large door before it was closed firmly. He sat back on his haunches and smiled. He would follow the girl. Obviously she meant something to these men—or at least the one man in particular. And if she meant something to them, the man who hired him would appreciate pictures of her. Which meant he could ask for more money.

—∿∿—

"You want to tell me what has all of you acting so tense?" Stryker asked after his cold shower. The men had finished cleaning the kitchen and gathered around the dining room table, talking among themselves. From the tone, he could tell it wasn't the best news.

"There have been more murders." Phantom watched him closely, playing with a rubber band in his hands.

"On American soil?"

"And Mexican soil. But there's a good chance it was the same killer."

"How did you come across this information?"

"News articles and messages I discovered this morning while digging around online," Buzz said. "The messages were posted on dark web message boards, though they weren't encrypted. It was almost as if amateurs were jumping on and talking to each other. The news articles just came out this morning, but it was only because of what I had already read on the dark web that I could connect the murders."

"This is why we're here. We're supposed to get ahead of this type of thing before it becomes a major issue." Stryker sat at the head of the table, running a hand wearily down his face. He had already been up for hours. But the work never stopped, not when you were on a mission.

"Haslett hasn't contacted us…yet. I have a feeling we'll be hearing from him soon, though," Brusco said in his deep, gravelly voice.

"Two low-level tech guys from a major software company were murdered a couple of days ago. The more I dug, the more information I discovered. Their company had been hacked shortly before their deaths. They must have gotten too close to figuring out who did it."

"Do *we* know who did it?"

"Not yet, sir. But I believe it's someone from within Mexico. Just a few days prior to these murders, another two men were killed in Mexico in what appeared to be an unusual drug transaction." Buzz folded his hands together on top of the dining room table.

"Unusual, how?"

"It appears they were tortured first. Usually with drug cartels, the transactions are quick, and you either live through them or you're shot between the eyes. Torture is usually only a form of retribution or retaliation against a rival," Santo said, his voice tense. "For these two to have been tortured during the course of a transaction…" He shrugged. "It doesn't seem to make any sense. Hell, none of this makes any sense."

"What other information do we have?"

"That's it so far. But things are heating up. If the murders are connected, we're going to have to take action, and soon. Our government won't sit still for long if there is a murderer crossing the border." Phantom frowned deeply.

"I'll get in touch with Haslett. There may be information to connect all this. In the meantime, keep alert, all of you. Buzz, try to dig into those messages on the dark web further and see what else you can discover."

"Yes, sir," they said in unison. Stryker's muscles bunched with tension. A new mission was headed their way, and soon. He could feel it.

The days went by quickly. Between clinic hours and late-night calving emergencies, Anya wasn't getting more than four or five hours of sleep a night. She knew she needed to get some genuine sleep soon, or her faculties would become impaired. She was tempted to close the clinic for a day just to sleep. Sleep would come on Sunday, she kept reminding herself. It was the one day of the week she'd close the clinic and enjoy a little personal time.

Her first calving call for the day had come in early Saturday night. It was six o'clock and the rancher was worried his heifer had been in labor for nearly four hours. Anya tried to reassure him over the phone that it was completely normal for a first-time mother to be in labor longer than the more seasoned heifers, but he wasn't going to feel comfortable until she came to check and make sure things were progressing normally.

Anya had driven out to the ranch, of course. The heifer progressed naturally, and she instructed the rancher just to stand back and watch. An hour later, a new calf was born and the rancher was breathing a sigh of relief.

It was after eight when Anya climbed back into her bed and instantly fell into a much-needed sleep. At ten o'clock, her phone rang and she fumbled for it in the dark. "Dr. Gutierrez," she managed to say, her voice husky.

"Anya, it's Stryker."

Instantly, she was awake and her heart was racing. He had occupied her thoughts all week long. She had even dreamed of riding with him again, wrapped in his warm arms. But this time she'd been awake as she'd allowed him to kiss her neck and had even pivoted in his arms to allow his full lips to capture hers. Had he truly kissed her neck when she had been there on Monday? Or was it all just a figment of her imagination?

"Stryker…what is it?" She was sitting up, running her fingers through her hair quickly as she searched for her boots at the foot of the bed.

"It's another one of the heifers you were worried about. She's only been in labor for a few hours, but already I can tell there's going to be a problem."

"I'm on my way." Excitement to see Stryker again had wiped the fogginess of sleep from her mind, and she maneuvered her truck down the old dirt road to reach his ranch quickly. Same as last time, he was on horseback when she arrived, and she didn't hesitate to reach up for his hand when she approached him.

Most of the other ranches she visited had four-wheelers to drive around in the thick south Texas brush, but Stryker seemed partial to his horse, and she wasn't about to complain. He wrapped his arm around her waist, and she gripped his forearm as they galloped through the brush and the trees, headed to the site where he had last seen the heifer.

They were fortunate enough to have a nearly full moon, which cast its glow down upon their path. It also caused shadows to jump out where she least expected, and Anya clung even tighter to Stryker's arm. During calving season, one of the biggest obstacles they faced was the abundance of coyotes prowling for young, help-less calves.

He slowed as they drew near, and she saw a heifer pacing back and forth, swishing her tail in agitation. "What made you concerned?" Anya asked before they dismounted.

"She's been bleeding. But there doesn't appear to be any amniotic fluid, which is good, right?"

"Yes, that's good. But I'm concerned about the bleeding. She may be tearing from the size of the calf."

He dismounted quickly and turned to lift her down.

They moved to the heifer slowly, but the heifer was already trying to lie down. Anya stopped walking, afraid to disturb the cow until it settled into a position so it could attempt to give birth. But she saw the blood trailing down its hindquarters and leg, and frowned. The placenta could be tearing away from the uterine wall, which would explain the blood.

The heifer had settled on the ground and was breathing heavily. "I need to examine her," Anya said, looking up at Stryker. "Will you hold her the same as you did the last one?"

He nodded, then took up his position, pinning the cow's head and neck to the ground. Anya moved in slowly, sliding on her long, latex gloves. She kneeled down behind the heifer and shifted her tail to the side. The cervix was fully dilated, and it was obvious her body was prepared to give birth.

Going by touch alone, Anya eased her arm into the birth canal and finally touched something. It was a tail. "The calf is in a breech position," Anya said softly. "I'm going to have to try to turn it."

"What can I do to help?"

"Just keep holding her down. This is going to be very uncomfortable for her." Anya focused on finding the legs of the calf, and slowly began to manipulate its position, carefully pulling the head forward as soon as she could reach it. "She's just about in the right position—"

"Anya! Look out!"

The words hadn't left his mouth before she saw the heifer lifting her hoof to kick. It was normal, especially given that what Anya was doing to her was incredibly painful. She jerked backwards to avoid the flying hoof,

tripped over a large rock, and gasped as she fell backwards, unable to regain her balance.

"Anya—"

His words were cut off as pain exploded in her head.
The ground had rushed up to greet her, knocking the
air from her lungs. She didn't know what she had hit
her head on, but it was hard and unforgiving. Nausea
instantly rolled through her stomach as the pain gripped
her head in a vise.

Bright explosions went off on the inside of her eyelids
as she struggled to draw in air. She could hear Stryker
talking to her, but the pain was blinding. Finally, she was
able to draw in a few breaths and force her eyes open.

Stryker was holding her in his lap, his face creased
with concern. "Anya, answer me, please."

"Stryker," she gasped out. She saw momentary relief
cross his face, but then he turned her head to examine
the damage.

"Looks like that rock caught your fall. You hit your
head really hard. You're going to have one helluva bruise."

"Thank my lucky stars for all my hair." She attempted
to be lighthearted about the entire situation, but pain
lanced through her when she tried to smile.

Anya struggled to sit up, but Stryker held firm. "Not
so fast. You nearly cracked your head open. You scared
the shit out of me. You need to stay still for a little while."

"Stryker, I'm fine. Just… just hold on to me in case
I'm a little dizzy, will you?"

Stryker frowned, but nodded in agreement and helped
her to her feet. She wavered for a moment, but then found
some stability, though she was immensely grateful for
Stryker's hands on her waist. Then she gasped in surprise.

"See? There was no need to rush," Stryker murmured against her ear. The heifer was licking its newborn calf, her eyes closed in motherly bliss.

"I'm so glad you called me when you did. We would have lost both of them if you hadn't." She carefully removed her latex gloves and wondered why everything looked so fuzzy. The dizziness was back, more vicious than ever. She needed to grab ahold of something... She needed *him*.

She lifted her head and slowly pivoted toward Stryker, reaching for him. "Stryker..." And everything went black.

Stryker caught Anya as she fell, curse words streaming from his lips. Holding her gently in his arms, he mounted his horse and took off at a fast walk, so as not to jar her any more than necessary, heading back to the house as fast as he could. He cradled her in his arms, trying to absorb the impact of each of the horse's steps himself to buffer her.

It seemed like hours, but only about fifteen minutes later, he was at the house and carrying her into one of the spare bedrooms. By the lamplight, she looked so incredibly pale, and his heart clenched.

He hated to leave her, but he needed help. He hurried down the corridor to Phantom's room and rapped on the door lightly. Within moments, Phantom was at the door, peering through the small slit that Stryker had insisted be placed on every door in the house. If they were going to be attacked in their own home, at least they could see who was coming.

"Shit, Stryker," he said as he opened his door. "Do you know what time it is? You're lucky I looked through the hole first." He walked back to his bed, no longer trying to conceal the sidearm that he held in his right hand. He opened his nightstand drawer and carefully placed it inside.

"I need your help." The urgency in Stryker's voice grabbed Phantom's attention, and he hesitated in closing the drawer.

"What's wrong? What's happened?"

"It's Anya. She's out cold. She doesn't look good."

"Shit." Phantom closed his nightstand drawer and didn't bother wasting time to get dressed. He followed Stryker out in just his boxer shorts.

"She took quite a tumble. I heard the thud of her head hitting the rock. The back of her head is bleeding only a little, but she's awfully pale."

In the short time that he'd been away from her, there had been little change. She still lay in the same position Stryker had placed her in. And she was unnaturally pale. Phantom nudged him aside so he could look at Anya, and frowned. "Help me turn her on her side, so I can look at the back of her head. Be careful."

Together they rolled her slowly to her side, and Phantom felt along the back of her head until he found the bump. He examined it carefully, then let out a sigh. "Damn. It's a bad one, but I've seen worse. And"—he hesitated, his fingers feeling up and down her neck—"it doesn't appear she injured her neck. We should still be careful moving her, though, at least until you can wake her."

Stryker ran his hands through his hair in frustration.

The closest hospital was over an hour away. But he trusted Phantom's assessment over any doctor's anyway. Phantom had served in medical for the first few years he was a SEAL, before they'd discovered he was a very talented strategist and could plan out just about any mission they wanted. Ever since then, he'd been their tactical ground operations specialist, and he had thrived in the role. But for now, he was the best medical help Anya could get.

"Do you have a flashlight?" Phantom held out his hand expectantly.

Stryker dug one out of his pocket, a small one he tried to always keep with him, and watched as Phantom aimed it at Anya's eyes. He clenched his hands into fists as Phantom gently lifted one eyelid and flashed the light in and out of her eye, then repeated the process on the second one. He knew Phantom was checking for any type of brain injury.

"Her pupils are responding as they should," he said softly and turned to frown at Stryker. "Did she pass out as soon as she hit her head?"

"No." Stryker shook his head. "It was about two or three minutes later."

"It's possible it was just the shock. Plus, judging by those dark circles under her eyes, I'd say she hasn't slept in days. She could have just hit her wall. Regardless, you need to try to wake her up. Given that she passed out on you, we need to be certain she can wake up. If she can't, we need to get her to the hospital ASAP. If you can wake her up and she talks to you, let her go back to sleep. It will help her heal faster. Now, I'm going to get dressed and start some coffee."

Stryker caught Phantom's arm as he was about to pass, making him pause. "So she's going to be okay?"

Phantom chewed on the inside of his cheek as he studied Stryker's face. "That all depends on how she reacts if you're able to wake her up."

"When I'm able to, brother. *When*."

Stryker turned all his attention on Anya and pulled her hand into both of his, patting it lightly, then a little harder. He sat on the edge of the bed and leaned low over her, placing his lips up against her ear. "Bella, I need you to wake up. Listen to me, Anya. It's time to wake up." He couldn't resist kissing her ear lightly as he spoke.

Still, she didn't move. He rubbed her hand between both of his, noticing how cold it was. "Anya, it's time to wake up," he continued speaking into her ear. "The clinic is about to open. We need you." *I need you.* He was startled as the thought flashed through his mind. He couldn't allow himself to feel such things toward a woman.

Especially Anya. He couldn't risk hurting her. She represented what was good and beautiful in the world, while he represented death and destruction, even if it was in the name of freedom. He couldn't—he wouldn't— contaminate her with his cynical poison.

But he didn't feel cynical when he was around her. He felt alive and powerful and more like a man than he could ever remember feeling. Though, blowing up that bunker full of terrorists that one time had made him feel pretty damn manly. But it was nothing compared to the way Anya made him feel.

He frowned down at her. She was making him think

and feel things he had been running from for years, and he didn't like it. He had to wake her up somehow. He couldn't shake her. If she was badly injured, he didn't want to take the risk.

"Anya, wake up for me. Please." She stirred, and he felt a flicker of hope. "That's it, bella, wake up."

Her eyes cracked open slowly and he could tell she was in pain by the grimace on her face. "Stryker?" Her voice was hoarse. Then a smile crept across her mouth. "I was just dreaming about you. You were kissing me."

Chapter 7

STRYKER ALMOST SWALLOWED HIS TONGUE. WAS THIS a sign that she needed to go to the hospital? She was still smiling.

"You were kissing me all along my neck. Your mouth is so very warm. You held me, and I didn't want it to ever stop. And then you woke me up." Her eyes were suddenly focused on his face. "Was that a dream, Stryker?"

Stryker had to work moisture into his mouth. He couldn't stop himself from reaching out and tucking some of her long, dark hair behind her ear. Her eyes reminded him of a kaleidoscope with every shade of brown and flecks of gold, and he felt he could get lost in them. "No," he said, his voice husky. "It wasn't a dream."

Her gaze searched his face, and he knew he should be focused on her injury. He needed to be assessing the damage. But when it came to Anya, it seemed all his training to control his emotions and always use his head flew away.

"Why did you stop?" she asked, her gaze now set on his lips.

He groaned low and couldn't resist her any longer. He dropped his head down and pressed his lips to hers, soft and gentle, then firmer as she responded to him. Her fingers reached up and curled into his short hair, drawing him closer to her.

He pulled back, reluctant to break the kiss, but worried about Anya's injury. He could imagine what it felt like. He had been at the wrong end of many things...fists, bullets, a grenade that had nearly killed him...

"Do you remember hitting your head?" His voice was soft and low as he did his best not to aggravate her injury any further.

"Yes," she said, her voice just as soft. "I remember. And I remember the calf being born and then...then nothing. Just you."

He ran his knuckles down the side of her face, and she gave him a smile. Then she added, "You have too many blasted rocks on this property. I think you need to hire someone to get rid of all of them."

"Did you *see* the size of the rock your head hit? It's bigger than me. Besides, you're practically dead on your feet as it is. When was the last time you slept?"

"I got a couple of hours before you called me."

Stryker frowned. "How long has it been since you really slept? And by that, I mean, you got more than five hours straight."

She closed her eyes for several seconds, and for a moment he was afraid she'd fallen asleep once more. When she opened them again, he was relieved that they looked clear and aware. "I can't remember. Two weeks maybe? But I catch an hour here and there, and I get refreshed."

"Good. She's awake." Phantom's voice at the doorway shattered their private bubble.

He brought in a steaming mug of coffee for Stryker, then set the a cup of cold water and another cup of apple juice on the nightstand. "Do you feel like you can sit up?" Phantom asked Anya gently, and Stryker began to move away, but Anya's hand suddenly grabbed his, squeezing it tight, and he stayed.

"Yes, I don't think anything else is injured too much, other than my pride." She gave both of them a smile. Slowly, she released Stryker's hand and straightened herself in the bed, pushing her back up against the headboard. She winced, and her hand flew to the back of her head, but Stryker caught her before she could touch the swelling.

"It's best just to leave that alone for right now," he said gently.

"That bad, huh?" She didn't seem surprised.

"Let me check that out," Phantom said, and he gave Stryker a pointed look. With reluctance, Stryker stood, giving room for Phantom to move in.

Anya watched him warily as he pulled out the flashlight that he had pilfered from Stryker. "Just follow the light with your eyes."

"Are you the resident doctor?" she asked with a crooked smile. But she did as he instructed and followed the flashlight.

"Good. Now turn your head so I can take a look at you here." His voice was very calm and patient, and Anya again followed his instructions. But when Phantom began to move his fingers through her hair to get a better look at the swelling, Stryker wanted to grab him by the shoulders and haul him out of the room. He was the only one allowed to touch Anya like that.

The possessiveness he felt for Anya took him by surprise. He had never felt such things toward a woman, not even his former wife. He'd loved her and he'd treated her like she was the most treasured person on the planet, but he wouldn't leave the navy for her, and she couldn't handle not having her husband home for dinner every night, even with the best intentions.

Bitter emotions fought to the surface, but he took one look at Anya and they faded away. She needed him, and he wasn't going to let his past keep him from her. He just wanted Phantom to finish up quickly so he could be back by her side.

She drew in a sharp breath as Phantom probed around her wound, and Stryker stepped forward. "Is that really necessary?" he asked, his voice coming out rougher than he had intended. Damn, this woman was getting to him.

Phantom glanced at him sideways with a disapproving frown and didn't answer his question. Of course it was necessary. Phantom knew what he was doing, and Anya couldn't be in better hands.

"The good news is that it appears all the swelling is on the exterior, and you don't have any broken bones. You've got a small cut from where you hit your head on the rock, but it's minor. You got lucky and don't have a concussion. But just to be safe, we'll still need to wake you every few hours so we can make sure it isn't any worse than what I can see."

"How do you know these things?" She watched him with curiosity, and there was no hint of accusation in her voice.

"I went to medical school for a few years. I learned a lot, but never pursued it further." He shrugged as if he didn't care.

"Phantom! You'd make a fantastic doctor! Why don't you go back to it? I know you love the ranching life—who doesn't—but I'm sure the guys would support you if you chose a different path."

Phantom smiled at her, revealing two charming dimples in his cheeks. "I'm happy here. This is where I'm meant to be."

Stryker was beginning to pace. He was relieved that Anya was going to be okay, but was past the point that he wanted Phantom to leave so he could have her to himself again. He wanted to enjoy her presence and bask in the warm smile she was currently bestowing on Phantom.

"How's the pain?"

Anya's smile slipped a little. "It hurts, but I'll survive. This isn't the first time I've been kicked or bitten or stomped on by one of my patients, or fallen from my own clumsiness."

"Yeah, but I'd wager it's the first time you ever got knocked out from something like this," Stryker offered, and her amazing eyes lifted to where he stood.

"Yes, this is definitely a first. I've certainly learned a lesson from it."

"What lesson could you have possibly learned?"

"That your ranch is booby-trapped with mesquite shrubs and rocks." She gave both of them a tentative smile.

"Hard way to learn a lesson," Phantom muttered, then turned to leave the room.

"Thank you, Phantom," she called after him.

"Anything for you, Doc." He grinned, then turned back to the door.

"Well, I have plenty of paperwork at the office to keep me busy and awake for hours," Anya announced, beginning to pivot out of the bed.

"No!" Phantom and Stryker spoke up at the same time. She looked shocked at their reaction.

"We can't let you go off on your own. You might pass out again or something else could happen to you. You need to stay here. You need to get your rest, but we still have to check you every few hours." Phantom's voice was emphatic.

Anya's eyes darted between Phantom and Stryker, and she folded her arms over her chest. "You can't force me to stay."

A slow smile spread over Stryker's lips, and he wanted to tell her "Try me," but instead remained silent, watching her the same as Phantom. She looked at both of them and threw up her hands in disgust, then winced as the movement disturbed her injury.

"I'm going to grab you some pain medication. Stryker, she's all yours now."

Stryker cast a stabbing glare in the direction of Phantom's retreating back, then turned his attention back to Anya. More than anything, he wanted to tuck her into bed and let her sleep through the worst of the pain. No, more than anything, he wished he were tucking himself into bed with her. And now that she'd shown she was alert and could communicate, he could let her sleep, for a few hours. *So stop thinking like an idiot and just let her sleep. She needs to heal.*

Stryker shook his head to remove the image of her beautiful, olive skin exposed from the roots of her hair down to her toes, and everything in between. He moved back to her side and cautiously sat on the edge of the bed next to her. "It won't be so bad." His gaze searched her face. "Staying here, you'll get to have more of Snap's good cooking, and I'm sure the guys will enjoy having you around."

"I have so much work to do at the clinic."

"Your rest and healing is far more important than anything you have to do at that clinic."

"*That* clinic is my life."

"Still, you're working too much."

"I'm sorry. I wasn't trying to upset you. I just—My clinic is my world. I've built this life here. And it was very hard to get where I am now."

"I'm not upset. What gave you that idea?"

"The corner of your mouth will turn down just a little bit when something bothers you. It's barely noticeable, but—"

"But you noticed it. You know me that well?" The corners of his mouth twitched, this time up.

The corners of her lips twitched as well. "*Do* I know you that well?"

"I think you do."

Her eyes widened at his comment, and her lips parted slightly. He wanted to kiss her. It seemed there was a magnetic force pulling him toward her, and he didn't want it to stop. He wanted to taste those sweet lips, to enjoy her in a way he had fantasized about.

"Okay, you need to drink plenty of water, and take two of these. They may make you a little drowsy, but that's probably even better since you need the sleep." Phantom came into the room talking, ignoring the fact that Stryker and Anya were in the middle of an intimate conversation. "Now, my job here is done, and I'm headed back to bed. Stryker, if anything changes, come get me immediately."

Stryker nodded firmly, and Phantom exited the room the same way he had come in—briskly. Stryker stood, followed him to the door, and watched him walk down the corridor, then took a step back and closed the door.

Stryker cleared his throat. "You need to take your medicine. If you don't, the pain is only going to get worse."

"Did you get kicked much in the rodeo?" she asked as she downed the medication, enjoying the cool wash of water down her parched throat. "I've seen some of those bull riders get thrown so hard, or trampled by the bull, or kicked so many times."

"I've been kicked plenty of times," he replied, though it had nothing to do with a rodeo. "But you forget all the protective gear we wear. I've never fallen and nearly cracked my head open, though." He sat next to her again, unable to get as close as he really wanted. He really wanted to take her face in his hands and kiss her until they were both breathless, and see where things led from there. "I've met plenty of veterinarians at rodeos, but none of them looked or acted like you."

"I go to rodeos to tend to the horses and cattle should they become injured or ill in any way during the show. The rodeo takes pride in making sure their animals are the healthiest and strongest in the circuit. Yes, I've been to some where they're cruel and mistreat the animals. But for the most part, they're good about caring for them. I used to rodeo myself. I competed in barrel racing and calf roping. I love the rodeo scene. But it isn't something I would like to do as a full-time career. What made you decide to join the rodeo?"

Stryker scratched at the scruff on his chin. "I really didn't care what it was. A rodeo, the circus, the psychiatric ward…any place to get away from my small town."

"And yet here you are, back in a small town again."

He shrugged. "You can take the boy out of the country, but you can't take the country out of the boy. I missed it. I never thought in a million years that I would. I got to travel and see so much, experience so much, and for that, I'm grateful. But there's just something special about knowing your neighbors, and knowing that the people around you are there for *you* and not what you might have to offer them. And then, of course, there's this incredible veterinarian that comes out to the ranch no matter what odd hour I call her…"

Anya began to shake her head at him, winced, and sat still. "Is this how… I mean, do you always…um… Never mind."

"What is it? I can see a question brewing behind those eyes of yours. It's a little too late to be shy with me, don't you think?"

She blushed a beautiful shade of pink. If she knew the things he really wanted to do with her, she'd be blushing dark red. He was suddenly very grateful. He didn't know what he would have done if her injuries had been worse.

"Do you talk to all your women in such a manner?" she blurted out rapidly, as if she would lose her nerve if she didn't get it out as fast as possible.

His lips twitched. "Do you think you're one of 'my women' now?"

"No!" She winced. "No, I just wondered if this is how you speak to women you are involved with—if this is all part of the charm you use."

He couldn't help but smile. "You think I'm being

charming? *That* alone is a huge compliment. I didn't think I had it in me anymore. Maybe you hit your head harder than we thought."

"Oh, you're very charming," Anya said seriously.

Stryker's heart rate kicked up. "Just so you know, I don't have any women. And the charm you speak of is more than likely a hallucination brought on by the medication Phantom gave you. I have been told many times exactly how much I lack charm."

"Whoever told you that is lying. Your smile, the way it's so easy to talk to you, your laugh… Well, I find them charming."

She blinked slowly, and he realized she was getting drowsy. He should let her sleep. But she had started a line of talk that he wasn't ready to relinquish yet. "And what of my kisses, bella? Do you find those charming as well?"

Her eyes widened and searched his face, as if she was trying to determine if he was being serious with her. "Very," she whispered.

He lowered his face to hers once again and hovered over her lips. He inhaled deeply and the scent of lilies filled his nostrils. *Must be her shampoo. She should smell like a cow. Although she was wearing latex gloves that protected her from much of the mess…* Slowly, he pressed his lips against her damp, parted ones and heard her soft moan of appreciation. He moved his lips over hers gently, caressing and teasing, but not demanding more. When her fingers worked their way up to his hair and began to tug him closer, he pulled back, feathering kisses down her jaw, wanting so much more, but knowing she had to be in pain.

"Slowly, Anya, slowly. Don't forget about your injury."

"To hell with my injury. I want you to kiss me…I want you to kiss me the way you would if I were your lover." Her voice was husky, and he wondered if she knew what she was actually saying. What the hell had Phantom given her?

But he was never one to turn down a request. Especially not one from a beautiful woman who made him feel things he had thought were long dead within him.

Gently, he slid his hand underneath her head, carefully avoiding the large bump at the very back, and cradled it as he returned to her lips, slanting his mouth over hers and pressing his lips forcefully against hers. She sighed contentedly, which parted her mouth for his tongue to taste her lips thoroughly, then slowly probe inside, darting in and out. It was his turn to moan in satisfaction when her tongue began to dance with his, meeting every thrust and caressing it lightly, before tangling with it once again. When she lightly sucked on his tongue, he knew his eyes crossed behind his closed eyelids, and he was hard in an instant.

One thing he had obviously gotten wrong was her experience with men. She kissed him back with enthusiasm, and he wanted nothing more than to continue. She had to know what she was doing to him.

Slowly, he pulled back from her, deliberately calming his breathing as he looked down at her. There was a soft smile on her face and her eyes were glazed. "Thank you," she said, her sexy, raw voice only making him harder.

He fought the chuckle that bubbled right beneath the surface. He had never had a woman thank him for a kiss. Being with her felt too damn right. Which meant it was probably a thousand ways wrong.

Chapter 8

THE SOUND OF KNOCKING AT THE DOOR WOKE HIM FROM a deep, dreamless slumber. For a moment, he didn't want to move. Somehow, during the early morning hours, he had let Anya convince him to lie down with her to relax as they talked about the ranch and her vet clinic. She had been awake for nearly thirty minutes, and he knew she needed her sleep. But she had wanted to talk, and he had been more than happy to listen. But when he saw the exhaustion pulling hard at her, he had encouraged her to lie down and try to rest.

How she had convinced him to join her, he couldn't remember. He was fairly certain it had something to do with her shimmying out of her boots and jeans, and curling under the covers, only to throw her shirt out after more movements under the blanket. She had laughed at the expression on his face, and he'd wondered again what kind of medication Phantom had given her.

Now, he lay with her, his back to the door, spooning her sweet body up against his. She made a sound of protest as he carefully moved away from her, not giving his body a chance to react to the feeling of her half-naked body nestled in his arms. The chill of the room greeted him as he pushed out from under the blanket, and he remembered taking his shirt off before sliding into bed with the woman who was quickly becoming the biggest temptation he'd ever faced.

Irritated that his time with her had been interrupted, he opened the door only partway, frowning. Phantom stood there, and he slowly took in Stryker's appearance. "Well, I suppose you chose to help her fall asleep," he drawled, and Stryker felt like punching him.

"That's not what happened," he said, feeling the need to defend Anya's virtue.

Phantom shrugged. "Whatever you say, boss. Admiral Haslett is on the line in the conference room. Apparently he tried calling you first but couldn't get through. Buzz patched him through but he's not saying much until you join us." The look in Phantom's eyes told Stryker all he needed to know. Playtime was over. It was time for them to face their first mission.

"We have Anya here," Stryker said in a hushed voice.

"She's asleep, isn't she? Those meds I gave her were bound to kick in at some point. You didn't keep her awake too long, did you?"

"No. And nothing happened between us. We talked for a little while, and then she, well, she just fell asleep."

"Good. She'll still be asleep long enough for the debrief." Phantom turned and walked away as Stryker went to grab his shirt. He found it at the foot of the bed and shrugged it on, all the while watching Anya sleep. She had been in a deep sleep as he had held her, but now she seemed restless, moving beneath the covers, her face contorting with emotions he couldn't decipher, as well as pain. He wondered if she still had nightmares about the car accident she was in.

He went to the bed and leaned over her, catching her chin lightly with his fingers and pressing a soft kiss on her lips. "Rest, bella," he whispered. When he pulled back, her eyes opened slowly, and he froze, transfixed by her gaze.

"Stryker," she whispered. She said only his name. But there was so much more in the way she said it. There was longing, and need, and a promise of things he thought he was only imagining she could give him.

"I'll be gone for a few minutes. You need to sleep now. You're exhausted. Let your body heal."

"Stay with me," she murmured. "I don't have nightmares when you hold me."

It was as if she had punched him in the gut, and he drew in a deep breath. He suddenly realized he hadn't had his nightmares as he had slept with her either. How many years had it been since he had slept without nightmares? Too many to count.

"I'll be back with you soon. Sleep." He pressed another soft kiss against her mouth, and she let her tongue taste his lower lip. He was going to have to take another cold shower before he crawled into bed with her again.

And suddenly he paid attention to what he was really thinking. He had no doubt he would climb back into bed with her. It was as if it were a foregone conclusion. She was like a balm to his wounded soul. And he couldn't get enough of her.

He pulled back from her and finished buttoning his shirt. "I'll be back before you know it."

He quickly walked out of the room, combing his hands through his short hair, making an attempt to look at least partially groomed in front of his team so early in the morning.

Once he reached the second floor, he heard the muted

sounds of the men talking, and Haslett's voice on the speakerphone. He hoped Haslett wouldn't give him a hard time. He had silenced his phone to make sure nothing disturbed him and Anya. Of course, it would be the one time he ever did such a thing that the admiral would try to call him.

"Good morning, Admiral Haslett," Stryker said, taking his seat at the head of the conference table. "I apologize for the delay."

"I understand from Phantom you had a bit of an adventure last night. How's the veterinarian?"

Stryker sighed with relief. Haslett understood and wasn't going to berate him. At least not in front of his team. "She's resting. Phantom said she should be fine."

"Good. Glad to hear you're getting out there and mingling with people. You never know when an important piece of intel will fall into your lap." Haslett paused for a few moments before continuing. "Which brings me to the reason for this morning's call. We've identified a suspect leading a drug cartel out of Nuevo Laredo who may be involved in the terrorist operations we're trying to dismantle."

"Doesn't Mexico already have an aggressive task force to take down drug cartels?" Snap asked.

"Yes. But this is about more than drugs. They are utilizing encrypted data unlike anything we've ever seen. Your mission will be not only to take down this cartel, but also to capture their leader, Benicio Davila. Ideally, we'd also like you to find their computer whiz and force him to explain his code to us. If we can't get him, we need the next best thing—a download from one of their main servers."

"Won't those files be encrypted as well?" Buzz asked, frowning at the speakerphone.

"That's where you come in, Buzz. We need you to crack this code."

"I take it this isn't going to be the usual drop in, extract people and information, and disappear all in one night?" Phantom asked.

"No. You'll go in undercover and become part of the cartel. All the information you need is uploaded to your secure server. Learn your cover stories inside and out. Stryker, Buzz, Phantom—you're headed for Mexico."

Benicio stared at the images in front of him. "*This* is the man you think I need to be worried about? He's a fucking vaquero kissing a girl. Show me maps. Show me guns. Show me proof this man is worth my time."

"The photographer I hired couldn't get into the house. But it is odd that a group of men all of a sudden purchase this ranch. Look at the photos of the house. It looks more like a fortress than a home. Whoever they are, they don't want anyone to know what they're up to."

"Or they're simply private men. Had that thought crossed your mind? Your job is to bring me information of value. And right now, you're wasting my time. Not to mention I had to come all the way out here to meet with you. Puto, people come to me, not the other way around."

"Don't insult me. You won't like the outcome."

"Is that a threat? You forget that you work for me, David. You do what I bid you to do. And if I choose to kill you, it won't be hard to replace you."

David snorted and adjusted the black-rimmed glasses

perched on his nose. "We both know I report to *your* boss. If you kill me, you've essentially signed your own death warrant."

Benicio's lip curled in anger and frustration. Beads of sweat dotted his brow and a drop slid down his back. It was hot in this part of Mexico. And David had insisted on meeting outside. At least they were in the shade. But that didn't help much.

David, however, looked cool and comfortable. He wore a lightweight linen shirt and cargo shorts, something Benicio frowned upon. If they were to have a business meeting, he needed to dress like a businessman. But that was the problem with David. He thought he was untouchable. He wasn't.

"Send his picture out to all our contacts so they are aware of him. If anyone sees him in Mexico, I want him alive. I want to know exactly who he is and who he's working for. I want information, something you clearly can't provide me with."

David's lips curled into a slight smile. "Sure thing. I'll be sure to keep our boss *informed* of what we're doing."

He wanted to kill him right then and there. It would be simple enough. David surrounded himself with technology and computers. He didn't have guards or protection. A single round to the heart, or between the eyes, and it would all be over. Or, even better, he could slash his throat and watch him bleed out, watch the life leave his eyes slowly.

David's smile broadened. "I caution you with your next actions," he said softly. He held up his hand, and there was a small device in his grasp. "There are twenty guns trained on you and your men. You make a single move toward me, or toward your gun, and all I have to do is flip the switch. You'll all be dead. Or wishing you were."

Fuck! He had underestimated the bastard. He should have realized the man would have a way to stop him, even without bodyguards. He stood slowly, forcing a smile to his face. "I'll take the pictures. What about the photographer? Can he provide us with any additional information?"

"No. Unfortunately, the photographer became greedy when I asked for their location and other details, so he had to be…removed."

"At least that's one problem out of the way. I'll have my men start searching." He forced a smile and nodded at David. "Until we meet again, amigo," he growled.

Benicio retreated with his men to the air-conditioned luxury of his car and they drove away. His right hand man, Hector, watched him closely. "What do you want to do with these pictures?"

"We may not know exactly where they are, but our contact in the U.S. should. Send them to him. He'll know how to scare them if they are indeed a threat to us."

He stared out the window and clenched his fists together, trying to control his temper. Benicio would kill David one day. Just not today.

Chapter 9

THE SOUND OF STRYKER ENTERING THE ROOM AGAIN brought Anya out of her restless slumber. Her head was pounding and her mind felt fuzzy. And she was more than a little embarrassed. She vaguely remembered wiggling out of her clothes and then diving under the covers. And then she remembered him sliding into the bed with her at her request, and the feel of his warm skin against hers had made her want so much more, but sleep had tugged her down.

She heard the rustle of clothing, then felt the dip of the bed as he got in under the covers and moved toward her. "Still not able to sleep?" His voice rumbled near her ear and his warm, calloused hand wrapped around her stomach, pulling her back against his bare chest.

Good grief. The man is built like a Greek god. She could feel the ripple of his muscles as he moved to place a kiss right behind her ear. She had never felt more like a woman, more desirable, more cherished. She wanted to touch him, to see him, and to know if she made him feel the same things he made her feel.

Slowly, she turned within his embrace, then winced as her swollen head made contact with the pillow. He gently maneuvered her so she was lying on her side, and he leaned over her, concern on his face. "Is the pain really bad? I can get Phantom..."

"No, no, I'll be fine." She stared up into his face,

studying his dark eyes, his high cheekbones, and his square jaw. There was a small scar about an inch long that ran along his jawline, and she couldn't resist the temptation to reach up and trace it with her fingers, feeling the bristle of his whiskers. "Stryker…I want you to know, I'm not the type of woman to hop naked in bed with a man. I don't know what came over me last night. I've never… I don't know why I stripped in front of you like that, and I'm sorry if I made you uncomfortable."

His lips twitched. "It was the medication Phantom gave you. And you could never make me feel uncomfortable. Watching you wiggle out of your jeans was hotter than hell."

"Oh." Anya felt the heat of a blush creeping up her face. "Having you hold me…feeling you against my skin…" She struggled to find the right words to say.

"It feels incredible," he said softly, finding the words she was having such a hard time saying.

Relief washed over her. He felt the same way she did. What they had was something unique, something special that she had never felt before. Knowing he was feeling the same eased her concerns and lowered her inhibitions. She pulled his head down toward hers, and she kissed his cheeks until she was able to lower her lips to the scar along his jaw. She kissed it tenderly, then tentatively ran her tongue along the scar, tasting the salty, earthy flavor of him.

A sound rumbled deep in his chest. "Remember what I said about playing with fire." His voice was deep, husky, and filled with a promise she wanted fulfilled.

"You already make me burn," she whispered, her eyes connecting with his, and she nearly gasped at the intensity of desire she saw. He wanted her. He wanted her the way a man was supposed to crave a woman, and her heart, already pounding heavily, began to beat faster.

"Anya," he groaned, before dropping his head and pressing his lips to hers, claiming her mouth in a way that made her gasp in surprise and pleasure. Her small gasp gave him the opportunity to slide his tongue into her mouth and she slid hers against it, and they both moaned as they began a rhythm that mimicked what they wished their bodies were doing.

His hand rubbed her stomach lightly, and with each circle his fingers got closer and closer to her breasts. She arched her back, letting him know what she desired as his thumb rubbed up against the underside of her breasts.

He pulled back from her, his breathing ragged. "Anya, you don't know what you do to me," he whispered, then peeled back the covers so he could view her body, and she suddenly felt very self-conscious. But she forced herself to relax, knowing she was safe with Stryker. She didn't know how she could be so certain, but something told her he would always be gentle with her.

His fingers slid around her back and plucked at the hooks on her plain bra. She suddenly wished she had something sexy to wear for him. But her undergarments were like her, simple and practical. He tossed her bra across the room and then slid his thumb down and hooked it in her underwear. She lifted her hips to help him free her of the garment, hoping he didn't pay any attention to how utilitarian they were. Finally, she was naked before him.

Stryker drew in his breath and let it back out slowly, his heated gaze taking in every inch of her body. She was beginning to wonder if he found her appealing or not, when his gaze finally came back up to meet hers. "You're gorgeous," he whispered, and his hand returned to her waist as his lips molded to hers, then traveled down her jaw and to her neck. She arched her neck to give him easier access, and a thousand butterflies settled in her stomach as his teeth nipped at her lightly.

She ran her hands anxiously through his thick hair, then, emboldened by his kisses, she let her fingers trail down to his thick, broad shoulders. She squeezed and massaged his tight, tense muscles, and she felt them slowly begin to relax under her ministrations. Then she slid her hands farther down and massaged his pecs. His sheer power seemed overwhelming.

"Anya," he moaned, when her fingers found his nipples and began to explore them. His lips and teeth were teasing the flesh of her collarbone, and she squirmed, desiring something more, but she didn't know what. He drew in a sharp breath when her fingers lightly plucked at his stiff nipples, and she was rewarded by his hands working back up to her breasts.

She drew in a shuddering breath when he pulled back and stared at her. She had never felt such sensations before. She didn't want it to ever end. He lifted one of her breasts gently, weighing and molding it in his hand, and she let out the ragged breath she hadn't even been aware she was holding. Her breast fit perfectly into his large hand, as if it were made for him to hold. When his thumb flicked over her nipple, she arched off the bed in ecstasy, her hands clenching the bedsheet beneath them.

"So perfect," he whispered, then lowered his head, his lips kissing her breast, though he teased her by avoiding the bud that craved the warmth of his touch so desperately. Her fingernails dug into his chest, and she was having a hard time catching her breath. Her hands wandered farther down his body until she was stroking the ripple of muscles of his stomach.

He moaned, and his tongue rasped over her nipple, then gently pulled it into his mouth, suckling at it as his tongue continued to circle it and tease it. Anya gasped, and her hands slipped from his stomach to curl into his hair, tugging restlessly. "Stryker," she beseeched, unsure what it was she was asking of him.

His hand that had been caressing her breast shifted lower, feathering over her lower belly. A quivering began deep within her, and she squirmed on the bed, feeling the sheets and blanket twisting at her feet, the cool contrast to Stryker's warm hands and mouth causing her to desire more of his warmth. Yet, at the same time, she felt flushed all over, down to the tips of her toes.

Stryker suddenly released her nipple and shifted to her lips, kissing her with a passion she matched, arching her back so her nipples brushed against his smooth chest, and she moaned into his mouth. His hand shifted to her hip and pulled at her leg as he nestled himself between her thighs. She thrilled at the feeling of his obvious desire for her.

The thickness of his erection pressed against her, and she felt his fingers slide around her hips, drawing her closer against him. She wanted nothing more than to feel all of him. She reached for his jeans to discover he'd already shed them and wore only his boxer briefs. He caught her hands in his waistband and pulled them up to kiss her knuckles.

"I want to enjoy this for as long as possible," he said softly to her, "and with your eager little hands, I don't know how much more I can take."

"Stryker...I need you."

He closed his eyes and rested his forehead against hers. "You are a temptation unlike anything I've ever known," he whispered. Her hands were caught splayed between them, and she flexed her fingers against the strength of his muscles.

"And you make me desire things...things I never thought I would..."

His lips pressed down on hers, and he released her hands, allowing her to slide her fingers under his waistband and carefully push his boxer briefs down, freeing his erection to press intimately against her core. She had never been more certain of anything in her life. She wanted him. She wanted him to claim her as his.

His hands gripped her hips, and he continued kissing her, his lips urgent and demanding. Then suddenly he paused, his breathing heavy. "I didn't think... This wasn't supposed to happen... I have to get a condom." He reached into a drawer in the bedside table and drew one out of his wallet.

He smiled down at her, the smile she so thoroughly enjoyed. "I haven't been with anyone in a long time. I'm very careful."

"Good, so am I." She smiled up at him and wrapped one of her legs around his, encouraging him to continue. The muscles in his jaw tightened as he looked down at her with unbridled passion.

His fingers slid down the length of her body and into the soft curls between her legs, and she gasped as his fingers found her moist folds. He moaned in approval. His fingers, slick with her excitement, circled the nub above her folds, and she nearly came off the bed. Her inner thighs began to shake, and she arched into his hand. "Stryker!"

Suddenly, he was pressing his erection against her, and she felt the intense pressure build up. "Oh," she moaned, her heart racing so fast, she wondered if she was going to have a heart attack.

He pressed into her farther, and she hitched her leg higher up his, spreading herself wider to receive him. He had barely entered her when he suddenly froze, his eyes flying up to her face. "Anya?" he asked, his voice strained.

Her hands tugged at his hips, trying to get him to continue filling the void she knew only he could fill. He was the man she needed, the man she had chosen to give herself to.

"You're a virgin?" He wasn't moving any farther, despite her insistence, and she froze too, her gaze lifting to his. He looked surprised and concerned.

"Yes," she whispered. "Is that… Does that…? I'm sorry, I didn't think that would be a problem. I'm sorry. I shouldn't have… I should have said something sooner…" Anya felt horribly exposed and vulnerable. She had never thought it would be a deterrent to a man to discover she was a virgin. But to a man like Stryker, who was probably very used to experienced women, an inexperienced woman in his bed was probably a major turnoff.

She wanted to get away from him. She wanted her clothes, and she wanted them immediately. She wanted to retreat to her clinic and cry her pain away. The first man she had ever offered herself to didn't want her. But when she tried to move, he held her in place.

"Anya, you're about to give me the greatest gift a woman has ever given me. Are you sure you want me to be your first?"

He wasn't angry. He still desired her. "Yes," she said, her voice throaty. "Yes, I want you, Stryker. I want to give myself to you."

He dropped his lips to hers and kissed her tenderly, lightly, then slowly increased the pressure until she could taste his passion again, could feel his desire pressing against her as he once again began to ease inside her.

He was slow and gentle, rubbing against her and barely penetrating her, driving her passion even higher. He continued to kiss her, then slid his lips down her jaw, her collarbone, and took a nipple in his mouth. She moaned in pleasure as he suckled on it hard, then gasped as he drove himself forward into her, breaking through her hymen and claiming her body.

He froze for several seconds, breathing heavily, and she could feel a fine trembling in his body. But he didn't move. Instead, he looked down at her, concern on his face. "Did I hurt you?"

"It…it was a surprise. And I feel very…full. Are all men as large as you?"

He chuckled, causing him to move within her, and she bit her lower lip to keep from making any sound. "I don't know. Though I have been told I am larger than some."

He continued to stay still, and her inner muscles rippled around him as she grew accustomed to feeling him within her. He closed his eyes and rotated his hips, and she gave an approving moan. Slowly, he withdrew and then eased himself back in until he was moving at a steady rhythm, and she was raising her hips to meet each thrust.

He began to move faster, his breathing ragged. With each thrust, he seemed to get deeper and deeper, touching more and more of her sensitive flesh until he was finally in her to the hilt, filling her completely. The tension in her lower belly seemed to be intensifying, coiling tighter and tighter, and she wanted everything he had to offer.

She began to meet his thrusts harder, gasping as he returned his attention to her breasts, suckling on one while rolling the nipple of the other one with his fingers. "Oh, Stryker," she moaned, feeling something building, feeling as if she were creeping to the top of the roller-coaster ride with the plummet just on the other side. "Stryker!" she cried as his last thrust sent her over the edge and she soared, the joy of her orgasm gripping her from the tips of her toes to her hair.

He thrust a few more times before his body tensed over her, and she felt the contractions of his body within hers. After several intense moments, he collapsed, breathing heavily, and rolled to the side, taking her with him.

"Thank you, Anya. Thank you."

He had thanked her. Was that what you were supposed to do when a woman gifted her body to you? He had no idea. He had never had a woman give her virginity to him. He *still* couldn't believe Anya had given him hers. He had been afraid he would hurt her, but she had responded to him with a passion he'd never expected.

He left her briefly to dispose of the condom and get cleaned up in the bathroom before returning and pulling her against him. She lay halfway across his body, her breathing even in sleep. He knew she needed her rest, but the feeling of her breasts lying bare against his chest and knowing that her soft, damp center was only inches away had him getting hard again rapidly. He wanted her again. He needed her again.

She sighed in her sleep, and her hand moved across his chest. He felt her press a light kiss to his shoulder. "Why did you thank me?" she asked softly, as if she didn't want to break the magical bubble they were in.

His hand made slow circles on her back, and he closed his eyes, enjoying this moment, this time with her. Because who knew, with the case they had to take on, he might not be returning home. It was that way with any new mission. "Because you chose me to be your first," he murmured, nuzzling her neck. She smelled like sweat and lilies and sex.

Anya made a humming sound low in her throat and turned her head to give him more accessibility to her neck. "You're the first man I ever desired so strongly, so passionately. And the more I got from you, the more I had to have."

He wanted to groan. He could take her again right then and there, but he was afraid it would be too much for her too soon. Her hand slipped down and rubbed over his strong, rippled stomach, and he drew in a deep breath as she continued to get closer and closer to his erection.

She hesitated, leaning up on her elbow to reach his ear and gently tugging the lobe into her mouth. She suckled at it, and he couldn't resist the temptation any longer. He pulled her farther on top of him and sank his hands into her luxurious hair, then sought and found her lips, pressing against her with the maddening desire coursing through his veins. He needed her, and it almost felt like he had never had her in the first place.

He maneuvered her body so she was straddling him and she could feel his erection pressing at her tender core. She gasped with excitement and her face flushed. She rotated her hips, and he felt his hard tip quickly get slickened by her renewed excitement. "Is it…normal…to want this again so soon?"

He smoothed her hair back and hooked it behind her ear. "With you, bella, I'm beginning to believe nothing is normal. And I like that." He fumbled in the nightstand drawer again and quickly rolled on another condom.

She smiled at him and lowered her hips, taking him within her sweet body. He clenched his jaw and held her hips in his hands, desperately trying to hold on to his control. Sweat beaded on his forehead as she began to take him within her body slowly, inch by agonizing inch. She threw her head back, arching her breasts out, and took him fully within her body.

Breathing raggedly, he began to guide her hips, lifting and lowering her, until they were both in a frenzy and moving in sync with each other. "Come with me, Anya," he whispered, as he felt himself tighten and edge closer to orgasm.

"Yes," she gasped. "Yes, Stryker, yes!"

Several minutes later, she stirred in his arms and ran her hand lazily through his thick, black hair. "I think it is my turn to thank you," she said with a smile.

He lowered his head and kissed her cheeks. "No, I still get to thank you. How does your head feel?"

She shrugged. "It's tolerable. You've managed to distract me from the pain. So I *do* get to thank you. Who knew making love had such powerful side effects?"

Make love. Is that what they had just done? In his mind he was under the impression they had just had mind-blowing sex. Making love was something entirely different. It meant there was something between them, emotions and feelings that he didn't want to feel ever again.

"I could have told you that," he quipped, though his heart was pounding with anxiety. "Now, I think I smell bacon, which means Snap is up and making us breakfast. Why don't you take a shower while I check on his progress?"

She looked at him with confusion as he slid out of her arms and went to the bathroom for a second time to dispose of the condom. He returned quickly and began to get dressed. "Stryker, is everything all right?" she asked, slowly sitting up in the bed. He knew she sensed something was off by the way she kept the sheet clutched about her body, hiding herself from him.

"I'm hungry." He forced a grin to his lips. "That's all."

She gave him a hesitant smile and nodded. "Me too. I'll be quick in the shower."

But she waited, obviously unwilling to walk to the bathroom in the nude. *Why do I suddenly feel like I'm ruining something great?*

He hesitated outside the door to the room they had shared for a moment to collect himself, and his heart sank when he heard the lock being turned on the door. Obviously she didn't want anyone coming in, including him. He shook his head at himself.

It was for the best. He didn't want a woman in his life. Even a woman as amazing as Anya. He had taken plenty of cold showers since meeting the beautiful woman, and he wanted nothing more than to lie in her arms and bask in the warmth of her smile. But apparently the intimacy they had just shared had a different meaning in her eyes. And he couldn't blame her. This was her first time. But he had to make sure her expectations didn't involve their relationship going any further than casual sex between two consenting adults.

He wandered into the kitchen where he found Snap and Phantom. Snap was cooking while Phantom was already munching on a pancake. "Oh, good," Phantom said, his tone dry. "We were beginning to wonder if we were going to have to rescue you from the evil clutches of the doc."

Stryker wanted to punch Phantom. He had no right to joke about Anya like that. He didn't know what they had just shared together, didn't know how beautiful it was. Stryker hadn't been with a woman since he and his wife had agreed it wasn't working and filed for divorce. Anya had been—amazing.

"Must not have gone all that well based on his face," Snap said, shaking his head. "We warned you, Stryker, that you needed to get back on the horse sooner rather than later or you were going to lose your touch."

"Anya is not your concern," Stryker said, grimacing at his tone. He sounded like a jealous lover. But he wouldn't let them talk about her in a degrading manner. "Leave her out of your filthy conversations."

Snap stared him down for several tense seconds, a muscle jumping in his jaw. "She's a good woman, Stryker. She deserves the best."

"You think I don't know that?"

"I think you may be a little confused," Snap replied, his gaze still intense. "I think you may be thinking with the wrong head when it comes to Anya."

"You sure are full of a lot of opinions this morning," Stryker said, his tone heavy with warning. "It would be for the best if you kept your thoughts to yourself."

Snap's lips pulled thin. "Yes, sir," he said, then turned back to making breakfast.

Stryker clenched and unclenched his fists. He had the desire to punch something, but he couldn't take his frustrations out on his men. They didn't know what had happened between him and Anya, but they could fairly well guess.

She had been a virgin, for fuck's sake! He had seduced a virgin not once, but twice, and had experienced more pleasure than he'd ever experienced with a woman. She hadn't held anything back with him. She had been completely uninhibited, trying her best to please him as he pleasured her. Her innocence had only strengthened the intense feeling of having her tight little body respond to him so passionately.

She had referred to it as "making love." Making love meant there were powerful emotions involved, and a couple was only steps away from actually declaring those emotions to each other. But he didn't feel that way about Anya. He couldn't feel that way. He cared about her and wanted to make sure she was safe, but anything more than that? His failed marriage showed how little he had to give her. And Snap was right. She deserved the best.

The rest of the guys began to emerge from wherever

they'd been hiding, as he knew none of them would've been able to sleep after they'd debriefed on their first mission together. Brusco was bragging that he had defeated Santo in pool three times in a row, and Santo was commenting that he felt sorry for Brusco and had let him win.

Phantom continued to hover in the kitchen, looking as tired as Stryker felt. His gaze flicked to Stryker, but he said nothing. Did he think the same as Snap? The obvious answer was yes. Somehow, Anya had won them all over, and they believed he wasn't good enough for her. Did his men really think so little of him?

Then they all lit up with smiles and good mornings when Anya walked in, finger-combing her damp hair. She smiled in return at all of them, though Stryker noticed it seemed hard for her to make eye contact with him. Surely it was normal for a woman to be a bit shy with the man to whom she had given her virginity. It was a gift he was going to treasure, no matter what the assholes on his team thought or said.

"How are you feeling?" Phantom asked, walking over to her and gently sliding her hair out of the way so he could look at her wound.

Possessiveness rolled through Stryker. *She belongs to me.* His thoughts startled him. How could he be so possessive of a woman he knew he had to let go? His heart clenched at the thought. He wanted her in his life. He *needed* her in his life. But how could he keep her happy when his life was devoted to the SEALs?

"It's tender, but much better than it was last night. Thank you, Phantom, for all that you did to take care of me."

"Now, let's get you some grub. You'll be feeling like

your old self in no time." Snap was pulling the last pancake off the griddle.

"Oh, thank you so much. But I really need to get back to the clinic. I've taken up too much of your hospitality as it is."

Stryker stepped toward her then, and the eyes she laid on him were cautious and wary. *What did I say? What did I do? There's no reason for her to look at me like this.* "You need your rest," he said firmly. "You don't have to work today. Stay here and get the rest you need."

She smiled at him, but the smile didn't reach her eyes. "I have too much to do back at the clinic. And I feel rested, truly. It's time for me to get out of your hair. I'm sorry I caused so much trouble as it is."

"You'll hurt my feelings if you don't eat my breakfast," Snap said, doing his best to get her to stay.

She laughed softly. "I think it takes more than that to hurt your feelings, Snap." Her genuine smile appeared, the one that reached her eyes as she looked around the room at each one of them. "Thank y'all for your kindness. I'll be back to check on the cattle soon and will be sure to stop in and say hello."

"We're going to hold you to that," Brusco said. He was frowning, his eyes on Stryker.

She nodded and turned to go, and Stryker followed her to the door. "I'll walk you to your truck," he said softly.

"Oh, that really isn't necessary," she said in the same hushed tone as his. "Thank you, for taking care of me."

"Anya, this morning—"

"Was incredible." She stood on tiptoe and placed a kiss on his cheek. "You made it wonderful for me, and I won't ever forget that."

"Anya…"

"I'll be back in a few days to check on the calves and new mamas. Call me if you need me before then."

Stop her. Stop her from leaving you. Let her know just how special this morning was for you as well. "Be careful, Anya."

She smiled again, and again it didn't reach her eyes. He felt as if he had broken something delicate and precious, and no matter what he did, he wouldn't be able to put it back together. And yet he didn't know what he had done wrong.

Maybe I should have reassured her, said sweet nothings in her ear—something to let her know I care. And I do care. I just can't give her more than that.

He couldn't think of anything else to say before she turned and left. He stood there at the open door and watched until her truck disappeared around the dirt road.

I'm a fucking idiot.

Chapter 10

ANYA DROVE HOME AND STARTED WORKING ON PAPERWORK immediately, eating a bowl of cereal, and diving head-long into numbers and documents. As she sat alone, remembering every moment with Stryker and wondering if he would call her, she realized she had to talk to Elena. Otherwise, she'd be left examining the previous night over and over again and getting nowhere.

Elena answered her phone on the third ring. "Hi, girlie," she yawned.

"Sorry to call so early. I didn't look at the clock. What are you doing?" Anya shoved a spoonful of cereal in her mouth as she waited for her friend to respond.

"I'm attempting to sleep in on a Sunday morning. What about you?"

"Working on a spreadsheet while eating a bowl of cereal. And no, I do not have ice in my cereal like some weirdos I know."

"Don't knock it until you've tried it. Now, I know you didn't call me to talk about a stupid spreadsheet and the way I like my cereal. What's going on?"

"I think I'm falling in love with Stryker."

Elena's bark of laughter hurt Anya's ear and made her head pound. "I could have told you that was coming. Is that it? That's what made you call me so early in the day?"

Anya remembered the feeling of Stryker's strong

arms around her and groaned, putting her head in her hands. "Oh, Elena, I think I really messed up this time."

Elena fell silent for several seconds. "Oh, crap," she said softly. "What happened?"

"I think I'm falling in love with him, and he doesn't want anything to do with me."

"What would make you think that? Anya, you are a prize! He'd be the luckiest guy in the world to have your love."

"I don't think he feels that way. He seemed really uncomfortable around me this morning."

"This morning? What were you doing with him… Wait, isn't that what you wanted? I'm confused."

"I thought it was what I wanted. Hell, who am I kidding? It's what I wanted. But I also wanted there to be something special about it. As soon as it was over…it was awkward." Anya swallowed hard. It had been the best and worst morning of her life.

"So, you want me to take revenge on him? I can go out there and slash every tire on every one of their trucks."

Anya couldn't help but laugh as she pictured tiny Elena slashing tires. "You probably wouldn't even be able to puncture them."

"I'll give it my best try."

Anya could tell Elena was serious, which only made her laugh harder. "No, no, you can't. I should have known a man like him wouldn't want to cuddle afterwards." But they *had* lain in bliss together until she had said they'd "made love." She squeezed her eyes shut.

Elena made a sound on the phone, and Anya pictured her blowing her curly hair out of her face. "I'm still ticked off at Stryker for making you feel this way," she grumbled.

"You warned me not to let him break my heart."

"No, I told you I would hunt him down if he did. Now, you aren't letting me. Not fair."

"Oh, Elena, what would I do without you?"

"Find a friend who really *could* slash their tires?"

Anya laughed again. "There's no better friend than you. Now, I'm going to get back to work. Thank you, Elena."

"Don't work too hard. Sounds like you could use some rest."

Anya felt better after talking to Elena and powered through her day, finishing most of her invoices and accounting before tumbling into bed, past the point of exhaustion. She was able to get two full hours of sleep before the first call came in from an anxious rancher. She was ready for calving season to be over.

Las Lomitas Café was quickly becoming the guys' favorite place to go in the mornings when they had to head to town for supplies. With incredible coffee and some of the best Mexican food Stryker had ever tasted, it also gave them a portal to the locals. The café always seemed busy, with ranchers coming and going, and even hunters leasing out some of the ranch land to catch exotic game like gazelles, buffalo, zebras, or their native wild turkey.

Ritz Feed Store was their usual destination, especially now that they needed a little extra feed and mineral blocks for the new mama heifers. Usually Snap joined them and asked to be dropped off at Lowe's Market so he could stock up on provisions. None of them had known of Snap's passion for cooking, and none of them were complaining.

"Been a bit busy the last couple of weeks," Snap said quietly, his cup of coffee hovering at his lips so no one would be able to tell what he'd said.

"Been noticing that," Stryker commented, also sipping at his coffee.

"Think they're all local?"

"More than likely," Phantom said. With his back to the room, he didn't have to worry about covering his lips to mask his words. "I think there are people here who are curious about us. We stick out like sore thumbs if you haven't noticed."

Stryker nodded, his eyes scanning the room quickly. No one was looking in their direction except a young Latina woman sitting catty-corner to them, who flashed him a bright smile when his eyes passed over her. He sighed heavily, thinking suddenly of Anya's beautiful eyes.

"Why don't you ask her on a date?" Phantom said to Snap, his face deadpan.

"Fuck off," Snap grumbled, and both Phantom and Stryker chuckled. It was obvious the woman had caught Snap's attention. But he was just as loyal to the SEALs as the rest of them, if not more so, and had decided not to have a relationship with a woman for years. In fact, Stryker couldn't remember him being with a woman the entire time he had known him, which was well over six years.

But Stryker quickly turned serious. "I'd like to know more about these people. I don't want us to be caught unawares."

"Already on it," Phantom said, leaning back in his chair. "I'll make sure we know more about them than they do about us."

—∿∿—

Stryker appeared at Anya's clinic the day after he had introduced her to pleasure she had never known possible. She was overwhelmed, but just seeing him had brought lightness to her heart and a smile to her face. He smiled back at her, hesitantly, almost nervously. She tried to restrain her reaction to him. More than anything, she wanted him to gather her in his arms and kiss her, but she couldn't tell what he was thinking.

He removed his cowboy hat as soon as he stepped through the door and raked a hand through his dark hair. She'd just finished with a dog that needed its vaccines and had been telling the customer goodbye. A horse had been brought in that she needed to check for potential colic next. She'd already sedated it and had it in a stanchion, so there was no chance it would roll and twist its intestines, as horses with colic were known to do.

She needed to tend to the horse, but she had a few moments, and she would give them to Stryker in a heartbeat. She came from around the counter and approached him slowly, almost desperate in her need to touch and be touched.

"I came to ask you something."

She paused at his words, and her smile faltered. Did he have business to conduct with her? Or did he want to discuss their personal life? "Come to the back," she said softly, glancing at her clients in the waiting room. If he had come to talk about their personal life, she didn't want the rest of the town speaking about it.

He followed her into the back room where she treated

the smaller animals, and she turned to face him, holding her breath. She couldn't hold back her smile, even though she didn't know his feelings. "How are you? I mean—how is the heifer and the new calf? There aren't any complications, are there?"

A genuine smile appeared on his face, and excitement coursed through her veins. "The heifer and calf are fine. Thanks to you. How are you feeling? I wanted to check on you yesterday, but I thought… I wanted to give you some room to breathe."

"I'm fine. A mild headache, but I'm sure it will pass by tonight or tomorrow."

"You're working too hard." He took a step closer to her, and her heart raced in her chest. *Yes. Come closer. Hold me. Kiss me. Let me know it was more than a simple conquest for you.*

She shrugged. "Calving season will be over soon. Then I'll be able to rest."

He drew a deep breath. "I wanted to ask—I came to ask if you have any time available next Wednesday?"

It was only Monday. Next Wednesday was nine days away. "I'll have to check my schedule, but I don't think it will be a problem. What do you need?"

"You. Time with you. I don't need you to come out to the ranch. I want to pick you up here next Wednesday evening and take you out for dinner. We can even go to another town if you don't want to be seen with me. I totally understand the small-town gossip."

Her heart had lodged in her throat, making it difficult to breathe. He was asking her on a date. She could barely contain her excitement. "Yes," she managed to say. "Yes, I'd love to go to dinner with you."

"Wednesday night. I'll pick you up at seven thirty. Will that work for you?"

All she could do was nod. Her mouth had gone dry. His lips had lifted into a grin, and he leaned forward, giving her a quick but firm kiss. "Try to rest, bella. I want us to enjoy our time together on our date."

He smiled and pressed one more quick kiss to her lips before leaving her to the rest of her work. She leaned against the counter and sighed contentedly. He had come to see her in person, which itself was far more than she had hoped for, though she had certainly wished for it. Next Wednesday couldn't arrive soon enough.

The Scorpions were relatively new to the drug cartel world, only on the scene for the last five years, but they already had a well-formed structure, with oversight into various areas of production, distribution, and selling. The halcones, or falcons as they were called, were the eyes and ears on the streets. Even though they were the key points in gathering information for the cartels, they seemed invisible and next to impossible to find.

They were the lowest rank within a cartel, but from the intel the team had been given, there were at least seventy-five falcons in operation for the Scorpions, which could make it difficult for the team to break in. Finding them was only the beginning of their problems. They then had to make it convincing that they were interested in becoming part of the cartel and weren't part of the policia.

It was late in the afternoon, and they had been poring over the information for a couple of hours already.

Sitting around the conference room table inside their communications room, they were all tired and tense. The more they dug into the life of the Scorpions, the more repulsed they were. They wouldn't just be bringing down a drug cartel. They would be bringing down a pack of wild beasts.

The sicarios, or hitmen, were next in the pecking order, and there were more than thirty hitmen in operation. Then came the lugartenientes, or lieutenants, the second highest in command in a cartel. The fifteen lieutenants supervised the hitmen and falcons within their own territory and could even carry out low-profile executions as they saw necessary. All of them ultimately answered to the capos. From the intel they had, there was only one capo in the Scorpions, and he made sure they all understood the direction he wanted them to go.

"How can this cartel be so young and yet already function at the level of the Gulf Cartel?" Brusco said with disgust, staring at some of the gruesome photos that had accompanied their intel. The Gulf Cartel was the oldest cartel in all of Mexico, with roots going back to bootlegging during America's Prohibition era.

"They have to have backing from someone very wealthy." Santo sighed. "You don't just start off as a cartel and immediately do the things they're doing. They have to have financiers. They need pathways for laundering the money. This usually takes years upon years to set up. From what I'm reading here, these guys were up and swinging their dicks around before they were even a full year vested."

"Santo is right. Something isn't adding up. We need to dig into everything we can before we head into

Mexico." Stryker's frown deepened the more his mind processed the enormity of the task they were taking on.

"That's what I'm trying to say, Stryker. We may go in there and remove a few top lieutenants and maybe even get the capo, but they'll all be replaced within forty-eight hours. If our mission is really to destroy this cartel, we have to cut them off at the knees. We need to take their infrastructure down with them." Santo was also frowning.

"Let's keep in mind that bringing down the cartel is not our only objective," Phantom spoke up from the corner of the table. Phantom wasn't much of a talker, so when he had something to say, they all paid attention.

"That's where I play my role," Buzz said, reviewing data uploaded from the admiral. "Am I the only one who finds it odd that there's a communications hub at their headquarters sending out encrypted data at an alarming rate?"

"We know the cartels have been using technology for a long time. The corrupt corporations have been buying in for years now. It was only a matter of time before they started using the dark web to outsource some of the work their men didn't want to mess with." Unlike the rest of the team staring at their laptops, Santo was deftly sharpening his KA-BAR fighting knife.

"But isn't that the point of having sicarios? They will do the dirty work no one else will touch." Buzz frowned.

"Only up to a certain point. With the war on drugs being waged by the Mexican police and military, they've had to go somewhere else to take out people in stations higher up."

"So, you think this encrypted data is for hired assassins and that type of shit?" Brusco asked Santo.

Santo paused his sharpening and looked at all the men seated around the table. "No. I think there is something much deeper going on here, and I think some key information has been left out of our intel. When was the last time we received intel that had redacted lines?" He grabbed Brusco's computer and turned it to face everyone, gesturing to the screen. There were several blocks blacked out so they couldn't read the information. "Anyone want to tell me why we're being sent into a war with one hand tied behind our back? Which means we may be in for a difficult fight. I agree with Stryker—we need to do some more recon of our own."

"If I'm hearing you right, it sounds like you're doubting who we can trust on both sides of the border." Stryker was tense. The same thoughts had crossed his mind when he'd first reviewed the information, but he'd thought he was just being extra paranoid.

"I always doubt who I can trust," Phantom said, talking around a toothpick. "Don't you?"

"Not when it comes to the five of you. You're my brothers in every way that counts. I know you'll have my back the same as I'll have yours."

"Hoo-yah!" came the resounding reply around the table.

"So, boss, what are you going to do about the info being redacted?" Phantom twirled the toothpick on his tongue.

"Let me worry about that," Stryker replied, his tone shutting down further discussion on that topic.

Buzz cleared his throat. "Now, with that out of the way, how do you propose we go after these sons of bitches?"

"We start making them hurt where it counts the most. We target their supply line. We do some major infrastructure damage, and then, when the timing is right, we approach a lieutenant. We'll be able to do most of that remotely. Buzz, I need you to start finding out their sources."

"And when we approach the lieutenant, we tell him what? 'Hi, we're the guys who have been fucking with all your fun. Let's be friends,'" Snap said sarcastically.

"I like that idea. You run with it. While you do that, the rest of us will approach them and let them know we have connections and the ability to help alleviate some of their problems—if they want to bring us on board." Santo had gone back to sharpening his knife.

"Oh, yeah, that won't raise any warning flags at all." Snap rolled his eyes.

"That's why we need to connect with our contacts over there." Stryker looked pointedly at Phantom and Buzz.

"Let's start establishing our stories and backgrounds," Phantom said.

"Some of it has already been done for us," Stryker said, as he pulled up their dossiers. "Phantom and Buzz, we'll be encountering the lieutenants and interacting with them to gain access to the cartel. Buzz, you're going to have to focus on getting a copy of their hard drive or as much off of their network as possible to allow us to begin deciphering their coded documents."

"Gotta love the covers they give us. Why do we always have to have facial hair?" Buzz grumbled and Phantom chuckled.

Stryker looked around at the men and felt a tightening in his chest. He could be sending his team into a death trap. Lacking information and unable to know who they could trust, they were in a difficult position. All he could do was lead them the best he knew how. "All right, team, we know what we need to accomplish. Let's get started."

Chapter 11

"WHO THE HELL ARE YOU AND WHAT ARE YOU DOING ON my property?"

Elena's breath caught in her throat. The voice was soft and calm, yet there was a tension she could almost feel in the air. She lifted her head slowly and had to look up—way up—the man was tall and muscular. But his face was expressionless. She would have preferred to see anger than a man who spoke in a threatening tone, yet gave no other clue as to his state of mind. It was disconcerting.

Every logical part of her brain told her to get away from him. This man was dangerous. It was in his eyes, so dark she could barely discern what color they really were. She didn't *feel* the need to run from him, though. There was something about him that rippled just beneath the surface, and she wanted to learn more.

Drawing in a shaky breath, she extended her hand to him. "I'm Elena Garcia. The horse trainer. You must be Phantom. Anya told me I'd run into you eventually since you are running everything with the horses now."

His eyes narrowed. "How do you know my name?"

Her hand fell back to her side. Things certainly weren't going as she as she had hoped. She had been so excited to work with someone who loved horses as much as she, but it seemed the positive feelings weren't reciprocated. "Anya told me to look for a tall, lean, dark haired man who loves horses. Aren't you Phantom?"

"You seem to know a lot about me. I'm at a disadvantage, I think."

Elena blinked slowly. "So is your name some kind of nickname or something?" She cringed. *Don't ask personal questions. It's probably best for you to know as little as possible about this man.*

"Or something. Anya told you about me? The veterinarian?"

"Yes. Anya and I have been friends for a long time. I've been the horse trainer at this ranch for many years. Didn't Stryker tell you? I presume you're the other new owner here?"

"Anya knows we are quiet people and like to keep it that way."

"Oh." Had she just gotten Anya into trouble? "I'm certain she thought it was all right. I was training the horses while your house was being renovated. I met the man who was overseeing everything—his name was Stryker. You *are* one of the new owners, aren't you?" He wasn't answering a single one of her questions.

"There are a few of us running the ranch. My focus is on the horses. It's my area of expertise."

"So you know something about horses! That's good to hear. The last owner loved to win ribbons and trophies, but had no idea how to care for them day-to-day. I had to make extensive lists for him. But he did have impeccable taste and purchased some of the most beautiful quarter horses I've ever had the pleasure to work with."

Phantom continued to watch her. "I've seen the trophies and ribbons. Are you the one who shows them?"

Elena ran her hand through her curly black hair and gave him a genuine smile. "Yes. It's an absolute pleasure showing animals that are this finely tuned. Though...I must admit, they seem a little more wired than usual." As if to prove her point, one of the horses kicked at the sturdy barn door near where they were standing, and she flinched slightly. "Have you, by any chance, changed their feed?"

"These horses were on coastal hay and oats. That's not enough to maintain their stamina."

Elena lifted her eyebrows in surprise. "So, you did what, exactly? You put them on sweet feed?"

"Homemade sweet feed. The stuff you buy at the feed store is overprocessed with too much molasses. I have a special recipe we used for our horses all the time."

"How long has it been since you've worked with quarter horses?" Elena asked as delicately as possible. He didn't seem the type to jump into a conversation willingly. Was he *that* irritated she was there, or was he just a difficult person to begin with?

"I've never worked with quarter horses. I had plenty of experience raising thoroughbreds when I was younger."

A light bulb triggered in her mind. "You raised race-horses, didn't you?"

The ever-so-slight lift of one eyebrow was the only indication that she'd surprised him. "Yes, that's right. How did you know?"

"Things you said. Plus, making your own sweet feed is something I usually hear about in the racing areas of the equine world. Then when you said thoroughbreds, I realized you must have worked with racehorses. It all adds up."

The corner of his mouth twitched, and Elena found herself holding her breath, wondering if he was going to bestow a smile on her. She had no idea why she wanted to see one so much. But there was something about the man that intrigued her.

The smile didn't come. "I take it you think I should be feeding the horses differently?"

Elena glanced into the stall at the horse pacing back and forth. "Absolutely. Quarter horses operate much differently than thoroughbreds, and require a different diet. That's why I had them on oats and coastal hay. We don't give them sweet feed until a few days before a show, in order to get them a shinier coat and the extra alertness a judge likes to see. Even with the small amounts of sweet feed that we give them, we have to exercise them extensively to burn off the energy."

"Good to know. Now, I appreciate the years you've put in here training these horses, but I'll be able to take over from here."

Elena felt as if she had been punched in the gut. "Excuse me?"

"I don't have need of your services."

"Surely you're joking. Training quarter horses to be winners in any of the categories we show them in—"

"I'll be showing them going forward. I know enough to manage. I thank you for your efforts and all that you've done up until now. We'll be just fine without you."

Elena felt tears burning the backs of her eyes. This was her favorite ranch. She had put her heart and soul into training these horses. It was as if he'd just told her she couldn't see her own children anymore.

"Mr.…I mean, Phantom, I don't think you know what

you're getting yourself into. Showing quarter horses is a very competitive sport, and—"

"Thank you, Señorita Garcia."

With her back stiff, she turned and began to leave the barn, refusing to let this man see her cry. But she couldn't leave without a parting remark. "If you ever change your mind, Phantom, just ask Anya how to find me."

That comment earned her a smug, knowing smile. He didn't believe he would ever need her. "I'll keep that in mind," he said softly.

Nodding firmly, Elena turned and made it to her truck before the first teardrops fell.

"Your woman could be a liability." Phantom focused on Stryker as he walked into the dining room.

Stryker paused, his fork halfway raised to his lips and his eyebrow arched. "What the hell are you talking about?"

"Anya. She's been telling some woman all about us. Or at the very least, all about me. It raises red flags."

"Some woman? Just a random woman? Why didn't you tell me sooner?"

"Was she good-looking?" Snap asked. "If so, I'll handle getting rid of her next time."

"There won't be a next time," Phantom said blandly. "She apparently used to be the horse trainer here before we bought the place. But she knew my name and that I'm managing the horses."

"The horse trainer. Yeah, I knew about her. She came out and worked with the horses the entire time we were remodeling this place. She knew I was involved with the place while she was out here, but we never really got a chance to talk. I forgot about her. She even took the horses to a few shows while I was around. Never asked for any help, though she made sure to deliver any prize money to me as soon as she returned. Seemed nice enough. What's your problem with her?"

"It should be everyone's problem with her. Why didn't you tell me about her? You had a fit when Anya showed up unexpectedly, but you didn't have any problem with Elena?"

"Elena. Pretty name," Snap spoke up.

"Pervert. You are way too much of a horndog lately," Buzz grumbled.

"What do you mean lately?" Santo ribbed.

"I did have concerns with her being around," Stryker said. "But she never went anywhere except to the barn, the arena, and her own truck. I ran a full background check on her, and even did some investigating in town."

"And?"

"She moved here when she graduated from Texas A&M. The owner of this ranch at the time personally reached out to her and offered her a lucrative job training his quarter horses. Rumor has it, he saw her competing at a couple of horse shows and he was blown away by her knowledge and experience. She's been showing horses since she was a child. But the deal wasn't enough for her to make a living, as sweet as it was. So she established her own business training horses around Hebbronville. She trains at four or five other ranches around the area, though she focuses primarily on roping, cutting, and reining with those ranches."

Buzz began to hum "Silver Bells" under his breath

and everyone at the table threw glares in his direction. "Seriously, Buzz?" Snap moaned. "Can't you go even one day without a Christmas carol? It's months away!"

Buzz lifted his chin, chewing on a mouthful of food, then swallowed and placed a hand over his heart. "It's constantly Christmas in my heart. I can't help it that the rest of you are so jealous."

The men groaned in unison, and tuned out Buzz's humming as they returned to the topic at hand.

"You fired her, didn't you?" Brusco asked, frowning across the table at Phantom.

"Yes. We have no need for her now. I'll manage the horses."

"So, who's going to take care of the horses when you're out on a mission?" Stryker asked, and Phantom's eyes dropped to the plate of food he'd just made, beginning to lose his appetite.

"I'll train one of y'all in what needs to be done. It's simple enough."

"In your mind." Buzz laughed. "I wouldn't know the head from the ass."

"Just because you're ranch-knowledge impaired is no reason to count yourself out. Working with horses can be incredibly rewarding."

"Yeah, um, you keep thinking that way, buddy. If it has hooves, I don't go near it. We had agreed on this, or have you forgotten already? I am your communications and tech guru. I like artificial lighting and have adverse reactions to hay, fur, and hooves. So, you won't be getting any help from me with this problem you've created."

"It's not a problem. The woman is not needed on our premises. She'd just be a liability."

Phantom felt Stryker's eyes on him for several long seconds and finally looked over at him. "That's how I felt when I first met Anya. As you well know, she's been extremely valuable to the ranch. Elena could be the same."

"I know how to take care of horses. There's no reason for us to keep her around."

"And show them? There's an expectation that this ranch will continue competing and drawing in breeding clientele who want to use that giant black stallion we have and the beautiful brood mares in the paddock right now." Stryker watched him closely.

"Why on earth is there such an expectation?" Phantom demanded, beginning to feel irritated.

"Because we need to actively participate in the ranching community. Not only is it part of our cover, it allows us to hunt for information that might be relevant to any of our missions. There's a reason we were placed here—to keep our ears to the ground and stay on top of anything concerning Mexico and Central and South America."

Phantom sighed heavily. "I'll give it some thought. Let's just get through this mission in Mexico. Oh, and, Santo, I'll leave the care of the horses in your hands while we're gone."

"Son of a—"

The men's laughter drowned out Santo's curse.

Chapter 12

STRYKER DIDN'T LIKE TO BE CONFINED. EVEN IF IT WAS a relatively decent-sized room, it was still too cramped for him. The admiral's waiting area needed serious remodeling. It could have been featured as a waiting room on an old episode of *Miami Vice*. He had grown up watching the reruns and could quote practically any episode. The biggest difference in the décor of this waiting area, though, was that it lacked any color other than awful cheap paintings hanging on the wall.

The only things that made it obvious he wasn't in a "normal" waiting room were the large glass case full of plaques, awards, and navy paraphernalia; the picture of the president prominently displayed; and the navy emblem and various insignia placed on the wall. A fake palm tree stood in one corner, and everything was polished and neat, nearly pristine. The carpet was a depressing shade of blue, and the obvious path marks where people had walked frequently showed the need for replacement.

He gripped the folder of printed data pages. He wasn't looking forward to this conversation. He didn't know how far he was going to get with the admiral, but he had to fight for information for his team. They couldn't be expected to go into these situations blind, and if this was precedent for how they were going to conduct things, he was going to let the admiral know he needed to find someone else to lead a team of SEALs. Stryker wasn't about to lead his men to their deaths because some bureaucrat wanted to keep certain things confidential.

He had debated talking to Admiral Haslett over the phone, but this type of conversation required face-to-face interaction. Haslett needed to know how serious Stryker was about the situation, and that couldn't be conveyed in a phone call.

Down a long hallway to his left, there was the sound of a door opening and a tall, middle-aged man with the standard buzz cut strode forward, a slight frown on his face. From the faint wrinkles in his skin, it was obvious the frown was a permanent feature. "Lieutenant Salas," he said briskly, then turned and headed back down the hall with clear expectations that he would be followed.

Stryker stood quickly, placing his hat in the back of his pants and cringing as the leather of his navy-issue boots pinched at his feet. He'd become far too comfortable in his ranch boots. Fortunately, the visit had only required that he dress in his fatigues and not his dress uniform. Those shiny black shoes would have had him limping by the end of the day.

Admiral Haslett stood at his desk as Stryker entered, and Stryker instantly saluted him. Haslett returned the salute then took his seat, irritation crossing his face as he watched Stryker sit. His eyes were focused on the folder that Stryker held. "When you took this assignment, I told you there would be a variety of situations. You don't get to pick and choose the missions you want."

"Understood, sir. My men and I are prepared for any mission you send our way."

"Then why have you come to see me today? What is the issue?"

Stryker pulled out several pages of the file. "My men and I are prepared just as I said. However, we won't go in with one hand tied behind our backs."

"What are you talking about?" Haslett snapped, his irritation visibly growing—until Stryker handed him the pages with the redacted information.

"What the hell is this?" he demanded.

"That's the same question I asked. I pulled this directly from the file uploaded to our server." Stryker watched Haslett with intensity, but Haslett's shock seemed real.

He hit a button on his phone and his secretary's voice came across the intercom. "Find me Commander Davis. Now." He punched the button to turn it off and then turned to his computer, quickly punching keys to open up a secure file on the screen. It took several long moments to load, but finally he pivoted the computer screen to face Stryker.

He stabbed at the screen, watching Stryker as he did so. "*This* is what you were supposed to receive."

Stryker looked at the document, and it was exactly the same as what they had received, except none of the information had been redacted. The entire document was clean. Stryker ran a hand over his mouth as he reviewed the new information. The key pieces that had been hidden from them could very well have cost them their lives.

"This begs the question, then, of how we went from this document"—Stryker pointed to the computer—"to this." He pointed at the redacted pages that sat on the desk.

"That's what I intend to find out," the admiral said with conviction. He looked from the redacted document over to the one that Stryker was reading. "How bad?" he asked softly.

"The changes could have meant death for me and my men," Stryker said. "Fortunately, we have Buzz. He was already gathering a lot of this type of information. But he couldn't get as much as what is here in this document."

"Shit. I was afraid you were going to say that." The admiral shook his head, then hit the button on his phone. "Where is the commander?"

"He's on his way. He should be over here in just a few minutes."

"Fine. Send him directly to my office when he arrives."

Stryker closed up the file, wanting to see how the commander reacted before getting a glance at what Stryker had brought with him. "What's the story on this commander?" He still watched the admiral intently, not wanting to miss any sign the admiral was trying to deceive him.

"To be honest, I don't know much about him. He transferred here from Little Creek, Virginia, about three months ago."

"Little Creek? Is he a SEAL?"

"A wannabe. He failed out of BUD/S training in the first few weeks at Coronado. But he wanted to stay close to the SEAL world and transferred to Little Creek a couple of years ago. I haven't looked too deeply into why he transferred here. We don't have an active SEAL team based here."

"Other than us." Stryker frowned deeply. "How common is the knowledge of our undercover assignment?"

"Need to know only."

"Let's keep it that way, then. When the commander arrives, I suggest we let him believe I'm from Coronado and here specifically for this assignment."

The admiral nodded. "I agree."

Within a few short minutes, the commander stepped into the doorway and both Stryker and the admiral stood. They saluted, and Commander Davis removed his hat and assumed an at-ease stance with his legs braced shoulder-width apart and his hands behind his back. "Reporting as requested, sir."

"Davis, do you recall the file you brought to me about a week ago? The one where you pointed out that your team had narrowed the search for the man who's been crossing over the border and is suspected of murdering individuals here stateside?"

"Yes, sir. I recall the file."

"Do you want to tell me how it ended up being transmitted to our SEAL team like this?" The admiral opened Stryker's folder and held up the redacted papers, his frown dipping even deeper than usual.

Commander Davis swallowed hard. "No, sir. I sent the file to your secretary as you requested, and I'm not familiar with what happened to it from there."

"My secretary sent me the file he was uploading for the SEAL team. I have it right here." He pointed to the image on the computer. "It doesn't look at all like what they actually received. I'm going to ask you one more time, Davis, and I encourage you to think hard before you answer: How did this file end up being transmitted like this?"

Sweat was beading on Davis's upper lip, and he

swallowed again. Stryker wanted to take him out to the training room and remind the man why he had failed BUD/S training in a slow, brutal way. He was clearly lying.

"Sir, don't you recall, sir?" His eyes were pleading with the admiral, and Stryker's attention shifted to Haslett.

The admiral's eyes narrowed dangerously. "Recall what, sailor? What am I supposed to remember?" he barked.

"I received a memo from your office, sir, outlining the information to redact from the document. Your instructions were very specific, sir."

"I never sent such a memo, sailor!" The admiral's face was turning red.

"It was on your letterhead, sir. It was on my desk when I came back from hitting the head, sir."

"Do you still have this letter?"

"No, sir. I was instructed to shred the letter, sir." Davis looked like he was going to throw up.

"Of course you were. Take a seat, sailor. You're about to be under military investigation. Salas, step out with me."

"Sir." Stryker grabbed the folder with the incorrect notes and stood quickly to follow Haslett out the door and into the hallway. Haslett slammed the door to his office shut with such force, a small cloud of dust fell from the ceiling.

"That little shit is telling the truth," Admiral Haslett growled.

Stryker turned to face him. "I know, sir. Which makes this problem much more complicated."

"Damn it all to hell. I'll personally upload the corrected document. Shit. I'm going to need them to investigate my secretary as well."

"It could be anyone, sir. It wouldn't be that hard to get ahold of your letterhead. What this does tell us is that there's someone with military clearance who wants this mission to fail."

Chapter 13

THE PACKAGE ARRIVED VIA FEDEX AND HAD HIS FULL NAME spelled out: LIEUTENANT AMADOR STRYKER SALAS. He never received packages with his handle included. Something felt wrong. Unease slipped down his spine as he looked at the thick envelope. Not that long ago, there had been a series of bombings in Austin, and a couple of the packages had come through FedEx.

Stryker frowned. He was being too paranoid. The bomber in Austin had been caught. Actually, he'd blown himself up when the police had closed in on him. Shaking his head at his morbid thoughts, Stryker tore open the package. The sender's address was in Corpus Christi. Which was even more disturbing. Was this from their mysterious "friend" in the military?

He had left the base in Corpus without any further information, other than the assurances that it was all going to be investigated thoroughly. That wasn't giving him any comfort. The team hadn't been comforted by the news, either. Discovering that mission-critical information had been deliberately redacted based on mysterious orders from within the admiral's office had left them all confused and frustrated.

The strange delivery he held in his hands presented a new dilemma. It was a large, flat envelope, the kind you use when you want to make sure that the contents won't get bent or damaged during delivery. Multiple slick photos came sliding out of the envelope and tension built within his body. He picked up the first one in the stack, and the rage that filled him caused his hands to tremble.

It was a photo of him with Anya. It wasn't just a random photo. It was a picture of her sitting in front of him on the horse, her head tilted to the side and a sleepy smile on her face as his lips pressed against her neck. This picture had been taken the first time she had come out to help with a difficult birth. Someone had been on their property, hidden within the shrubs, taking pictures of him with Anya.

The next several pictures weren't quite as disconcerting, but they were still upsetting. There was at least one of every member of his team working on the ranch, even photos of the few times Buzz had wandered outside to join them in a task so he could learn not to be such a greenhorn. The number of pictures of him with Anya disturbed him deeply. Whoever had taken these photos and sent them, if they were one and the same person, was obviously trying to get a point across.

The team had been immersed in preparing for their infiltration of the drug cartel, and he hated to pull their minds off that important task. But they needed to know what was going on, and they needed to be wary of someone trespassing on the ranch with unknown intentions.

He called the team together and tossed the photos on the table. "Someone is watching us," he said bluntly. "And I doubt it's for friendly purposes."

"You never know, boss. It could be they just want some photos of the sexiest men in Hebbronville and are considering us for model gigs," Snap said cheerfully.

"Yeah, right, pendejo. Nobody would want a picture of your ugly mug," Santo replied with a growl. "How did they get on the property without our security going off?"

"That's the first problem we need to address. Buzz, before we leave, do a complete systems check of all security, and search the tapes to see if he's getting in somewhere and we've just been missing it. Look at the perspective of some of these pictures. He had to have been in the barn with us, or in a tree nearby us, to get the angle of shots he got. That's way too close for my comfort."

"So, what do you think this is?" Santo asked, tossing his picture back on the table with an expression of disgust on his face. "You think it's Big Brother letting us know he's always watching us?"

"No," Phantom said softly. "They're not watching us. Whoever this is, they're watching Stryker."

"What are you talking about?"

"Look at the pictures, Stryker. You're in every single one of them, either talking to us or working alongside us. It's the only consistent thing in every picture."

Stryker sorted through the pictures and realized Phantom was right. He was in every single one of them. *What the hell?* He looked up, and the team was watching him expectantly. "Buzz, do as I said and look into our security. From now on, we need to be on high alert. Someone is watching us, and I'd sure as hell like to know why."

"Today can't finish soon enough." Anya grinned as she began to prep the clinic to receive clients. It was hard running the clinic by herself, but, if she kept growing her clientele, she would be able to hire a receptionist soon. Elena rolled her eyes, kicking back in the chair at the front desk and propping her boots up on the counter. "You're acting like you've never been on a date before."

Anya scrunched her nose and frowned at Elena. "You seemed happy for me when I told you he came by and asked me out."

"You're right. I'm happy for you. I'm sure you're going to have a good time. Just ignore me."

Anya paused in drawing the blinds up on the windows and looked at Elena closely. "Something's bothering you. You've been acting strange the last few days, but you change the subject every time I try to get to the bottom of it." She walked over to the counter and sat down next to Elena's boots. "You can't get out of it anymore. What's going on?"

"The Bent Horseshoe Ranch is what's going on. Or should I say it's what isn't going on?" Elena wouldn't make eye contact with Anya, instead focusing on a fingernail.

"What are you talking about? You aren't making any sense." Anya swatted Elena's boots, forcing her to look up.

Elena sighed heavily. "One of your new pals out there decided the ranch doesn't need me anymore and I have been fired as their horse trainer."

"What? You can't be serious! You're the best horse trainer in south Texas, if not all of Texas."

"Apparently this guy doesn't think my expertise is needed. Goes by the name of Phantom. I can see why, too. He moves so quietly you don't even know he's there until he's right on top of you." Elena looked back down at her fingers. "With just a few short sentences, it was all over, and I'm not needed back at their ranch."

"Elena, I'm so sorry. Maybe I can try to talk to Phantom—"

Elena held up a hand and gave Anya a sharp look. "I didn't tell you about this to get you to do anything. I can look out for myself."

"Do you want me to reach out to some of the ranchers I know to see if they could use your services?"

"No." Elena shook her head emphatically. She straightened in the chair and set her feet back on the ground. "Like I said, I can take care of this on my own. I see your first customer of the day pulling up right now. I'm off to go get some new clients. Wish me luck!"

Anya embraced her friend quickly. "You just let me know—"

Elena laughed and returned Anya's embrace. "I've got this. I'll be fine. And you better be sure to tell me all about your date tonight. Every juicy detail."

Anya's day went by faster than she had expected. She was busy trying to help a cow dog that had been trampled by one rowdy bull and was in the middle of setting its broken leg when the phone rang. She tuned it out. The poor dog was whimpering, but she'd given it enough sedative that it wasn't feeling much of anything. Her phone buzzed and vibrated in her pocket, alerting her that she had a voicemail.

She began wrapping the dog's leg, focused and intent on her work. The dog had stopped whimpering and appeared to have fallen asleep. The wet plaster was drying quickly, and she cleaned the table and straightened up the other areas of the exam room where she had worked. She peeled off her latex gloves, scrubbed her hands diligently beneath the warm water at the sink, and turned back to the dog, drying her hands on a towel.

The dog was slowly waking up and sluggishly lifted its head off the table to look at her more thoroughly. "You're a good dog, aren't you, Ralphie? Such a good dog. Now, stay put for a little longer while I go get your owner for you."

She opened the door that led into the waiting room and was relieved to see the rancher was the only one sitting in the room. It was six o'clock at night, but it was normal to have these last-minute emergencies. She still had enough time to get ready for Stryker.

She nodded to the rancher and smiled. "Ralphie's going to be just fine. He just has to wear this cast for the next six weeks. That means no cattle rustling for him for a while. I'll give you some painkillers for him—give him a dose in about four hours, and then every eight hours or so after that, or whenever he seems to be in pain."

The rancher smiled and stood, walking into the room and stroking the dog's head. "We can make it just fine. As long as Ralphie's okay.'" He turned and shook her hand. "Thanks so much, Dr. Gutierrez. You always come through for me."

Anya smiled as she watched him pick up the dog gently, then begin to carry him out. "Come back in six weeks, and of course, call me if you need anything in the meantime," she called after them, and the rancher nodded as he left her office.

She sighed heavily, still wiping her hands on the towel as she began to peel out of her scrubs and head for her bedroom. She stripped down to her tank top and underwear and lay down on her bed, battling the exhaustion that tugged at her as she picked up her phone and listened to her voicemail.

"Hi, Dr. Gutierrez...I'm sorry to bother you at this hour, but one of my heifers is down. Please call me back as soon as you can." Anya cringed. No, not today, not when she was supposed to have her first date in years. She squeezed the phone in her fist, wanting to throw it across the room.

What could she possibly do? She had to take care of the heifer. She had to hurry. *Maybe things will progress quickly and...* She realized she was just fooling herself. There was no way she would be finished and ready for a date with Stryker. Not the way she wanted to be.

With a heavy heart, she hit the redial button and connected with the rancher. He was relieved to receive her call and asked for her urgent arrival. The headache that had nearly disappeared since the accident at Stryker's ranch came back, pounding in rhythm with her heart, a dull and steady thud. She had to call Stryker.

She couldn't deny her desire for the man. She had always wondered what it would be like, and Stryker had taken every fantasy she'd ever had and made it ten times more erotic than she could have imagined. She wanted to taste that pleasure again. But it had probably meant more to her than it had to him. What if he had politely asked her on a date because he thought that was the "proper" thing to do after taking her virginity? *What did you expect? A declaration of love?*

With trembling fingers, she hit the numbers on her cell and connected with Stryker's phone, listening to the ringing on the other end. Her heart was racing in her chest and she felt flushed from her chest to her cheeks.

"Anya?"

Just the sound of his deep, husky voice seemed to wash over her, and she shivered, remembering the way he had talked to her as they had made love. *Made love.* That's what it had been to her. But she supposed the accurate description of it was sex. "Hi, Stryker. I'm sorry to tell you this, but I'm not going to be able to meet you tonight."

"Did something happen? Are you all right?"

"I'm fine. It's just... There's a heifer down calving right now, and it doesn't look good."

"I understand. It's what you do."

Is that it? He won't even pretend he's disappointed?

"What ranch are you headed to? Will you be any-where near here?"

Her heartbeat picked up. "I'll be about fifteen min-utes away. But, Stryker, I have no idea how long it will take. You know how it is. It can go quickly or it can take hours."

"You're worth waiting for. I'll be ready for you whenever you get here."

How could she respond to *that*? Maybe he really had enjoyed his time with her and wanted to see her as badly as she wanted to see him. "I-I... I'll see you as soon as possible."

What was she about to head into? Frowning at the now silent phone, she quickly got dressed in a pair of blue jeans and a button-down blouse that was a little dressier than she usually wore on her trips to take care of a vet call. She wanted Stryker to be surprised and at least a little impressed. She could give him so much more than he realized. She could love him.

Anya stared at herself in the mirror where she had been concentrating on brushing her hair. Was that what she really wanted? Was that how she really felt? *Oh, no, this is a bad idea. I can't fall in love with this man… Too late.*

Anya struggled to control the trembling in her hands as she set down the brush. She didn't let most people impact her too much. She was friendly with just about everyone, but she didn't let her emotions flow that strongly for them. Her heart pounded in her chest and she shook her head at herself. *I've fallen in love with him. How did I let this happen? And now, what do I do about it? The man clearly doesn't want love or anything that will tie him down to anyone or anything. I'm alone.*

She'd never really thought of her life that way. Her clinic had been her baby. It had been her dream ever since she had graduated veterinary school. When she had found the need in Hebbronville, she'd put all her energy and every last dime of savings into building the clinic. She had done it all on her own. Alone.

But now her heart yearned for the strength and comfort offered by Stryker's arms. She longed for the security and pleasure he brought into her life. He was a good man. He had shown that in the way he had taken care of her both when she had suffered a panic attack, and then when she had hit her head.

Tears suddenly burned at the back of her eyes, but she fought them back and stood, grabbing her truck keys. Stryker had touched her heart, and she would never be the same.

She drove out to the ranch quickly, and luckily, the

heifer was progressing naturally. A little over an hour later, with Anya keeping a close watch, the heifer gave birth to a beautiful calf.

She was a little frustrated that the rancher had called her out unnecessarily, but it was a good outcome for the animals and she was going to see Stryker, even though it wasn't quite a date now. Would he take her out to eat from the ranch? Where would they go?

She drove directly to his ranch, and as she stepped out of her truck, she heard the crunch of hooves on the gravel.

She turned and saw Stryker standing close behind her, holding the reins of two horses. "This is a change," she said with an eyebrow lifted. Then her heart sank. "Is it another calf?"

"No," he said softly. "But trust me, I need you."

His face was serious and focused on hers, and there was something else hovering in the depths of his eyes. She didn't know what it was, but she was afraid to ask any questions. Without arguing or taking any additional time, Anya went to the horse he'd provided for her and mounted quickly. He checked to make sure the stirrups were the right length for her, his hands sliding along her calf muscle as he slipped her boot back into the stirrup after a quick adjustment, and Anya's heart pounded. She felt too much when it came to this man. She needed to rein in her heart.

He mounted his horse effortlessly and turned toward a part of the ranch she hadn't been on in a long time. Her horse automatically followed his, and soon they were traveling in silence toward Stryker's destination. Anya drew in a deep breath, smelling the mesquite and the sage and the scent of dirt on the air, threatening an upcoming storm. The dry soil desperately craved the moisture, and she silently prayed for the rain to come, to wash their world, to make it clean again, and give the ranchers hope for a decent year for grass and hay.

She let her eyes slide closed as the last rays of sunlight beat down on her face, warming her. It was what she needed after a day cooped up in the clinic and the tense hour she'd stayed in the barn watching a heifer go through labor pains. But no matter how good she felt, she could sense the power of Stryker's presence, and that made her heart race.

"Long day?" His voice cut through to her heart.

She opened her eyes and turned her attention on him. There were dark circles under his eyes, and she could tell he hadn't slept well in days. But there was caring in his eyes as he focused on her. There was genuine concern. "Yes," she said softly, giving him a half-hearted smile. "In fact, it's been a long week."

"Did you rest at all since I've last seen you?"

Her lips twitched and she lowered her head. "No. There's been too much work to do."

"That's what I thought. You were far too eager to leave me that morning."

"I wasn't trying to leave you…"

He chuckled softly, and the sound wrapped around her like a soothing blanket. "When you called me today, I was afraid it was to back out of our date. But I couldn't go this long without seeing you again."

"Now you're just being dramatic," Anya said, feeling her lips pull into a smile.

"There it is," he said softly, staring at her as if he

hadn't ever seen a person smile. "That's what I've been needing. Your smile."

She could feel a blush creeping up her cheeks, but she didn't turn away from him. "Is that all you've been needing?"

A slow, very male smile began to spread across his face. "I need a lot, Anya." His smile faltered some. "And I'm not very good at expressing my thoughts and letting anyone know…how much I need."

Chapter 14

STRYKER FELT A LITTLE LOST. THIS WAS UNCHARTED TERRITORY for him. Even when he first met his former wife, he hadn't felt so far out of his comfort zone. She had been at a mixer for Navy SEAL graduates. She had come along as a plus-one and had been left high and dry. He'd made short work of getting to know the beautiful woman and found her enchanting.

They'd given it their best effort. Both of them had been young and foolish in love. But she had the need to have him home every night for dinner, and he had the need to devote himself to the SEALs. Finally, she threatened to divorce him if he didn't quit the navy — more importantly, the SEALs. He had helped her pack. She had tearfully admitted that she couldn't live with the fear and uncertainty. She had thought she could handle being a military wife, but the stress was killing her. He supposed he could understand on some level, but she'd never understood that being a SEAL was his heart, his soul, his true identity. He wasn't going to abandon that for anyone. Shaking his head to clear out the past, he looked at Anya, so gentle and kind and dedicated to her own career. Was it possible that she would understand? "Did everything go okay at the other ranch?"

"It was a normal birth. The rancher was just being a little anxious."

"I can tell by your face you're in pain. You haven't been resting like you need to."

"I'm fine. It's just been a long week already. Calving season is always taxing. But I'll make it through. Just having a headache makes the day a little harder."

He frowned. "You still have a headache? Anya, you really need to slow down. You have to take it easy."

"If you knew how little sleep I get during this time period, you would understand. I just go on autopilot, I suppose."

"You must be very successful."

"For a small-town veterinarian, I do okay. One day I hope to expand my practice and have a full team and a clinic large enough to serve the surrounding small towns as well. Right now, I'm stretched too thin, and there are outlying areas that just never get any help. They're the ones that need it the most."

"How long have you had that dream?"

"Since I used to live in one of those areas that desperately needed a veterinarian."

"I thought you saw a veterinarian save a horse when you were young." Stryker looked at her with confusion, and she bestowed another one of her mind-blowing smiles on him.

"You remember!" She had shared that story with him when she'd been recovering from hitting her head. "Yes, that shaped my decision. He was the first veterinarian we had seen in years. We'd lost countless animals to disease and birth defects. He made such a difference on the whole farm."

"I can see how that would shape a dream. This… this"—he gestured to the land around them, the occasional group of cattle clustered together—"is my dream." He returned his eyes to her and a warmth spread through his chest. This was his dream, wasn't it? If so, then why did he feel like he was missing the most critical piece? Someone to share it with. It was also his dream to stop terrorists. But he could have the best of both worlds, couldn't he?

Anya deserved to know how he felt. She deserved to know so much. She had to know about his failed marriage and how terrible he was at so many different key compartments of his life that revolved around feeling anything for a woman.

Anya was smiling at him, but he could tell from the look in her eyes that she was still wary of him. He had totally fucked up when she'd left after they had been together so intimately. He had wanted to keep her in his arms forever, and at the same time, he'd wanted to put as much distance between them as possible. He couldn't have a relationship, not now, not ever. Could he?

Yet, as he had prepared for the undercover mission they were leaving for the very next day, all he could think about was Anya. He had to make things right with her now. He might not get another chance.

It was a risk they all took when they went on missions, and they all understood that death was always lurking nearby. All it took was a word said in the wrong tone of voice, taking a step in the wrong direction, or looking someone directly in the eyes when their culture forbade such an action.

Added to that was that they were walking into the unknown. Their research had revealed a much deeper story about the cartel, though it hadn't yielded as much as he would have liked. Still, it was disturbing that key information had been redacted from their debrief files. Someone in the admiral's office had made sure they received incomplete information. How much did that person know about their operation? Or could it be that the person giving the admiral the information was working both sides?

Then the mysterious photos had appeared. Santo and Phantom had ridden the fences and found an area where someone could have slipped onto their property and avoided detection by the security cameras. They'd repaired the hole and then added more cameras to the perimeter of the property, the barn, and around the exterior of the house. Whoever was fucking with them would be caught this time.

Regardless, Stryker and his team studied intensely, making notes, sharing with each other, practicing together and in solitude, until they actually *became* the men they were supposed to be on the mission. They had their backstories memorized, they had their mannerisms down to perfection, and they knew their marks. Buzz had already successfully disrupted their supply chain in Colombia through his vast network, and the cartel was beginning to feel the pain. It was a matter of time before they became desperate.

But tonight wasn't about the mission. Tonight was about making things right with Anya. And he was going to try his best. He needed to show her how much he valued her, how much he valued what she'd given him, and that she was an incredible woman for any man to have.

He didn't know why she'd decided to gift him with her virginity. He didn't know what he'd done to earn it.

Maybe it had been the way he had held her through her panic attack. Maybe it had been the way he had treated her as his equal, had valued her opinion. Maybe it had been the way he'd cared for her when she hit her head. Whatever the reason, he was grateful. Her innocence was something he was going to treasure for the rest of his life.

Finally, they came upon the small clearing where Stryker had placed a thick blanket and a basket with food and a bottle of wine. Anya turned to look at him with surprise and a half smile on her lips. "*You* did this?" she asked incredulously.

He gave her a lopsided grin. "Why are you so surprised?"

"I-I just never thought you would do something like this. You're so…rough. I figured you would think such a thing too corny."

His smile broadened as he dismounted and quickly went to help her dismount. She turned within the circle of his arms, and he saw her draw in a sharp breath at how close he was to her. She was having an impact on him as well, and he never wanted to let her go. That thought alone was frightening. By holding on, he could end up hurting her even more.

"So this was why you decided to ask me out here?" He saw her swallow as her gaze searched his face.

"Yes, and we'd better hurry or the wine will be too warm."

A nervous chuckle escaped her, and she ran a hand through her long, dark hair. "Are you trying to get out of paying one of your vet bills?"

He winked at her and grabbed her hand, leading her over to the blanket. "Have a seat, señorita," he said, bending at the waist and taking off his cowboy hat as he leaned forward for her.

"Gracias, señor," she said with a soft roll of her *r*'s that made him want to kiss her at that very moment and find the honey of her lips.

She sat near the basket and waited for him to join her. He suddenly felt nervous as he joined her on the blanket, but he knew he had to finish what he'd started. He couldn't leave tomorrow with a clear conscience if he didn't.

He pulled out meats and cheeses, and carefully opened the wine before pouring her a glass. She shook her head and smiled up at him. "So, was this your plan all along, or were you actually going to take me to dinner somewhere?"

"Which would you prefer?"

Her eyes searched his, and he knew her answer before she said anything. "Here. Anytime. I would pick here over any restaurant."

"You told me to call whenever I needed you." His smile slipped. "And I do need you, Anya."

She drew in a shuddering breath and looked at him with startled eyes. "I didn't think... I mean, after the other day..."

"I don't often make mistakes, Anya. But when I do, I make it colossal. The way I behaved toward you the other morning... I'm sorry." Anya was staring at him like a woman who was afraid to trust what he was saying, and for the millionth time, he wanted to kick himself in the ass. Why had he reacted so sharply to her words? *Because the idea of "making love" with anyone scares the shit out of me.* But that was exactly what they had done. They had made love. It'd been magical — it'd been surreal.

In hindsight, he wished he had been gentler, caressed her more, whispered soft words in her ear, made her feel his gratitude for the gift she was giving him.

He nearly shook his head at himself for the fool he was. She hadn't said a thing and had left with the dignified grace of a true lady. Going to see her the next day wasn't soon enough to behold her beautiful face.

Anya was still watching him, and the hope he saw in the depths of her eyes made his heart clench. No woman had ever affected him this way. And he doubted one ever would again. "Anya."

He began slowly, picking up her small, delicate hand in his oversized one. He marveled once again at how perfectly their bodies had fit together as they had — made love. It was still hard for him to think about it that way, but he knew that was exactly what it had been, no matter how much his male brain fought against it. "Anya, there are things you don't know about me."

"I've known you had your secrets about your past, Stryker. I've told you that before."

How is she so damned perceptive? Am I losing my ability? Am I that easy to read now? "Yes, I've carried around secrets about my past. I think most people do."

"Trying to justify it doesn't make it any better," she said with a raised eyebrow, and he felt as if his grandmother had just chastised him for telling a lie.

"No, it doesn't. You're right. Anya, I was married once a few years ago."

She looked at him warily. "Was? As in, past tense?"

He smiled slowly as he realized she was afraid she

had committed the sin of adultery. "Yes, *very* past tense. But I haven't known how to trust a woman…how to be myself with a woman…"

"I'd say you do fairly well for yourself," she complimented him as she took a sip of the wine.

"Only with you, Anya. With you, I want to prove that I can do anything. That I'm stronger, I'm faster—I'm *better*—than any other man you've ever met. I want to impress you, Anya. Only you."

Again the hope blossomed in her eyes, and he wished desperately he could kiss her, but there was still so much to be said. "But I know…beyond a doubt I know, I will disappoint you. I will let you down. I will make you hurt. Same as I made you hurt the other morning. I was… I'm not the man you deserve."

Her gaze searched his face for several long moments, and he wondered if she could hear his heart beating. This wasn't how he'd expected everything to happen. He'd needed this last night with her. Just one more night. But he hadn't expected the apology to be so difficult, to be so taxing on his emotions. He hated that he'd hurt her, and was afraid he was only making things worse.

"I'm not good at this, Anya. I don't know how to say I'm sorry. I don't know how to warn you that I'm not the right man for you. Because my mind is clouded by the fact that I want you…I need you, and…"

His words ended abruptly as she leaned forward and pressed her warm, supple lips to his. He responded automatically, moving his lips against hers slowly. Her hand reached up into his hair, combing her fingers through the locks that were growing out and weren't their usual short crop. Slowly, she ended the kiss and pulled back from him, staring into his eyes.

"Why do you say that you aren't the right man for me? You don't even know what kind of man I want."

He smiled at her, something he found himself doing frequently around her. It wasn't something he was used to, and it made his cheeks hurt. "I know what kind of man you deserve," he said softly. "You deserve a man who is dependable and reliable, who will always be there for you and put you on a pedestal. A man who will treat you right, and do everything in his power to make your life perfect every moment of the day. I can't give you those things. I'm a rough man, who is more than rough around the edges. I have limited patience, and I can be a surly cuss to deal with."

"First of all," she said, as she moved forward on the blanket, getting closer to him, "I'm not about to be put on any pedestal. I'm afraid of heights, so that would be a bad idea for me. And I don't care about someone trying to make my life perfect every moment of the day. That's up to me. I'm sturdy and able to take care of myself. I midwife cows, for heaven's sake! I haven't given much thought to what I want in a man. All I know is that right now, you're the only man I want."

"Bella," he whispered, and his hand came up behind her neck, supporting her as he brought his lips down fiercely against hers. Unlike their previous kiss, this one was demanding, giving and receiving with the passion he'd been trying to hold back but couldn't any longer. Hearing that she wanted him was like setting a fire within him, and he knew only Anya would be able to soothe the burning ache.

She made a soft sound of appreciation at the back of her throat and leaned into him, one hand settling on his chest while the other moved up into his hair again. He slanted his mouth hungrily over hers, running his tongue along her lower lip, encouraging her to part for him. And she did, with a soft sigh, allowing him to taste the sweet depths her mouth offered.

Her tongue met his, teasing and gliding in an effortless dance, one they both seemed to know so well, though their kisses hadn't been anywhere near enough for that to be the case. It's as if she was made just for me. *She belongs just to me.* It caught his breath again as he felt the possessive desire to hold her and claim her as his and his alone. Why did he feel this way every time he was with her?

Slowly, he eased away from her and stared down at her kiss-swollen lips, then at her soft, shining eyes that were watching him under heavy lids. She was incredibly beautiful and was the temptation he couldn't deny. But he had planned to treat her the way she deserved, not to take advantage of what she offered.

"Why? Why, Anya? You could give yourself to any man in the world. Why did you choose me?"

She looked at him, and her fingers smoothed down the facial hair he had started to grow in. "Because you make me feel more like a woman than I've ever felt before. You make me feel desired and feminine, something that is very rare these days. I've never had a man look at me the way you do."

"Anya." He shook his head. "I don't know how to thank you for giving me your innocence. And I don't know how I can really expect you to forgive me for last week."

Anya's eyes dropped slowly and she stared at the blanket where her fingers picked at the fabric. "What *did* happen last week, Stryker? I was a bit foggy when I left Sunday morning."

Stryker ran a hand through his hair, then repositioned his hat on his head. "I don't really have a good answer for you, Anya. Not one that I'm proud to say, at least."

Her eyes searched his face, and he could tell she wasn't willing to take his noncommittal response as an answer. He had hoped the week and a half of being away from her would have given him the chance to realize that they'd just been two consenting adults who had enjoyed their time together, and that he owed her nothing. Instead, the longer he was away from her, the more he craved her. He sighed heavily and shook his head.

"You don't know me very well, Anya. I've done some terrible things in my life. And I won't ever speak of them. I'm not a good man."

She frowned at him. "I don't give a damn about your past. I care about the man who is sitting in front of me this very moment. And this man—the one I'm looking at—is a good man." Her eyes searched his face. "What haunts you, Stryker? I can see it in your eyes. I've seen flashes of it before. And it isn't the rodeo. That wouldn't leave such a dark mark."

"I wanted to spend tonight with you because I have to leave town tomorrow. I shouldn't be gone long, but it is to take care of some business that I can't talk about."

Her eyes searched his face, and she smiled slowly. "Then we should make sure tonight counts for something."

Chapter 15

ANYA WASN'T USED TO BEING THE ONE IN CONTROL. She wasn't used to any of this. But she knew what she wanted. And that was Stryker. She craved his touch, his scent, his arms, all of him. And if he wasn't willing to make the move, she would. Even though she was certain she was going to make herself look quite the fool.

She leaned into him, resting her hand on his chest, and looked up into his eyes. They had become so dark, and, with the faint streamers of the setting sun behind her, they looked like a fire blazed within their depths. Should she ask him to kiss her? No. She was in charge.

She stretched forward and placed her lips to his, tentatively at first, and the taste of him was intoxicating. She moved her lips leisurely over his, taking her time to enjoy him. The smell of his cologne filled her nostrils and the spicy scent seemed to wrap all around her. She could drown in this man. His lips responded to hers, moving just as lazily, while her heartbeat seemed to double.

The fire that had been in his eyes seemed to have settled deep within her. She felt warm, flushed, and excited at what she knew was to come. She pulled his lower lip between her teeth and sucked on it gently. He drew in a deep breath, and she felt a smile pull at her lips, interrupting their kiss.

"What are you so smug about?" His voice rumbled around her.

"Just knowing that I can make you feel some of what you make me feel is a very nice experience. Is this what it feels like when, well, whenever you do this?"

"First off," he said, stretching out on the blanket and pulling her along with him so she lay partway on top of him, "I don't do 'this' with any woman. She has to be incredibly special. She has to be smart, and funny, and beautiful, and sexy as hell."

"Oh." Anya suddenly felt very self-conscious. Did he really think all of those things about *her*?

"And B, I'm not sure what you're feeling. You might have to describe it to me."

"Oh, no," she groaned and dropped her head to his chest. She tried not to laugh, but the chuckles slipped out.

"What's so funny?"

"You're one of *those* people. You can't keep track of your logic."

"What are you talking about?" He lifted his head and stared down at her as if she had lost her mind.

"You said 'first off' and then you said 'B.' When you should have said, 'second off.'"

"Oh, so you're the leading authority on the way a person should keep track of their logic, are you?" He was laughing with her, but his hands reached down to her ribs where he found her sensitive sides, and his fingers moved quickly, until she let out a peal of laughter that caused the horses' heads to jerk up from where they'd been tethered and grazing nearby.

He rolled her onto her back so he could stare down at her, and the laughter on his face was the most handsome thing she'd ever seen. "You really need to smile more often," she said softly, her fingers reaching up and tracing his lips.

"*You* make me smile," he said, his voice in the same hushed tone as hers. "And I can't remember the last time I laughed like that."

She sighed heavily, though a smile still clung to her lips. "*You* make me smile all the time."

"I wish that were true, bella. I know I've hurt you, but I hope I'm making up for some of that."

"You've made a good start."

His eyebrow lifted. "Did you have something else in mind?"

She could feel her cheeks burning with a blush. "Well, I wouldn't mind a repeat of the other morning."

His eyes widened as he looked at her, and a slow, very masculine smile spread across his lips. "Oh really, señorita? Are you sure you really remember the other morning that clearly? You had a pretty bad knock to the head if I remember correctly. And…" He turned her head to the side where the bruising was fading. "The proof is still there."

"Oh, I know exactly what I have in mind." She bit her lower lip to try not to smile, and her desire to beam at him faded quickly at the look of hunger that moved across Stryker's face. "Kiss me, Stryker. Kiss me the way you've always wanted to kiss a woman. I want to taste your passion."

He let out a soft moan before lowering his head to hers, pressing his lips to hers with intensity, so firmly she thought he would bruise them. But she didn't mind. She kissed him back with the same ferocity, one hand sliding into his hair while the other hand worked to pull his shirt out of his jeans so she could touch his skin.

His hands joined hers at his waist, and he quickly pulled at his shirt. She slid her hand up underneath the material and sighed heavily as she touched the smooth skin of his back. He used her sigh as the opportunity he needed to slip his tongue into her mouth. She moaned in the back of her throat and opened her mouth for him, allowing him to take as much as he wanted, and she gave just as much in return.

Their tongues danced together, and she distantly became aware of the howl of coyotes in the far-off fields, but it wasn't loud enough to overpower the pounding of her heart in her ears. The things this man could make her feel were beyond words. All she could think about was having him skin-to-skin with her.

She pulled her hand from his thick hair and her other hand from underneath his shirt, and he groaned at the loss of her touch. But he drew in a sharp breath when he felt her fingers on the buttons of his shirt, and he shifted his weight to give her the room to unbutton it all the way. He pulled back from her and shrugged out of his shirt and dropped back down on his hands, hovering over her to kiss her again, but her hand pressed against his chest, stopping him.

"So...you're doing this for me?" she asked, her lips lifting in a hesitant smile.

He drew in a deep, shuddering breath. "Yes."

"Then at least give me a little time to admire," she murmured, pushing him over and onto his back. She lay alongside him and stared down at his muscular torso, from his broad shoulders to his narrow, tapered waist.

He smiled up at her. "I don't know that I've ever had a woman ask to 'admire' me."

"Any woman would admire you for many reasons. They'd admire your intelligence, your wit, your humor…and certainly your body." She ran her fingers along his shoulders, pressing and testing the strength of his muscles. When her hand ran down to his smooth chest, a slight shiver ran down her back. He was the most perfectly made man she had ever laid eyes on.

When her hand slid down to his abs, his hand caught hers, holding her fingers in his. "I think there's only so much admiring from you that I can handle." His voice was strained and thick, and her gaze shifted to his face.

His eyes were on hers, and his hand reached up into her hair, brushing the strands away from her face. "Are you even remotely aware of how beautiful you are?"

Anya felt her cheeks burning again. "Stryker, I only feel beautiful when I'm with you. You make me feel so many different things…" Before she could say anything else foolish, she lowered her mouth to his and took his lips as aggressively as he had taken hers when he had kissed her only minutes earlier.

His fingers instantly went to work on the small buttons on her blouse, but he made a sound of frustration, as his large fingers couldn't work the delicate pearls. Licking her lips, she pulled away from him and lifted the shirt over her head and tossed it to the side.

She leaned down toward him to kiss him again, but his large, calloused hands caught her slender shoulders, stopping her. "It's my turn to admire," he said, his voice husky.

Anya drew in a shuddering breath as his fingers quickly released the clasp at the back of her bra, and the light material slid away, revealing her breasts for his desire-glazed eyes. His fingers feathered along her collarbone, a gentle caress, and she knew she was blushing to the roots of her hair.

His hands slid down her sides, and the feeling of his calloused fingers rubbing against her smooth flesh made her eyes close in delight. This was what she wanted. She wanted to be with this man, in his arms, protected from the world, without a single care.

"Open your eyes, Anya." His command wasn't harsh, but more of a request. "I want to see your eyes while I touch you."

The air rushed out of Anya's lungs, and she felt a strong tingling between her thighs. This man knew how to say the right things to turn on a woman. She opened her eyes slowly and was staring into a face full of desire, as her body quivered with anticipation.

His hands moved inwards, rubbing lightly over her stomach, and she moaned softly, but never took her eyes off him. She didn't understand how he could maintain such control. She wanted to feel him, every inch of him on her, around her...in her. She needed to be one with the man who was stealing her heart.

She could feel in her soul that he was a good man. She could tell by the way his buddies respected him, by the diligent way he cared for his animals, and by the tenderness he'd shown to her, over and over again. He may not want marriage or children...things she had craved to have one day in the future. He may not even want to have a long-term relationship with her. But she would treasure what she had now and cherish the memories always.

His hands spanned her waist and his thumbs brushed the undersides of her breasts. She bit her lower lip to hold back her cry of excitement. His fingers moved smoothly, slowly inching up her skin until his palms cupped her breasts, but he deliberately kept his fingers away from her nipples, the part that ached for his touch so much they nearly hurt.

"Stryker," she moaned.

"Tell me what you want," he whispered.

Saying the things she wanted him to do to her out loud was incredibly erotic, and she was afraid she would sound like a fool. "Touch me," she gasped.

"Where? Where do you want me to touch you, bella?"

"My...my nipples. Oh, Stryker, I ache for your touch."

And then he was touching her, his fingers lightly circling the pouting buds, then his rough palms rubbed over them and she gasped, arching her back so her breasts filled his hands. He squeezed and pinched, rolled and pressed, until she was squirming against him, eager for more.

"Tell me what you want next, Anya. Tell me. This is your night. I want to do whatever you want."

The feeling of control was as much of an aphrodisiac as his touch and his voice. "I want..." She licked her lips. "I want to undress you."

He drew in a deep breath and let it out slowly. "Do I get to keep touching you while you do that?"

"Oh, yes, of course!" she replied, nodding at him, and he chuckled.

"At least I know you like the way I touch you."

She gave him a soft smile. "I suppose I was a little obvious about that, huh?"

"You don't hear me complaining," he murmured as he squeezed one of her nipples and she gasped, her mind suddenly back on getting him naked as fast as she could.

Her fingers slipped under the waistband of his jeans, and he sucked in a sharp breath. She smiled to herself. Two could play this game. She could make him burn the same as he made her burn. She unfastened his belt slowly and let her fingers linger at his low waist, feeling the thin trail of dark hair that led down to his erection.

Finally, she slipped the button at the top of his jeans free, then pulled at his zipper. Her pulse was racing as she could feel the heat of his body through his jeans. When she finally had the zipper lowered, she gripped the waistband and began to pull his jeans down.

"Let me help." His voice was thick and husky, and her eyes flew to his face. The desire was so strong, it caused her heart to skip a beat, then lurch forward at a nearly painful rate. He wanted her. He craved her as much as she craved him.

Lifting his hips, he slid out of his jeans and boxer briefs, tossing his boots to the side along with his clothes. Then he lay back and he was hers to look at, enjoy, and pleasure as she felt like it. She wanted to pleasure him to the point that he lost all control.

His desire was obvious, and she couldn't tear her eyes from the part of him she knew could bring her so much pleasure. She reached for it, and he moved quickly, catching her wrist, stopping her from touching him.

"Anya," he said, his voice strained, "I don't know how much more I can take. I need you."

Her gaze searched his face, and she licked her lips before dropping her head down to his, pressing her lips against the pulse beating rapidly at his neck. "I need you, as well."

"Good," he growled, and he made quick work unbuttoning her starched slacks, which she had slid on before driving over to Stryker's ranch, and he lowered the zipper before her small hand on his stopped him.

"You said this is my night, right?"

He let his breath out slowly. "Yes. But I want to pleasure you."

"This is all still so new to me, Stryker. Let me pleasure you. We have all night."

He swallowed, and his hands slid back up to her neck. He pulled her down to him, pressing his lips urgently against hers. "What did I do to deserve you?" he whispered against her ear as his lips traveled along her cheek and jawbone. She tilted her head back, giving him access to her neck, and his hands slid lower, lifting and molding her breasts.

When his fingers plucked her nipples, she gasped and pulled back from him. "You're distracting me," she said with a light smile, and while she kept her gaze on his face, her hand traveled down his chest, across his abs, and her fingers combed the hair that surrounded his sex.

He closed his eyes and moaned as her hand slowly wrapped around him, measuring him as she moved up and down his length. Anya's gaze dropped to her hand, and she marveled at what she held. It pulsed with his heartbeat and filled her palm.

Moisture gathered at the tip, and with curiosity she touched it, smoothing the silky substance around the head. "Anya," he groaned.

She felt as if she were melting in her very core. She

ached between her legs, in the spot that she knew only he could pleasure. Breathing heavily, she stripped out of her slacks and her lace underwear, underwear she had gotten specifically with the hope that she would be with Stryker again. Her clothes and boots landed in the pile next to Stryker's.

"What…what do I do now?" she asked, suddenly feeling very shy and nervous.

He gave her a soft smile. "What do you want?"

"I want you inside me. I need you, Stryker."

He unwrapped the foil around a condom and slid it on quickly. Then he reached for her waist and pulled her up and over him, maneuvering her until she was straddling his body, with his erection pressing against her aching core. "Oh, Stryker…" she moaned, and rocked her body against him. His hard length rubbed against the sensitive nub of desire, and she gasped as sensations exploded through her body.

"Does this feel good?" Stryker asked, his voice tense.

"Yes, but I want more. I want…" He reached down and positioned himself so the tip of his arousal pressed against her core, and she shuddered. "Yesssss," she groaned. "I want that."

She moved her body back and forth, testing the feel of him just barely penetrating her. Breathing heavily, she began to press down on him and threw her head back in ecstasy. Slowly she took him within her body until she felt she couldn't take any more. Then she arched her back, and he slipped into her to the hilt. Her hands were clenched on his chest, her nails digging into his skin.

"Anya." His voice was hushed and raw. "Anya, are you all right?"

If she hadn't been lost in a world of pleasure, she would have laughed. But her body was overloaded by sensation as she felt her inner muscles ripple to adjust to him, sending additional shivers through her body. "I'm more than all right," she replied when she was able to find her voice.

Slowly, she lowered her head and looked down at him. His face was intense, the features pulled tight, showing his strong jaw and high cheekbones. But there was something in his eyes…a blaze that burned bright just for her. He was such a handsome man and could have any woman he wanted. And he had chosen her.

She smiled softly and traced his eyebrows, his nose, his lips. And then she moved, and she gasped loudly at the sensation. "Stryker!" she whispered urgently.

"Slowly, bella, slowly."

She did as he said and began to slide her body up and down his length, raising up on her knees until just the tip of him was in her, then slowly descending back down on him, shuddering each time as his cock filled her completely. A rhythm began in her body, and she began rocking up and down on him, grinding on him when she had him at the hilt. She arched her back and raised her hands into her hair, moaning softly, chasing the pleasure she knew he was going to give her.

She looked at him through hooded eyes, and he was watching her with similarly hooded eyes. He reached up and his fingers lightly flicked her aching, pouting nipples. She cried out with pleasure, throwing her head back and riding him faster.

His hands gripped her hips, and he began to thrust up into her, the urgency having apparently caught him as well. She felt as if she were at the edge of a very high cliff and was about to tumble over the side. "Stryker... Stryker..." She breathed his name like a mantra.

"Come with me, Anya. I want to see that sweet face of yours when you come with me."

His words made her entire body feel hot as she lowered her head and looked at him. He began to thrust into her harder, faster, and her hands fell to his chest, her nails digging into his flesh again. "Oh, Anya... Come with me, Anya!"

She felt the tension suddenly vibrating through his body. It sent her over the edge, and she was falling, flying down the side of the giant cliff. "Stryker!" she yelled his name, nearly screamed it as her whole body convulsed and fell apart in spasms.

He was still thrusting into her as he leveraged himself up on one hand and pulled her to him for a kiss hotter than any they'd had before. His tongue matched his movements inside her body, and she felt herself climbing again, and she began to grind against him hard, seeking the next peak. It slammed into her, and she screamed into his mouth as she fell apart in his arms.

Chapter 16

"Anya."

"Mmm."

Stryker smiled. Even in her sleep she was absolutely amazing. He wanted more of her. But his time was up. They had to leave for Corpus to fly into Matamoros, where they would assume their new identities and attempt to infiltrate the cartel.

He didn't know how long he would be gone, but he wanted to be back already. He needed Anya in his arms, in his life, as much as possible. And the sooner they were finished with this mission, the sooner that would happen.

"Anya, bella, I must leave, remember?"

"I have selective memory problems," she mumbled. Lying on her side, her naked rump nestled up against his crotch, she was making him desire her all over again. He slowly turned her in his arms until she was lying on her back, his arm as her pillow, and he was able to look down at her.

"You are terrible at playing possum. You know that, right?"

She cracked one eye open to look at him. "Do you really have to leave?"

"Unfortunately, yes. But I'll be back as soon as I can."

She sighed heavily and opened both eyes, lifting her arms to run her fingers through his thick hair. "What made you decide to go caveman on me?" she asked, rubbing his short beard and tugging gently on his longer locks of hair.

He chuckled and pressed a kiss to her forehead. "I'm just enjoying a life where I don't have to shave every day, and I can go for a couple of months without getting a haircut."

"I've seen plenty of bull riders with facial hair. There's no rule against it."

Stryker had to think fast. "Yes, but being shaved and clean-cut was the desired appearance for most of the bronc and bull riders. There were always a few rebels."

"Hmm. Whatever you say, cowboy."

"I don't want to leave you." He couldn't believe he'd just confessed that out loud. He had lost his mind.

She looked up at him, her face very serious. "Then don't."

He lowered his head and pressed his lips firmly against hers, and kissed her until they were both breathless. "I'll have last night to think about while I'm gone. And then I'll be back in no time. You'll see." How he hoped that were true. He had never felt more at home than he did at that very moment, and all he could think about was how right it seemed.

Could this be what was missing in his life? Could it be that he had needed a strong, independent woman around to hold him, to kiss him, to need him in more ways than one? He shook his head at himself. It was a foolish notion. He had never needed anybody. Other than around his SEAL brothers, he liked to be alone.

"We need to go, bella. I still have to get ready for my trip, and I'm catching an early flight out this morning."

She sighed dramatically, then smiled up at him. "Last night was…amazing."

Stryker felt the possessive need to grab ahold of her and never let her go. He didn't want to leave this magic bubble they were in. He didn't want to face the ugly, violent world he knew existed. He just wanted Anya and her joy and her smiles. But he had a duty to fulfill, and that was exactly what he was going to do.

They fumbled around in the dark until they found their clothing, and Stryker was disappointed when Anya was all covered up again. Seeing her lying nude before him had been so incredibly erotic, because she had held nothing back.

For the second time, as he held her in his sleep, he hadn't been tormented by nightmares. He felt more refreshed than ever before. Anya was good for him. But was he good for her? He didn't know.

To the east, a faint glimmer of pink showed on the horizon, and Stryker knew they had to get moving, even though every part of him wanted to stay exactly where he was. It wasn't that he was dreading the assignment ahead. He was just dreading the time apart from Anya. Which was a very new sensation for him.

They had everything packed up faster than he had expected, and he untethered the horses and led them to where she stood waiting for him. The first rays of light were stretching, and in the pale glimmer, she seemed to glow. He couldn't believe his fortune. This incredible woman wanted to be with him. *Him*. And she had slept out under the stars with him, snug against his body, chasing away his demons.

He caught her chin and pulled her in for a gentle kiss before turning and helping her mount her horse. He swung up on his, and they headed back for the ranch in a comfortable silence. It seemed right that the only sound was the cattle calling to each other in the early morning light.

They arrived at the house far too soon, in Stryker's opinion. They both dismounted and the horses stood by lazily, still half asleep, as Stryker walked Anya to her truck. She turned and leaned against the cab of her truck, a sleepy and satisfied smile on her face. "Thank you for last night," she murmured.

"I'm the one who should be thanking you," he said, his own lips twitching into a smile as he leaned against her, brushing her hair out of her face and hooking it behind her ear. The idea of not being with her for the next several days suddenly seemed unbearable. It came with being a SEAL, though. Once they left for a mission, all communication went dark. He'd have to wait until he had finished things in Mexico before hearing her sweet voice again. "I won't have time to call you while I'm away," he said softly. "I'll call you as soon as I'm headed back. It may be from a number you don't recognize—just promise you'll answer?"

She bit her lower lip and smiled up at him, her fingers hooking in his belt loops. She tugged him closer to her. "Give me one last kiss before I go, cowboy?"

"Anything you ask for, señorita." He leaned down, brushing her lips lightly, then more firmly, until she sighed and her lips parted for his tongue to take a sweet taste of her. She was just as intoxicating as she had been the previous night, and he was growing hard remembering.

With reluctance, he pulled back. "Goodbye, bella."

"Goodbye, Stryker. I love you."

———◆◆◆———

Cell phones had been used for communication within cartels since the day they'd been invented. But the cartels had become so talented with cell phones that even modern search tactics utilized by international agencies weren't able to keep up.

The cartels had learned quickly how to disable GPS and voice recognition software, as well as any distinguishing characteristics that could allow law enforcement to track them. Over the years, they had become creative with their methods of communication, creating their own unique language that they were constantly changing up to keep everyone on their toes.

A company in Canada had finally realized the market they could capitalize on. They began manufacturing various smartphones that came fully prepared for the cartels to use, encryption codes included.

But after months of gathering damning information, the feds had brought the company to a screeching halt. The CEO was in prison, and the assets of the company were worthless. So the cartels were back to coming up with their own communication plans. Fortunately for the Scorpions, they had "acquired" a man gifted in coding and cyber intelligence and had changed their communication across the board. And it was paying off for them in ways they hadn't expected.

Benicio had proudly taken charge of a section of a large cartel operating out of Nuevo Laredo as a young man, one of the youngest lieutenants in the business. He had worked hard and been recognized quickly for his cunning abilities and ruthless pursuits of adversaries.

Within five years he had moved up to become a capo's second. The cartel was so large, they had multiple capos to oversee the regions. Too large, in Benicio's opinion. He had watched how fat and content his capo had become—how many of the capos had become—and knew they'd lost touch with the way it was on the streets.

It had all been just a matter of time.

More time than he had wanted, but his time came. He had been the capo's second for nearly seven years when the perfect opportunity presented itself. Several of his lieutenants were dissatisfied with the capo, and he had already secured the sicarios to back him up. That was when the capo had been in an unfortunate accident that had left him, his driver, his treasured Rolls-Royce, and his mistress at the bottom of Lake Casa Blanca in Laredo, Texas.

Benicio had quickly stepped up to fill his role of capo and carry out his grand plan: to separate from the cartel, form his own, and slowly but surely bring down all the capos who hadn't taken him seriously before. Less than three years later, he had succeeded and launched the Scorpions.

The Capos from other cartels weren't challenging him, at least most of them weren't. One Capo had died a year after Benicio had created the Scorpions, and as much as Benicio would've liked to take credit for it, the man's death hadn't been by his hand. And only a couple of months ago, the Capo of another cartel had been captured by the Mexican military and the feds. Many cartels were falling to pieces, and he was picking up the top performers and absorbing them into the Scorpions. If they kept growing, he might need to consider making

Hector a capo and managing the cartel like the well-greased machine it was becoming.

It had been a stroke of good fortune that had brought David Castro to head up their intelligence division. He was already working for a major leader in Colombia, and his talents with the computer were being farmed out to various criminal organizations throughout Mexico and Central and South America. His skills had been obvious to Benicio when he and his friend in Colombia had used him to make their network more powerful than they had ever imagined. That had been years ago. David seamlessly assisted their operations, and they grew stronger every day because of David's talents.

David didn't report to Benicio directly, the only thing that frustrated Benicio. His friend in Colombia held all the power and approved all David's assignments. Benicio didn't like reporting to anyone. He was a drug lord, a king in the industry. He would find a way around his Colombian friend.

Over the years, with David's work, Benicio's level of encryption on the dark web had yielded them a new opportunity to offer protection to small stores and shops near the border that had recently been left defenseless after the large cartel continued to disintegrate. The opportunity to spread their fingers closer and closer to the border only furthered his goals. And, he knew, it would please his friends in Washington, D.C., who were watching his movements so closely.

—⁓—

Stryker showered quickly and tried to think about the things he had left to do before they hit the road to

Corpus. His go-bag was packed, and he had his fake identity well mapped out in his mind, and... *I love you.* Her voice had sounded so sweet. He knew she hadn't planned to say it, the way her cheeks had turned bright red and she'd slid into her truck rapidly.

The words had stabbed straight to his heart. When was the last time he'd heard those sweet words? Years. Back when he and his wife had been besotted with puppy love and thought the real world wouldn't interfere with the life they were creating. But the longer they had remained married, the longer the time went without her saying she loved him. And the further he had pulled away from her.

Focus, sailor! Focus! Damn it to hell, he was going to lose his mind reliving the moment Anya had whispered the words, as if they were natural for her to say. As much as he had enjoyed hearing them, he'd believed that the likelihood of her truly loving him was far-fetched. He was her first. He was the man who had claimed her innocence, and he knew he'd taken her to ecstasy not once but twice the night before. She must be confusing love with lust.

He turned the water all the way to cold and welcomed the pelting jolt to shake his thoughts back to their rightful place. In his go-bag, he carried a variety of things that he'd learned never to go without on a mission. That included his point-and-shoot camera that looked and felt like a simple mint tin and had been crafted for him years ago by an undercover agent. An all-purpose tool was a no-brainer, as were a couple of hydration packs to carry water.

Thinking about his go-bag while under the icy water

from the showerhead was finally pulling his mind off Anya. When he started to shiver, he turned the shower off and sluiced water from his body before grabbing a large towel. He was moving quickly because he knew they were going to need to leave soon.

He wore a simple pair of jeans and an untucked, name-brand T-shirt that shouted money. That and a pair of expensive boots completed his ensemble. In order to play like a big-time drug dealer, he needed to look the part. He scanned his room one last time and glanced longingly at his bedside drawer. He wanted nothing more than to bring his gun with him. But he had no doubt there would be a pat down as soon as they arrived in Matamoros, and he wasn't about to lose that weapon. It had seen him through far too many tough situations.

He entered the dining room and was surprised to see Snap already awake, beginning preparations for breakfast. He looked up when Stryker entered and nodded to him silently. It was an unspoken rule that you left a sailor to his thoughts right before he was about to leave on assignment.

A few minutes later, Phantom entered, his face lost in concentration. Stryker watched Phantom as he finished his preparations, and knew his friend was fully immersed in his character's backstory. Which was exactly where Stryker needed to be, but he kept getting jerked back to the moment when he was leaning against Anya at her truck and she had whispered such sweet words so softly into his ear.

Buzz came into the dining room and nodded to all the men. Stryker looked at his two teammates closely, and they returned his gaze, then nodded in acknowledgment, and without saying another word, the three of them left the house, ready to tackle their new project. They piled into Phantom's truck and were silent for the first thirty minutes of the drive.

Buzz was the one who broke the silence from the back seat. "I'd like to go over our key points in our assignment—a high-level overview."

Stryker shifted in the front passenger seat so he could look at both Phantom and Buzz. "We arrive at Corpus to meet with Admiral Haslett for any final intel. We'll have some downtime on base until twenty hundred hours. Then we'll take a private chopper down to Matamoros. We should arrive in Matamoros around zero two hundred, roughly.

"We'll meet our contact at the drop zone, and he'll take us to a safe house where we'll get our disguises, as well as our vehicle to make the drive to Nuevo Laredo. It will be over a four-hour drive to Nuevo Laredo. There's another safe house for us there, and then we begin hitting the streets and determine the best way to crack into the Scorpions. We're on our own out there, so we need to watch each other's backs."

"That's about as generic an overview as I've ever heard," Phantom said, his voice dry.

"He asked for a high-level review, and that's what I gave him. If you want more details, ask." Stryker was clenching and unclenching his fists in his lap, trying to control his temper.

"Maybe if you had your head in the game, we wouldn't be asking for clarification from you for anything."

"What the hell is that supposed to mean?" Stryker growled.

"You shouldn't have seen her last night," Buzz spoke up from the back seat.

Stryker felt like he'd been punched in the gut. "What the fuck gives you the right to say such shit? What I do is my business."

"Not when it causes you to have your head up your ass hours before we go into a kill zone."

"Watch what you say, sailor. You're overstepping."

"Sir, I mean no disrespect," Buzz said while Phantom gripped the steering wheel so tight that it looked like he was going to crack it in half. "The thing is, we all know she's getting to you. We all know you care for her, though you may not admit it. We just need to know you're ready for this mission and we aren't being led into jeopardy."

"My awareness has not been compromised, and you have no need to question my ability for this mission. She isn't a problem. What *will* be a problem is if you talk about her again."

It was silent the rest of the way to Corpus.

Chapter 17

THEY ARRIVED IN MATAMOROS, TAMAULIPAS, CLOSE TO TWO
o'clock in the morning via a private helicopter con-
tracted by the navy. They met up with their contact outside the airport, and he drove them to a small apartment
complex. The apartment looked like a junkie's home,
with mismatched, ragged furniture, holes in the carpet,
and filthy walls. There was even the smell of marijuana
smoke clinging to the air.

Vidal, their contact, made no apologies for the shabby
location, nor did they expect anything different. They'd
been in places far worse as they dropped into their
undercover locations. In the dirty bathroom, a couple
of roaches skittered into the shadows as Stryker flipped
on the light, and he carefully began grooming himself to
slip into his role.

He had been growing his beard out for the past week,
and it was already thick enough to cover his face. He
fought the memories of Anya stroking his beard and
forced his mind to stay in character. He used a thick gel
to slick back his hair, which he had been growing longer
for weeks, and with the hair gel, he was beginning to
take on an entirely different appearance. He applied the
small rubber prosthesis that was his new nose and used
the makeup that had been given to him to blend it in
with the rest of his skin, to make it appear to be his own.

With the final touch of light hazel contacts, he barely recognized the man who stared back at him. Which was exactly what he needed.

He left the bathroom so Buzz could go in and apply his cover, and he pulled off his shirt, ready for Vidal to lay down some creative artificial ink around his body, including some gang symbols, which were critical for them to be considered legit.

By the time Vidal had finished applying all the tattoos, Stryker's arms were covered, as was part of his chest, and his back was covered in a large tattoo that even crept up to his shoulder. Within an hour, all three of them were in their new clothes, tattoos, and various facial hair and slicked-back hair.

The initial goal was to take down this new cartel. But it wasn't as simple as finding the leader, removing him from the operation, and dropping him in a dark hole where he would never be found. They had to get in with the lugartenientes—lieutenants—and bring them down too. It was impossible for them to get to everyone. The sicarios and halcones would find ways to win loyalty into other drug cartels. And the production operations would never end.

But Buzz would be working on their computers, and would cripple the Scorpions financially. Then he would delve into their communications. The encrypted messages to phones, Facebook accounts, Twitter, and the few pieces of correspondence over email that Buzz had been able to collect were unlike the encryption they'd experienced in the past. And they needed to break the code. Fast.

Vidal provided them with a dark red Ford Explorer,

and Stryker was shocked that the rims were still intact. They were spinners, and in this kind of neighborhood, those rarely stayed attached to a vehicle for long. The interior was leather and decked out with all the bells and whistles that would be expected of a high roller in the drug-dealing world. The car would be left alone if people knew it belonged to somebody high up in the ranks of a cartel.

Vidal gave them directions to their new home, a four-hour drive away, and let them know the house had many critical hiding spots where they would find a bevy of weapons. Before they left, he handed each one of them a loaded HK45 compact handgun, which they all tucked into side holsters. It was go time.

They were silent as they entered the car, each one thinking about the intel and his own backstory. One false move could kill them all. When they were pulling out of Matamoros, the streamers of dawn were feathering across the sky.

"I don't know about you—" Phantom, whose words were always so carefully chosen, was cut off by Buzz's sharply raised hand. Buzz reached over and turned on the radio, taking it to a level loud enough that having a conversation would be difficult, but not impossible.

Phantom moved to sit close between the two of them, so their conversation could be held without him shouting to be heard. "You think we're bugged?" he asked, his face a dark mask.

"Hand over your guns," Buzz said, his voice rough and gravely, the way he'd been practicing it for days.

Silently, they did as he asked, and his fingers made quick work disassembling the weapons. With a deep frown on his face, he held up three small microphones, each one having come out of their guns. He tossed them out the window before turning back to them. "The obvious answer is, yes, we were bugged. I ran my scanner over all our equipment as we loaded up, and the guns spiked high readings. So far nothing else is coming up on the scanner, but we need to be aware that someone is trying to listen to us. The question is, who? Do we trust that little snake Vidal? Is he loyal to us or is he loyal to someone else? He's been undercover for years. That fucks with your mind after a while."

"He started off as an informant. So his original allegiance is with the cartels. He's not one of us. He has no reason to be loyal to us."

"Other than the fact that he knows we'll come and cut his balls off before we kill him if he really is betraying us," Phantom growled.

"Regardless, we know Vidal is not the mastermind behind having us bugged. It's someone higher up the food chain, either on our side or theirs. Either way, I don't like it one fucking bit." Stryker was glaring at the road ahead of him.

Phantom's jaw clenched and unclenched. "This means the house is bugged too. It's going to be nearly impossible for us to debrief."

"Not if we take it off local and do it our own way. We'll go through different channels to reach Brusco at home base. We can't trust the cell phones they gave us, or any other item. From here on, we are code silence unless I say otherwise. Now, Buzz, put the guns back together. We've got a job to do."

———

Anya buried herself in her work. If she didn't have patients lined up for the day, she was out at the ranches, checking the newborn calves, giving vaccinations, and helping any of the ranchers or ranch hands who needed to know how to care for an injured or sick heifer.

Mastitis, an infection in the teat of a heifer, was the most common problem they had to deal with, and that just took some antibiotics and hand milking for a few days until the infection cleared. A few of the heifers needed more urgent and diligent care, but most of them were easy enough to care for.

It had been a week since he had left. A week since the most incredible night of her life. She had made her way home that morning, that beautiful morning, enjoying the lingering feelings of tenderness and warmth that flooded her when she thought of her time with Stryker. It had been just as magical as the first time…more so. His whispered words of encouragement, of praise, of passion, had made her fall apart in his arms. And she couldn't wait to experience it again.

That is, if *he* wanted to experience it again. She couldn't believe she had slipped up and admitted that she loved him. She wasn't going to say it out loud. It had been a huge mistake, and from the look on his face, she could tell it had shocked him. But she couldn't tell if it had turned him against her. That was the part she agonized over.

She had fallen victim to his smooth voice, his gentle touch, and her own attraction to the tall, dark cowboy. The anticipation of seeing him again, of feeling his calloused hands touching her cheeks so tenderly as he dropped his head to place a kiss on her lips… Just thinking about the man had her worked up.

He had warned her it would be difficult for him to call. She wondered what he had to do that took him away from the ranch and why he hadn't told her anything about it. She shook her head at herself. They were hardly at the point in their relationship where he would share everything about his life with her, right? She gnawed on her inner cheek. *She* wanted to be at that point in their relationship. But it was probably too soon for him. She couldn't wait to hear his voice.

She headed out her back door and stopped when she saw a FedEx envelope lying at her feet. She frowned. Normally the deliveries were made at the front desk. For a moment, apprehension gripped her.

But this was just an envelope. She shook her head. They had caught the bomber in Austin. She picked up the envelope and turned it around in her hands. It indicated that it had originated in Hebbronville. She frowned. They didn't have a FedEx office in Hebbronville. She hesitated again, debating whether she should open it or not.

Finally, after drawing a deep breath, she ripped open the cardboard tab and looked inside. Confusion clouded her mind. Inside were pictures. Who would send her pictures?

They were all full-sheet pictures and she pulled them out to get a better look. The apprehension came back as she saw picture after picture of Stryker and the men from the ranch. Then she saw the picture of Stryker with her, placing a kiss on her neck as she slept in his arms.

She gasped. It hadn't been a dream! But who had taken these photos? And why were they being sent to her?

She flipped to the next photo, and she gave a strangled cry, dropping the photos to the ground. It was a gruesome picture of a mutilated body. It was unlike anything she'd ever seen before, and she never wanted to see it again.

With trembling hands, she made herself pick up the pictures. She flipped through the rest of them, forcing herself to see the terrible, unspeakable things. As a veterinarian, she had become used to blood and to the bones, tendons, muscles, and tissues of an animal's body. But nothing could have prepared her for the sight of those gruesome photos.

She stuffed the photos back in the envelope and rushed to her truck. She needed to see Stryker. Surely he would know something about the photos—at the very least, he should know something about all the photos of him and her together, as well as the ones where he was with his fellow ranchers. That much she was almost positive about. Her palms were sweating as she drove out to the ranch, and she focused on breathing deeply to calm her racing heart.

What could possibly be the explanation for what she'd just seen? Obviously Stryker was involved, because he had been in every one of the first set of photos she'd looked at. Stryker hadn't come home yet, though, or, if he had, he hadn't called her as promised. As she drove up to the large ranch house, she noticed that one of the trucks wasn't there. He may not be home, but surely someone could give her answers. They were a tight-knit group and needed to know what had been sent to her.

She wished Stryker could be there with her. She

hoped he was thinking about her and craving her just as much as she was him.

She couldn't stop her hands from shaking as she stepped down from her truck and grabbed the hideous envelope. She took another deep breath as she turned and headed up the path toward the ranch house and wiped her hands on her jeans to dry her palms.

She stood on the shaded porch for a minute after she rang the doorbell, and waited to hear the familiar sound of boots on their hardwood floors, but there was just the sound of a hot spring day settling into the trees and foliage around her. She waited a few moments longer before ringing the doorbell again and knocking on the large door. Her knuckles hurt afterwards, and she was certain there was no way her knocking had even sounded within the house.

She chewed on her inner cheek, agitated. She didn't want to leave without seeing one of the men. She needed answers. She needed to know what the pictures were and why they had been sent to her.

Suddenly she heard footsteps approach the door. Brusco opened the door swiftly and appraised her from head to toe in one quick flick of his eyes. "What's wrong?"

How did he know something was wrong? She had schooled her face so he wouldn't know she was disturbed by anything, so she could judge his reaction—not so he could judge hers. "Has Stryker returned yet? It's urgent that I see him," she demanded.

"He's going to be out for a few days."

Anya's trembles settled in stronger. "May I come in?" Was that the wisest move to make? What if someone was trying to warn her about them?

She covered her mouth with one shaking hand,

trying to hold back the bile that had risen in the back of her throat. *I've done some terrible things in my life.* Stryker's words came back and seemed to slap her. Had he done *this*? Was this the type of man he was?

Brusco hesitated only a few moments. And then he waved her inside and closed the large, heavy door behind her. "What are you doing here, Anya?" His voice lacked warmth. There was something menacing, something deadly, to the sound of it.

Oh, what if they are a cult of killers? Anya swallowed hard several times, trying to regain the ability to speak. "I—I—this is a mistake. This is a terrible mistake. I'll go…"

Anya tried to sidestep him to get to the door, but Brusco grabbed her around the waist as she tried to flee past him, and he set her back in front of him as if she were as light as a feather. "Why are you here, Anya?"

"Anya, what is it that has you so shaken?" Snap's voice made her jump, and she turned to see him standing behind her, a deep frown on his face, his hands on his hips. There was no hope for her to escape them. She never should have come in the house.

Finally, barely able to hold the envelope any longer because of her tremors, she held it out to the men. "This was delivered to my office today. Well, not to my office. It was just at my back door. Th-those pictures… How… I mean, why…?"

Brusco took the envelope and pulled out the photos. His frown deepened as he flipped through them. He handed them to Snap, but kept his eyes on her.

"I should just go. I don't want to know what it's all about. Keep the pictures. I don't want them."

"Anya, it's not that simple."

She was going to throw up. She was almost certain of it. They were going to kill her and dump her body out on this vast ranch, and no one would ever know. She backed away from Brusco, a cold sweat breaking out across her skin. *This can't be it. This isn't the way I'm supposed to die, is it?*

Snap exchanged glances with Brusco and shook his head. "Let's go into the dining room, Anya. We need to talk."

Chapter 18

IT HAD TAKEN A WEEK FOR THEM TO GET INVITED TO A MEET, actually faster than Stryker had expected. But they'd put the word out on the street that they were new in town and looking for a new "home." A runner had quietly passed the information along to them that one of the lieutenants wanted to meet with them.

It wasn't as high as they needed to go, but it was a start. The lieutenant was a thin man with a goatee and tattoos that covered his neck and arms. He had questioned them civilly, simple chitchat for the first hour as they drank in one of the private booths at a club.

The music had pulsed loudly, and frequently he had two or more women seated around him. They were obviously women of the gang, because he didn't try to disguise his questions when they were around. Stryker had bided his time, waiting for the banter back and forth to slowly stall out. And then he'd asked the burning question. "So, are we going to talk business or is this just a meeting for pleasure?"

The lieutenant's smile slowly faded, and he slapped the women on the ass, telling them to leave. "In my opinion, my business is about pleasure," he said confidently, leaning forward and bracing his arms on his knees, clasping his bejeweled hands in front of him, staring directly at Stryker.

Stryker gave him a lopsided grin. "I can agree with

that. But there's always the business end of our work. That never goes away, no matter how much pleasure we sell."

The lieutenant lifted his chin and smiled. "True. The work never goes away. I've heard rumors about you boys. Word on the street is you took down a capo in Matamoros. You've got to have balls to pull off something like that."

"The boss wasn't supporting us the way we needed," Buzz said, taking a swig of his beer. "Once your boss loses sight of the prize, he has to go. We backed his second…a younger man who knew what it was going to take to get us higher up the food chain. He was a great capo to work for."

The lieutenant raised an eyebrow but made no comment. "Look," Phantom spoke up, "we've been through all this before. We were lieutenants in Matamoros. We played with the big dogs. And we were damn good at it. We're looking for a home that will appreciate all we've given to get where we are, and be ready to take us in as brothers."

"We'd like that to be the Scorpions." Stryker carefully set his beer down on the glass table in between them. "But we'll go somewhere else if we have to. We'd just hate to have to face you from opposite sides."

Turf wars in Nuevo Laredo were at an all-time high. The number of gangs in the area was insane, and they all wanted a piece of the pie. But none of those gangs were using the level of encryption and high-powered technology the Scorpions were.

"We've already been building our street team." Stryker kept his eyes focused on the lieutenant. "We just need to coordinate getting the product to them. We'd already have sicarios, hitmen, in place too, but a meet with your capo is critical before we proceed."

"What made you leave Matamoros if you had such a good thing going there?" He was sipping his beer, but his eyes were laser focused on them. This man didn't play. He took his job very seriously. "How do I know you're not still working for your capo in Matamoros and are looking to expand your territory by taking over the Scorpions?"

"It's getting too hot in Matamoros. The policia are cracking down on the cartels no matter how much we grease their palms. Half our lieutenants have been killed or arrested. It's just a matter of time before one of them flips on all of us. We decided to get out while we could."

The lieutenant ran his tongue along the front of his teeth before taking another long swig of his beer. "The Scorpions are already successful. We move a lot of product. We have an extensive network already in place. So, tell me, what can you offer?"

Stryker looked over at Buzz. Buzz pressed his lips together tightly, then leaned forward. "The entire northeast section of your territory between Venezuela Street and Madero Street is in jeopardy of going to the Zetas. Your lieutenant running that section of the city is playing both sides and is pocketing money that you aren't even aware of."

"José has been with us for a long time and is as loyal as they come. He wouldn't double-cross us."

Buzz looked over at Stryker, and Stryker nodded his head. Buzz slowly pulled out his phone, keeping his other hand open and wide so they wouldn't shoot him, thinking that he was pulling out a weapon. They had already been patted down and their sidearms removed as soon as they had arrived. But the hitmen were always on edge, especially when it came to protecting their lieutenant.

Buzz got to the screen he was looking for and handed his phone over to the lieutenant. He swiped through the pictures, his frown deepening with every picture he saw. Finally, he handed the phone back to Buzz, his lips pressed into a thin, tight line. "We'll take care of the problem," he said, and, even though the music was loud and his voice was quiet, the deadly menace in it still carried.

"I'd like to take that area," Phantom said, his eyes penetrating and his face strong. He didn't look like a man who would accept a negative answer easily.

"You should know that you don't just take over an area. You have to buy in, first. And I need to see your established street crew. This is one of our busiest sections in the city. I can't lose out on the area because you aren't competent."

Phantom's eyes narrowed. "My past speaks for itself. But you know that because you've already done the research on me or we wouldn't be sitting here talking. And I have the cash to buy in right now if you want it. But I get the feeling there's more you aren't telling us. Perhaps it has something to do with the problems you're having with your supply right now."

The lieutenant shifted in his chair under Phantom's intense gaze. "I'm not sure I know what you're talking about."

"Of course you do. We've heard things on the street.

You have problems with your supply line, and that means you have problems with your business altogether."

"And you think you have a way to fix it?"

"There are other suppliers I've worked with. They can help us out until we're back in line." Stryker's gaze never wavered, and he maintained his relaxed, confident position reclined in the chair the entire time he was talking with the lieutenant.

"We have very high standards for what we expect in our product." The lieutenant rotated a shoulder, another sign he was uncomfortable with the direction of the conversation.

"I wouldn't take anything but the best."

"In order to consider this or even to move you all into territories, there are going to have to be shifts, and obviously we're going to clear out at least one problem, leaving room for someone to step in. But nothing gets done without the capo giving his approval."

"And what is the problem with that?" Stryker asked, leaning forward into the same position as the lieutenant.

The lieutenant smiled slowly. "Why don't you come along to the meeting? I think the capo will find you all very interesting."

Stryker exchanged glances with Buzz and Phantom, who each gave him agreeable nods, before returning his attention to the lieutenant. "Just tell us when and where. We're ready to get to work."

Benicio always enjoyed a scotch on the rocks as he wound down from a long day. And it had been an incredibly long day. Their supply lines had been tied up for over a week. What seemed to have been a minor breakdown had been held up by time locating parts for processing the drugs and measuring them out. Every provider they usually went to seemed not to have the main piece they needed, until they had finally located the part today. Now it was just a matter of rushing the part to get it to the supplier.

He sighed heavily and pressed the tumbler of scotch against his forehead. The heat in the city was getting to the point of sweltering, but at least it wasn't the humid heat that was closer to the coast. And it wasn't even May yet.

There was a quick rapping at his door, and he glared at it. Hector Cruz, one of his most trusted lieutenants, flipped open the peephole as Benicio casually reached under his desk, gripping his semiautomatic that was taped to the side of the drawers. There was caution, and then there was preparation. Benicio firmly believed in being prepared for any scenario possible.

Hector flipped the peephole closed and looked over at him. "It's my cousin. She says she has some information from the streets."

"Tell her to take it to you tomorrow."

"She says it pertains to you…and it's urgent."

Cursing under his breath, Benicio inclined his head toward Hector and the lieutenant let in his young, attractive cousin. He sat up a little straighter in his chair. Hector had neglected to inform him it was *this* cousin. Elsa Domingo was one of the most coveted women on the street. But she kept close to her Scorpion family, and in turn, they made sure to keep her protected from all of the filth that lusted after her.

"Elsa, my dear. What a pleasure you are to my eyes

and my heart." He stood and greeted her, pressing a kiss to each one of her cheeks.

Elsa gave him a tentative smile. She was just as strong and brave as most of the men he had working for him. And she was far more intelligent. He could have any woman in the city he wanted. Including Elsa. But he wouldn't put his lieutenant in that kind of position. Family was always first. And that meant you didn't mess with the members of your cartel, or their families.

"I hope you still feel that way after you hear what I have to tell you," she said softly, as she sat down in the plush chair opposite his desk.

Benicio balanced himself on the corner of the desk and folded his hands in his lap. "Why would I ever feel differently, bonita? You truly do make a man's day brighter."

"Ay, Mr. Davila, you certainly know how to charm a woman. I wish I had better news to bring. But there are some new men in town, and I believe they intend to bring you harm."

"We are constantly facing new competition. But have no fear at this, bonita. We always come out winners in the end."

"These men are not your competition. They are here to shut you down. They are from the U.S. They are el gobierno. The government."

Benicio fought hard not to grind his teeth together. He thought he had settled things with the U.S. government officials already. Were they angry because he had come and stolen from some of their CEOs? If so, they didn't need to send men over in secret. These types of problems could be handled over the telephone, and usually a wire transfer settled any disputes.

He couldn't stop the frown that was forming on his forehead. Slowly, he crossed his arms over his chest and tilted his head from one side to the other, his neck popping loudly. "What exactly do these men want?"

"The Scorpions. From what my source tells me."

"Who is your source?"

Elsa gave him another one of her smiles, but it was tilted. "Do you always give away your sources, Jefe?"

"What do they want with the Scorpions?" he asked, frustrated. He would be able to find out her sources soon enough.

"To take them down. They're out to destroy you."

This time he did grind his teeth together. "Tell me everything you know."

Chapter 19

"BRUSCO."

"'Bout damn time you contacted me. It's been ten days without a word from any of you."

"You know how it can be. This is the first chance we could get to a secure line." Stryker rubbed his eyes wearily.

"Good to hear your voice. How's the progress?"

"We're in. I've got several names I need you to run to find out exactly what we're up against."

"Sure thing, boss. Fire away."

"Antonio Fernandez. Hector Cruz. Raul Ortega. Juan Alamedas. Castro Gamboa. Franco Morales. Those are the top leaders in the organization."

"So you met the capo already?"

"No. He's a very reserved man and reclusive, and from what we've learned, hardly any of the lieutenants spend time with him. But we know his location, and we now know where his main hub is. We need you to check the area via satellite and see if it is transmitting data. He's having a meeting with all of his lieutenants tomorrow night. We need to know everything pertinent so Buzz can locate their transmission room and get as much data downloaded as quickly as possible. We need to know the facility layout, any movement in or out of the place over the next twenty-four hours—anything and everything you can dig up."

"Yes, sir." Brusco's fingers were already flying over

the keyboard in their communications room. "How are all three of you holding up?"

"We're fine. All is running smoothly. How…how are things there at the ranch?"

"Good. Cattle seem to be developing just fine, and Snap and Santo have been diligent about checking on them."

Stryker's hand tightened into a fist as he hesitated over his next question. "Anybody seen Anya?"

Brusco was silent for several long moments. "She may be a problem."

"What do you mean? What happened to her?" Stryker's heart rate kicked up. If something happened to her while he was gone, he would do everything in his power to get back to her.

"This is probably best discussed when you get home."

"Is she safe? Brusco, you need to tell me what has happened."

"She's safe. But she's going to be a problem."

Ice settled in Stryker's stomach. "What do you mean?" All emotion had left his body. He was numb. He was prepared for anything. He was dying a slow death. Hell, he didn't know what he was anymore.

"She turned up here at the house a few days back. Someone sent her the same photos that were sent to you. And whoever sent it also sent it with the cartel pictures. There's a leak somewhere, and whoever this dick is, he's causing a major problem."

"What did you do when she showed up?"

"We had to take the necessary precautions. She asked for you first, and wanted to talk to you about everything. Don't know what kind of spell you cast over her, boss, but—"

"What the hell did you do?" This time there was emotion. There was anger. There was fear. There was need. Buzz and Phantom cut him a sharp look, and both of them became tense, but he signaled for them to relax. He knew what protocol would demand, and his gut clenched. To put Anya through such a thing…sweet, innocent Anya…

"We had to question her, Stryker. You know we had no choice but to follow the proper steps in the protocol."

"And? Did you follow procedure and contact Haslett? Did he take her for further questioning?" There was another long pause by Brusco, and Stryker felt like screaming into the phone. "Where is Anya, Brusco?" he demanded when the pause went on too long.

"We tried to get hold of Haslett, but he's out of pocket. I left a message for him. In the meantime we improvised."

Some of the tension eased in Stryker's body. "What do you mean you improvised?"

"We told her that Snap and I worked for the DEA before retiring a few months ago. But that part of our retirement required us to stay on as consultants on some of their more difficult missions. We told her we didn't know who had sent her the pictures, but that they were confidential."

"Did she buy it?"

"To be honest, Stryker, I think she was so shaken by the entire experience that she would have believed anything we had to say by the time we were done questioning her."

Stryker squeezed his eyes shut. "How hard did you go after her?"

"Shit, Stryker, it isn't as if we broke out any torture devices."

"We don't have much more time on this secure line. I'll contact you tomorrow to get that intel. It's critical we have it before the capo's meeting in two days. And, Brusco, if you've hurt her in any way imaginable—"

"Stryker, we gotta blow," Buzz said softly, and Stryker realized he had already stayed too long at their temporary location. He could hear Brusco trying to make another apology, and he hung up just to kill the sound of his voice.

———ᴧᴧᴧ———

"Your cousin's information has proved incredibly helpful." Benicio was carefully grooming his goatee in the ornate mirror that hung in the restroom of his private residence. He lived in one of the more affluent homes in the neighborhood. His neighbors knew who he was, and knew to leave him alone.

He had taken special care with how he decorated the interior. He didn't want it over the top, as he had seen so many other capos do in the past. But he wanted it to declare the level of stature that he held at the same time. So the house was adorned with marble floors and granite countertops, rich wood cabinets, and top-of-the-line furniture picked out by an interior decorator who had been given an unlimited budget and told to make the home a modern powerhouse.

Hector grunted from where he sat in an overstuffed chair nestled into a nook in the bathroom. "Good. At least I know she's good for something."

Benicio hesitated in his trimming and his eyes met Hector's in the mirror. "I'm going to pretend I didn't hear that," Benicio said, his voice dark and threatening.

"So you trust her. I'm sorry, capo. I meant no disrespect."

Benicio nodded and went back to trimming. "It turns out there are three new men in town from Matamoros. But we're having a hard time digging very far into their past more than the last few years. Something feels wrong about them."

"Are these the three who are coming to the meeting tomorrow night? The ones who Franco met with?"

"Yes. He has no idea of the suspicions I have about them. And right now, their background looks ironclad. I can't find anything to indicate they are from the U.S. The only thing is—one of the men looks like the picture of that rancher from Texas. But it's hard to tell, and I can't find anything that proves they aren't from the U.S. either. So I'm going to go to Matamoros."

"Today?"

"Tomorrow. I won't be here for the meeting. I'm going to rely on you to conduct it."

"I'm honored, capo, but you know the men like to see you, to visit with you at these meetings. They so rarely see you throughout the year—"

"Which is why I've hired someone to be there in my place."

"You've *what*?"

"Hector, let me introduce you to Benicio Davila. Or, at least, a decent representation of me." He made a flourishing gesture as a man walked in from the bedroom. Hector did a double take. The man walking in looked like Benicio's twin. The features, all the way to the trimmed goatee, were almost uncanny.

"This is Samuel. He's my first cousin and has been

working as a sicario for Antonio for years. Antonio has no idea we are related, as we have kept it very silent. With a little help from a makeup artist, it wasn't too hard to get Samuel to look just like me. He already has my eyes and nose. The rest was simple."

"No, primo, you have *my* eyes and nose."

Benicio laughed and slapped his cousin on the back. "He's perfect to have in front of the men tomorrow night. But the only one who's going to know what's going on is you, Hector. And, of course, Samuel. I've already directed Antonio to bring one of his other sicarios tomorrow, and he didn't challenge me on the decision. We're in a perfect situation here with Samuel."

"So, you want these mystery men to meet Samuel and think he is you?"

"Precisely. And if they check out, then there is nothing for us to do except begin building a relationship with them. But if they don't check out, then I'll contact you and let you know they need to die."

"It will be my pleasure," Hector said, a smile stretching across his face.

Stryker was in hell. He adjusted in his bed, but it just wasn't comfortable, no matter what position he got into. Finally, he stood and paced out onto the small balcony that was attached to his bedroom, and welcomed the slight breeze that cut through the heat of the night.

Their house fit the lifestyle of a lieutenant. It was two stories, with all three of the bedrooms on the second floor. On the first floor was a comfortable living room, small dining area, and decent-sized kitchen.

Far off in the distance, he heard gunfire and the sound of police sirens wailing. He wondered if it was cartel-related. He shook his head at himself. He had buried himself so deeply in the role he was playing, he imagined everything pertained to his mission. He could just as easily be in a highly populated city in America and hear the same things.

He ran a hand down his face and felt the rough texture of his beard. *What made you decide to go caveman on me?* He could almost hear her voice. It was as if she were standing right next to him. His skin tingled as if she had just touched him.

Who had sent her those fucking pictures? Why would they? What game was being played, and what role did Anya factor in all of it? He needed to know the full story. And not from Brusco. He didn't know what he was going to do when he saw Brusco next. But he was more worried about Anya than anyone else.

Standard protocol required intense questioning, almost to the point of torture. How far had they taken it? How much had they scared her? Had they hurt her? There would be hell to pay if they had.

He didn't consider the possibility of her being a spy. Anya was gifted and talented in many ways, but he knew she would never use her intelligence to hurt the country she loved. She'd made a poor choice to come to the house, but, given the pictures she'd received, where else could she turn? How much of it did she even understand? Was she buying the story that Snap and Brusco were former DEA agents?

He looked at the street below him and saw a cat wandering along the alleyway. The rest of the street was silent, and the immediate area was asleep by all appearances.

He was desperate to know she was okay. His hands gripped the railing. Going a week and a half not hearing her sweet voice was torture, and he didn't know how much longer he would be on the mission before he could see her and hold her in his arms.

He wondered what she had thought when she had first seen the pictures. She had to have been horrified. She was a hardworking woman who had a business riding on her shoulders. She didn't need added stress with bizarre excuses from his teammates.

He longed to hear her voice, raw and sensual without her even trying, telling him once more that she loved him. He longed for her cool fingers upon his body. He longed to see her beautiful face and stare into her eyes that seemed to change from every shade of brown and gold imaginable. But he would have to wait a little longer before he had access to her like that, access to touch her and caress her and make sure she was truly okay.

He frowned down at the alley. He needed to know she was okay. He would send Snap to check on her in the morning and report back to him. It was all he could do until he could reach out to her himself. Things had drastically changed, though, now that she had been exposed to the unpleasant world he worked in. He needed to talk to Haslett right away and get permission to let her know his true identity and purpose in Hebbronville.

But what the hell would he say to her when he got back home?

Anya's hands were trembling as she brought the coffee mug to her lips. She took several long gulps, then set it back down on her desk carefully. Mornings were the hardest. It was when the nightmares were still the freshest, and she could only do so much to get them to fade.

She had thought she had nightmares before this. Those had been simple, faint dreams compared to what she was living through now. Now, she was haunted by the faces of people she had never met staring at her with the vacant expressions of death, their bodies mutilated.

Then, she was haunted by the nightmares of Snap and Brusco questioning her over and over again. They warned her that they were being gentle with her compared to what she would face with the authorities.

They never elaborated on whether it would be the DEA or some other organization that she didn't even want to learn about. Regardless, she didn't want to go to any authorities. She wanted to take back all the missteps she had already made and never enter their home to talk to them in the first place.

Was Stryker part of all of it? Was he former DEA as well? Was that why he'd told her he had done bad things in his past? Did she know who he really was? She felt so foolish, so blind and naive. She had taken for granted that he was a simple cowboy who couldn't tell her all about his past because it was painful. The more likely scenario was that he couldn't tell her about his past because he was afraid he would frighten her away.

He had been right to think that way. She was terrified of the things she had seen in those pictures, of the questions Brusco and Snap had asked her. Stryker had to be involved in some form or fashion. He couldn't be the leader of that ranch without having knowledge of the activities of his fellow ranchers.

She glanced at the clock. Five thirty in the morning. She had always been an early riser, but this was early even for her. Especially since she was supposed to be catching up on her sleep after weeks of the calving season keeping her on her toes. She buried her face in her hands and rubbed her eyes with her fingers. Maybe she could go back to sleep for a couple of hours. Heaven knew, she needed it.

She had just slipped back under the covers when her phone rang. Sighing heavily, she glanced at the screen, and recognized the number of one of her ranchers. It seemed she wouldn't be getting the sleep she so desperately needed after all.

Chapter 20

AFTER ANOTHER SUCCESSFUL CALF BIRTH, ANYA BEGAN THE long drive back to her clinic, her windows rolled down to keep the air blowing in her face so she would stay awake. She tried desperately not to think about the images that had been sent to her, but it was as if they were permanently etched into her mind. Her body longed for sleep, but she feared the nightmares that would come with it.

She wondered if Brusco and Snap had somehow been in touch with Stryker and let him know what had happened. If so, how had he reacted? How would he react when he returned home? Would he be angry? Would he be worried about her? Would he pull her into his protective arms and never let go?

She rolled her eyes at herself. She was being a complete sap. Her gut told her that Brusco and Snap hadn't told her everything. She had thought it odd for six men to go into a partnership to run such a large ranch without any ranch hands. Perhaps there was even more going on than she suspected. Perhaps they were involved in something illegal, and she had stumbled right into it.

What if Stryker returns with the intention to permanently silence me for meddling in his affairs? Anya shook her head at herself. She'd been watching far too many spy movies. Her heart was pounding in her chest and her throat was tight. Her thoughts certainly made it easier to stay awake.

Just thinking about Stryker made her heart beat a little faster. How could she still be so excited about seeing this man who had clearly misrepresented who he really was? *Because you've seen the good in him. He has been gentle with you and kind to you...* She missed him. She wanted to see him as soon as possible and have him reassure her that everything was going to be okay.

Anya's mind flashed back to that afternoon at the ranch, sitting in the dining room at the head of the table with Brusco on one side and Snap on the other, effectively cutting her off from every attempt at escape. They hammered her with questions nonstop, relentlessly trying to determine if she was a spy of some sort.

She had never felt such fear, and never wanted to feel it again. Stryker wouldn't put her through more questioning, would he?

She pulled into the parking spot behind her clinic and climbed wearily out of her truck. She had to open up the office in less than thirty minutes. Perhaps she could get just a quick nap. She prayed her dreams would be happy ones, filled with Stryker's arms wrapped around her in a passionate embrace.

Much to her disappointment, she hadn't been able to sleep once she entered the clinic. Her mind still raced, and for once she hated her overactive imagination. The scenarios about the type of illegal things Stryker and his friends could be involved in seemed endless.

She took a long shower to try to wake up. She felt as if the bubble of joy and happiness she lived in had been popped beyond all repair. She would never look at things the same again. But she could get it back. She was determined to get it back. She needed to find her smile again.

She dressed quickly and was towel-drying her long hair as she walked out into the bedroom. Instantly, she felt that something was different in the atmosphere. There was the faint scent of a man's cologne clinging to the air, and she dashed quickly to her nightstand where she had stashed her handgun. She had been around guns her entire life. It came with living on a ranch. She had been taught early how to use them, and had always enjoyed target practice.

She knew she had a full clip of bullets and one in the chamber, ready to fire as soon as she flipped off the safety and pulled the trigger. She was already releasing the safety when she saw the shadow of a man stretch on her floor as he walked from the clinic area back into her personal quarters.

She gripped the gun tightly with both hands and waited for the man to show himself, staying crouched on the other side of her bed. When he entered her room, she swallowed her gasp. What was *he* doing here?

"Not another step, asshole," she spat, and Snap stopped, his eyes settling on her.

"Are you going to shoot me, Anya?"

"I'm thinking about it."

"I'm not here to hurt you."

"Why are you here, then? Oh, no. Let me guess. You talked to Stryker and he told you to check up on me. To make sure I'm not causing any trouble."

An eyebrow lifted on his handsome, youthful face. "I'm here to check on you, yes, but I wasn't worried about you causing any trouble. I did talk to Stryker early this morning and he wanted me to make sure you are okay—he wanted to make sure that Brusco and I weren't too harsh with you."

"And? Do you think you were harsh with me?"

"Anya…" He sighed heavily and ran a hand through his hair. "Please understand—we had to know for sure that you weren't—"

"What? A spy? A threat to whatever you're doing here? Which one is it? Are you one of the good guys or one of the bad?" She shifted on her feet but she didn't change the aim of her gun. If he made one move she didn't like, he would need serious medical attention quickly. The strange thing was that she seemed to be blanketed in this eerie calm. She wasn't shaking; she was laser focused on him.

"Anya, put the gun down. There's no need for any of this. I was legitimately coming to check on you. I know we were hard on you the other day, and I wanted to make sure you're holding up okay."

"How can I trust you after what I saw and what you told me?"

"Please…" He took a step toward her, and she cocked the gun, making him freeze halfway into his next step. He sighed heavily. "I can see why you don't trust me. I can understand it, even. But I wouldn't harm you, Anya. I couldn't hurt you. I could never hurt you."

She stood slowly, steadying the gun with both hands, and while maintaining eye contact with him, she flipped the safety back on the gun. Gradually she lowered it, but she made no move to get closer to him.

Snap didn't move either. Instead, he stuffed his hands

into his jeans and watched her with curiosity. "You were seriously considering shooting me? Hell, Anya. You are full of surprises."

"You should know that if you break into a home in Texas, you're likely to get shot. That shouldn't come as any surprise at all. And given recent events, I'm even more grateful that I know how to shoot a man between the eyes if I ever had to."

Snap frowned, but didn't comment. "I know what you saw has you shaken up. And I know talking to Brusco and me didn't make things any easier. I'm sorry for that. How are you? Seriously."

"I don't know, to be honest. I'm having a hard time telling which way is up and which way is down. Everything feels like a jumbled mess." She shook her head, unwilling to talk about herself any more. "How is Stryker? Is his trip going well?"

"Yes. He's good. But when he heard what had happened, he was livid. He didn't like the idea of us trying to question you."

"Perhaps he trusts me more than you do," Anya replied back sharply.

"I understand you're angry with us. But can you try to step back from this and look at it through our eyes?"

"Through your eyes?" Anya was incredulous. "Given what I saw, I don't want to see *anything* through your eyes."

Snap pinched the bridge of his nose with his thumb and forefinger. "Look, I'm sorry for everything we had to put you through. But we had to be certain. I'll leave you to your day. But know that we all still view you as a friend, and you're welcome at the ranch at any time."

Anya swallowed hard, feeling the weight of the gun in her hand. She nodded to Snap, but made no further move toward him. He was frowning deeply as he turned and left her room, and she heard the door open outside as he left the building. She realized then that she hadn't asked him how he'd gotten in.

With a heavy sigh, Benicio opened his eyes to greet a new day full of unlimited possibilities. The faint rays of light beginning to penetrate through his shades told him it was later in the morning than he wanted it to be. He had a long journey ahead of him, and he needed to get on the road.

He had an odd feeling when he thought of going to Matamoros. The city was even more dangerous than Nuevo Laredo.

The policia were cracking down hard on the cartels in Matamoros, making arrests as well as engaging in gun fights. If certain people knew he was coming, he could easily become a target. But he hadn't gotten as far as he had without using his brain.

He had greased the palms of many influential people over the years, even in Matamoros. From politicians to detectives to leaders in the cartels that he despised, he had made certain that no man would question who he was or why he was there. He hoped. He had to be careful nonetheless. With all the upheaval and changes, the people he'd won over to his side might need additional persuasion to keep him safe.

He hated giving money to those lowlifes. They were all a waste of oxygen. None of them had the balls to take their organization to the levels he was taking his. And none of them deserved a fucking bribe from him.

Already irritated, he rolled out of bed and headed to the restroom. Nearly thirty minutes later, he emerged, and his mind had returned to the business ahead of him. Matamoros was a long four-hour drive from his home. But it would be worth it if he got the answers he needed.

Information coming from Matamoros was taking much too long to reach him, and it couldn't be trusted as it was usually third- or fourth-hand accounts. No one disputed that a capo had been displaced in Matamoros, but no one could agree who'd done it.

Some agreed that it had been a group of three lieutenants who were very close in their friendship and bond with each other and had decided it was time for the capo to go. Others said it was the capo's second who had made the dramatic move and had enlisted the help of three lieutenants to make it happen. Still others said the capo was murdered by an unknown assassin and the second had taken over reluctantly, fearing the target would be on his back next.

Any of these scenarios was disturbing to Benicio. If these three lieutenants had the power to unseat a capo, what would stop them from doing it to him? What if Hector wanted his position? He was second in line for it. Was he already plotting for a takeover? Had he enlisted the help of these three men? Was Elsa involved in the plot?

The third scenario was the least worrisome of all of them. An unknown assassin was a common way that other cartels took out a capo who was getting too powerful for his own good. It was a danger they faced nearly every day. But it still didn't sit right with him that these three men would be as pulled together as they were and able just to slip into his organization after being in high levels with another crew.

He dressed casually, so as to come across as a lieutenant, but nothing above. He needed the sicarios to fear him and respect him, but feel comfortable enough to talk to him and not worry about retribution if they told him some of the secrets of their cartel.

He didn't even know which cartel to start with. But, fortunately, he had contacts in nearly every cartel, and would be able to find someone who could help him with his search. He sighed heavily as he slid behind the wheel of his Land Rover. He preferred this vehicle whenever he wanted to get around without his driver. He couldn't even risk taking his driver with him on this mission. The fewer who knew about it, the better his odds of getting facts.

The sun was just beginning to creep up, the rays growing brighter, as he headed out the gates to the road. It was going to be a long day.

Chapter 21

"GIVE US SOMETHING GOOD, SNAP," STRYKER SPOKE INTO the phone, with Buzz and Phantom sitting around him.

"You're messing with some tough fuckers, that's for sure."

"Good thing we're just as tough," Buzz said.

"You calling me from that burner phone, Stryker?"

"Yes. We couldn't take any chances. Buzz thinks they could be trying to track our calls through the phones they gave us."

"Good thing you were able to find a burner phone. Let's just hope no one saw you get it."

"You're talking to a pro here, Snap, remember?" Stryker grinned. "I've got moves some of you have never seen."

Buzz and Phantom groaned and rolled their eyes. Stryker knew he had the respect of his team—they simply enjoyed giving him a hard time. Snap cleared his throat, drawing their attention back to the conversation at hand.

"So, do you have anything we can act on?" Stryker asked.

"Yes, but I wanted to update you on something first. I went to see Anya this morning."

Stryker tensed. If he could, he would be calling her directly, reassuring her personally that everything was fine. But once they went dark on a mission, their only communication was with the team. "How is she?"

"She's still rattled. I can't say I blame her. After the things she saw and then all the questions Brusco and I asked… I finally heard back from the admiral and let him know about the situation."

Stryker was clenching and unclenching his fists under the worn table in the small dining area in their safe house. Buzz had already scanned the area for bugs and had removed the two he'd found. It was the safest place for them to have the conversation that would give them the intel they desperately needed. He knew the discussion with Haslett was unavoidable. They had to follow protocol. "What did he say? Does he want to bring her in?"

"No. I let him know everything. He's appeased for now, but he's concerned about this package being delivered first to us, and now to her."

"Does he think she's in danger?" Stryker asked, a deep frown pulling down the corners of his mouth.

"He didn't say so directly, but you know how Haslett can be," Snap replied. "He wants us to keep a close eye on her until we find out who is behind this security leak."

"We should be home soon," Stryker said, and prayed he was right. "Will you watch over her in the meantime?"

"We've already worked out rotating shifts between me, Brusco, and Santo. Don't worry, Stryker. We aren't going to let anything happen to her."

Stryker swallowed hard. "Thanks Snap. It means a lot to me. Now, should we get to the pressing news of the day?"

Snap sighed heavily on the other end of the line. "Do you want to run through each guy? Their lists are fairly extensive."

"Why don't we hit the highlights?" Phantom suggested. "Let's identify age, years in the cartel, status, and specialty. Does that sound good?"

"Perfecto. First, let's start with Antonio Fernandez. He's one of the low guys in the organization. At thirty-two years old, he's fairly young to be a lieutenant, though we've all seen them even younger. He's been working in cartels since he was a teenager, starting off as a runner. He slowly worked up the ranks. His specialties are with a knife—he's done some real nasty carving on people over the years. And they lived to talk about it, which makes it just a bit worse."

"So he takes joy in causing pain. Good to know." Buzz shook his head in disgust.

"Raul Ortega makes Antonio look like an amateur. He's between thirty-eight and forty years old, depending on which birth certificate in the various states of Mexico you choose to believe. Same as Antonio, he's been involved since he was a teenager. He takes a lot of pleasure in torturing people and carries out some of the more important kidnappings ordered by the capo. He especially seems to delight in sending body parts to the people they're trying to get ransom from, or trying to send a message to."

"Real stand-up kinda guy," Phantom growled.

"Juan Alamedas is forty and has been on the scene for the last fifteen years. He bounced around among a variety of cartels before landing a spot with the Scorpions. He's their main extortion man. He seems to share that responsibility with Castro Gamboa, thirty-eight, and fifteen years with the Scorpions. Franco Morales is forty, been involved for about twenty years, and specializes in laundering the money."

"They seem to have it all organized very well. But what I don't understand, Snap, is that our research showed this cartel has only been in play for about five years at the most. How can these men have more years invested?" Stryker frowned down at the phone.

"Yeah, I should clarify that. So, all these guys have been working for the capo, Benicio Davila, for at least fifteen years, prior to when Benicio broke out war against his old cartel and split from them. All of these guys followed him, as did quite a few others. He had his own cartel ready to go before his old capo knew what had hit him."

"That explains a few things," Phantom muttered.

"Which leaves us with Hector Cruz. He's the capo's second. The capo doesn't take a shit without Hector knowing about it. He manages one of the most contested territories in Nuevo Laredo. He's thirty-nine and has been loyal to the capo since Benicio first began to rise in the ranks of the old cartel. It didn't take them long to become tight."

Stryker nodded, digesting the information. He ran a hand wearily down his face. "What about Benicio? Did you get any information on him?"

"C'mon, boss," Snap said beseechingly. "You know me better than that."

The three men sitting around the table chuckled and leaned in closer to the phone to hear Snap's description. "The man is in his midforties and has been building this cartel in his mind for who knows how long. Probably since he first joined the oversized cartel and caught wind of the opportunity for a hostile move. The man is smart. Incredibly smart. He runs the cartel like a well-oiled machine. After Buzz 'disabled' his supply line, he had people taking action to get it back up and running within hours of the first hiccup, when it usually takes days for such coordination. Fortunately, Buzz did such a good job that their line is still down."

"Thanks, brother. He has an elaborate team in place. It is going to take all our focus and teamwork to make this happen. Any description of the man himself?" Buzz asked.

"He's a bit of a recluse. He interacts mainly with Hector from what I've been able to dig up. But he does hold periodic meetings, which explains the one you're having tonight."

"What about the communication hub?" Buzz asked, folding his hands on the table. "Were you able to locate anything that looked like it could be a match?"

"Yes. But you're going to hate where it's located."

The old, familiar Matamoros that Benicio had expected to find was gone. Instead, it was obviously an active war zone, and every single citizen of the town seemed to be paying for it, except for the capos who were the actual targets.

He knew his arrival in town could cause tremendous turmoil and trouble for him, so he parked his Land Rover on the outskirts of the city, pulled on a baseball cap and a pair of dark sunglasses, and kept his head down as he hopped onto a bus to take him deeper into the city.

He was going to have to aim low. If it was found out he was questioning a sicario or a lieutenant, he would be subject to their justice for intruding on another capo's affairs. If he had Hector with him, that would make the situation a bit different. As it was, he needed to do this on his own. So he would have to take a Falcon, or even a drug runner, to try to gain insight into these men from Matamoros.

He grew more and more suspicious as he asked around about them, and no one seemed to know who they were. Unfortunately, he didn't have a photo to share, so he was going strictly by the names he'd been given. They could have changed their names when they changed their location, but he doubted it.

But the farther he got into the city, the more the names were recognized, and the more the runners and even the falcons were reluctant to say anything other than that they knew of them. He had finally found their territory, and, if he was to believe the reactions by the people he questioned, they were men not to be trifled with. But something still gnawed at his gut. Elsa wouldn't have given him information this far off the mark.

Finally, one of the runners led him to a run-down apartment complex and told him he'd find the answers to his questions on the fourth floor. Then the runner disappeared quickly, obviously not wanting to be seen in his presence any longer. Benicio shifted his ball cap on his head, desperately wishing he could take it off, but unable to risk the chance that someone would recognize him.

Once inside the apartment complex, he had to pull off his sunglasses. He hadn't been in a place this trashed since he was in his late teens. Since then, he had been climbing higher and higher. The place stank of urine and cooking grease.

He searched frantically for the elevator, only to find it out of order. Covering his mouth and nose with a rag, he rushed to the stairs and moved quickly. Fortunately, the farther up he went, the less the odors mingled, or he was becoming accustomed to it. He was going to burn his clothes when he got home.

The distinctive scent of marijuana soon overcame the smell of the rest of the building, and he knew he was getting close to the apartment he was meant to find. He paused outside the door where the scent was the strongest and knocked on it. No answer. He pounded on the thin, wooden door harder a second time, and there was a clattering inside the apartment.

A thin man dressed in baggy clothing and sporting a goatee and long, slicked back hair opened the door partway, his eyes scanning Benicio from head to toe. "¿Quién eres? Who are you? What the fuck do you want?"

Benicio was tired. He was hot. And the damn ball cap was making his head sweat. He hated sweating. With more force than was needed, he slammed the door open, smashing it into the man's surprised face, then quickly drew his gun from where he had kept it stuck in the holster hidden under his lightweight windbreaker.

He scanned the interior of the small apartment quickly and saw that no one was in the immediate room with them. He closed the door with his foot and motioned for the man to move with him.

The man's hands covered his face and blood was dripping from between his fingers. "You broke my fuckin' nose, puto!"

"And I'll put a fucking bullet in your brain if you call me a bitch again. Now, move. Sit down on that shit pile you think is a couch while I look around."

The man suddenly seemed properly subdued and sulked over to his "couch" where Benicio could keep an eye on him while quickly checking the rest of the small apartment. He snatched a towel out of the bathroom and returned to where the man sat, satisfied they were alone.

He tossed the towel at the man and then sat on a coffee table that had obviously been used recently to cut cocaine. There were even small bags stashed under the table hastily, and he thought he saw a scale stuffed under the couch. That must have been what the dick had been doing before opening the door.

The man must be a lowly street dealer. That was exactly what he needed. "I have questions for you," Benicio said softly, "and you're going to answer them for me."

"I don't know anything. I just work the streets. That's all. I don't have any answers for you." The pathetic man was whining.

"Three men have come into my territory. And I need answers about them."

The man's pupils dilated before shrinking to pinpoints. "I don't know what you're talking about."

"Oh, but I believe you do. What's your name?"

"M-my name? I'm nobody. I just work the streets, hombre."

"Well, hombre, this could be your lucky day. If you have the answers I'm looking for, your life could be spared. But if you don't, I'll make sure your death is slow and painful. Now, what's your name?"

"V-Vidal."

～∼∼～

Stryker wanted to punch something. He was used to the rush of adrenaline and the tension before a big mission, but he was wound even tighter than usual. All they knew was that they were to meet Franco and he would escort them to their meeting.

He was glad Snap had gone to check on Anya. But, damn it, that was *his* job! He was supposed to be there to soothe Anya, to take away her fears. Now, inadvertently, he and his team had only added to them.

He sat on the edge of the bed and shook his head. There was nothing he could do for Anya now. His mind was already on the bigger picture, and that was taking down Benicio Davila. They had to dismantle his operations and question him. He knew too much to kill him, even though that was what he deserved. The man was ruthless and heartless. But they needed him alive.

He went to the mirror and straightened his Gucci shirt, smoothing out the faint wrinkles. Then he used a little more gel to slick back his hair. He looked the part. But something in his gut felt wrong. This entire meeting felt off.

There was a rap at his door and he opened it, stepping out in the hallway to join Buzz. "Ready?"

"Depends," Buzz replied.

"On what?"

"Exactly what I'm supposed to be ready for."

"Same shit, different day," Stryker said.

"I didn't hear how this conversation started, but I concur," Phantom said, as he stepped out of his room. He nodded to the others, and the three of them filed out of the house, driving over to their designated meeting spot with Franco.

"Hope you understand the need for this, amigos," Franco said just before dark bags were shoved over their heads. "Don't try to take them off, por favor. It will be much easier on all of us if we don't have to shoot you."

Stryker, Phantom, and Buzz remained silent as they were loaded into a large SUV and it took off with a screech of the tires. The entire time they were traveling, Stryker was mentally keeping track of the number of turns they were making, though he could tell they were making several that formed a tight circle. It was a tactic to confuse them.

But the sounds around them gave him clues, and soon he realized they had traveled to the far northwest end of town—in the direction of where the communications hub was located. Surely their meeting wasn't being held at the same location? If it was, their job may have just been made exponentially easier.

They were shoved up some steps, stumbling as they were rushed, then pushed through a doorway. Suddenly, the bags were ripped from their heads, and they all blinked their eyes, squinting against the bright lights in the room. Several men circled them, arms folded over their chests, watching them closely.

Stryker made sure to smooth back his hair before gazing determinedly at all the faces, including Franco's. "Did we pass the test?"

"That remains to be seen," said a voice from the far corner of the room, and the group parted to reveal a tall, well-built man with a small beard that ran along his jaw-line and connected to a goatee. He stepped forward, but didn't extend his hand in any form of greeting, nor did his eyes invite any warmth. "I'm Benicio Davila. I trust you know who I am."

"Your reputation precedes you, Mr. Davila," Buzz spoke up.

"Good. Spend time getting to know the lieutenants.

I'll be counting on them to let me know if and when we should move forward with you joining the Scorpions."

"Shouldn't we spend some time with you too?" Phantom asked quietly, and Benicio turned and gave him an appraisal from head to toe.

"If you make it through meeting my lieutenants, then you'll earn a meeting with me."

Unease slithered down Stryker's back again. Something didn't feel right. And he saw more than one of the lieutenants exchange confused glances. Something was definitely off, but he couldn't put his finger on what. They had already been frisked for weapons, and he suddenly craved the comfort of his HK45 compact handgun.

The men around him seemed to be well armed, some with more than one handgun in holsters at their sides. A couple of the men standing on the outskirts of the group had M14 EBR assault rifles slung across their shoulders. He immediately sized them up to be the sicarios, the hitmen of the group, there to provide protection.

Gradually, Stryker took in their surroundings. The warehouse environment fit in with exactly what he'd expected. They *were* at the communications hub that Snap had described to them in their morning phone call. He cautioned a sideways glance at Buzz who made eye contact with him and gave him a slight nod, bending to tie his shoe to mask the motion and also signal to Stryker that he was on it.

Stryker drew in a deep breath and began to move slowly around the room, casually introducing himself to the lieutenants as if they weren't important to him. Each one wanted to question him about his background and his knowledge, and he fed them his cover story over and over. He had to steal as much time as he could for Buzz. He had to make it seem as if all was good and they were ready to enter into business with the Scorpions. And if he failed to buy enough time for Buzz to do what he needed, they were all dead.

—◆◆◆—

Usually he thoroughly enjoyed the process of killing someone. But this time he had been so pissed off, he had garnered only minimal enjoyment out of killing the man. The pathetic scrap of a human being now lay at his feet, his body contorted oddly, his bloodstain slowly spreading farther and farther out on the filthy carpet.

Vidal had proved far more useful than he'd expected. But the information wasn't what Benicio had wanted to hear. He had wanted to believe Elsa on one hand. But on the other hand, he'd wanted to believe that it would have been much harder for someone to infiltrate his business, especially at such a high level. But now he knew the truth. Which meant more men were going to die. And, unfortunately, one of them would have to be his lieutenant, Franco.

He cursed under his breath as he left the stench of the apartment complex, only to realize it had soaked into his clothes. Franco was a good lieutenant. He had been with him a long time and seemed to be as loyal as they could come. But no one was beyond suspicion at this point.

Fuck! U.S. Navy SEALs. He thought he had greased all the appropriate wheels within the U.S. Apparently there was a squeaky wheel somewhere, and he needed to take it out of the equation. Who would target him? Was it because of the recent murders he had committed in the U.S.? He thought all worries and any qualms around that had been satisfied. Maybe not.

But there was an immediate issue that needed to be resolved. He pulled his phone out of his pocket, then grimaced when he saw blood on his hand. It wasn't his, even though Vidal had put up a valiant fight for his life. He was usually so much more controlled and never got dirty. But his rage had made him neglect some of his usual tact and decorum when it came to the artistic process of murder.

He hit a number on his phone and kept walking as the line rang. Finally, Hector's voice came across the line. "Bueno?"

"Take them out. I won't be back for a while. I have business to attend to in Texas."

Chapter 22

AS SOON AS STRYKER SAW HECTOR TAKE A PHONE CALL, he knew they were blown. There was no way to explain how he knew, but his gut clenched in preparation for battle. A war was about to go down. And he was without a weapon.

As if in slow motion, he watched Hector's eyes scan the room, registering where Phantom stood, and then finally where Stryker stood. Stryker was able to look away quickly enough that Hector wouldn't know he'd figured out what was going down. They had a little bit of time. They would want to kill them slowly and painfully and leave their bodies as examples for anyone else who wanted to try and bust apart their cartel.

He just needed to know where Buzz was before he could act, or Buzz could easily be collateral damage. He turned slowly and made eye contact with Phantom. The only sign that Phantom gave was a slight downturn of his mouth. Other than that small motion, his face remained impassive, listening to one of the lieutenants talk about a recent kidnap-for-ransom mission.

Stryker had successfully conveyed to Phantom that he needed to be ready for the shit to hit the fan. But he needed to find Buzz, and quickly. Otherwise, being separated, they were at even greater risk.

Suddenly, there was commotion at the far end of the room, and one of the sicarios walked out with Buzz in front of him, a gun pressed to the back of his head. Buzz walked into the room but didn't make eye contact with anyone. Buzz was a much larger man than the sicario who had a gun to his head, and could take him down in seconds. Stryker had watched Buzz do it. But he had to continue playing into their game…at least for a little longer.

"On your knees, puto!"

The entire room drew quiet, and all eyes shifted to the center of the room where Buzz obliged and got down on his knees. "What's going on here?" Benicio asked, stepping forward from his protective circle of sicarios and lieutenants.

Buzz lifted his eyes, and they connected with Stryker's. Stryker gave a slight inclination of his head. Buzz knew the situation they were in, and knew the odds weren't in their favor. They were going to have to take drastic steps, and soon.

"He was in the communications room. He was doing something on the computers."

"Shit. We need to get David here, pronto," Hector growled.

Fuck. Their technology guy isn't here. We need to take him along with Benicio. Stryker doubted they would have the time to get David there before the cartel decided to kill all of them. His fists clenched and unclenched, and he felt Hector's gaze on him. Slowly he looked up.

"What was your man doing in there?" Hector demanded, his gaze fixed on Stryker.

"I have no idea. He's not my man. We just run together."

Hector tilted his head to the side. "Now that's funny.

Because the entire night I've been thinking you were the leader of your little three amigos group you have going on here."

Chuckles broke out around the room, and Stryker's muscles began to tighten in anticipation of the battle they were about to fight. They were outnumbered five to one. They'd had worse odds before. But then, during those times, they'd been armed. He needed to buy enough time for Phantom to get into a good position. He was trying to think through the various ways he could do that when Hector spoke up again.

"Tell you what," Hector said, stepping toward Stryker. "Why don't you show us your new loyalty to the Scorpions by killing the man who has betrayed both of us?"

He pulled one of the guns out of his holster strapped across his chest and handed the weapon to Stryker. "Now, shoot him in the head."

Stryker walked over to Buzz, took the place of the sicario, and placed the gun to the back of Buzz's head. He could tell by the weight of the gun that it lacked bullets. Nothing could have told him more strongly that they were on to his team. They weren't willing to give him a loaded weapon. At least, Hector wasn't. But no one else knew what had transpired in the phone call from a few minutes earlier.

"No offense, Hector, but this isn't my preferred gun." He motioned to the sicario to trade guns with him before Hector could react. "I've always liked one with a little more heft to it."

Hector made a motion like he was going to step toward them, but he stopped when Stryker aimed the weapon at Buzz's head once again. "Do it, then. Prove yourself to us."

Stryker smiled at Hector. "You already know the answer to that, Hector. I don't have a damn thing to prove." He lifted the gun and fired, and Hector stumbled backwards as Stryker threw himself to the floor, taking out two more men as they all began to draw their weapons.

Bullets struck the concrete near him, and he and Buzz lunged forward from their position on the floor. Buzz grabbed one of the sicarios who had his back to him and kneed him in the kidney, making him lose focus and giving Buzz the opportunity to take his gun away from him. Then, he joined Stryker, shooting the man nearest to them and then using his body as protection from the bullets flying at them. Buzz and Stryker didn't stop shooting.

"Heads down!" Phantom yelled as warning to Stryker and Buzz, and Stryker knew that Phantom had been able to get hold of one of the automatic weapons from a sicario. Both Stryker and Buzz quickly dropped before the other men knew how to respond, and Phantom was peppering them with bullets from the M14 he'd just taken. Silence followed the ear-blasting volley. No one who was still alive wanted to give away his location.

Stryker slowly eased out from beneath the body of the lieutenant named Antonio. There was movement in the far corner, and he spun rapidly, then pivoted to continue scanning the room. It had only been Buzz easing out from underneath a sicario's body.

Another movement caught his eye, and he fired off a round into the body of Lieutenant Raul before he could reach his gun again. Phantom moved slowly, holding the M14 at the ready. But the one who was moving the most drew Stryker's attention, and he stepped over dead bodies to reach him.

"Do you want to know why I didn't kill you, Hector? Do you want to know why? Because you and Benicio have some information I need."

Hector was bleeding profusely from his wound and stared up at Stryker with hatred. Next to him, however, Benicio was still scrambling for a gun, having lost his when Hector had jumped in front of him to protect him from the gunfire.

"Focus now, Hector," Stryker said, aiming his gun at Hector's head. "Who is David? Where do I find him?"

"Rot in hell, motherfucker." Hector attempted to spit on Stryker but missed.

"You'll be there soon enough. Just answer my questions. I may have mercy and try to save your sorry ass."

Hector gave a weak laugh. "We both know I'm past the point of saving, pendejo. I'll take my secrets to the grave with me."

Stryker hadn't expected much from the man. He reached into his pocket, then, the one he had seen him put his cell phone in. He pulled it out and grabbed Hector's hand, pressing his thumb to the key pad to unlock it. Within moments he was in Hector's contacts. "Well, would you lookie there—David Castro. Only David in your phone." He made a tsking sound. "You really should make more friends."

"You…son of a…bitch," Hector wheezed out, before his head fell back to the floor.

"Now, we just have you to contend with," Stryker said, turning his attention on Benicio, who was sweating profusely. "You're coming with us."

"No, no. You have the wrong man. Por favor…listen to me…"

"Sure thing, Benicio. We'll listen to everything you have to say once we get out of this hellhole," Phantom said dryly.

Together, Phantom and Stryker hefted Benicio to his feet, despite his struggles against them. Stryker turned to look at Buzz. "Where do we stand on the communications room?"

Suddenly there was a gargled sound. "We've been… betrayed. All of us."

"Fuck!" Stryker spun around and saw Hector talking into a separate cell phone, probably Benicio's. *Who* he was talking to was the critical question. He snatched the phone out of the man's hand and heard Hector expel his last breath of air. At least that problem was solved.

He looked down at the caller ID and his stomach clenched. "Jefe" was the name on the caller ID. Who had been on the other line? Didn't they have the boss already with them? His eyes reconnected with Buzz. "The communications room?" he asked curtly.

"Heavily encrypted, as we expected. Whoever is doing this work has a lot of experience in the dark web. But I wasn't able to get everything. I need more time."

"Our time is up," Phantom said, looking at his watch. "It won't be long before the policia arrive and we have a real problem on our hands."

"I was able to get about seventy-five percent on this flash drive. If you can just buy me five minutes, I can yank one of the hard drives."

"Move fast, sailor. We're living on borrowed time now."

They began to propel toward the door with Benicio attempting to twist and turn in their arms. He dug in his heels, and for a relatively trim man, he was also strong, and temporarily halted Stryker and Phantom. And then he began to laugh, the twisted, demented laugh of a man who knew he was going to die.

"Are you truly the best that America has to offer? *This* is it? You men are clueless. You have no idea what is even going on around you."

"Yeah, sure. Tell us all about it on the drive home."

"Too late. Jefe knows everything now. And he's only the tip of the iceberg. You have no idea how deep and far this goes. It isn't just Benicio. He reports to someone else, who reports to someone else, and so on and so on. You'll never be free of us."

"He's stalling," Stryker spat. "Let's get him out of here." They began to drag him forcefully, but suddenly he lunged forward. They were able to keep a tight grip on him, but he hit his head into one of the ornate carvings that seemed so out of place in an industrial building.

The floor of the building shook violently, and the men staggered their stances, trying to gain better footing. Benicio turned on them and gave a hysterical laugh as blood trickled down his forehead. "It's over now. There's no escape."

"The whole place is collapsing!" Phantom yelled over the cracking sound of concrete and the crashing of giant blocks of the wall and ceiling down onto the floors.

"The computers!" Buzz began to charge off, but Stryker tackled him from the side.

"We have to get out of here," Stryker yelled at him. "Forget the computers."

Benicio turned back to the carving that he had smashed, and, too late, Stryker saw the red flashing light. "They've killed everyone and have a flash drive. There are three of them—"

Stryker lunged at him and slammed him back against a wall that was beginning to crack. "Who are you talking to, you sick fuck? Who are you partnered with?"

Benicio laughed in Stryker's face. "You'll never know. You won't figure it out until it is too late for you to do anything about it. There are great plans in place. But you'll be too late."

Stryker drew back his fist and smashed it into Benicio's jaw, sending him sliding back toward the blood-drenched room they had just left. Benicio sat up and spat blood on the ground. "You dumb, stupid—" A massive piece of cement fell from the ceiling, crushing Benicio, and then there was complete stillness.

"We have to go now!" Phantom yelled, grabbing Stryker by the arm.

Dodging falling debris as they ran, they threw themselves over cement blocks and raced for the exit. A piece of concrete fell so close to Stryker that he felt the air move the hair on his neck as it went down. "Hustle, boys!" he yelled. "This whole fucking place is coming down around our ears!"

"No shit!" Phantom yelled back in frustration.

They jumped through the door and were thrown forward as the interior of the building collapsed in on itself, and they fell down the steps they'd climbed up what seemed like hours ago, hooded and unaware of the way the night was going to play out. Dust plumed around them, making it hard to see. Stryker scanned through the dust and floating debris to make sure his men had made it out alive but it was too hard to see.

"At your six," came a cough directly behind him, and he whirled to see Phantom walking forward, Buzz's arm slung around his shoulder. Buzz limped beside him, grimacing.

"Damage?" Stryker demanded, his heart rate pounding, but he forced it to slow through paced breathing. This was what he and his men trained and lived through constantly. But he wasn't about to lose a man on a mission that shouldn't have been nearly this complicated.

"Busted my leg when we were thrown down the steps, but I'm going to be just fine. Ready to go home, though."

"You and me both, sailor. Let's grab our shit and get out of here."

∗∗∗

Getting across the border was as easy as usual. Benicio knew which border patrol officers he could count on to look the other way as he slid by. He'd stopped at his home as he had prepared to leave and had found the security video his cousin had recorded as the building had collapsed around him. He had broken the security monitor as well as a fifteen-thousand-dollar vase in his rage.

How could these three men have come in and done so much damage to his team? He had trained his Scorpions himself! He had even recruited men from the Mexican marines into the sicarios to train his men. They were considered elite, even by other cartels. What had happened?

He'd changed clothes while at his home and packed a small bag. He had gathered some items he knew were going to be critical to his business in the U.S. Elsa had been the last thing on his mind as he had gone out to his Land Rover and loaded in his bags. When the headlights had drifted through his gate, he had yanked his gun and held it by his side as he stood behind the Land Rover, waiting with his breath held.

Elsa's car had slid up into the driveway, and she'd stepped out, looking determined. He knew why she was there. She had told him she would stop by and find out what he had discovered in Matamoros. He had walked around the Rover, startling her.

"I knew you were looking forward to me coming, Benicio, but I wasn't expecting you to be waiting for me." She'd smiled brightly at him.

"Not tonight, Elsa. There have been…complications."

Elsa's eyes had widened in surprise, then they'd narrowed quickly with concern. "*Tío* Hector? Please tell me he's okay. He's the only family I have left."

"I'll avenge him, Elsa. I'll avenge him. But until I know how far this goes, stay here. I want you safe."

"It comes back to you! That's how far it goes. They're after you! ¡Dios mío! I can't stay here. They'll come right here." She'd turned and raced away from him back to her car.

Benicio realized she was probably right. When word got around that his cartel was crumbling, they would be coming for him, if they didn't think he was already dead. He hoped the death of his cousin bought him some time until they realized it wasn't him.

Now, as he drove east from Laredo, his mind raced with all that lay ahead of him. He not only had business to conduct, he had revenge to exact. And he needed answers more than anything. He needed to know what had gone so horribly wrong.

———∿∿∿———

They had barely crossed the border when Stryker pulled out the burner phone to call Anya. He hated disturbing her in the middle of the night, but he needed to hear her voice and have the reassurance that she was truly okay. He knew the team had been watching over her and making sure she stayed safe, but hearing it from her would make it real to him.

"Dr. Gutierrez," her groggy voice came across the line and he suddenly felt everything was right with the world.

"Anya, it's Stryker. I'm sorry I woke you, I just—"

"Stryker!" Her voice filled with energy. "I'm-I'm glad you called. I didn't realize your trip would last so long. I've missed you."

His heart beat faster and he forgot about Phantom and Buzz riding in the SUV with him. "I've missed you, too. I'm on my way home now. Is it okay for me to come see you in the morning?"

"Yes. We need to talk." Apprehension tinged her voice, and he knew she had a lot of questions.

"Yes, we do. I'll see you soon." He disconnected the call and quickly dialed the admiral. It was past time to talk to him about Anya.

Chapter 23

"THE AIR NEVER SMELLED BETTER, AND ALL I CAN SMELL is cow shit and hay."

"See, we're going to make a country boy out of you after all, Buzz." Stryker chuckled, patting the man on the back. Buzz gave him a weak smile. They were all exhausted and in desperate need of showers and fresh clothes.

They'd taken the SUV that had driven them out to the communications hub back to where they'd originally met Franco and traded back to their own vehicle. They left the SUV burning behind them, erasing any indication that they'd ever been in the vehicle. They'd waited nearly half an hour before finally entering their "safe" house, unsure whether it had been breached.

Fortunately, Benicio's foot soldiers hadn't hit the place yet, and they were able to grab their go-bags and leave the place quickly. They had zigzagged out of the city, avoiding major territories they knew would be crawling with Scorpion runners. It'd taken them longer to reach the checkpoint and leave the city, but they'd finally made it out. Stryker's mind ran over the conversation with Anya and, subsequently, Haslett, and he couldn't wait to go see her.

Now, the small town of Hebbronville was the best thing they had ever seen, even though it was shrouded in darkness with only a few streetlights showing how empty the town was at this time of night. It was late when they finally pulled down the long dirt road to their ranch.

The light at the front door flipped on before Stryker had a chance to insert his keys. Snap yanked open the door, his face a mixture of relief at their return and anxiety over Buzz as they helped him hobble into the house. "It's nothing. Seriously. Phantom's the doctor around here, remember? And he says I'll be fine. It's just a bruise on the bone. Hurts like hell, but it will heal, and quickly too."

Brusco came around the corner, eager to make sure they were all okay. He paused as his eyes settled on Stryker.

"How are things here? Have you gotten any leads on those photos?" Stryker asked, eyeing Brusco. He realized it wasn't his fault that Anya had been pulled into things. He couldn't take his frustrations out on his team.

Snap shook his head. "The envelope she received indicated that it originated here in Hebbronville, but we don't have a FedEx here. The one you received was from Corpus. Someone is playing some major head games with us."

Stryker's eyes landed on Brusco. "How far did you take it with Anya?"

"Nothing more than you would have, Stryker. I had to make sure to protect the team."

Buzz leaned against the wall, watching the interaction. "You do realize that Brusco was following protocol, right? That's all this is really about. He was doing his job."

"Good. Then, are we all cleared up?" Phantom asked, and Stryker felt some of the tension leaving his body.

"Yes, we're cleared up."

"Great. Now, let's go into the dining room. We need to take care of Buzz, and we need a debrief."

As a group, they moved into the dining room, giving an extra chair for Buzz to prop up his leg. Snap got him a bag of ice, and then they all focused on Stryker. Stryker let out a heavy sigh. "The immediate mission is over. But whether that is truly the end of things, I doubt it."

Benicio made his way to his first stop. Even if his cartel was crumbling around him, he was going to make sure he still had the infrastructure in place to be able to rebuild. It would take him a long time, and he was going to have to dodge the other cartels that would be fighting to take over everything he'd built. But he had plenty of people to step in who just needed training.

He should be in Nuevo Laredo doing damage control. But this was more important. He was going to make sure the U.S. learned they couldn't take him down so easily. He was a powerful man, and they had no idea the hornet's nest they'd just disturbed.

It was close to two o'clock in the morning, and he knew Frederick would not be happy at being disturbed at this hour, but there was no way around it. Besides, he was his boss. He expected to be received pleasantly, regardless of the hour. He went to work on the lock on the man's door, and within moments had the door open. Fortunately, Frederick wasn't paranoid enough to have a security system in place. Pendejo.

The layout of the house was predictable, and Benicio slowly moved down the hallway to where the bedrooms were. Fortunately, Frederick didn't have any kids. That could have been a huge complication, and even though he was pissed off, he didn't feel like killing any kids today. Now, the man's wife, on the other hand, was someone he wouldn't mind killing. She was a nagging bitch who seemed to have him by the balls far too often, which hindered some of their business negotiations.

But deep down, he wanted to savor the anger and desire to kill for a little longer. He had other obligations while he was in Texas, and he wanted to draw upon those feelings for that event. So, if he could, he would avoid killing Frederick's wife. But he wouldn't be heart-broken if she was collateral damage.

He could hear snores traveling down the hallway and shook his head. If the guy didn't get a security system after this visit, he was even more of an idiot than Benicio already suspected. He moved into the bedroom silently, feeling the weight of his gun in his hand, reassurance that he had the upper hand. Frederick was big and could wake up swinging, but Benicio knew he could stop that with the simple click of his gun cocked at the man's head.

He stood over him for several moments, watching him in his deep sleep, before clamping his hand firmly over Frederick's mouth and pressing the barrel of the gun against his forehead. Frederick's eyes flew open, startled and fearful. He was breathing heavily through his nose as his eyes adjusted to the dark room. When he saw who it was that stood above him, his eyes widened even farther.

Benicio slowly pulled the gun away from his fore-head and held it to his lips, motioning him to stay quiet as he got out of the bed. He made a point of giving a direct look at Frederick's wife, making it clear that she would die if he didn't follow Benicio's instructions carefully. He nodded in understanding as best he could under Benicio's heavy hand.

Benicio took a step back, allowing Frederick to stand, and encouraged him to move forward by tapping the gun against his back. Wearing only boxer shorts, he straightened his back at the touch of the cold metal and walked rigidly down the hallway and into the small dining room.

"Can I get you something? A beer?" Frederick asked, obviously trying to make Benicio feel welcome, even at this insane hour.

Benicio shook his head. "We need to talk business."

Frederick sat at the dining room table across from Benicio, apprehension clear on his face. "The runs have been going according to plan," he said, his fingers picking at imaginary lint on the tablecloth.

"That's good to hear. Here is your latest payment." He placed the large envelope on the table, and he could tell that Frederick was itching to count it but was being respectful. "There will be another run for you coming up very soon. This one will be the last for a few months."

Frederick's eyes widened. "But—I don't understand. We've been doing so well."

"There's been a bit of a shake-up in the cartel, and it's going to take me some time to get all this worked out. In the meantime, I'm going to need you to lay low. And you can't take any orders from anyone other than me. Is that understood?"

"Completely, sir. But I have to admit to you…using my cattle hauler to run the drugs has allowed me and my wife to live our lives comfortably. I don't know what I'll do without that extra income."

"I'll need other things from you in the meantime. It isn't going to pay as much as what you've been earning, but it will be easier than being cut off completely."

"Thank you, Jefe. What—may I ask what happened?"

"Some authorities in the U.S. decided to go rogue and infiltrate the cartel. And now, I'm trying to do damage control."

"I'm here to help if you need it, Jefe."

"That's good to hear. You might be able to help me right now. What do you know about the new ranchers who recently moved here? The ones who took over that old, abandoned ranch to the north of you."

Frederick looked surprised. "The Bent Horseshoe Ranch? I don't know much about them, other than that they're aggressively building their stock of pure Santa Gertrudis cattle. That and they had an impressive selection of trained horses."

"Where did they come from? How many are there?"

"They've really kept to themselves. I believe there's six of them altogether. I see them in town from time to time. Clean-cut, business-oriented. They're friendly, and are gradually getting to know everyone around here."

Benicio's hands clenched into fists. "Who *would* know something about them? Who is someone they interact with frequently?"

"The same person all of us ranchers interact with. Dr. Anya Gutierrez. She's the veterinarian who treats all the livestock around this area."

"Dr. Anya Gutierrez. Thank you, Frederick. You've been more helpful than you realize. Now, go back to your wife, and forget I came by to see you tonight. For now, it's business as usual until you hear from me next."

Frederick nodded, obviously relieved. "Thank you, Jefe. Thank you."

Debriefing the team was harder than Stryker had thought it would be. They had to get all the information out and recorded, so they would be able to deliver an accurate report to Admiral Haslett.

"How do you think Hector discovered you weren't the real deal?" Santo asked, his face pulled into a deep frown. None of the men looked pleased. The leader of the Scorpions was still alive and on the loose, which meant their mission had failed, even though they'd taken down the other key players in the cartel.

They hadn't been able to get all the critical data from the computers. On top of that, they hadn't been able to catch the man responsible for all the encoding and encryption that currently plagued them. While that hadn't been part of their assignment, it would have been a real win for the team.

"It's hard to say for certain." Stryker sighed. It was a question that had haunted him the entire drive home. "Something or someone must have tipped off Benicio that we weren't all that we seemed. Then Benicio assigned Hector to look into us, and something this person found made him doubt us."

"Do you think he could have sent someone all the way to Matamoros to check your background?"

"I wouldn't put it past him. Benicio struck me as one

paranoid fucker," Buzz replied. He was on his third bag of ice on his leg, but hadn't complained about it once.

"Did either one of you get the feeling that Benicio was a bit…odd?" Phantom asked, shifting in his seat. It was the first time he'd moved since they had all sat down hours ago. Stryker didn't know how the man did it. But his ability to stay still and blend into his surroundings like that was what had earned him his nickname.

"I would've been surprised if he wasn't odd," Buzz replied, shaking his head. "The man had to be a bit twisted to have created the cartel he did at such a young age."

"That's just it. For someone who had so much power, he seemed to lack the confidence I would have expected from a man in that position."

"You have a point," Stryker said thoughtfully. "It almost seemed like he was hiding behind his lieutenants and sicarios most of the night. He even let Hector take a bullet for him."

"That's normal in the cartel world—the second would always protect the capo with his life," Santo pointed out.

"Has anyone thought any further about the pictures that were sent to us? And to Anya?" Brusco asked, his gaze locking with Stryker's.

"It's another part of the mystery. Someone got on our property and took pictures of all of us—though it is curious that Stryker is in each one. Was it someone trying to send us a message that they could see us no matter where we are? That we aren't as undercover as we think we are? Could that person have told Benicio everything about us?"

Stryker shook his head at Santo's theories. "I think

it's bigger than that. Think about it… Who had the cartel pictures that were sent to us?"

"Admiral Haslett had the ones of the cartel that were included in our debrief files," Snap answered.

"So, those pictures should have been in the safety of the navy office, inaccessible to someone on the outside."

"You think there's a mole."

"I think there are a lot of things that just don't add up. Someone got their hands on those cartel pictures and sent them to Anya. That same person had the pictures that were taken of us here at the ranch. Other than the leadership in the navy, who knows we're here? Add to that the redacted file, and I think there's a major problem. But who would know about Anya?"

"Buzz, have you done a sweep of this place for bugs, the same way you checked the safe house in Nuevo Laredo?" Phantom asked, his tone tense.

"The same day I moved in, and once a week ever since those photos arrived. We're clean."

"We can't trust anyone," Brusco said. "Not even the admiral."

Stryker shook his head. "I've known Admiral Haslett for a long time. He isn't the type of man who can be corrupted. He bleeds red, white, and blue."

"Money can be a powerful influence." Snap shrugged.

"Not for him. But you're right. We have to tread carefully with everybody. And we need to get to the bottom of who sent those photos to us…and to Anya."

"Already on it," Snap said softly. "I've been turning over every rock I can. I'll find the son of a bitch. And then we'll know where the corruption is coming from."

The room fell into silence for several long moments

as everyone absorbed the information. Then Stryker picked up telling the rest of their adventure in Nuevo Laredo. "When we arrived at the meeting location, the lieutenants removed the bags over our heads and we were facing what appeared to be the entire upper echelon of the cartel. All of the lieutenants and most, if not all, of the sicarios."

"None of them seemed thrilled to see us there, which was odd, considering we were supposed to provide them with help with their supply line, and we were also going to fill one of the gaps they had open in their territories," Buzz said, tapping his fingers on the table.

"Perhaps they weren't happy about you uncovering the problem with that lieutenant they had to remove from their team. That probably didn't go over well." Snap shrugged.

"Perhaps," Stryker admitted. "Regardless, the reception was less than warm. And the lieutenants seemed surprised when Benicio said we had to go through them first before he would spend any time with us. There was a vibe of confusion in the air the entire time we were there."

"I think that's what made it so easy for me to sneak off into their communications room." Buzz leaned forward.

"What did you find there?" Brusco asked.

"A very elaborate setup for a drug cartel. There were five laptops all equipped with high-speed internet. Their IP addresses all traced back to false company fronts, but no longer. I changed them to trace back to that location. The level of encryption was unlike anything I have ever seen, though. I couldn't access even a fourth of the computer's data. But I was able to back up about seventy-five percent of it on this flash drive before I was discovered. Now, I just need to pore through this data to try to make sense of it."

"You were caught?"

Buzz, Phantom, and Stryker all exchanged glances. Sometimes reliving the events of a mission wasn't easy. But it was best they did it that way in order to make sure the entire team knew of the report and could check it for anything they might have missed.

Stryker cleared his throat and began to tell the team how they'd brought down one of the most dangerous cartels in Mexico. Including every gory detail. "It was only because of Phantom that we made it out of there before the entire place collapsed."

There was silence around the table for a few long minutes as everyone digested the information. Finally, Brusco spoke. "Do you have any idea who Benicio was talking to?"

"None. But it makes me wonder if there is someone in an even higher position pulling strings in Mexico… and even here. There's the possibility that Vidal is the one who gave us up. Buzz found bugs in the guns he gave us. He also found bugs in the safe house. Either Vidal was behind it, or there's a bigger player involved."

"Or both," Santo said softly. "And someone had to have taken those pictures of us. I still don't understand why all of that was sent to Anya."

"I think at this point any suspicion is one we should take into consideration. Nothing is too far-fetched."

"Even one where our own government could be setting us up for failure?" Phantom asked, his gaze intent.

"Especially that one. *Especially* that one."

Chapter 24

STRYKER TOOK A HOT SHOWER, WASHING OFF ALL THE GREASE in his hair and the fake tattoos. He shaved and put on his aftershave, a scent he knew Anya liked. He was even able to convince Snap to give him a quick haircut.

The debrief had taken far longer than expected. There had been a lot of questions, and all of them were very important. They helped clarify the details of the mission, and they made progress that wouldn't have been possible if not for the additional insight. It was all necessary, but he'd felt the time ticking away as he anticipated going to see Anya.

The drive into town seemed to take forever. The town was still asleep, and there was no traffic on the road. His heart thudded with the need to see her, and he hoped she'd put aside her fears and confusion briefly to greet him with the warmth and love he craved from her.

He had never thought he would be capable of feeling anything other than lust toward a woman ever again. But it was different with Anya. She was beautiful inside and out. And she gave of her heart so generously. Did he deserve such an incredible gift?

Finally, he pulled up to the back of her clinic, and his hands clenched the steering wheel. It was four in the morning. Would she be shocked to see him so early? She knew he was coming, but she probably assumed it would be right before she opened her clinic. He couldn't wait any longer. He needed to hold her in his arms, to breathe in her scent, to be reminded that good still existed in the world. And he needed her to know he was there for her and would protect her from anything.

He ran a hand through his shorter hair and drew a deep breath. He had just faced down men with automatic weapons, a crumbling structure, and almost certain death. And yet, he was so nervous about seeing Anya, he couldn't bring himself to step out of his truck and go knock on her door. He drew another deep breath, turned off his truck, and opened the door.

Instantly, the hair on the back of his neck stood on end. Something didn't feel right. There was a tension in the coolish spring air, and he looked around. There was nothing amiss that he could see. Everything was where it belonged, and there was nothing there that he hadn't seen before. The paranoia from Mexico must still be in his system. But he knew how to fix that. Anya.

He went to her back door and rapped on it gently, waited for a few minutes, then knocked again. Finally, Anya's sleepy but nervous voice came through from the other side. "Who is it?"

"Anya, it's me. Stryker. I know it's early, but I couldn't wait any longer to see you."

He could envision her on the other side of the door, chewing on her lower lip, trying to decide what to do. Then, he heard the lock being released, and she was there, wearing an adorable pajama set, her hair tousled from sleep. With the light of her room beaming from behind her, he had a hard time seeing the gold flecks he knew were in her eyes. Then she motioned for him to come inside, and that was when he saw the handgun she held.

"Anya! What are you doing with a gun? Do you even know how to use it?"

She frowned, uncocked it smoothly, and slipped the safety back on. "I've lived with guns my entire life. Did you forget I grew up on a ranch?"

"Shooting a coyote or a rattlesnake is very different from having to use one to defend yourself from a person."

"You sound like you're speaking from experience," Anya said softly, as she walked over to the side of her bed and opened her nightstand drawer, placing the gun inside.

"Anya, we have a lot to talk about."

She crossed her arms over her chest. "That might be the understatement of the year. I've missed you so very much. But I'm also terribly confused. Who sent me those awful photographs? And how are you mixed up in all of it? I've known all along you haven't told me everything about your past. I never imagined it could involve something this horrific, though."

"I just need you to listen. That's all I'm asking of you. I've made a lot of mistakes, Anya, and I want to make up for those."

Anya ran a hand through her hair and drew in a shaky breath. "Stryker...I don't know what to say. I don't know what to believe. I want to trust you—I've always felt safe with you. But after this—"

He took a step toward her and grabbed one of her hands in his. "I'm a very private man. You know that about me. Talking about my past...about who I really am...it doesn't come easy for me. Trust is a luxury I can rarely afford. But I want to trust you. I just...I just haven't told you everything about my team and what we do."

"What *we* do? So you are former DEA as well?" She didn't sound terribly shocked.

"No. I'm… It's very complicated. I don't even know how to tell you everything. But you need to know the truth."

Anya squeezed his hand and moved a step closer to him. "You can trust me, Stryker. There is nothing I want more than to know you. The real you."

Stryker reached for her and pushed a piece of her wayward hair behind her ear. "All I've been able to think about is holding you again. I couldn't wait to touch you again. It's what's gotten me through the last two weeks."

"Stryker," she whispered, her voice hoarse, and suddenly she had wrapped her arms around him, and he was burying his face against her neck, inhaling her sweet, intoxicating scent. He had dreamed of her, but his dreams couldn't even come close to this.

She pulled back, her eyes searching his face as his thumb rubbed over her cheek. "I want to know you, Stryker. Everything. The good with the bad. I won't judge you."

His ex-wife had wanted to know everything too. And they had shared everything in the beginning. They had been lost in young love and had plunged forward without a care in the world. But he hadn't realized he already had a first love, and that was the Navy SEALs. Soon his missions kept him away from home, and he poured his heart and soul into his work. And soon, young love wasn't enough to hold them together anymore.

But Anya wanted to know everything. And she

committed to him that she wasn't going to judge him. If only she knew…

"I had to get clearance to be able to have this conversation with you. There are rules I have to follow in a situation like this."

She looked at him with wide eyes. "I don't understand."

"I'm a Navy SEAL, Anya. My entire team is composed of Navy SEALs. We were handpicked to come undercover here in Hebbronville to try and take down some forces in Mexico and Central and South America that are threatening us here in the U.S. Our mission is to integrate into the community so we'll be among the first to hear about anything brewing. Hebbronville is ideal because we're close to Laredo and the border, and the chance of information passing through the surrounding communities is high. It is dangerous. And it's dangerous for you to know about us. But you need to know, since someone is obviously reaching out to you too." He stared at her intently, wanting her to understand the gravity of what he was saying.

Anya was staring at him with a mixture of confusion and anxiety. "Is that where you've been? You've been on a-a mission?"

"Yes," he answered bluntly, watching her expression closely.

"Could you have been killed?" There was a slight tremor to her voice.

"Yes. But my team is really, really good. I never feel safer than when I'm working with them." He gave her a slight smile, hoping to relieve some of her anxiety.

"Are all the missions like that? Where you could die?"

"We all take calculated risks with every assignment or mission. But we're careful, Anya. And like I said, the team is good. We're all trained by the best." He brushed her hair back from her face again.

"Do you...do you kill other people?" She looked nervous and worried at the same time.

Stryker's mind flashed to the bloodbath they had left in Mexico. Killing other people was putting it lightly. "Only when necessary," he said softly. "It isn't something I'm proud of, but sometimes we have no choice."

"I could have lost you. Just like that."

"You can't think about it that way. This team is made up of some of the most highly trained Navy SEALs America has."

She drew in a shaky breath. "Those pictures that were sent to me—is that what you were doing? Were you going after whoever had done those horrific things?"

Her eyes searched his face intently. She was smart, but then, he already knew that. "Yes."

"Did you catch them?"

Stryker hesitated. They were all dead except for Jefe. "Most of them," he said reluctantly. "There is more to be done, but for now our mission is complete."

She swallowed hard and laid her head against his chest. He smoothed her long hair. This was what he had needed. This is where he had needed to be, with this woman in his arms.

"We stop the bad guys, Anya. That's what our job is."

"Why couldn't you tell me before now? Why did you keep it secret?"

"I had to get approval from my commanding officer to tell you about everything. We're undercover out here, and have to be very selective about who we bring into our circle. But the situation has changed with you being pulled into it. And I trust you. Because I want to have you in my life, and I know I can't if I don't share everything with you." He looked down into her eyes, pressing a kiss to her forehead.

"I have so many questions. And I have to admit I'm scared."

"Why, bella? What are you scared of?"

"I'm scared for you and your men. But I'd be proud to serve my country backing up a man who's doing what you do. I'd be proud to back you up as a rancher. I don't care. I'm just proud of the man you are."

Stryker felt lighter than he had since he'd seen her last. His heart halted, then lurched forward. He needed her in his life, and she had just made it clear she wanted to be a part of it.

He turned her face up to his and dropped his head, molding his lips to hers. The taste of her was so incredibly sweet, and he finally felt like he was officially home. His kiss was soft and gentle until her tongue licked his lower lip and she moaned lightly.

He angled his mouth over hers and drew a gasp from her as he pulled her body tight against his body. His tongue swept into her mouth and tangled with hers, gliding back and forth, in and out, mimicking what he craved for their bodies to be doing. Her arms slid around his neck and up into his short hair, her fingernails digging into his skin.

It was his turn to moan, and he pulled her closer to him, allowing her to feel exactly what she was doing to him. He had never craved a woman as deeply as he craved Anya at that very moment. But it wasn't fair to her. She needed her sleep, and he had to help Buzz and Phantom put together the debrief to be sent off immediately.

She deserved to be made love to slowly and

passionately, to be treasured as the amazing woman she was. He pulled back from her gently, feathering kisses on her cheeks, then her nose, then each eyelid. "What does your day look like?" His voice was husky, showing the desire that raged within his body.

She sighed heavily. "Busy. I need to make my rounds to the ranches today. Then this afternoon is booked with appointments."

"Can I come see you for lunch?"

She gave him an almost shy smile. "Yes. I would like that very much."

"I have to get back to the ranch and finish drafting our debrief that goes to the admiral today. Otherwise, you probably wouldn't be able to get me to leave your side."

"What makes you think I would want to?"

He groaned and placed a quick, fierce kiss on her lips. "I'll be here around 11:30 to take you to lunch. Does that work?"

"Yes," she whispered breathlessly.

"Good." He smiled, then pressed one more kiss to her lips. "Now go back to bed and get some sleep. I'll see you soon."

As he was climbing back into his truck, the same icy feeling slipped down his spine and a chill spread over him. His eyes scanned the area thoroughly, but there was nothing. He was still on an adrenaline high from their mission. It would pass soon enough.

───

It was early—very early—in the morning, when there was a banging on her back door. Very few people knew that it was the entrance to her private quarters. She had thought only Stryker knew, but after Snap's visit, she realized he also knew where her private quarters were located.

Fear jolted her wide awake. Who would be trying to get her attention this early in the morning? The next thought that crossed her mind brought on an even more intense fear. What if something had happened to Stryker? What if they needed to let her know, or if there was some way possible for her to help him?

Then her heart leapt for another reason altogether. What if it *was* Stryker? What if he'd changed his mind and had come back to spend the rest of the morning with her? Both joy and apprehension made her palms sweat and caused a fine tremor to set in her hands. She rolled over quickly and pulled her gun out of her nightstand drawer and flipped the safety off. She was shaking so hard, she nearly dropped the gun when another loud knock sounded at the door.

Her feet hit the cool tile of the floor as she shoved out of the bed quickly, holding the gun down at her side. She came to the door and paused, her grip tightening on the gun. "Who's there?"

"It's me, Anya. I'm sorry it's so early, but I need to talk to you."

She didn't recognize the voice. Then again, it was so early in the morning, and she didn't know very well what some of the men from Stryker's ranch would sound like at this time of the day. Still, something pulled at her, warning her not to open the door.

"Come back in the morning. During office hours. Now is not the time to talk." She wished her voice

sounded firmer than it did. If it was one of Stryker's
men, there was nothing for her to fear. But if it wasn't…

"It can't wait that long. It's important, Anya. It's
about Stryker."

Anya's hands began to shake harder. Stryker. He had
just come back into her life. If anything had happened
to him… She struggled with her conscience only a few
moments longer before she unlocked the door. Before
she could open it, the door slammed open against her,
sending her staggering backwards.

A man she had never seen before strode toward
her. Terror seemed to grip Anya, and she felt as if she
were watching herself from a distance as she raised the
gun with both hands and pulled the trigger. The smell
of smoke and gunpowder surrounded her, filling her
nostrils, and the man fell to the ground, grunting as the
bullet struck him.

Anya's shakes became so violent, she could barely
hold the gun. *I just shot a man!* The man lay still on the
floor, and her heart pounded in her ears. If she didn't do
something soon, he could very well die. She couldn't be
a murderer. She wouldn't be a murderer.

She needed her phone. She needed to call the sheriff as quickly as possible. Turning, she began to race
toward her nightstand for her phone, only to cry out in
surprise when an arm stretched out and looped around
her leg, yanking her to the ground.

Her knees hit the tile first, and then she pitched forward. She used her hands to break her fall, while one
thing repeated in her head over and over. *Don't let go
of the gun. Don't let go of the gun!* Somehow she was
able to maintain control of the gun. She whirled around,

aiming the gun again, but the man had raised himself to his knees, and with one hard strike with the back of his fist, he knocked the gun from her hands.

He's going to kill me. Icy fingers slid down her back. This couldn't be happening to her. *I have to fight back. I can't give up!*

With a feral cry in the back of her throat, she lunged at him and scraped her nails down his face. He growled in fury and in pain and drew back his arm. She threw her arms up to protect herself and heard a harsh sound. Suddenly she realized it was the man's laughter. But it didn't last long. She heard the man get up, heard him swearing fluently in Spanish.

When she opened her eyes again, he stood above her, pointing her gun at her. There was an odd grin on his face. "You're like a doctor, right?" he asked, his accent thick. How had she not noticed that when he'd spoken through the door? Had he disguised his voice to fool her? That seemed to be the only logical answer. Either that or she was losing her mind.

"I'm a veterinarian," she answered, and damned her voice for trembling.

"Good. Then you can treat the wound you just gave me." He reached down, and she flinched away from him. He chuckled, a sound that made Anya think of a horror film. He grabbed her by her arm and forced her to her feet. Anya did her best not to cry out, though she couldn't prevent the grimace of pain on her face. It felt as if he were going to pull her arm from its socket.

When he had her on her feet, he pulled her close to him. "Now, you're going to fix my wound, and you're going to be a good girl the entire time, aren't you?"

She glared at him. "I'm not a girl," she spat, looking at him with disgust.

His hand tightened around her arm, and he sneered at her. "You're my girl right now. And you'll do as I say. Do you understand me?"

She was silent until he shook her. "Yes, I understand," she growled.

A slow smile spread across his face. "I can see why he likes you. Your personality is very…appealing."

Anya wanted to spit on him. If it weren't for the ugly sneer on his face, the man might be thought of as attractive. With the fine features of his Spanish ancestry and a well-built body that he obviously worked hard to maintain, he could be considered quite the catch by many women. But his light hazel eyes were soulless, only revealing a deep-seated cruelty that made Anya's stomach cramp in fear.

"I need to grab my supplies," she said, attempting to turn from him, but his tight grip on her arm stopped her from moving. She looked back at him with exasperation. "I need to—"

"I'll go with you," he said firmly. "Lead the way, Anya."

She hated the sound of her name on his lips. But with no other choice, she turned slowly and led him into her clinic, where she gathered gauze and a needle and thread and antiseptic. She hesitated for a few moments. "Did the bullet go all the way through?"

"Fortunately for you, yes. So you won't need to dig around to try and find it. I'm sure you were looking forward to stabbing me with the instrument."

The thought had crossed her mind. How could he have known? She swallowed hard and tried to gain

control over her tremors. She needed to think. She had
to get away from him, but she didn't know how. At the
moment, he held the upper hand. But maybe she could
change that. She needed to change that. Because she had
to warn Stryker there was a madman in town.

Chapter 25

SHE MOVED TOWARD ANOTHER DRAWER WHERE SHE KEPT her sedatives and anesthesia. Just a small dose of horse sedative would be enough to knock him down. And then she would race to the only place she knew was safe: Stryker's ranch.

He yanked on her arm, pulling her away from the drawer. "What are you getting?"

"Local anesthesia," she lied. "It will numb the area that I'm going to need to treat."

"Cute. Nice try, but I don't think so, *Doctor*. I don't need you sticking any needles in me."

"It's going to be incredibly painful."

"Ah, sympathy from the bitch comes a little late. You already shot me, don't you remember? If you were worried about me being in pain, you should have thought of that sooner." He pulled her back toward her private quarters. She'd missed her chance.

He sat sideways on the bed and eyed her from her sleep-mussed hair to her bright pink toenails, and a slight smile curled his lips. Anya thought she was going to be sick.

"What are you waiting for, Doctor? You have a patient to tend to. And I expect you to be gentle."

She felt her lip curling in revulsion at him, but she slowly moved closer to him. "I'll need you to remove your shirt." She waited as he shed his shirt, clasping her hands together to try to stop her tremors. "What do you want with me?" She kept her face impassive as she asked the question. He probably already knew she was terrified, and she imagined he was getting great joy from it. But she didn't want to give him any more satisfaction than she could control.

He looked at her, again with the same sickening smile. "There are many things I could want with you, girl. What do you think I want with you?"

"I honestly have no idea. I don't carry much cash—"

His bitter laugh caused chills to slide down her back. The man was evil. And there was definitely something missing upstairs. "Do I really strike you as a petty thief? What gives you the impression I need money?"

"I-I don't know. What else could you want?"

"Answers. Revenge. Justice."

Anya poured antiseptic on his wound, and he hissed in pain. The antiseptic hadn't been needed, but she had hoped it would be uncomfortable enough he would lose his grip on the gun. Unfortunately, her plan failed. She blotted at the wound with bits of gauze, and the fabric quickly soaked with blood. Maybe he would lose enough blood that he would weaken and she could overpower him. She glanced up at him and was startled to find him watching her intently as if he could read her thoughts.

"I can hold pressure to the front while you treat the back," he said harshly, grabbing a few of the gauze pads and pressing them tightly against his wound.

Swallowing hard, she focused on his back. *Answers. Revenge. Justice.* What did he mean? How could she be involved in anything like that? She pressed the gauze against his back where the round had exited and caused the most damage.

She paused to thread the needle and realized her hands were shaking so badly, she wasn't going to be able to do it. She closed her eyes and drew a deep breath through her nose, willing her hands to be still long enough that she could get the thread through the needle. She held her hands in her lap, and with deep concentration, she was finally able to do it.

She didn't warn him before she pressed the needle through his flesh. "Damn it, puta! A little warning would be appreciated."

"You didn't warn me before you smashed into my home," she snapped back at him, then bit her lip, remembering he held the gun. What did he want? *Answers. Revenge. Justice.* Stryker.

Anya's stomach clenched. That was the only possible answer to all of this. It had to do with something Stryker was involved in. Could it be the last assignment he had just completed? That explained why he'd mentioned Stryker's name at the door. He'd known she had some form of relationship with him. To what extent, she didn't know.

If this man was connected to the people who'd committed the horrific crimes she'd seen in the photographs, he would have the ability to do many gruesome things. Hadn't Stryker mentioned they hadn't caught everyone? She felt bile rise in her throat. That had to be the connection. He was out for revenge for what Stryker's team had done to his crew in Mexico.

She finished his stitches and realized she needed scissors to cut the thread. It would be the perfect weapon.

"I need to grab my scissors to cut the thread," she said casually, beginning to slide off the bed, but his arm snaked out and grabbed her around the waist, hauling her painfully close to his body.

"Do you think I'm stupid?" He was shaking his head at her. "Use your teeth."

"My teeth? To cut the thread?" She was incredulous.

"Yes. It's how it's been done around the world for centuries. There's no way I'm putting a weapon in your hands. Now, finish your damn job."

Anya leaned down and took the thread in her lips and tugged at it until it snapped off. She shuddered and wiped her tongue with a piece of gauze. He laughed at her, then turned farther so she could easily access the entry wound.

Her aim had been good. Just not good enough. The bullet had entered just a couple of inches above his heart. If only her shooting had been more accurate. The blood flow had reduced significantly, making it easier for her to stitch the wound closed. Much to her relief, she didn't need to "cut" the thread again. She pressed fresh gauze to his front and back, then grabbed the surgical tape she had and secured the fabric in place.

"We're done," she said, sitting back as far away from him as she could on the bed.

He turned to face her more fully, and the corners of his mouth lifted again in that twisted smile that made her stomach churn. "Oh no, girl. We're just getting started."

"What I'm asking you isn't difficult. I know you're familiar with this man: Stryker. I watched him come in here for a short time in the middle of the night. Also, you wouldn't have let me in if it hadn't been for me mentioning his name earlier. So, either you know him, or you *really* know him. Either way plays well for me. So, who is he?"

"I've already told you. He's a rancher. He was in the rodeo circuit before now—"

"Let's try something different," he growled. "Why don't you tell me about the men Stryker works with. How many of them are there? Do you know anything about them?"

"Go to hell." She readied herself again. It was easier to get slapped around by him than to face his onslaught of questions.

Instead, he grabbed ahold of her hair and yanked her head backwards, holding a blade at her throat, a blade she hadn't noticed before. This was it. This was how she was going to die. Her heart thundered. Was it going to hurt?

"No wonder he likes you. You're the same as him. Arrogant and overconfident. Do you think I won't kill you? Do you think he will protect you? No one can protect you now. You belong to me."

"I belong to nobody. You have me confused with someone else. I never belonged to him either." The comment was far from the truth. *I belonged to him the moment I gave him my heart.*

"You need to tell me the truth, girl. Your answers about him could save his life. And possibly your own."

Save Stryker's life? Good grief, what has this madman done? Is he holding Stryker captive somewhere? Did he grab him when he left my clinic only a couple of hours ago? How can my answers save him? "I've told you everything I know. If there was something more I could tell you, I wouldn't. You don't even hold a candle to Stryker."

Anger flashed in his eyes once again. "Why don't you tell me where you hid the flash drive he gave you earlier today? Show me where you hid it."

"Hid *what*? Stryker didn't give me anything."

"There are few reasons a man gets involved with a woman. The sex is good"—he eyed her up and down— "she is rich and he's milking her for every dime she has, which obviously isn't the case here, *or* he's using her for something. The first could be true, but if he was here for sex with you this morning, you must not be very satisfied because he left so quickly. The second we've already decided isn't true. That leaves us with the third as the most likely."

"You're disgusting. I have no idea what you're talking about. There is nothing that he gave me. And your assumption about a man's relationship with a woman is preposterous. You've probably never had a decent relationship with a woman in your life."

"Very well. Let's just hope he doesn't feel the same about you. Otherwise, you'll be left to die a very, very painful death."

———

Lunchtime hadn't come anywhere near early enough for Stryker. When he'd gotten back home, he'd found Buzz already working on the report to send to Admiral Haslett and Phantom jotting down notes to help jog his memory as he read through the report in case they needed to add anything. While all three of them were running on zero sleep, they knew there was a critical time period to pull out information from memory, and they had to take advantage of it while they could.

Once Buzz was done preparing the report, they would then all take a look at it to make sure nothing was missing. It was a failproof method they'd used for handling debriefings for years, and Stryker was grateful for the way his team worked so seamlessly together, listening and probing where appropriate.

Finally, they were able to get the document completed, all of them agreed to it, and Buzz uploaded it to a secure drive for Admiral Haslett. And now, lunchtime had rolled around, and he was on his way to see Anya. Her sweet words still floated through his mind. *I love you.* Oh, how he prayed that she still did. Because he had come to the shocking realization that he couldn't make it without her. He needed her in his life, no matter what.

He'd told her a great deal more than he had originally planned early that morning. But he hadn't wanted to keep anything from her anymore. For her safety, he was going to need to convince her to move out to the ranch. She could still be a veterinarian. That was part of who she was. But it would be too dangerous for her to be on her own. He knew she wanted to expand her clinic. If they could just hire someone else to assist her, someone that he knew could protect her...

He was getting ahead of himself. He first needed to get her to forgive him for keeping his life secret from her. And then he needed to convince her he was still a man worthy of her love. *Am I worthy of her love? Wouldn't she be better off if I wasn't in her life at all?*

No. I'll give her everything her heart could ever desire.
I'll hold her every night and drive her nightmares away.
But can I give her my heart?

Stryker hadn't given much thought to his former wife in the past few weeks. Instead, he'd been obsessed with Anya. His life before Anya seemed insignificant and lacking. He knew Anya was nothing like his ex. Anya had her own life and was independent, almost to a fault. He didn't need to worry about her telling him to leave the navy to devote more time to her. If anything, he may be asking her to cut back her hours at the clinic so he could have more time with her.

The thought brought a smile to his lips. He doubted she would view that request favorably. He could just see her reaction—fists on her hips, one foot tapping, her lips pursed in disapproval. He already knew her better than he knew himself. And he needed to bury his face against her neck and breathe in her heady scent and know there was still good in the world.

It was close to eleven thirty in the morning by the time he pulled up to the clinic. He knew she was probably already back from her rounds at the ranches and open for business and went to the front door, not surprised when it swung open for him. But everything changed as soon as he stepped inside.

Immediately he drew his gun from where he kept it tucked safely at his side and calmed his breathing, taking into account everything around him. File cabinets had been dumped on their sides, with papers spilled all over the floor. The main computer monitor in the reception area had been tossed to the floor, and he carefully stepped around it to avoid the crunch of the glass beneath his feet. He knew the business wasn't large enough to afford a receptionist, so he wasn't surprised to find no one there.

He entered her treatment room cautiously, checking behind the door and in each corner before moving farther in. The medicine cabinet and drawers stood open, and it was obvious from the many vacant spaces that medication had been taken. Was this a robbery? Had someone hit her clinic to get drugs? It didn't make any sense, though. A person had to be very desperate to take medication from a veterinarian.

He eased his way through the room slowly, finding more broken glass. That was when he noticed the bright blotches of red on the floor. He didn't have to check to know what the substance was. He'd seen it often enough. A cold sweat broke out on his body. Was it Anya's blood?

He shifted his attention to her private quarters, easing through the door that separated the room from the rest of the clinic. Goose bumps covered his entire body and the hair on the back of his neck stood on end.

Her bed had been slashed with a knife. Her desk was turned upside down, with the drawers hanging out and papers strewn everywhere. Someone had been searching for something. And then, he saw, beneath one scattered pile of papers, a large pool of blood. *Let her be okay*.

He walked farther into the room, scanning every inch carefully, keeping his gun raised, prepared for anything. He rounded her bed, hoping to find her hiding on the other side, hoping to find her shaken but safe. But there was nothing.

Finally, he entered her bathroom, and when he

yanked back the shower curtain, he froze and icy fingers clutched at his chest. *Turn over the flash drive or she dies.* The words scrawled across the bathroom tiles were written in blood.

Stryker's hands trembled as he lowered his gun. Despite their best efforts, someone in the cartel had survived. Either that, or they were dealing with the person in the shadows who was orchestrating the cartel's movements, and that was even more terrifying. But Stryker made a promise to himself in that very moment. Whoever hurt his Anya would die slowly and painfully. By his hands.

It was inevitable the sheriff would be called out. When her first client showed up and saw the disaster of the place, he had called the sheriff. By then, Stryker was observing everything from a distance. He had combed through the entire clinic, but there was nothing to show what had happened to Anya, other than the fact that she was gone, a lot of medication was missing, and there was a lot of fucking blood all over the place. He'd been able to clear the writing on the wall with a bottle of Clorox and some hard scrubbing. He knew it would leave a forensics team puzzled and scratching their heads, but he couldn't risk having such a note discovered.

The sheriff had a better chance of identifying where the blood had come from, of identifying fingerprints, and of trying to piece together what had happened. Stryker had been able to collect samples and was going to have them expedited to the navy crime lab in Corpus. It would help them to take care of things, and it would be a helluva lot faster than what the sheriff in this tiny town would be able to pull together.

As soon as he had seen the message on the wall, Stryker had contacted Admiral Haslett. His CO needed to know that things had gone seriously sideways. Fortunately, Haslett had answered himself.

They had already discovered there was a problem within Admiral Haslett's ranks somewhere. The extent of it was beyond him. He was driving himself mad trying to think of who had the power to pull off this type of kidnapping. It was obvious it was someone with ties to the cartel. Whether that person was in the navy or not was a question that disturbed him a great deal.

His next call was to his team. He hated waking Buzz, but he needed his expertise. He briefly filled him in and asked Buzz to gather the team and start trying to find any information that could point them in the right direction.

A crowd had gathered to watch, and for the true busy-bodies of the town, it couldn't get any juicier. There was a crime scene, and the area's veterinarian was missing. Of course, her clients were genuinely concerned for her and were checking in periodically to find out if there were any updates.

Finally, realizing that he wasn't doing Anya any good by hovering around, he left, speeding back to the ranch. The heat of the day beat down on his back as he walked up to the ranch house. Now, more than ever, he needed his team. He had never felt so out of control in his life. Fuck, he didn't even know where this madman wanted him to drop off the drive. How was he supposed to save her when the man who'd taken her clearly wasn't operating with a full deck?

He could hear the men in the dining room. His gut clenched as he walked toward the room. Had they been able to uncover any information? If so, why hadn't they contacted him yet? What if what they had uncovered wasn't something they wanted to tell him over the phone?

Stryker looked around at the men that were his family and fought the anger and fear that raged within him. "The sheriff's at her place, but they have no leads. Anything here?"

Buzz shook his head. "Not yet. I'm combing through satellite imaging and anything else I can get my hands on to see if I can pick up anything."

Phantom stood and approached him. "We're here for you, brother. We're going to catch the bastard who did this."

Stryker nodded even though his gut churned with apprehension. "I've been giving it a lot of thought. I think it's Jefe who took her."

Chapter 26

ANYA HAD REMAINED STRONG. SHE DIDN'T CRY AND SHE didn't plead for any mercy, which only seemed to infuriate the man. He used duct tape to tape her hands together behind her back, then placed some over her mouth. She had glared at him furiously, but it did her little good.

He'd tossed her over his shoulder and hauled her out to his SUV. To her shock, he placed a black hood over her head. She heard him loading things in the back of the SUV and shivered when the back door slammed shut.

He started the SUV, and suddenly they were moving. They seemed to be driving around forever, and, even though her nerves were fried, the darkness of the hood and the rocking of the vehicle lulled her exhausted body into a restless sleep.

Anya came to with a rush of adrenaline and a barely suppressed scream. Her head was throbbing, and it was a struggle to lift it, but she did so, slowly. The pounding behind her eye sockets increased, and she tried to work the muscles in her jaw.

"Finally back to play?"

That voice…that horrible voice with the heavy accent was back. And very close to her ear. She tried to swing her arm to bat him away, only to find her hands were bound to something. She forced her eyes open.

Daylight struck her in the face, and she winced at the

intensity of the brightness. Judging from the direction of the light, it was past noon, at least that much she could tell. How far past noon she wasn't certain.

She tried to scream around the duct tape over her mouth and make as much noise as she could.

"Tsk, tsk, tsk." The madman laughed at her. "No one can hear you for miles. So I suppose we don't need this anymore." He ripped the tape off her mouth, and she couldn't help but cry out at the pain.

He came into focus slowly as she tasted blood on her torn lip. "Help!" she screamed. "Someone, please! Help me!"

He stood by watching her, a satisfied grin on his face, and she shuddered. For him to be so smug and confident, there truly must be no one around to hear her. "Where have you taken me?" she demanded.

He leaned down in her face, and she realized he had his knife out again. "Far, far away. Which isn't that far away in this shitty little town."

He had just given away a valuable clue, even though he hadn't realized it. He'd revealed that they were still in town, though out of earshot of anyone. Which left a million possibilities. Her mind raced.

"So, what do you plan to do with me?" she demanded. "You've brought me out here so no one can hear me scream. Why? I've already proven to you that I have nothing to offer you."

His eyes traveled down to the lace of her nightshirt, and he slid the knife underneath it, slashing one of the straps, allowing the blouse to flutter open, revealing the top of her left breast. "Oh, I wouldn't say we've exhausted all possibilities."

"You're a sick, perverted bastard. I doubt you can even get it up."

He jerked his hand back, and when she flinched, she felt her world momentarily tip, then right itself again. Confused, she looked down and realized he'd taped her securely in a chair that he had found in this...this warehouse? Was that where they were? It had to be one of the old warehouses located along the old train line.

"Such a filthy mouth for such a beautiful girl," he said softly. "Now, I thought we had a discussion earlier where we agreed you were going to be my good girl. Do you remember that conversation?" He looked at her with concerned eyes, as if he were talking to a child.

"I remember. And I'm not a girl, and I will never be yours."

"Oh, such a pity. You have far too much anger for one so young. If you were mine, I would never let you feel the pain you are going through now. But because you fight me... Well, it is only worse for you in the long run."

"Who are you? Why are you even here?"

"Ah. How rude of me not to introduce myself. My name is Benicio Davila. Until very recently I ran one of the biggest drug cartels in Nuevo Laredo. But, then, for some reason, your *rancher* friend and his associates decided to take me down. They think they've destroyed me. They know so little."

"You wouldn't be here if they didn't do at least some damage, and for that, I'm grateful. The drug trade is illegal and must come to an end one way or another."

Rage crossed his face, and he gripped her chin tightly between his thumb and forefinger, his face just inches from hers. "You would think that, puta. But it is my drug cartel that is giving so many young men a future. They have jobs, responsibilities, power. All the things a mother could ever want for her son."

"And all the death? All the people who overdose on your drugs? What of them? What about their grieving parents? What about the parents of the men you murder?"

"Necessary business. If your country would only see the fruitlessness of the war on drugs, there would be a lot less death, trust me. But as long as they continue to be fools like you…" He squeezed her jaw hard one last time and then released her.

Anya decided that if she could keep him talking, she could buy some time to come up with an escape plan. "For some reason, I get the impression that you like talking. About yourself, your plans, your gang—"

"Cartel. I run a drug cartel, puta. Very different than a mere gang."

Anya shrugged with indifference. "Whatever you say."

"Yes, it is. Whatever I say. That's what you need to remember right now. Whatever I say is what you listen to. Do you understand me?"

She didn't know what was prompting her to continue testing him. She was actually grateful for the tape at the moment because it hid how badly she was trembling. She couldn't let him know he frightened her. She had to keep up the false bravado as long as possible.

"There actually is something I'm looking forward to more than putting you through hell," he said, his face close enough to hers that she could smell his breath and was certain she smelled alcohol.

"What? What is it you expect?"

"I expect to torture and kill your boyfriend…your

rancher…and all his fucking partners. I'll let him watch me torture you and ruin you first, so he can watch me destroy something that he cares about the way he destroyed something I cared about. Then I'll kill them all."

"Walk us through everything. Starting with this morning." They sat in the communications conference room, everyone watching Stryker anxiously.

Stryker looked down at his clasped hands, trying to think of how to answer Brusco's request. His mind was a jumble of things at the moment. All he could think about was how good she smelled, of how warm her embrace had been, how happy he'd been when he had left her, knowing that he was going back to her within a few short hours.

And then there had been fear. Immense, overwhelming fear.

Icy fingers tickled his spine, triggering a memory. "When I pulled up to her place this morning, something felt wrong. Something felt off."

"Wrong how? What was off?" Snap fired questions at him. Santo smacked Snap on the shoulder, and Snap turned to him, a bewildered look on his face. "What the fuck, man?"

"Let him talk," Santo said calmly. "Give him a chance to say what he needs to say before you hit him with your fifty million questions."

Snap opened his mouth as if he were going to protest, but the look from Santo must have been strong enough to make a difference. Stryker wanted to thank Santo, but he couldn't find the strength in his voice at the moment. Anya trusted him and believed in him. He had asked for her trust, and she had given it to him in spite of everything he'd put her through. She'd given him her heart, and she'd given him more than he could ever have asked for. And now she was paying the price for it.

"I don't know. I thought it was just the adrenaline from the mission. But now I wonder…" he finally said, his voice thick with emotions and frustration.

"Shit," Buzz said softly. "The fucker must have followed us out of Nuevo Laredo."

"No." Stryker shook his head. "I was watching our six the entire time. There wasn't a single car that followed us from Nuevo Laredo or any point in between."

"Then how did he know to come here? And who is he? We took down all the lieutenants and sicarios. There shouldn't be anyone left." Phantom's face was contorted with frustration.

"I counted all of them that were there last night. It added up to the exact number we were targeting," Buzz said softly.

"Except Jefe." Stryker lifted his eyes to look at the team and met expressions of confusion. "Look, Buzz, Phantom, you saw the same thing I did. Benicio was talking to someone in that camera. Someone had to receive that message."

"Even so, he wouldn't know where we're located. He wouldn't know…" Buzz's voice died away, and then he began to shake his head, as if he didn't want to believe what he was thinking.

"Speak up, Buzz," Brusco said. "It's not going to help any of us if you retreat into that nerd brain of yours."

Buzz cast Brusco a go-to-hell look, then focused on Stryker. "Vidal," he said softly.

"You think Vidal is behind all of this? The man didn't strike me as smart enough even to know how to cross the border, let alone find us." Phantom scowled.

"I agree," Stryker said, shaking his head. "Vidal didn't have the mental capabilities to pull off something like this."

"I'm not saying he did. But someone got to him. How did Hector know we weren't who we said we were? He got a phone call right before everything went to hell. Someone had found out information about us. It was damning information, and made our stories, our carefully crafted backgrounds, *everything*, worthless. Who would have had that kind of information?"

"The navy, for one," Stryker replied in a monotone.

"Okay, that's obvious, but let's just pray for one moment that we haven't been compromised that severely. Who else knew everything about us, had our dossiers, and would have access to the cartel?"

"Vidal. And we all had suspicions about him." Phantom was listening intently to Buzz.

"But why would he turn on us? There's no reason for him to." Stryker was shaking his head. It still didn't add up. "And exactly who did he betray us to? Like Buzz already said, every head was accounted for, other than my mysterious Jefe, and none of you seem to believe he even exists."

"That's not true, Stryker. We believe you. We just don't know who he could be. And that puts us in an even more difficult position." Snap glanced around at the group, looking for consensus.

"You seem to think there's someone operating at a higher level, and that this person is involved in more than just the drug cartel." Buzz frowned.

"That's exactly what I think," Stryker said, his voice adamant. "Even if it was one guy attached to the cartel directly, I think there's a strong possibility someone is out there coordinating things between the cartels and other entities. And I believe that person has contacts within the navy, if not directly into the U.S. government."

"Those are some really big allegations you're making," Phantom said in a room that had suddenly gone so silent, the only sound was the click of the air conditioner turning on.

"You guys weren't with me to witness the total clusterfuck at the naval offices over the redacted file we received when we first started the mission. We know the admiral has launched an investigation. What that tells me is that someone with the appropriate clearance wanted to make sure we were headed into Mexico without the latest, most accurate data."

The men exchanged glances around the dining room table. "I think this will be a deeper question to dive into once we have Anya back safely. But, for right now, she's our number one priority," Buzz said, though his expression was grim.

"Let's go back to the beginning. So, you felt like you were being watched this morning." Snap led him off in the dialogue once more.

"Yes. But I looked around, and I couldn't see anything out of the ordinary. The town was fast asleep. It was too early for any cars to be on the road, and from what I could tell, there was no one within the immediate vicinity. I should have looked closer. I should have trusted my gut." Stryker pounded his fist on the table.

"None of that is going to help her now. You went inside to be with her. Was there anything unusual then?" Phantom asked.

"No. Yes! She had a handgun."

"Anya? Our little Anya?" Santo asked in astonishment.

"She grew up on a ranch, and she's a native Texan," Stryker said, feeling a little bit of pride that Anya was his woman. "It's practically in her blood."

Stryker flexed and stretched his hands slowly, curling them into fists. He was angrier with himself than with anyone else at the moment. "Her place was pristine as usual. She was groggy, but came fully awake after she saw it was me. I was there for about fifteen minutes, and then I asked her if I could come back for lunch. When I left, I had the same feeling—as if something was off."

"What time was it that you left?" Buzz asked.

"Twenty or thirty past zero four hundred hours… right in between there."

"And what time was it that you got to her place later today?"

"Eleven thirty hours."

"That means whoever took her could have over a seven-hour lead on us by now. Would he take her into Mexico?" Santo asked.

The thought made Stryker sick to his stomach, but he immediately dashed the idea from his mind. "No. Whoever did this knows about the flash drive that Buzz took and wants it back as quickly as possible. He wouldn't risk taking her to Mexico and asking us to follow him."

"You got that from the message you found on the shower wall, right?" Phantom asked.

Stryker pulled out his phone and opened the photos folder. He passed his phone around, and each man frowned grimly as they looked at the picture. "Is that…?"

"Blood? Yeah, Snap, it is. There was a whole puddle of it on the floor near her bed. And it trailed through the clinic. Also, a lot of her medicine and supplies were missing. Scroll through the pictures. I documented everything. I even got samples of the blood and hair off her brush to run through DNA testing if we decide we can trust the naval labs."

"Let's hold off on all that for right now. I'm still running searches from all the surrounding cameras, and even those coming across the border to help us narrow down the search. Was there anything indicating where to take the flash drive or directions of any sort?" Buzz's fingers were already twitching, ready to go back to his computer keyboard.

"No. Which gives me hope. He wouldn't have taken her with that threat if he intended to kill her, right? He has to have something to negotiate with." Stryker clasped his hands together under the table, silently praying for her safety. She had to make it home to him. He couldn't lose her after finally realizing he was in love with her.

Chapter 27

"THE LOVELY LITTLE TOWN OF HEBBRONVILLE HASN'T jumped forward into modern times," Buzz said as his hands flew across the keyboard. "There are only a few security cameras I can tap into, and they're located at the grocery store, Ritz Feed Store, and Extreme Ranches, Inc. None of those are anywhere near Anya's clinic."

"What about any vehicles that passed Extreme Ranches? Anya's clinic is just farther down Smith Avenue from there." Stryker leaned over Buzz's shoulder to get a look at the surveillance videos.

Buzz hesitated, his fingers poised over the keyboard as he cast an annoyed look at Stryker. "Personal space, man. I needs me my personal space."

Stryker frowned down at him. "You don't get personal space, sailor, not when—"

"All right you two lovebirds, break it up." Snap stepped into the room and handed out sandwiches. "Everyone knows how testy Buzz is around his toys. Let's just give him his space and let him work his magic."

Stryker raised his hands in acceptance and stepped back, though he still glowered at the back of Buzz's head. "Give me something good to work with, Buzz. Give me something good."

"Unfortunately, none of the cameras are pointed out toward the streets. They're all focused on the doors of the establishments, which makes sense if you're trying to keep the bad guys from getting in."

"But?" Stryker asked, apprehension clawing at his throat. He needed answers. He needed solutions. He needed Anya.

"But, our pals at the border patrol may have come through for us."

"Really? Never would have thought that would pan out... How did you make that happen?"

"Well, I didn't really ask them for their help. I just hacked into their database and pulled up footage of the last twenty-four hours of people crossing the border in Nuevo Laredo. You're not going to believe who popped up on one of the screens."

"Don't keep us in suspense, Buzz. Stryker's ready to put his foot up your ass already." Snap's words were muffled around a mouthful of sandwich.

"I'm pulling it up right...now." An image popped up and flashed a few times before it became a semi-steady, pulsating picture of a face.

"What the fuck?" Phantom nearly spat out his food, but instead, swallowed it whole without chewing. "How is that even possible?"

Stryker's blood ran cold. "It's not possible. We need to think back through everything that happened last night, Buzz, Phantom. Something has gone terribly wrong."

They all stared at the images Buzz had pulled up and had flickering on the various screens. Sliding across the border in a Land Rover was none other than Benicio Davila.

~~~

Anya felt ill. The last meal she'd eaten was breakfast the day before. Then her day had just become too hectic and she'd tumbled into bed exhausted.

Now, she sat in front of a madman who was so bent on his own agenda that he was clueless to the world around him. Or, so she thought. He had vanished for a short time, and in that period she had worked frantically to free her hands from the binds of the tape. It had only served to tighten them further.

She decided to focus on her surroundings, trying to identify exactly where she was. The familiar scent of corn and oats kept teasing her nose, so she thought it must be the old feed mill. She looked around the large, vacant room with old equipment piled in a corner. The doors that used to open directly to the train were closed. The glass windows at the top of the building were long gone or left in jagged ridges from where kids had chucked rocks or fired BB guns, or worse, at the windowpanes.

No one ever came to this area unless they were looking for trouble. Or to cause trouble. It was frequently where teens hooked up to make out on weekends, or to share a few joints, or just to escape. But it wasn't the weekend, and she was in serious trouble.

The heat was climbing, and sweat rolled between her breasts and down her back. Yet her body felt cold and numb.

She would give anything for some water. The idea of the cool liquid sliding down her throat made her close her eyes with a delicious daydream of the fresh beverage that could coat her parched tongue.

A sudden noise jolted her out of her daydream. Had she fallen asleep? She glanced up at the sun and realized it hadn't moved far since she'd closed her eyes. She may have dozed off, though. She felt confused and lost and…frightened. She wanted Stryker desperately.

She wanted his arms around her, telling her everything was okay. But more than anything, she wanted him safe.

"What kind of fucking whore are you? You fall asleep as soon as I'm gone? You disgust me."

He laughed. She wished she could kick him in the balls and make his laugh turn into a cry of pain. How she hated his laugh. How she hated his face. She never thought she could feel such anger toward another human being in her life. But he posed a direct threat to Stryker. She'd be damned if she ever let him hurt the man she loved.

"I still have use for you, stupid puta. I just need your thumb…" His words broke off into more laughter. "Did you really think you could escape me? You learned your lesson, didn't you, puta?"

"You're the only bitch here." She spit in his face, using what little moisture she was able to work into her mouth. He drew back his hand as though to strike her again, but he drew in a deep shuddering breath, and gradually lowered his arm. "You're lucky I'm in a generous mood right now. I just want your thumb. Don't make it so that I have to cut it off you."

Anya tried to suppress the shudder that ran through her, but she knew from his smile, she wasn't completely successful. She knew he was the type of man who would have no problem cutting off her thumb and would probably even enjoy it. He pulled her phone out of his pocket, and she stared at it in confusion, before it suddenly dawned on her what he was about to do.

He grabbed her thumb and pressed it to the phone, unlocking it. After several silent moments, he smiled brightly. "Tsk, tsk, tsk," he said, shaking his head at her.

"How terribly unoriginal. I would have thought you would have programmed him as 'lover' or 'boy toy.' But instead, you just put him under his name. You disappoint me."

"You disgust me."

He hit the speed dial button for Stryker and put the phone on speaker so she could hear it ringing. There was a click on the other end of the line, but there was no greeting. "I assume I've reached the infamous Stryker," Benicio said into the phone.

"And who am I speaking with?" Stryker's deep voice came across the line, and Anya wanted to cry at the sound.

"Let's just say it is the man in control."

"His name is Benicio Davila! He's from the drug—"

"Ah. Benicio. I've heard so much about you."

"This little puta you've been with doesn't have any discipline. But I'll fix that for you. It just may take more time than I had planned."

"What is it, exactly, that you have planned? Because you aren't really acting like a rational man right now."

"You're not in a position to talk, Stryker. I'm the one in power right now."

"You only have the woman. I have the drive you so desperately want. How are you going to rebuild your empire without this?"

"I have the programmer ready to do as I bid when I return to Mexico. The drive only gives us a starting point. What your men destroyed in Mexico was far more valuable. So, you see, the drive is just a bonus at this point. Knowing you've suffered because of this woman's death will be the true reward."

Anya choked. She had to stop Stryker from trying to save her. Benicio had a streak of evil in him a mile wide.

They couldn't stop him. Not even if all of the men from the ranch came to help. She didn't want them to be hurt by this one man's madness.

"Put her on the phone for me." Stryker's voice didn't leave room for discussion.

"She's not really in a position to talk right now," Benicio said, looking over at Anya, whose head was hanging to the side, but she sat up straighter and blinked back her tears.

"Unless I talk to her directly, I'll not be able to give you whatever it is you want."

"I thought I'd already made it clear what I want from you. Do I need to repeat myself?"

"Put her on the phone."

A muscle twitched in Benicio's jaw, then he held the phone out toward Anya. She couldn't stop the tears that slid down her cheeks. "Stryker," she said with as firm a voice as she could muster.

"Anya. How badly are you hurt?"

"I'm fine, Stryker, there is no need for you to—"

"Now you've had your chance to talk to her. I expect you to deliver on my request. Bring the drive to the old mill facility near the abandoned tracks within thirty minutes. I suspect you'll try to bring those men of yours along, but that is pointless. I can see far around me and will be able to take them out long before they get me in their sights. You have thirty minutes starting now."

"We should storm the place."

"While I appreciate your enthusiasm, Snap, Benicio

is right. As soon as he sees us coming, he'll draw a bead on us. It's best for you to stay back."

"And let you take the fall for all of us? We're going to back you up, Stryker; we just have to make a plan for how all of this is going down."

Stryker ran a hand through his hair and paced the small room. The bastard had to be stopped. But his team was right. If he went in there alone, neither he nor Anya would make it out alive.

"Buzz, can you pull up a detailed map of the town?"

"I can do you one better. I can pull up a live satellite image of the town." Buzz's fingers flew across the keyboard, and within seconds, they were watching him zoom in on the little town they now thought of as home.

"He said the old mill, right? What would that look like?" Buzz asked, and a couple of the men chuckled.

"City boy, through and through," Phantom muttered as he looked at the images Buzz had pulled up.

"Yeah, well, this 'city boy' is helping your happy asses, so just can it right now."

There were a few more chuckles in the room, then silence as the men studied the images. They were all tense, and the lighthearted banter helped ease some of the nervous energy that gripped the room.

"There." Stryker pointed at a building on the edge of town near the abandoned railroad tracks. "It's the perfect size for a feed mill, and its location makes sense. But there are very few buildings around there. Team, this is going to be virtually impossible."

Phantom slapped Stryker on the back. "We're not known for taking the easy jobs, brother."

Stryker looked at the guys, knowing how fortunate

he was. These men were his brothers in more than arms. They were his family. And they were ready and willing to help him save the woman he loved.

"All right, Phantom, we have ten minutes to make a plan and gather gear."

"Not a problem." Phantom nodded firmly. "She's going to be okay."

Stryker looked each one of them in the eye, hoping to convey how much he appreciated all they were doing for him. "Then we roll out."

"Hoo-yah!"

━━━━

"You're not going to get what you want. You never will. He's too smart for you." The wise thing for her to do would be to say nothing. But, for some reason, she couldn't control herself. All she wanted was to point out to the man that he was inferior to everyone…especially Stryker.

Because she knew Stryker was coming. She felt it in her bones. She knew beyond a doubt that he was going to come for her, and that he was going to try to save her. But Benicio had the upper hand. He had pulled her to the second-floor landing of the building. From his vantage point, he would be able to hit Stryker as soon as he entered the building.

She had to do something to protect Stryker. He would be walking into certain death if she didn't do something to warn him. Benicio had turned his back on her and was pacing back and forth, looking at his watch every few seconds. She ground her teeth together. This drive they were talking about meant far more to him than he had revealed. In fact, he was desperate for it. That was the angle she was going to have to play with him.

"Benicio," she said, attempting to make her voice sound as defeated as possible. "Benicio, please, I can't take anymore."

Benicio spun on his heel and faced her. At first she thought he had sunk so far into his madness that he wasn't even aware of what he was doing. But then, his eyes focused on her and a slow, animalistic smile came to his face. "So, you are finally cracking, eh, my ice queen? Tell me… What is it you can't take anymore?" He leaned down in her face.

"Please, I'm just so thirsty, and tired…"

"That's it, puta? You're tired and you're thirsty?"

"And…and I'm scared. I don't want to do this anymore. I'm ready to tell you everything I can."

"It's a little late for that. I'm about to have all my answers delivered to me."

"No. You're not. Stryker gave me the drive when he came and saw me this morning."

His look of triumph faded slowly and an expression of anger crept into his features. "What? Tell me the truth, you fucking whore! I destroyed your clinic looking for that flash drive. It wasn't there."

"You didn't know where to look. I saw you take boxes of my medications. I hid the drive in one of the medicine bottles."

"You couldn't have. There's no way you had time."

"You came into my clinic a couple of hours after he left. I had plenty of time."

Suddenly his blade was out again and pressed against her throat. "You better not be lying to me this time, puta.

I know you're worried about your precious boyfriend, but if you are lying to me, I'll make you watch while I torture him, slowly and very, very painfully."

His blade dropped down and slashed at the tape at her ankles, then at the tape at her wrists. Before she could move, his hand was in her hair and the blade was pressed against her neck. "Stand. Slowly."

Anya did as he said, knowing she was not only buying Stryker time, but also giving him a better advantage when he came inside. She stood slowly. "If you don't move down these stairs fast enough, I'll push you down them," he threatened.

Anya drew a deep breath and began to move down the stairs, clutching the rail tightly. She was having a hard time pulling air into her lungs as he ushered her forward, her chest tight with anxiety.

She stumbled along, gasping. He was going to kill her. The realization brought about a sudden calm in her. If he took her life instead of Stryker's, it would all be worth it. She squeezed her eyes shut against the fear that clawed at her from inside. She could do this. She could fight him just a little longer.

He dragged her outside into the hot sun to a Land Rover. The SUV should have plenty of room to hold the boxes she had seen him take from her clinic. She focused on the SUV instead of the sharp pain in her side or her bare feet treading on the rough ground. She stumbled forward until he yanked her to a stop and opened the rear of the Land Rover. The boxes of her medication filled the back of the SUV.

"Find it." He pointed to the boxes and shoved her toward them.

Anya's heart was racing and her hands were shaking so violently, she didn't know if she'd be able to go through the contents of the boxes. How much time had passed? At least fifteen minutes. That meant she had another fifteen to burn before Stryker arrived. She had to keep Benicio distracted.

Her legs were trembling as she leaned into the back of his Land Rover and began to dig through the contents of the first box. Why had he pilfered her medications? The answer struck her instantly. He intended to give them to his crew to sell on the black market as soon as he returned to Mexico. The medications were hard to come by, which was why she always kept them locked up in her cabinets.

With determination, she dug through the box, trying to find anything that could help her. But all she could find was bottle upon bottle of simple pills that she gave to animals in need of help. She needed syringes and a vial of horse tranquilizer that she could quickly stab into Benicio's thigh, but she had to find the right items. And her time was quickly running out.

As if in response to her thoughts, Benicio's voice cut through the hot, humid air. "Hurry up!" he barked.

"You're making me too nervous," she said weakly, hoping he would believe her.

"If you're lying to me, puta, you'll live long enough to regret it. Because I will make you cry for mercy before I kill you." His voice was a low growl behind her.

She reached into another box and felt the glass medicine vials, and for a moment, her heart soared. "I'm looking, I'm looking," she pleaded. "Did you bring all the bottles with you?"

He took a step back from her, cursing under his breath, and she knew she had found a potential weak spot. She turned to glance back at him. "You *did* take all the bottles, right?"

"Keep searching. You have a few more minutes."

Her heart was pounding so hard, she was certain he could hear it. She turned back to the SUV, and with one hand dug through the bottles, making the appropriate rattling sound, while the other hand, the one she concentrated on, carefully maneuvered the vials until she found the one she needed. Now she could only pray he'd been greedy enough to grab syringes too.

Time was slipping away, and she knew he was going to take her back soon. Feeling through the boxes blindly, she nearly cheered when her hand wrapped around a syringe. She didn't even look at it before she plunged it through the thick rubber stopper of the vial and began to draw out medicine.

"What are you doing? You stupid, fucking whore!" He spun her around and lifted his hand to backhand her, but she plunged the needle into his stomach. She had gotten a decent amount of the medication into the syringe, but he knocked it from her hand so fast, she doubted she had gotten much into his system. But it would slow his movements. It would cause him to be less aware and give Stryker the upper hand.

He grabbed her arm and pulled her up close. "You want me to hurt you, don't you?" She felt a slight tremor in his grip and wondered if he was already feeling the impact of the tranquilizer. She may have just saved her own life, and Stryker's too.

Chapter 28

GRABBING HER HAND, HE HAULED HER BACK INTO THE MILL and let go of her so suddenly she fell to her knees. She had to remain strong for Stryker. Everything she did, every choice she made, must be to try to protect Stryker, if at all possible.

She knew she would do everything in her power to protect him. Even if it meant sacrificing her own life. She wavered as she climbed back to her feet in front of the man responsible for her grim thoughts, and wanted nothing more than to punch him in the face. She needed to distract him. That was the best way to provide help for Stryker.

"Why is this drive so important to you? What's on it?"

His smile was mirthless. "You wouldn't understand."

He was doing something that was making a lot of noise, but she was too disoriented with fear and thirst to figure out what it was. "I actually know quite a bit about computers," she lied. "What does this drive have on it that is so important to you that you're willing to kill for it?"

"My dear, I would kill someone if they failed to bring me the right item I requested. Killing you means nothing to me. Killing Stryker, on the other hand, is very important to me. As I'm sure you know, he went into Mexico and virtually destroyed my leadership team. What he doesn't know is that I've had leaders in training for years, in case just such a thing would happen. He hasn't crippled me. He's merely made me adjust my timetable."

"Then why the fixation on this drive? If you have a plan in place, why not just go ahead and move forward with it?"

"And this is why I say you know so little. Do you want to know why I'm one of the youngest leaders out of all the drug cartels, hmm? Because of that drive. It has encrypted data on there that no one else can see. So, I simply must have it back. And if it costs two foolish American lives to make it happen…" He shrugged nonchalantly. "Now, back up those stairs. I want to see him coming."

"Too late." Stryker's voice was cold, hard, and full of anger. But it was sweet music to Anya's ears. Before she could react, Benicio grabbed her and pressed the muzzle of the gun directly against her temple.

"I can see why you came," Benicio said, hiding behind Anya's body. "She certainly is sweet."

She was afraid to move. She was afraid to do anything. Benicio had the gun pressed so tightly to her head, she knew the slightest move could have her brains splattered across the floor.

Despite the heat and the fact that she was sweating, a chill slipped down her spine.

"Let her go, Benicio, and I'll give you the drive."

"Your little whore claims you gave it to her when you went to see her early this morning. Which one of you is lying?"

Stryker hadn't looked at her since he had entered the building. He'd kept his eyes fixed on Benicio. But at Benicio's words, his eyes flicked to Anya briefly. She pleaded for his forgiveness with her eyes, but his eyes quickly darted back to Benicio.

"I gave her a copy of the drive this morning for insurance. I was afraid you had gotten it when you destroyed her office. But I found it where she had shown me she would hide it."

Anya's heart was pounding. Would Benicio believe their story? Now that he had no use for her, was he going to kill her?

"Let her go and I'll give you the drives."

"No, no, no. It isn't that simple. There is a laptop in the corner over there. Put the flash drive in and cue it up."

Stryker stared at him for several long moments, without any expression on his face. "I'm not the tech savvy one," he said softly. "I'm just the one who gets things done."

"Then you'll get this done, won't you?"

"You'll need to turn on the laptop for me. Like I said, I'm not the tech savvy one."

Benicio jerked Anya closer to him. "I don't believe you. Get the laptop and turn it on."

Stryker turned slowly and marched to the corner at an angle, keeping his eye on Benicio. He grabbed the laptop and turned, walking back toward them with purpose.

Stryker stopped and set the laptop down on top of one of the stairs that led up to the second-story landing. "You can stop," Benicio said curtly, and he laughed, letting go of Anya so suddenly that she fell to her knees on the floor.

"How do I turn this thing on?"

"You're serious? You really don't know?" Benicio began to laugh again. "Puta!" he snapped at Anya. "Go and turn on the laptop. My gun will be on his head the entire time, so make one mistake, and he dies."

Anya's gaze connected with Stryker's, and she saw his strength and determination. Nodding, she made her way forward, drawing in a deep breath.

She reached the laptop and was so close to Stryker, she could smell the scent of his cologne and closed her eyes briefly as the wonderful aroma wrapped itself around her, comforting her. She wanted to say something to him. She wanted to tell him to leave, to get away now. He couldn't save her. No one could. And if he stayed any longer, he would be dead too.

"Turn on the damn thing and get back to me!"

"Just do as I say," Stryker said without moving his lips.

"What?" Anya was confused.

"Get down!" Stryker shouted, and he dove to the side, pulling a pistol from the side holster he had hidden beneath a casual vest. A bullet pinged the metal railing of the stairs.

The sound of gunfire tore through the air. Anya rolled onto her stomach. Stryker had taken up a position behind a thick pillar. Benicio was searching for a safe place, and his gaze slammed into hers.

Suddenly Benicio ran toward her, his hand holding the gun level at her head. "Anya, run!" Stryker shouted out, and her quivering muscles propelled her into motion, but not fast enough.

Benicio grabbed her again, pressing the gun against her chin. "You stupid little whore!" he spat, his anger unlike anything she had seen. "I should have known you would do something so foolish. Now you're going to die."

Before he could pull the trigger, she slammed her fist

into his nose, and he yelled out in surprise. He reached for his nose as it spurted blood. Anya couldn't believe her weak attack had broken his nose.

"Anya!"

She scrambled toward the sound of Stryker's voice. With an angry growl, Benicio lunged for her, but Stryker was suddenly upon him, slamming his body up into the stairwell. A shot went off. Anya screamed.

Benicio loomed large and angry in front of her. Blood dripped from his nose. She was doing everything in her power to remain focused. Anya was going to kill him with her bare hands if he'd shot Stryker.

It was dark underneath the stairwell as the sun was beginning to set. Too dark for him to see the gun that he'd knocked free of Benicio's hands. Silently he pulled himself from under the stairs. His blood went cold then flaming hot as he saw Benicio advancing on Anya. He had to stop him. He had never felt as protective of a woman as he felt at that moment. Anya was his. He would do anything to keep her safe.

He threw his entire weight forward and slammed into Benicio.

They collided with fists flying. He slammed his fist into the nose Anya had already broken. Benicio's fist collided with his ribs, and he grunted at the pain. He was going to destroy him. Benicio had hurt Anya. His beautiful, precious Anya. And who knew what else he had done?

Stryker threw an uppercut that sent Benicio staggering backwards. Where was Anya?

Anya came flying from the corner, tackling Benicio on the back. He stumbled under the onslaught and tried to free himself from her clutches. She grabbed at his hair and shoved him hard…directly into Stryker's arms.

"It's your turn to answer questions," Stryker growled at him, pinning his arms behind his back and wrestling him to the ground. "Be careful what you do now, Benicio. There's a man outside who's had a bead drawn on you for the last few minutes. He can take you down anytime I give him the signal."

"Then give him the fucking signal already," Benicio barked. Hatred and something else was in his eyes. Was it fear? Benicio didn't strike him as the type of person who was scared of anything, not even death. Perhaps it wasn't what he was scared of, but *who*.

"Tell me who you're working for, Benicio."

And there it was. His eyes flooded with fear and darted around him in desperation. Abruptly, he seemed to gather himself again, and his eyes narrowed into slits as he glared up at Stryker. "I don't know what you are talking about."

"Bullshit."

"You fucking Americans think you're so much better. You're worthless."

Stryker stood, keeping one foot on Benicio's hand. He glanced back at Anya. "Are you all right?"

Instead of replying, her eyes widened in fear, and his gaze flew back to Benicio. He was struggling, reaching for something near him. When his fingers circled around the butt of the handgun, Stryker lunged.

He grabbed Benicio's hand, smacking it down against the concrete to knock the gun from his grip. Stryker wanted to pound the man's skull into the cement. But he needed answers more than anything. Killing Benicio wasn't going to give him what he needed.

Suddenly the sound of boots on the cement drew his attention, and his team was rushing in.

"Stryker!" Anya screamed, her voice hoarse and raw.

In slow motion he saw Benicio smile, saw him draw his hand upwards. And then bullets struck Benicio from several directions as his team went in for the kill. "No!" Stryker yelled, as Benicio's head fell backwards, the gun dropping from his hand. Stryker grabbed his collar. "Who do you work for? Who? Answer me, damn you!"

Benicio didn't answer. Stryker released his grip on him and let the man's lifeless body fall.

Hands gripped his shoulders and pulled him away from Benicio's body. "Where is Anya?" he asked, desperate to know she was safe.

"Stryker!" she cried out, pushing through the men to reach him. She threw herself into his arms, holding him tightly, so tightly his bruised ribs protested but his heart soared. "You're okay? You're not shot?"

He glanced down. "I'm not shot." He smiled at her hesitantly, running a hand through her sweat-dampened hair. "And you? He didn't... Did he hurt you, bella?"

She shook her head. "I had to be strong. I knew he wanted to hurt you more than me. I was able to tranquilize him—"

"You did *what*?" Phantom looked at her incredulously.

"I-I thought it would help. I didn't know that you were going to kill him, but I couldn't take the risk that he would kill any of you..." She swallowed hard and glanced at Benicio's dead body. "Stryker—I think I should sit down…" He caught her in his arms as she crumpled.

"Phantom?" Stryker said, his voice sounding frantic even to his own ears. If the bastard had hurt her… If he had done *anything* to her…

"She's just passed out. Probably from shock. We're taking both of you to the hospital to get looked at."

When Stryker began to groan, he was silenced by a wave of Phantom's hand. "You want to make sure she's all right, don't you? And the rest of us would like to make sure you check out as well. Physically, at least. Mentally, we all know the answer to that after this little display of heroism."

A slight smile tugged at the corner his mouth. Then Anya stirred and whimpered softly in his arms, and he pinned Phantom with a hard look. "Take us to Laredo."

———

They were bruised, battered, and exhausted, and Anya was suffering from mild shock. But she quickly came around as they drove to Laredo, lying in Stryker's arms. "Bella," he said softly, smiling down at her.

"Stryker!" She threw her arms around him, holding him tightly. "I was so afraid… I thought you were shot. When I heard the gun go off…" Her voice wavered.

"He missed," Stryker said. He swallowed hard. "Are you hurt? Did he… Are you hurt in any way?"

"No. I think he enjoyed tormenting me mentally more than anything. I fought him off, and when I gave him the tranquilizer, it slowed everything down."

"Yeah…about that. Care to explain to me how you *tranquilized* the man?"

Anya smiled at him, and he wanted nothing more than to be alone with her at that moment, to kiss her and touch her and show her how much she meant to him. "I was able to get my hands on some horse tranquilizer, and I stabbed him in the stomach with it."

Stryker nearly laughed and shook his head. "Do you have any idea how incredible you are?"

Her smile slowly faded. "Because of you. I fought because of you. I couldn't bear the thought of something happening to you."

His brows furrowed. "What do you mean?"

"After he called you, I knew you were going to come looking for me. So, I had to try to incapacitate him somehow before you got there. I couldn't take the chance that he'd hurt you."

Stryker felt his throat closing up. She had put herself at risk for him. She could have been hurt, or worse, killed. And all for *him*. He pulled her close and buried his face against her neck.

"Are we headed back to the clinic?"

"No, Doc, we're headed to Laredo," Phantom said from the driver's seat.

"Laredo? I don't understand."

"We want to make sure both of us are okay. Phantom wouldn't let us get by with his inspection. We're headed to the hospital."

"Are you okay? Did you get hurt?" Her eyes began to search his body frantically.

"Only bumps and bruises. I know I'll check out fine. You're the one who gave us a scare when you passed out."

A blush tinged her cheeks. "I was so afraid that you—it all hit me at once."

He leaned down and pressed a kiss to her forehead. "Everything will be fine now. You'll see."

―~~~―

As Stryker had predicted, he only suffered from bruises, though some of them were worse than others. One bruise was to his ribs, and that one was a bit more painful. Another on his stomach was already blossoming into a colorful hue that he knew would last for weeks.

The doctors decided to keep Anya overnight for observation as she was still showing signs of shock. Stryker had insisted on staying in her room with her, and the rest of the men had retreated to give them privacy. She had fallen into a deep slumber, and, against his will, he had too.

When he woke up, Buzz and Phantom were walking in, and there was a beautiful arrangement of flowers sitting on the small table at the side of the bed. "Wow, you guys didn't have to bring her flowers. Just seeing you here is going to be enough of a joy for her."

"We didn't bring them. We just got here," Phantom said, his eyes narrowing.

"Who else would know she's here?" Stryker demanded in frustration.

"Only our team. There isn't anyone else."

"There's a card in it. Buzz, read it to us." Phantom nudged Buzz forward.

Buzz worked moisture into his mouth, and then began to read off the card: *Roses are red, violets are blue, you may have won the battle, but you can't win the war too. Stryker and team, this one is for you.*

"Fuck!" Phantom pulled out his phone and immediately began to dial.

"Who are you calling?" Stryker demanded with ferocity. They couldn't risk any further exposure than they already had. Someone knew about their location, and it could have been given up by anyone—doctors, nurses, general staff—it would be virtually impossible to identify who had leaked the information.

"I'm calling Admiral Haslett. He needs to send down protection for the two of you."

Stryker groaned, but he knew it was the right thing to do. They needed to let the navy know what was going on. He just wished he had more answers than questions.

The navy reacted quickly to the news. Two masters-at-arms showed up within hours of Phantom making the phone call. Less than an hour after that, much to Stryker's surprise, Admiral Haslett arrived and cleared the room of everyone except him and Anya. He looked at Anya for several minutes, and the way Stryker was holding her hand, then grunted.

Anya had awoken for a couple of hours and chatted with the men, oblivious to their new concerns. Later in the morning, she had slowly drifted back to sleep. Stryker hoped his conversation with the admiral wouldn't wake her.

"I didn't quite believe you when you told me you had fallen for a woman here. Now I have no doubt." Admiral Haslett gave him a wry smile.

"Yes, sir. I care for her very much."

"How did she react when you told her about being a SEAL?"

"Better than I expected. She seems ready to embrace who I really am."

"I'm concerned that someone breached your security around the ranch in order to take photos of you and the team." The admiral's grin turned to a frown.

"Yes, sir. It shocked me just as much. I don't know what anyone had to gain from such a thing other than to let us know we're being watched. We've tightened our security and haven't had any breaches since."

"That you know of," the admiral said, his voice tight with frustration.

"Correct, sir."

"Brusco informed me about all of the photos being sent to her."

"Brusco and Snap questioned her intensively. But there was no concrete evidence to suggest she was a spy or was anything more than an innocent civilian caught in the crosshairs."

"Not an innocent civilian caught in the wrong place at the wrong time. She was targeted. Same as you were, from what I can tell."

"Yes, well, every member of my team was also in those photos. So I feel it is a threat to my entire team. Someone out there is trying to scare us away, but it isn't going to work."

Admiral Haslett was silent for several moments as he stared at Anya. "That bastard really traumatized her, didn't he? How the hell did he find out about her?"

"I believe it's all my fault. I went to see her when we got back from the mission, and I suspect he was following me. I led him straight to her."

"That's one of the risks you take when you get involved with a civilian. What do you plan to do now?"

"I hope I can convince her to come live out on the

ranch with us, that is, if she'll still have me. And we need to hire someone to work at her clinic with her who will be able to defend her if things ever go sideways again."

"I have a new man who just came off a mission. He'd be the ideal sailor to put in a role like that with her."

Stryker lifted an eyebrow. "You're going to help me with this, sir?"

"Unless you don't want me to." Admiral Haslett pursed his lips and appraised Stryker with knowing eyes.

"No, no, sir. I greatly appreciate it."

Admiral Haslett sighed, then sat in the uncomfortable reclining chair. "I reviewed your full report this morning. It goes on like a bad movie script. But I could read between the lines and gather that you think there's someone else out there…someone pulling the strings on this cartel and possibly other operations." He looked down at his hat in his hands, then finally back up at Stryker. "I have a few suspicions of my own, but it's nothing I can put on paper. Why don't you tell me what you think is going on, and then I'll tell you my version of this sordid story."

Chapter 29

ANYA WOKE UP SLOWLY, FEELING THE NEED TO STRETCH OUT all the aches in her body. She knew her panic attack had been vicious, but she hadn't realized how much it would leave her aching. She opened her eyes a crack and saw Stryker's handsome face staring back at her. Memories poured back, and she sighed heavily.

"I think he wanted to die," she said softly, watching his face.

He lifted his eyebrows, showing surprise at her choice of topics. "What makes you say that?"

"Because he would prefer to die than answer any of your questions. He was terrified of them."

"You caught on to that too, huh? You're incredibly perceptive. I may be able to convert you into being a spy."

"No." Anya shook her head adamantly. "No, I don't want to have anything to do with that. I'm happy just supporting you from the sidelines."

His smile faded, and he stroked her hair back off her forehead. "Do you know what you're saying, Anya?"

Her eyes were beginning to droop, and she gave him a hesitant smile. "Am I saying the wrong thing again? It seems I have a terrific knack for that."

He leaned down and pressed a kiss to her forehead. "Rest, *bella*. If you have recovered enough, we may be able to take you home this afternoon. Sleep. Heal."

She clung to his hand against her cheek as she slipped off into a refreshing slumber.

—⁓⁓—

Anya had a thousand thoughts running through her mind and didn't know which one to address first. Stryker had told her about the destruction to her clinic, and she knew it would take weeks for her to get it back in order.

She hadn't even been able to tell the full story to Stryker yet. He knew what he'd walked into when he had come into the mill. But he didn't know what had happened before that. Did they know she had shot Benicio and then stitched him up? Did they think she was weak and a failure for falling prey to him? How much would he even want to know? *One step at a time. Crawling, if I have to. I will not let that bastard define who I am as a person. He can no longer hurt me.*

When they turned down the dirt road that would take them to the ranch, Anya was jarred back to the present. "I thought you were taking me back to the clinic?" She leaned forward in her seat, looking at Stryker and Phantom, her head pivoting back and forth.

"You'll be safer at the ranch, Anya," Stryker said softly.

"Safer? What do you mean 'safer'? Benicio is dead. He can't hurt me anymore."

"No, he can't. Just trust me, Anya. Please don't fight me on this. There are things I need to explain to you. Things about who Benicio was and what we're really up against."

Stryker's eyes looked up at her with concern and something else…something warm that reminded her of their night together before he had left for his mission.

Before both of their lives had been impacted so violently. If she could only have that night again... *Heaven help me, I still love him.*

The realization was like a lightning bolt. She drew a deep breath and slid her hand into his offered one, and she stepped down from the large truck. Much to her surprise, the rest of the team was waiting outside on the porch, their faces anxious. These were Navy SEALs. What did they have to be anxious about?

"Welcome back, Anya," Brusco said softly as she approached.

"Glad to see you looking so much better," Buzz said, reaching out and embracing her. "You gave all of us quite the scare."

"Welcome home," Santo and Snap said together, both nodding to her in greeting.

"Have you all been drugged?" Anya asked suddenly, feeling as if she were in a surreal experience.

Stryker chuckled behind her and placed his hands around her waist, guiding her into the house. His touch felt incredible. He was the man she had always dreamed of, but had never realized it.

She needed to tell him how she felt. She needed to confess her love to him. She wanted to be alone with him so badly, it was all she could do not to demand his immediate and undivided attention away from the entire house.

He guided her into the living room, a part of the house she hadn't spent any time in before. She realized he was doing it for her. It would be easier for all of them to sit around the dining room table, but he knew she would be uncomfortable being back at that table after her last experience. Why couldn't they be alone? She needed to kiss him for everything he was and everything he did with her in mind.

They all took a seat on the large leather couches that wrapped around the room, and Stryker pulled her into a love seat with him, keeping his arm firmly around her waist. She didn't mind. In fact, she used it as an excuse to nestle up closer to him, to have his body pressed along her side. She could tell that pleased him as he looked down at her with a soft smile and gently pressed her in a hug.

They were all finally seated when they looked at her with expectation. And some looked at her with concern, which made her grab hold of Stryker's thigh without thinking. He covered her hand with his and squeezed her waist.

"I know who you are. You are all Navy SEALs. You're undercover here, and you're going after the bad guys. I won't tell anybody about y'all. I promise. I didn't even tell Benicio anything about you."

The men exchanged glances, then returned their eyes to Stryker. "All right, Anya—Joseph 'Buzz' Gomez is an expert in communications and technology," Stryker informed her.

Anya looked over at Buzz with a slight smile. "Joseph. It suits you. But I still like Buzz better."

"Enrique 'Phantom' Ramirez runs tactical ground patrol and does a damn good job of it. He saved our asses in Mexico. He was training to be a doctor in the navy before they realized his strategic abilities. But, as you've seen, we rely on Phantom still for his medical knowledge. Hunter 'Santo' Gonzalez is an expert sniper. He's also one helluva tracker."

Anya nodded to both of the men, flashing a smile at Phantom. She owed him a lot. Then again, she needed to set him straight. "Phantom, you may be a badass, but you did something really stupid." He arched an eyebrow at her, his expression unreadable. "You fired my best friend."

His eyes widened slightly. "Elena," he said softly, and a slight smile lifted the corners of his lips.

"Yes. She'd be good for you. She's one of the best horse trainers I've ever known."

"Why do you say she'd be good for me?" His expression became unreadable again.

"Because you could use the influence of a strong woman in your life." She smiled at him, and the men chuckled at his expense.

Stryker cleared his throat before he continued, temporarily taking Phantom off the hook. "Derek 'Brusco' Delgado is our spotter and on-the-ground specialist. He works closely with Santo when taking down a target and evaluating our surroundings for potential threats. And Isaiah 'Snap' Flores is our operational and tactical officer. He oversees every piece of our missions."

Anya swallowed hard. "You all sound very…talented. And lethal."

"Only when we have to be," Phantom said quietly, leaning forward with his elbows braced on his legs, his hands clasped loosely in front of him. Anya looked around the room and saw all kind, friendly eyes watching her. It made her feel proud and brave. She could make a difference with these men, and in so doing, make a difference for her country. "Do you only go after drug cartels?"

The men all looked to Stryker, and Anya's eyes

followed theirs. "Several months ago, our admiral reached out to me and told me he was pulling together a special ops task force and he wanted me to head it up. The details for this task force are limited, so it isn't that I'm keeping information from you; it's just the way we work.

"I lead the task force, and it was my honor to pick these men. I've worked with all of them before, and I trust my life with each one of them. Our assignment is to become part of the community and keep our ears to the ground about activities in Mexico and Central and South America. There are a lot of bad things going down right now, and, I'm sure you know, they're having repercussions in the U.S. We don't know how far the corruption goes."

"So you think some of these crimes could be linked back to the U.S. government?" Anya asked, searching his face for answers. The thought was disturbing.

"We aren't ruling it out."

"I traced the paper those photos were printed on and it's common stock," Buzz spoke up. "But it is most widely used in the United States. Not in Mexico."

"Why would someone in the U.S. government be spying on all of us?" Phantom mused.

Anya drew in a deep breath. She had fallen in love with a Navy SEAL on a special ops assignment. A question suddenly popped into her head, and, involuntarily, her hand squeezed his leg. All muscle and no give. She nearly lost her train of thought. "H-how long are you going to be here?"

"It's hard to say. For however long the admiral decides our work is needed. A handful of years at least."

"Will it always be the six of you?"

Stryker's jaw worked for a few moments before he finally spoke. "About that—we don't feel it is safe for you to continue your clinic by yourself."

"What? Why not? Benicio is dead, isn't he?"

"Yes, Anya, but ask yourself this—who took those pictures of us here on the ranch?" Santo said in a voice that was like rumbling rocks and gravel tumbled together.

"I... Well, I hadn't given that much thought. All I've been able to think about was Benicio and the horrible things..." Her voice died off and she shuddered.

"Anya, you now know who we are and what we do. Will you please tell us about Benicio and what happened between the two of you? It's time to get your story out."

Chapter 30

A LIGHT DRIZZLE WAS FALLING, TYPICAL LATE-SPRING weather. Soon, they would be battling the heat of summer and suffering through rolling brownouts of electricity across the city as everyone cranked the AC down into the sixties. The city was a cesspool.

The sound of the drizzle striking the canvas of his two-hundred-dollar Gucci umbrella was beginning to get on his nerves. With the position he held, he never knew when he was being watched. The longer he was out in public the more attention he could draw to himself. The location he had selected for the meeting was secluded, and he had made certain he wasn't followed.

Finally, a sleek black Rolls-Royce pulled around the corner and stopped beside him. The driver's side back door opened, and an elegantly manicured hand gestured for him to get in. For a moment, he almost reached for the handgun he had tucked under his custom jacket in its holster, but realized that would be a telling sign. He knew it was there, and knew he could draw it quickly should he find it necessary.

He slid into the car and carefully closed the door so it wasn't latched. He wouldn't take the risk that he would get locked inside, subject to whatever madness his new partner had in mind. "Traffic must have been a bear," he said, in an attempt to begin a friendly dialogue. His new partner wasn't interested in chitchat.

"Benicio Davila is dead."

"We're well aware that his cousin was killed by the team the navy sent in. But we received communication from Benicio shortly afterwards that he was alive and well."

"Your intel is out-of-date. He was killed a couple of days ago in the U.S. Whoever this navy team is, they're savvy enough to take down one of your top men. Whether they have realized you had a fool bumbling around their residence is hard to say. Though it wasn't very intelligent to send pictures. It only served to complicate matters."

"I was unaware he had sent pictures." His blood pressure was going up. He could feel it by the pounding in his ears. He needed to take his medication.

"Are you even aware of their location?"

"Benicio hired someone to take the pictures and never told me the location. Though I held a gun to his head, he still wouldn't tell me the location."

"A pity. All I've been able to gather is that they're somewhere in south Texas near the border. But I've just begun to dig. Given time, I'm certain I'll know everything down to the size of their dicks."

The congressman nearly recoiled at the foul language. He was used to being around politicians all day who watched every single word they said. With reporters lurking around every corner, one never could be too careful. "Let's hope you won't need to get into that much detail. But we need to move quickly. They ruined my business with Benicio. I can't afford to have them get involved in any more of my operations."

"Do you have an inside man?"

"Where?"

"Good grief, man, how have you functioned? Without

an inside man at the navy, you're practically on a stranded island. You need information, and that is the place to get it."

"I'll find someone. It shouldn't be too hard."

His partner eyed him skeptically. "Get your shit in order. Once you have better control over the situation, call me. Until then, don't fucking waste my time."

His partner reached across him and opened the door, an obvious statement to leave. He ground his teeth together. No one got away with talking to him like that. No one. But at the moment, he was at a significant disadvantage.

He popped his umbrella open and stepped out of the car. He was turning back to make a scathing statement, when the door slammed in his face and the car sped away, spitting pieces of mud up on his designer suit. His jaw clenched and unclenched rapidly. He had just added another person to his list of people who had to die, along with the navy team that was making his life hell. They would all pay. And in the end, he would come out looking like the hero.

Stryker listened with intensity as Anya explained the way Benicio had forced his way into her clinic, and he wanted to hug her when she told them how she had shot the man. But from there, everything seemed to go downhill. Relief flooded him as she continued on with her story.

The men listened intently, leaning forward with elbows resting on their knees. Their faces were grim, though they never once interrupted her.

Anya had kept her eyes closed the entire time she'd been speaking, as if trying to pull everything from the deepest recesses of her mind. When she finally opened her eyes, she looked at them with apprehension.

"You did great, bella." Stryker kissed her on the forehead, wishing he could end the meeting immediately and take her off to his bedroom. His heart skipped a beat as he thought about the conversation he was about to have with her. It could quite possibly change his life forever.

"You said he had a plan to get his team running again quickly, is that right?" Phantom asked.

"Yes. He said he had a group who he'd been training for just such an occasion. But he needed that drive. He made that clear when Stryker got there. That drive was the reason he was so successful."

Buzz shook his head. "I've got my work cut out for me trying to decode this bitch—er, this problem."

Anya smiled at him. "I have faith in you."

"Santo, Brusco, do you think you can recap everything from this conversation? The admiral is going to want to see it," Stryker said softly.

"From what *I* said? I'm just a veterinarian. Surely he doesn't want to hear anything from me."

"Anya, you were the hostage of one of the most notorious drug lords in all of Mexico. Anything you learned about him and his organization is going to be incredibly valuable to the admiral. Hell, it's valuable to us," Phantom said with conviction.

Anya nodded slowly. "Well, then, if you don't need me for anything more…"

"Anya, you can't go back to your clinic. Not yet. You're still recovering, and it just isn't safe. We have a new SEAL starting with us in a few weeks. He's going to work with you at the clinic and be there as your protection."

"My…protection."

Stryker could tell Anya was about to go on overload. The rest of the team must have sensed it as well, because they all began to exit the room. Each one of them nodded to Anya and expressed his gratitude for her bravery in telling her story.

"Come with me," Stryker said softly against her ear, picked up her hand in his, and began heading back to the large room that belonged to him. He closed the door behind them and watched her walk into the room, taking in the manly décor.

"Your room, I presume," she said softly, turning back to face him, her hands clenched in front of her to hide her shakes.

"How did you know?" He forced a grin onto his face, moving toward her.

"It smells like you."

"Oh? And how is that?"

"Earth. And horses. And man."

He paused directly in front of her, his pulse racing. "I never feel more like a man than when I'm with you, *bella*." He finger-combed her hair away from her face. "And I've waited too damn long for this." He lowered his head, his lips hovering over hers to the point that he could feel the heat of her breath blowing against his skin.

And then they were kissing, finally kissing, and she was the sweetest tasting thing in the world. He never wanted to let go of her. He needed her in his life now and always. He slanted his mouth over hers and let his tongue swipe along her lower lip. With a sigh, her mouth parted for him, and he played with her tongue, sliding his alongside hers and gently sucking on it. When they broke apart, they were both breathless.

"Is this safe for you?"

"I'm not hurting you, am I?"

They both laughed, as they had spoken at the same time. It felt so good to see and hear her laugh.

Watching her with hooded eyes, he led her to the bed, where he sat her down, then proceeded to take her boots off for her. His boots quickly followed, and then he moved up to lie beside her, fully clothed, on top of the bed linens.

"This is a bit different than our past," Anya said, and a teasing but sad smile touched the corner of her mouth.

"Yes. But I need to talk to you."

Anya rolled onto her side, worry on her face. He wanted to alleviate all her fears. He didn't want to make her have even more concern than she already had.

"Anya," he began softly, lifting his hand and brushing a wayward strand of her dark hair away from her face. Her hazel-and-gold eyes watched him intently, with an anxious expression. He could imagine she had a lot that bothered her lately. But he shouldn't be like those other worries. He was ready to be the constant in her life. He just had to figure out how to do it.

"I didn't know what to do when I found out Benicio had taken you. I nearly lost my mind. And I had no idea where to look for you. And what devastated me the most was knowing you were in danger because of me."

"Stryker, you don't know that. You don't know how he came to pick me—"

"No, Anya, I know. I *felt* him watching me that morning I went to visit you. I didn't know what it was at the time, but I felt something. Now, I know it was that bastard watching me and planning how to hurt me the most."

"Oh, Stryker. You can't blame yourself for this. It wasn't your fault."

"Yes, Anya, it was in a roundabout way. He wanted revenge on me, so he took you." His eyes searched hers, wanting her to understand. "If I step away from you right now, you might be able to go back to your old life, to easier and simpler times. But if I don't step away from you, your life is going to have to change. And I can promise you there will be days you want to murder me for being so protective of you. But I can't live through this again."

"Is that what you want? Do you want to step away from me?" Her gaze was as intense as his.

"Absolutely not. Anya, you're what got me through those terrible two weeks in Mexico. You're all I could think about on the drive home. And I became a man obsessed with getting you back when you were taken. Because, in my mind, Anya, you're mine. You were meant to be mine all along, and I wish it hadn't taken me this long to find you."

"Stryker," she whispered, smiling at him as tears formed in her eyes.

"Don't cry, Anya," he whispered in reply. "Please, don't cry. I only want to see joy on your face from now on."

"These are happy tears, Stryker." She smiled.

He smiled and began to kiss the tears, taking them off of her skin, then he slowly kissed her eyelids, taking away the tears that hovered on her lashes. But the kisses didn't stop there. His arm slid around her waist, pulling her closer to him as he kissed her nose, then her chin, then down along her jawline. Her breathing hitched as she arched her neck, giving him access to her sensitive skin.

He pressed gentle kisses against her throat. "I'm so sorry I wasn't there for you."

"You were with me the entire time, Stryker. You were in my heart, giving me the courage to keep going."

He moaned softly and pressed kisses to her collarbone as his fingers began to work quickly and deftly to unbutton her shirt. Soon, he had it opened, and he paused for a moment to pull back and admire her breasts wrapped in the clingy lace of her bra. He had picked it out for her when he had gone to get her fresh clothes to wear home from the hospital. "Anya, you don't realize—you just don't see… You're beautiful," he murmured.

She reached up to unbutton his shirt, her fingers moving just as quickly as his had done only seconds earlier. Her only hindrance was that he was attempting to remove her bra at the same time.

Finally, they were both completely nude, and Stryker was trying to maintain control. He had been craving Anya for weeks. He needed her so he could feel whole again.

He gently lapped at her stiffened nipples, causing her to moan and writhe on the bed, her hand tangled in his hair. When he drew one of the firm peaks into his mouth, she gasped and arched off the bed, and he smiled to himself. Yes, she was his. She belonged with him, together forever. If she would take him.

His fingers trailed along her side, and he caressed

the sensitive skin of her hip bone. She had lost weight while he'd been gone. He would need Snap's help to get her health back on track. With Snap's cooking, she was certain to gain back the weight she had lost.

His fingers moved farther inward, and she drew in a deep breath as they played with the dark curls at the apex of her thighs. She trembled as his fingers dipped lower and slid over her slick folds. His own breath hissed out of him as he felt how excited she was, and it took all his control not to make his move at that very moment.

Instead, he continued teasing her nipples as his fingers played with her, until he slid one finger into her tight canal. "Stryker!" she cried out, her fingernails digging into his scalp as her hips leaped beneath his hand.

"Anya, I want to go slow. I want to make love to you. I want to—"

Her hands caught his face, drawing his eyes up to hers. "And I want you. Now."

The passion in her face nearly sent him over the edge. He grabbed the condom he had set to the side in hopes that things would progress this far and rolled it on quickly. He carefully settled his body between her legs and moaned as the head of his erection moved across her desire-soaked triangle. "Stop me if I'm hurting you," he said, staring deep into her eyes, and she nodded, licking her lips in anticipation.

Slowly, slowly, he eased into her and hesitated when just the head was inside her. She moaned and wiggled her hips, trying to take him farther, but he held perfectly still, not allowing her to get what she wanted so badly. He eased in a little farther, and she groaned, her hands pulling at his hips.

When he was halfway sheathed, he pulled back and she whimpered at the loss of him within her body. Urgency was burning within him, but he wanted to make sure she was pleasured before he found his own release. He once again entered her, going in halfway then pausing. He began to thrust gently, never going past the halfway point, unsure of how much longer he could maintain control.

"Stryker, please…"

Her throaty and breathless plea nearly sent him over the edge. He surged forward, filling her to the hilt, and she cried out in pleasure. The feeling of her body adjusting around his girth was almost more than he could take. He was breathing heavily and had braced himself on his forearms so he wouldn't put too much of his weight on her. He looked down at her and groaned as he saw the passion across her face.

"Did I hurt you? Am I hurting you?" he asked, struggling to talk as his body throbbed with pleasure and the need for more.

"Oh, no, Stryker, no…you feel so incredible…so good. Please, Stryker, please don't stop."

It was his final undoing. He began to thrust into her rapidly, and she arched her hips to meet each one of his thrusts, her fingernails digging into his ass cheeks as she encouraged him to go faster—harder.

"Anya…Anya, I don't know how much longer I can last…"

Her breathing became more rapid, and she began to make the small sounds in the back of her throat that he'd come to learn meant she was on the verge of coming. "Come with me, Anya. Come with me…" His words broke off, and his voice joined hers in a cry of pleasure as her body began to clench around him and his body tightened just before he released in her.

His orgasm was powerful, and he struggled to continue thrusting into her, but his legs seemed to have lost all of their strength. He felt her continuing to pulse around him and knew she had found her ecstasy too, and he moaned as he rested his forehead against hers, still breathing heavily.

"Anya, I'm sorry. I had wanted to go slow. I had wanted to make love to you the proper way. I had wanted to—"

Her soft chuckle interrupted his words and his thoughts. "What, exactly, is the proper way? Because if it is anything different than what we just did, I don't think I want it." She lifted her chin and pressed her lips to his briefly, and he shivered as another wave of desire washed over him. Would he ever have enough of this woman?

With a low groan, he rolled off her and pulled her against his side tightly, quickly discarding the condom in the nearby wastebasket. She lay sprawled limply across half of his body, still trying to gain her breath. "I've said it before, and I don't know if you heard me. And if you did hear me, you might have thought it was a mistake. But I mean it. With all my heart, I mean it."

Stryker's heartbeat had been about to return to normal, but it picked up in speed at her words. "What did you say?" he whispered.

She lifted her head and looked down at him with satiated eyes. "I love you, Stryker. I love you more than life itself. I love you so much my heart aches when I don't get to see you. I love—mph!"

He kissed her deeply, passionately, intensely. "I

heard you say it before," he admitted when he finally pulled away from her. "And I was too afraid to believe it. But I wanted to believe it. I wanted to believe that you could love someone like me. I don't deserve it. But I will treasure your love till the day I die. Because…" He smoothed her tousled hair back away from her face. "I love you, Anya. I love you more than I ever thought a human being could love. You are my heart and soul. Without you, I'm just a shell of a man."

"Stryker," she breathed his name as a promise, as a prayer. She pressed her lips to his, and they spent several long moments tasting each other again, as if they would never be satisfied.

Stryker ended the kiss and ran his fingers along her delicate features. "I have something very important to ask you, Anya, and I don't know if now is the right time, and this probably isn't the right way to go about it. But, will you move here to the ranch? It's for your safety, but it's also because I can't imagine going to bed every night without you in my arms, or waking up every morning without holding you tight. I need you in my life, desperately. Will you move out here to be with me?"

She smiled at him and pressed a kiss to his forehead, his cheeks, and lightly on his lips. "I'm yours, Stryker. Forever and always. I love you. And I can't imagine being without you either. Yes, I'll move out to the ranch."

"Will you tolerate me being overprotective of you? At least until we catch the guy behind all this chaos?"

"Somehow, I have a feeling you will be overprotective no matter what, regardless of whether you catch this person or not."

"Oh, we'll catch him. It's what we're good at."

"I'd say you're good at many things," she murmured, a slight blush tinging her cheeks.

"Mmm. I may be good, but I'll only get better with practice. A lot of practice."

She giggled, a sound that warmed his heart, and he rolled her onto her back and stared down at her. "You know what comes next, right?"

"Umm…some more practice?"

His eyes widened, and then a burst of laughter escaped him. "Yes. That will happen in the very near future. Very. But I'm talking a little further out than that."

She drew in a deep breath and her gaze searched his face. "What?"

"Marriage. Then children. Lots of children."

She licked her lips, then gave him a sly smile. "You're getting ahead of yourself, sailor. Don't you have to ask the question first?"

"Oh, I'm getting to that. Have no fear, bella. It's coming."

*Keep reading for a sneak peek at the next book in
Holly Castillo's thrilling Texas Navy SEALs series!*

A SEAL ALWAYS WINS

*Coming February 2020
from Sourcebooks Casablanca*

Chapter 1

THE SOUND OF SHOTS FIRED IN THE DISTANCE stopped him in
his tracks. He listened carefully before dropping and
rolling into the nearby shrubs. He paused, his body tense
and ready to move the moment he heard a sound. The
crunch of dry brush underfoot brought a smile to his
face.

He pivoted toward the sound and aimed through the
shrubs. His target let out a startled shout a split second
after he fired. Chuckling, he stood, lifting his safety
goggles.

"Shit, Phantom! You didn't have to hit me where it
really hurts!" Santo groaned, glaring at his close friend
and BUD/S partner in crime.

Phantom's grin only broadened. "You should have
been paying attention to your surroundings."

"As if anyone ever knows where you are," Santo
fired back. "Your name is Phantom for a reason."

"Over here!" another voice called out. "Phantom brought him down."

"You know, just wait until it's your turn, pal. I'm going to hit you right in the cojones," Santo muttered as he glared at the paint gun splatter from Phantom's shot on his upper thigh.

"That's if you can find me, punk."

"No, that's *when* I find you. Care to make a wager on how fast I make that happen?"

Phantom held up his hands and shrugged.

"Did I hear someone say 'wager?' If there's betting going on, I need a piece of the action." A large man walked into the small clearing where Phantom and Santo stood, the afternoon sun beating down on them.

"Buzz. Nice of you to join the party." Phantom clapped the big man on the back, earning a glower.

"Nobody said this was a race. You could have given the rest of the team a chance to catch up." As Buzz finished ribbing Phantom, several other men stepped into the clearing and began to laugh at Santo's frustrated expression.

"He took you down in less than eight minutes. That's a new record," Stryker, their SEAL team leader said, joining in the laughter.

Santo shook his head, though he, too, started to smile. "Glad you're all having a good laugh."

Together, the six men teased and joked their way back to their equipment shed to put up the paintball guns and goggles. Stryker held Phantom to the back of the group, giving them some distance, and Phantom's gut told him his team leader didn't plan to chat with him about his record-setting target practice for the day.

He sighed. After four hours of intense PT and a run through the hot Texas sun for their paintball training drill, he had looked forward to a hot shower and a cold beer. He shook his head at himself. He must be getting soft if such a light day made him ready to ring out before the afternoon was over.

If a new mission had come up though—his gut clenched at the thought. They had just wrapped up their last mission nearly a week ago. A surge of adrenaline pulsed through him at the thought they could be headed out again.

"How are things going in the horse industry?" Stryker asked, surprising Phantom. It was the last thing he had expected to hear.

"Good. I've got to say, working and training quarter horses is a lot different from the thoroughbreds I grew up with."

"When are you planning to get out into the community with them? You know that's a critical component of our assignment here."

Several months back, Admiral Haslett had approached Stryker to put together a team of SEALs to go undercover in Hebbronville, Texas, a small town near the border with Mexico. Their cover was as a group of close friends who had gone in together to purchase the massive ranch to raise cattle and horses, all while covertly keeping their ears to the ground for illegal activities in Mexico, Central and South America that posed a threat to Americans. The more they could do to eliminate crime south of the border, the safer it would be for immigrants, asylum seekers, and everyone else at the border itself.

Their last mission had involved taking down a

drug cartel that obviously had connections within America, but they hadn't yet identified the players on the American side. The team had succeeded in bringing down the cartel and the drug lord, but it was obvious that there were larger stakes involved.

"To get out into the community with the horses means competing them. I'll need to understand quarter horse shows a lot better before I take that step." Instantly the image of a determined, energetic woman popped into his head. Elena Garcia had been the horse trainer for the ranch's prior owner, up until two weeks ago when Phantom had told her they were no longer in need of her services. His intentions had been to secure their undercover mission, but he was beginning to doubt his hasty decision.

Stryker paused and turned to face him, a knowing look on his face. "You need to talk to Elena."

Phantom scowled. "I can make it without her help. I just need a little more time." Even to his own ears his argument sounded weak.

Stryker shook his head. "Admit that she's your best chance at being able to network and get involved as quickly as possible. Things in the criminal world aren't going to slow down while we get our shit in gear. We can't waste any time. Your job is to gather intel in the community. You can't do that working the horses out here on the ranch. We're SEALs. We're the experts in our field, but outside of it, we go to the experts in theirs, and Elena is the expert you need."

Phantom gripped his paintball gun tightly. He suddenly wished they had another drill to run so he could take out his frustration. "I'm not sure the best tactic to approach her."

Stryker smirked. "Business is business. Anya talks about her all the time, and it sounds like the woman is smart as hell. If you come at it as a business proposition, I'm sure she'll take us back as a client."

When it came to business, Phantom often deferred to others who had a gift for such things. He knew how to track an enemy for miles and sneak up on him in total silence. He knew how to be a deadly force in nearly any situation. His experience outside of an assigned mission tested his nerves. He had to remind himself it all served their ultimate goal—defuse a hostile situation with minimal casualties. He'd have to take one for the team.

"I'll call her tonight," he relented. Stryker's fiancée Anya and Elena were best friends, which meant he had to handle the whole thing even more delicately.

"It's best to handle this type of transaction face-to-face. Calling her could put you at a disadvantage. Who knows—she may demand double the previous fees."

"That could still happen if I meet with her in person." Phantom doubted Elena would try to double the fees regardless. She didn't strike him as a person driven by money.

"Not as likely. Go out and meet with her tomorrow. Maybe you can even convince her to come back to the ranch to see that you haven't destroyed her years of hard work training those horses. I'm sure Anya would be thrilled to visit with her for a little while."

Phantom nodded. One way or another he was going to convince Elena to take them back as a client. He cringed. He just hoped she didn't hate him for cutting her loose in the first place.

—◦—

Elena barely lifted the reins and the horse jumped forward, moving swiftly and smoothly beneath her to cut out the heifer from the small herd gathered in the arena. She balanced her weight in the saddle, shifting left to right to guide the horse, barely touching it with her heels. She had trained it to respond to her body's movements, not to the feel of spurs against its side or the bite of the bit in its mouth.

It wasn't the way some cowboys she knew worked the range. There were bad ones out there who were notorious for digging their spurs into a horse's flesh until its hide became tough from misuse and a horse could become nearly unresponsive to a bit in its mouth because of being yanked around constantly. Those practices were outdated, and with the use of proper training for both the horse and rider, a lighter hand could be utilized.

Fortunately, the ranch she worked today employed her methods and style out in the field, and none of the ranch hands wore spurs to guide their horses. She smiled as the horse began to move without cue from her, having honed in on the heifer she wanted to cut from the herd, and aggressively pursued moving it out. A few short minutes later, the heifer had been separated from the herd and she chuckled, patting the horse's neck as a reward.

A couple hours later the sun had climbed, and she decided it was past time to take a break. She dismounted smoothly and led the horse, the third she had worked with already that morning, over to the trough for a long drink of water. She began to scratch it between the ears, a favorite with horses as it was always a difficult spot for them to scratch on their own.

The horse cocked one leg in relaxation and leaned its head against her and she chuckled. "That's a good girl. You did some hard work out there. I'd say you deserve an extra share of oats."

"Do you sweet talk all of them like that? Is that how you get them to do what you want?" A deep male voice nearby startled her. It wasn't anyone she immediately recognized, and unease slid down her spine.

She turned and let out a small sigh of relief. "Do you always sneak up on people like that?"

"My name *is* Phantom, you know."

"Ah, yes. The name suits you. Are you friends with Henry?" she asked, referring to the owner of the ranch.

"I just met him. I came out here hoping to find you."

She led the horse out of the arena and started walking to the barn, Phantom falling in alongside her. She dug her phone out of her back pocket and waved it in the air. "Easiest way to find me." *Why is he here? What could he possibly want?* She couldn't say she was glad to see him. Just watching his granite features reminded her of the way he had tilted her world on its side with a decision that changed everything for her.

He shrugged. "Too impersonal. I prefer to look people in the face when I'm talking to them."

"You were born in the wrong time, then, I hate to tell you. Texts, email, social media…that's how everyone stays in touch. It's rare even to hear a voice these days, let alone see a face."

"Call me old-fashioned."

"Okay. I just might. Why are you looking for me

anyway?" Her words came across a bit stronger than she had intended. She couldn't conceal her frustration at the way he had so quickly and casually told her he no longer needed her services with his horses. In a few brief sentences, he had cut her off from quarter horses she had been training for years and had practically come to think of as her own. In that same move, he had destroyed the main reason she had come to Hebbronville—to work with some of the finest quarter horses she had ever seen.

The Bent Horseshoe Ranch had recruited her as soon as she graduated from A&M to train the quarter horses to be some of the best in the nation. She had jumped at the opportunity, and it had been her main source of income—up until two weeks ago. Once Phantom had fired her, she'd had to act fast to find new clients. She found a couple close to Falfurrias, but the cost of gas to drive out to them barely made it worthwhile.

"For someone who loves to brag about her tech world, you don't check your phone often."

Surprised, Elena clicked open her phone and found she had missed multiple text messages from Anya. "Is she okay? Did something happen?" she asked, quickly scrolling through the texts.

"Everything is fine. She'd like to see you, that's all. She wanted to know if you could come out to the ranch today. If we go soon, Snap will probably be making lunch."

Elena looked at him skeptically as she began to undo the cinch on the saddle. "Snap? Who else lives at your ranch? Crackle and Pop?"

For a moment she thought he was going to smile, but the face carved from granite stayed serious, though his tone seemed amused. "Good one. Never heard that before. We admit our nicknames are…interesting…"

"And yours? You specialize on sneaking up on people, so you're called Phantom?"

"That, and I can make like a ghost and disappear."

"Right." She chuckled. "Good to know. So did you really come out here just because Anya wants me to come out to the ranch today?" She grabbed a soft brush from a bucket of cool water and began to wipe down the horse in long, smooth strokes. The horse looked half-asleep.

"That and I wanted to see my competition at work."

She hesitated mid-stroke, then resumed quickly. "Your competition? Does that mean you've decided to start showing the horses?"

"Yes."

Elena felt a dull ache in her heart. She should be the one showing his horses. She had trained them, guided them, prepared them to be their absolute best. *She* wanted to show them. "Good luck. I hope everything goes well for you."

"I've done a lot more research since I saw you. I appreciate the tip about the horses' feed, by the way. It made a world of difference when I did what you recommended and switched them from sweet feed back to coastal and oats."

Elena laughed as she remembered how hyper the horses had been on the sweet feed and his dismay when she told him what to do about it. "Glad I could help." She dropped the soft brush back in the bucket of water and led the horse into its stall, sliding the bridle off and turning it loose with a pat on the withers.

"There are still plenty of things I have to learn," Phantom said, stepping closer as she came out of the stall.

Hope blossomed in Elena's heart, making it thud hard in her chest. Could he be re-hiring her? Was that why he had come out to the ranch to watch her work? Was this some sort of test?

"Always will be," she said with a bright smile. "The day you think you know everything about raising or showing horses is the day you find out you're wrong. I just got thrown by a two-year old filly last week. I certainly learned a lesson that day." She nearly bit her tongue. She needed to tell him about all the things she was great at, not her misadventures.

He raised his eyebrows. "Are you okay? You didn't get hurt, did you?" She sensed genuine concern in his voice. Was there a human being beneath all that granite?

"I would think you'd be happy if your competition got side-lined for a few shows," she teased.

"Not my idea of fair competition. Seriously, are you okay?"

"I've got some bruises that are fading into lovely colors; other than that, I'm fine. Thanks for your concern." She forced herself to look away from him. Something about him drew her in and made her curious to know more about him, especially this glimpse of a softer side she didn't think existed. "How soon are you going to start showing?" She hated talking about herself, and wanted to hear more about her—his—horses.

"I'm not sure. That's another reason I'm here today. I wanted to pick your brain about the best horse shows to take them to. Given that it is your area of expertise and all."

Elena grinned at him. "So you *do* need me after all."
Yes! I'm going to get him back as a client!

He gazed at her intently, then slowly nodded his head. "I could use some help."

She ran a hand through her thick, curly hair and fought back the cheer threatening to burst from her. She wanted to see the horses she loved so much. She had come to miss them greatly in the two weeks since he had dismissed her.

Did he really want her help, or was he simply on a mission for Anya and decided to take advantage of her expertise at the same time? The hope inside faded slightly, but she clung to it tightly. She wasn't going to give up on pursuing even the smallest crack in his shell.

"You know, my prices are generally pretty steep," she grinned, teasing him once again. "*But*, if you're throwing in a free lunch, I might be able to help you a little."

"Good. Anya's missed you since she's been out at the ranch."

"I've missed her, too. Since she closed the veterinary clinic temporarily, things haven't been the same."

"She'll be back soon. She's itching to get back to work."

"I know it may not seem like a long time to you, but for the two of us to go a couple of weeks without seeing each other seems like an eternity." Elena studied the ground as they walked toward their trucks.

"Good. Then it's settled. You'll join us for lunch?"

She looked over at him and gave her brightest smile. "Wouldn't miss it." Elena was on a mission. She was going to win back her client.

Chapter 2

THE DRIVE OUT TO BENT HORSESHOE RANCH WAS SCENIC, though bumpy. The road had suffered from the late spring rains, and county maintenance had yet to repair it. Phantom watched Elena's truck bobbing along behind his and smiled to himself. So far his plan seemed to be working.

Watching her ride the horse earlier had been like watching a choreographed dance routine. He realized more than ever how critical she would be to his success with the horses and furthering his work out in the field as Stryker had mentioned.

He knew she had a real passion for his quarter horses and had put her heart and soul into developing them into well-trained competitors. He could tell she still held some resentment toward him for cutting ties with her, and he couldn't say he blamed her.

He admitted to himself he had made the decision to dismiss her too hastily. Having grown up working and training horses most of his life, it was a bit of a hard pill to swallow to ask for help. It was the right thing to do, though. He had watched a few quarter horse show videos online and realized he was in over his head.

They arrived at the ranch house close to one in the afternoon, with the Texas heat in full force. The humidity made it feel ten degrees hotter. He parked quickly and headed over to her truck, surprising her at her door. She looked up at him with a smile and he saw that her brown eyes held flecks of gold and tan within them. There was something about the way her smile lit up her face that made him want to see it as often as possible.

They had barely stepped onto the small covered patio when the large wooden door to the home flew open and Anya rushed out, grinning from ear to ear. "You found her! Phantom, you're the best!"

Elena brushed past him and he caught her unique scent of Texas wildflowers. He had noticed it when he first met her, and it had lingered in his memory. Phantom watched as she embraced Anya as if it had been years since they had seen each other instead of just a couple of weeks. "You know, those first couple of days when I didn't hear from you, you had me worried sick!" Elena scolded Anya. "I had to hear from the gossip-mongers in town that your place had a break-in, and you know how my imagination gets carried away."

"I know, I know. I'm sorry. I should have called you as soon as it happened. I was so rattled I didn't know up from down. If it hadn't been for Stryker, I probably would have fallen to pieces."

Elena shook her head. "I should have known you'd be with him. The way you've been mooning over him the last two months, I'm not surprised."

"I have not been 'mooning' over him," Anya shook her head back at Elena. "Who even says such things anymore? I swear, you and Phantom should compare notes. You both are old souls."

Elena looked up at Phantom, her eyes assessing him. "Is that what you are? An old soul?"

"So I've been told. Anya has been educating me. I did tell you I'm old-fashioned."

Anya laughed. "Yes, you are. Sometimes that can be a good thing, though."

"And other times?" Elena asked, an eyebrow raised.

"Other times can bore you to tears."

Phantom rolled his eyes and headed toward the front door. "Let's get out of this heat and see if Snap is working his magic in the kitchen."

He held the door open as the two women walked past him, lost in conversation. He watched Elena and plotted his next steps to get her out to the barn and back with the horses she loved.

"You're going to *live* here?" Elena wasn't sure she had heard right. Anya wasn't making any sense.

"Yes. I can't wait for you to meet the rest of the guys. They're such an amazing group. But Stryker…he owns my heart. I can't imagine life without him. I'm in love, Elena."

"You're joking with me, right? Love? I thought we agreed we'd be certified bachelorettes the rest of our lives. You're changing the rules on me."

"I'm just living with him, El. We're not making any wedding plans…" Anya's voice trailed off.

"…Yet. You practically said it. It's on the tip of your tongue! No way—Anya, has he *asked* you?" Elena stared at Anya, holding her breath.

"No, not exactly." Anya smiled slyly.

"Either he has or he hasn't," Elena demanded. She sipped her coffee, the delicious brew warming her from the inside out.

"He's hinted the question isn't far away."

Elena nearly choked on her coffee. "Okay, now I know you're messing with me. Anya! You've known him for two months! How can you possibly consider marriage? I mean, moving in with the guy alone is a huge step."

Anya shrugged and smiled. "If I were in your seat right now I'd say the same thing." She leaned forward in her chair and grasped Elena's hands in hers. "I don't know how to explain it. Somehow when it's right you just know. He's the one, El."

Elena stared at Anya in a moment of stunned silence. "Okay, who are you and what have you done with my best friend?"

Anya laughed just as Snap arrived with a tray of bite-sized sandwiches: turkey and cheese, ham and cheese, and cucumber salad. On top of that he had made a dreamy creamy tomato bisque soup. Elena tasted the bisque and her eyes nearly rolled back in her head. "Snap, where did you learn to cook like this?"

Snap beamed proudly. Of the men she'd met so far, he appeared to be the youngest. There had to be others around, given the interesting nicknames Anya had been using, but so far she'd seen only Phantom and Snap. Apparently the rest were out working on the ranch. Snap disappeared back into the kitchen, giving them their privacy.

The sound of boots on the hardwood floor drew their attention and Anya's eyes lit up as Stryker came striding into the room. At first he had eyes only for Anya, but Elena saw his gaze flick over to her briefly. He leaned down and pressed a tender kiss to Anya's lips and she leaned up into the touch, her hand resting on his chest for a moment.

"Stryker, I want you to meet my best friend Elena."
Anya gestured toward Elena and she smiled brightly.
So this was the man who had claimed her best friend's
heart. She had interacted with him months ago when he
and his friends had first bought the ranch and had begun
remodeling the outdated ranch house into the beautiful
home it had become. Their conversations had been limited to her work with the horses.

Elena stood and extended her hand. He smiled at her.
"I seem to remember you lurking around when we were
remodeling this place."

"Lurking isn't the term I would use," she replied with
a smile. "I was working quite hard."

"That was around the time you won the Grand
Champion trophy in Corpus, isn't it?"

Phantom's voice came out of nowhere, gentle, and
could that be appreciation? He hadn't made any noise
to alert her he had come into the room. She turned and
found him leaning against the dining room wall. How
long had he been there?

"Yes, it was," she said, watching his face for a reaction. If she wanted him back as a client, she needed him
to know how good she was with his horses. Knowing
that he had seen the trophies she had won was a step in
the right direction.

He watched her for several long seconds, finally
breaking eye contact to glance over at Anya and Stryker,
who seemed to be in their own world. "When you have a
moment," he said, returning his gaze to her, "I'd like to
take you out to the barn. It won't take very long."

About the Author

Holly Castillo grew up spending many lazy summer days racing her horses bareback in the Texas sun. But whenever Holly wasn't riding her horses or competing in horse shows, she was found with pen and paper in hand, writing out romantic love stories about Texas heroes.

Today, Holly lives in a small community just south of San Antonio, with her husband and two children. On the family's eighty-acre ranch, surrounded by cattle during the day and hearing the howl of coyotes by night, Holly has endless inspiration for her writing. Holly's current romantic suspense series about heroic Navy SEALs is set in her own backyard of south Texas.